CONSTANTINE

DISTORTED ILLUSIONS

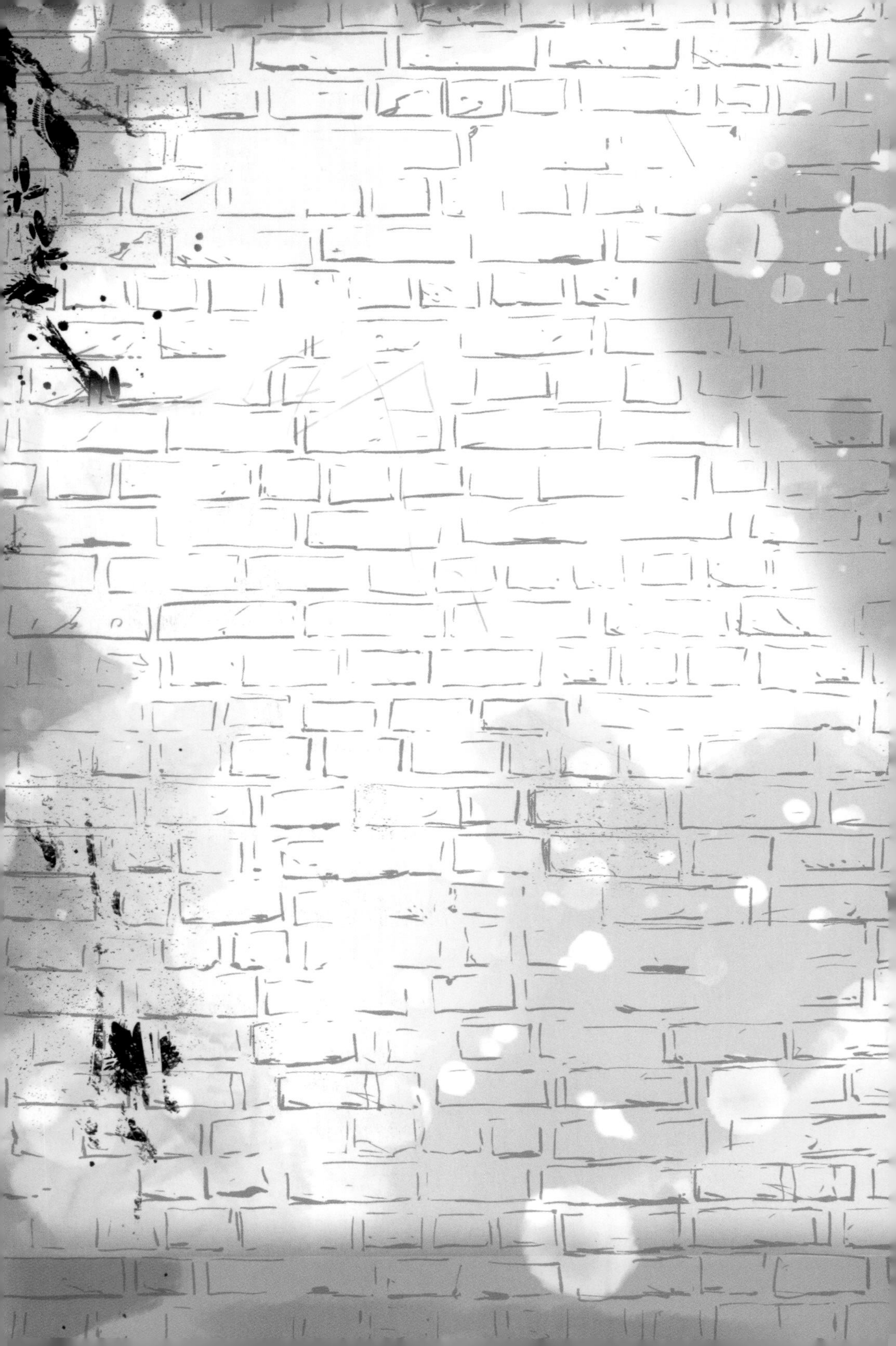

CONSTANTINE
DISTORTED ILLUSIONS

WRITTEN BY
Kami Garcia

DRAWN BY
Isaac Goodhart

COLORED BY
Ruth Redmond

LETTERED BY
Steve Wands

John Constantine created by Alan Moore,
Steve Bissette, John Totleben,
and Jamie Delano & John Ridgway

KRISTY QUINN Editor

COURTNEY JORDAN Associate Editor

STEVE COOK Design Director – Books

AMIE BROCKWAY-METCALF Publication Design

SANDY ALONZO Publication Production

MARIE JAVINS Editor-in-Chief, DC Comics

ANNE DePIES Senior VP – General Manager

JIM LEE Publisher & Chief Creative Officer

DON FALLETTI VP – Manufacturing Operations &
Workflow Management

LAWRENCE GANEM VP – Talent Services

ALISON GILL Senior VP – Manufacturing & Operations

JEFFREY KAUFMAN VP – Editorial Strategy & Programming

NICK J. NAPOLITANO VP – Manufacturing Administration & Design

NANCY SPEARS VP – Revenue

CONSTANTINE: DISTORTED ILLUSIONS

DC Comics, 100 S. California Street, Burbank, CA 91505
Printed by Worzalla, Stevens Point, WI, USA. 8/19/22.
ISBN: 978-1-77950-773-0

Special Edition ISBN: 978-1-77952-161-3

MIX
Paper from
responsible sources
FSC® C002589

Library of Congress Cataloging-in-Publication Data

Names: Garcia, Kami, writer. | Goodhart, Isaac, illustrator. | Redmond,
Ruth, colourist. | Wands, Steve, letterer.
Title: Constantine : distorted illusions / written by Kami Garcia ; drawn
by Isaac Goodhart ; colored by Ruth Redmond ; lettered by Steve Wands.
Description: Burbank, CA : DC Comics, 2022. | "John Constantine created by
Alan Moore, Steve Bissette, John Totleben, and Jamie Delano & John
Ridgway" | Audience: Ages 13-17 | Audience: Grades 7-9 | Summary: John
Constantine, a magician of the highest caliber, accepts an
apprenticeship in the United States to become the lead singer of his
best friend's punk band, but when a complicated spell gets out of hand,
the disastrous consequences might be more than Constantine can handle.
Identifiers: LCCN 2022021795 | ISBN 9781779507730 (trade paperback)
Subjects: CYAC: Graphic novels. | Magic--Fiction. | Friendship--Fiction. |
Punk rock music--Fiction. | LCGFT: Paranormal comics. | Action and
adventure comics. | Graphic novels.
Classification: LCC PZ7.7.G366 Con 2022 | DDC 741.5/973--dc23/eng/20220506
LC record available at https://lccn.loc.gov/2022021795

For anyone who feels alone—
we all have demons.
Some are harder to slay than others,
but they can still be slain.
—Kami

For Klaus, Phil, and Edwin.
Thanks for being great teachers,
friends, and inspirations.
—Isaac

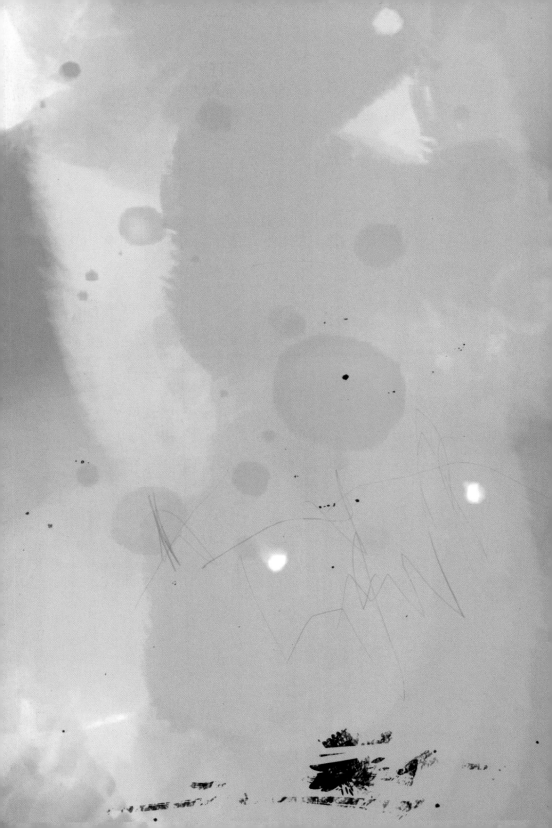

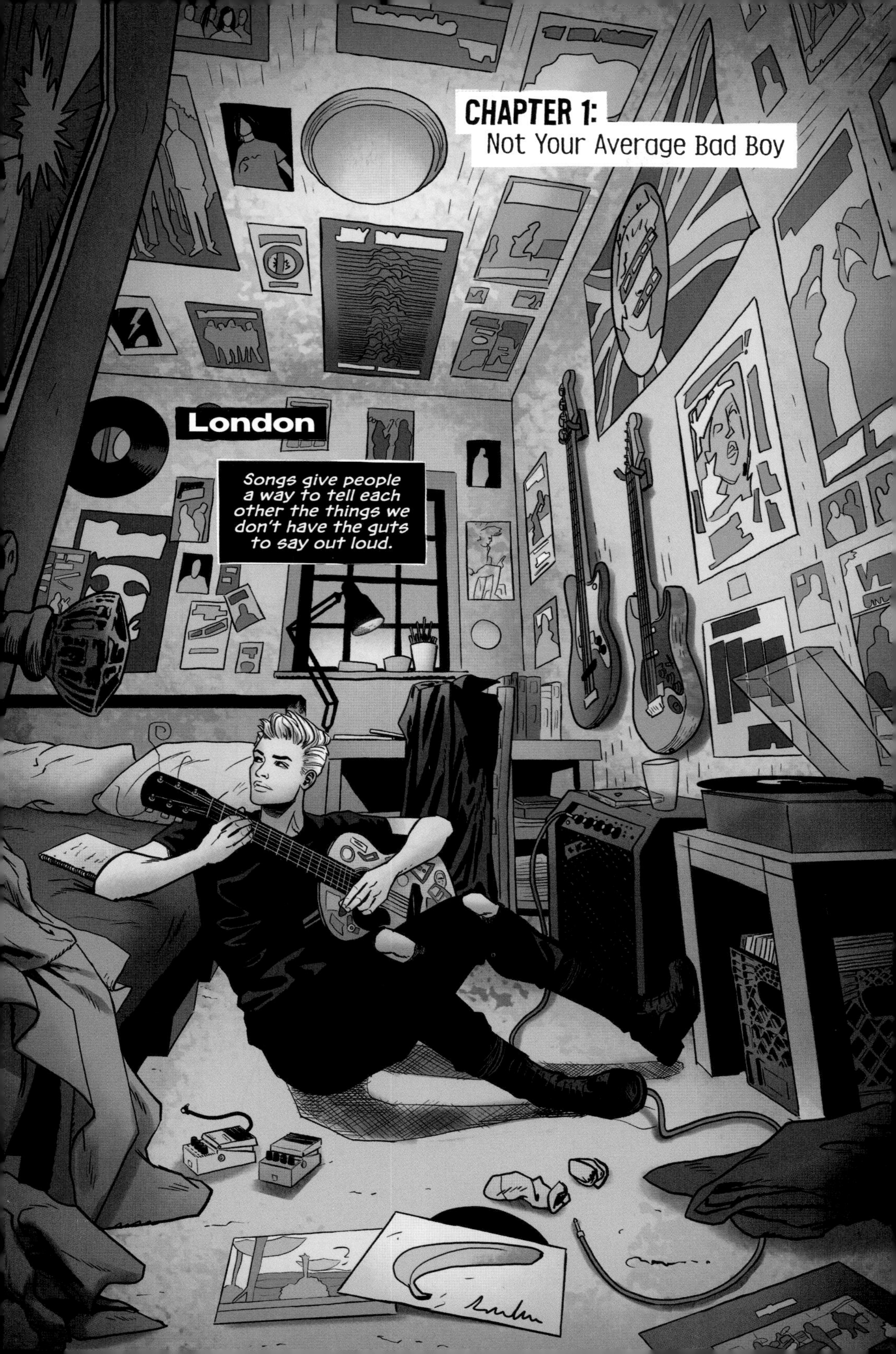

CHAPTER 1:
Not Your Average Bad Boy
London
Songs give people a way to tell each other the things we don't have the guts to say out loud.

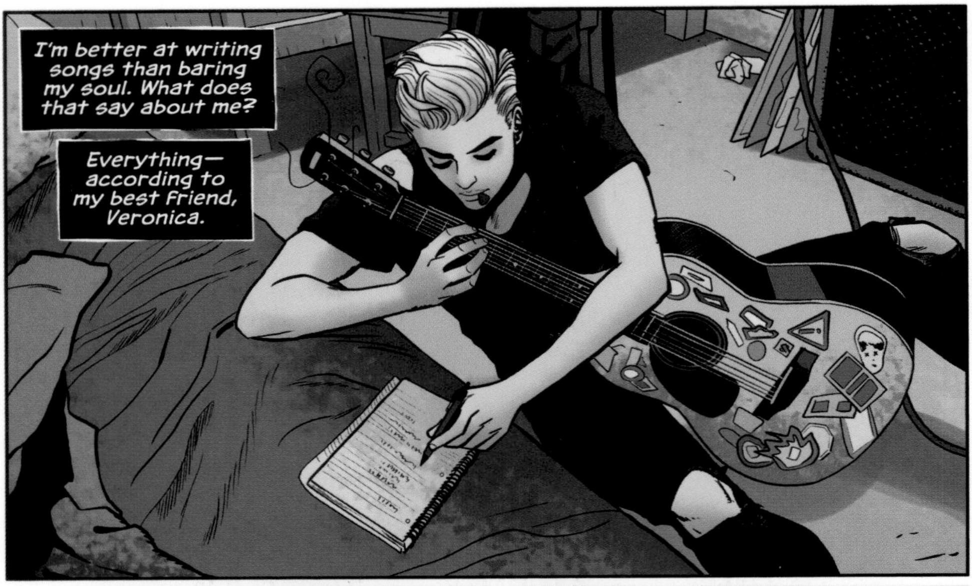
I'm better at writing songs than baring my soul. What does that say about me?
Everything—according to my best friend, Veronica.

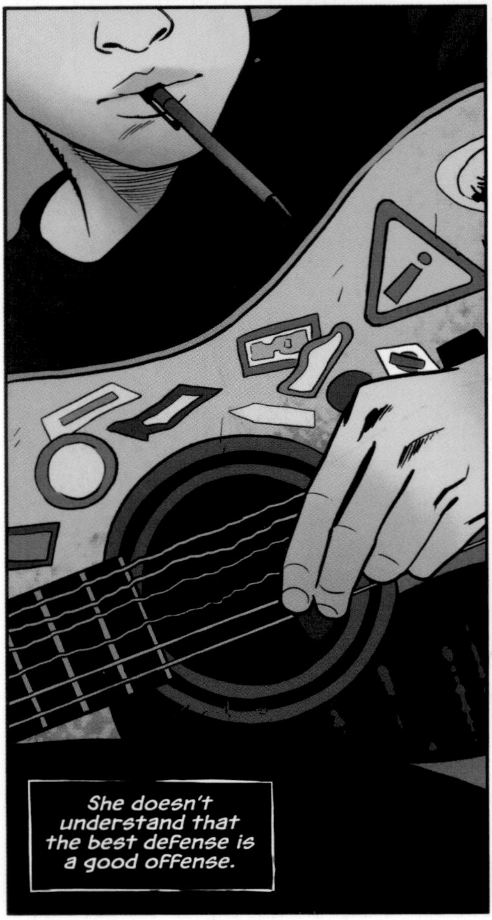
She doesn't understand that the best defense is a good offense.

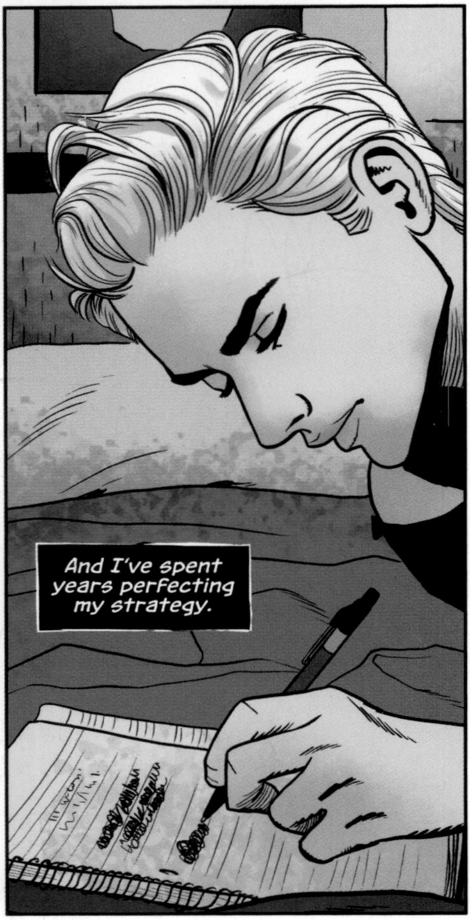
And I've spent years perfecting my strategy.

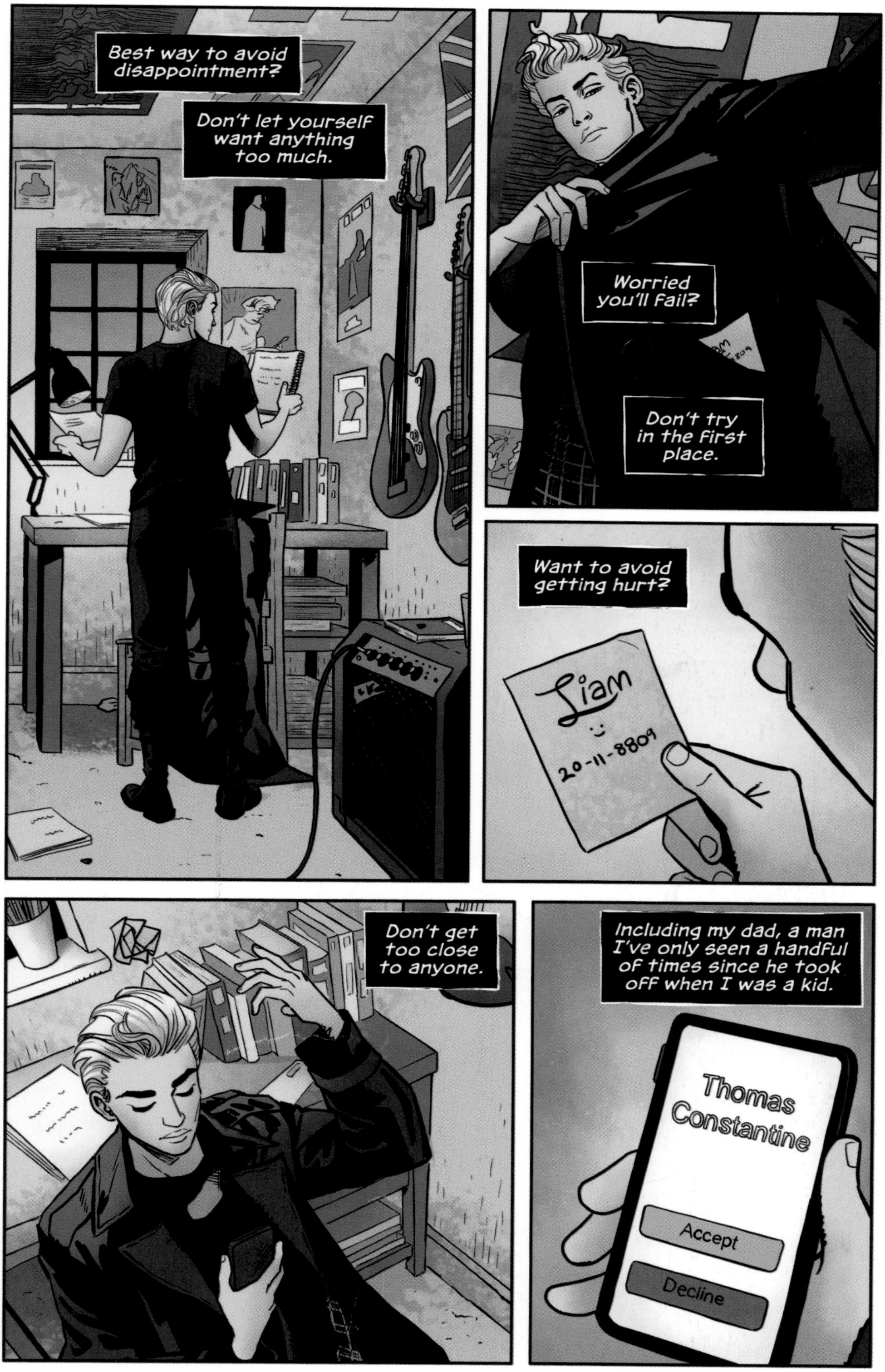
Best way to avoid disappointment?
Don't let yourself want anything too much.
Worried you'll fail?
Don't try in the first place.
Want to avoid getting hurt?
Liam
20-11-8809
Don't get too close to anyone.
Including my dad, a man I've only seen a handful of times since he took off when I was a kid.
Thomas Constantine
Accept
Decline

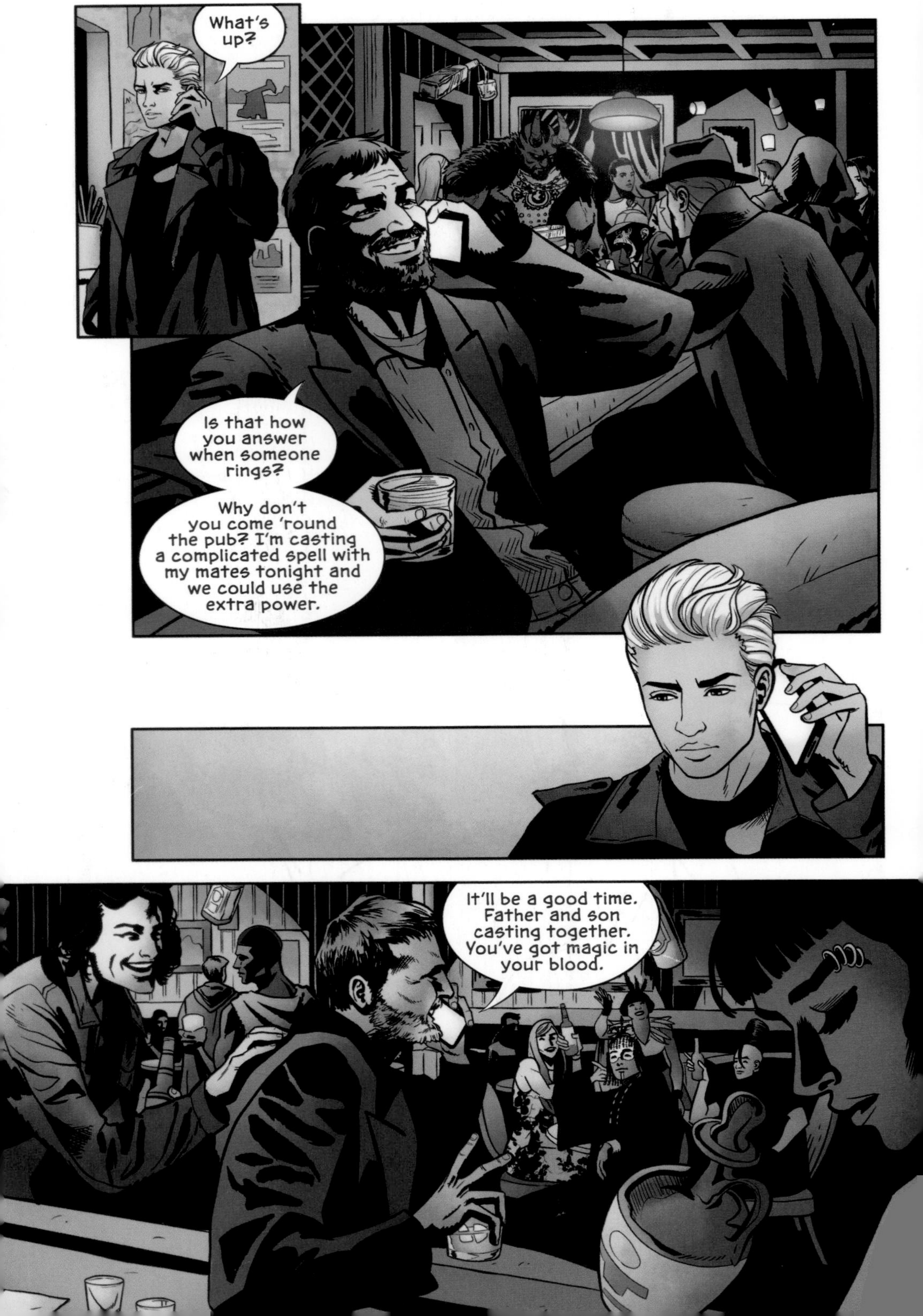
What's up?
Is that how you answer when someone rings?
Why don't you come 'round the pub? I'm casting a complicated spell with my mates tonight and we could use the extra power.
It'll be a good time. Father and son casting together. You've got magic in your blood.

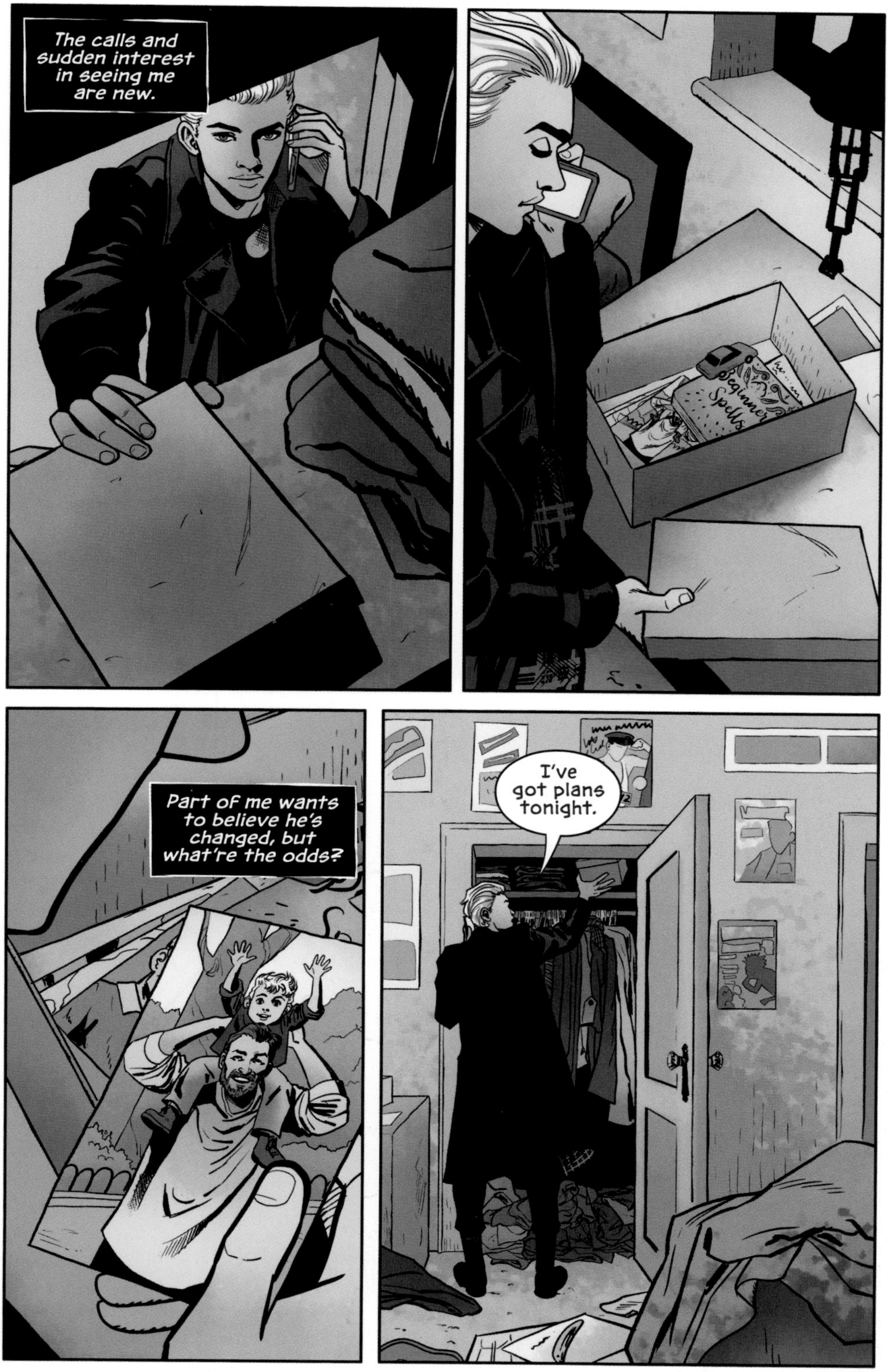
The calls and sudden interest in seeing me are new.
Beginner Spells
Part of me wants to believe he's changed, but what're the odds?
I've got plans tonight.

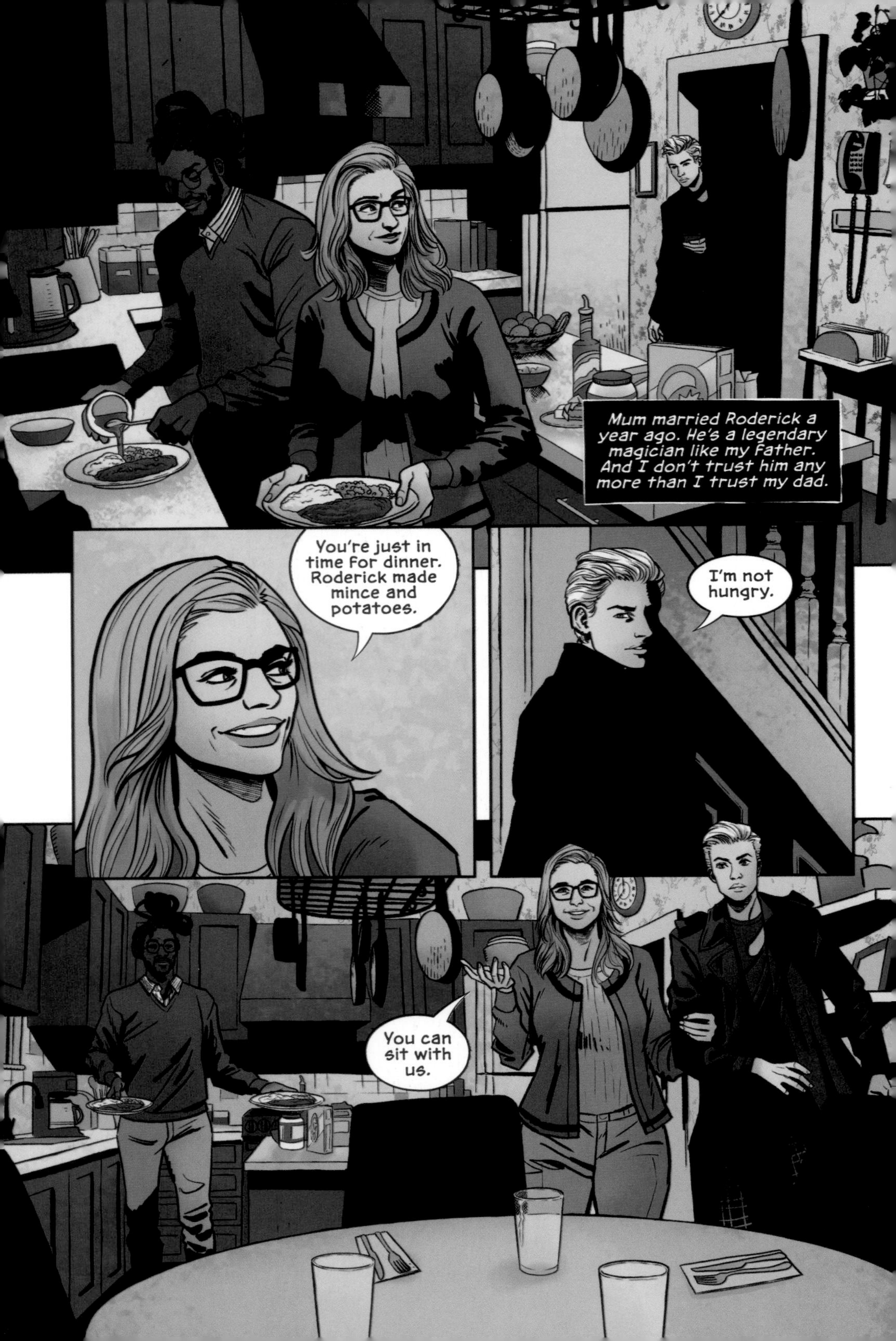

Mum married Roderick a year ago. He's a legendary magician like my father. And I don't trust him any more than I trust my dad.
You're just in time for dinner. Roderick made mince and potatoes.
I'm not hungry.
You can sit with us.

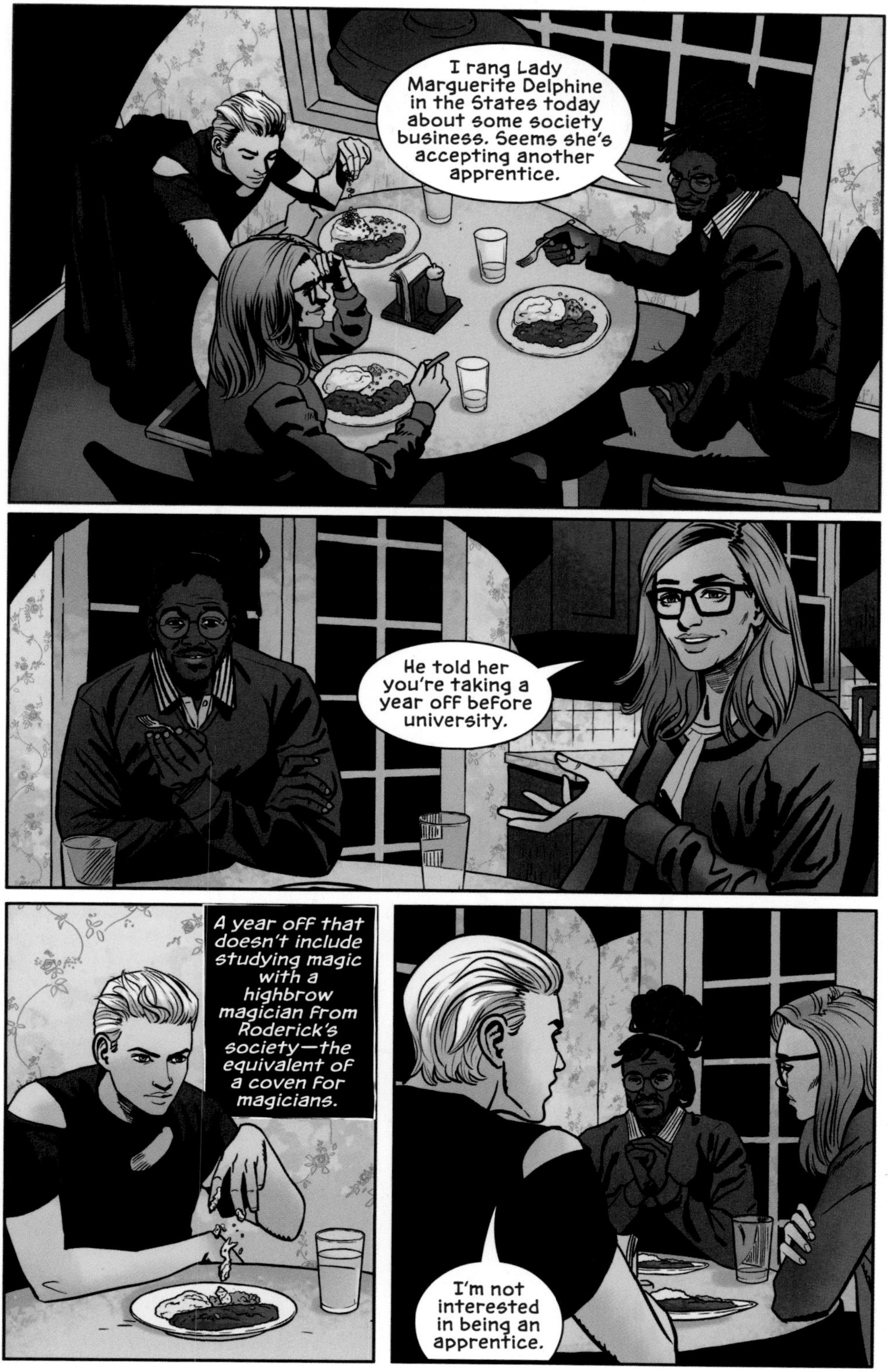
I rang Lady Marguerite Delphine in the States today about some society business. Seems she's accepting another apprentice.
He told her you're taking a year off before university.
A year off that doesn't include studying magic with a highbrow magician from Roderick's society—the equivalent of a coven for magicians.
I'm not interested in being an apprentice.

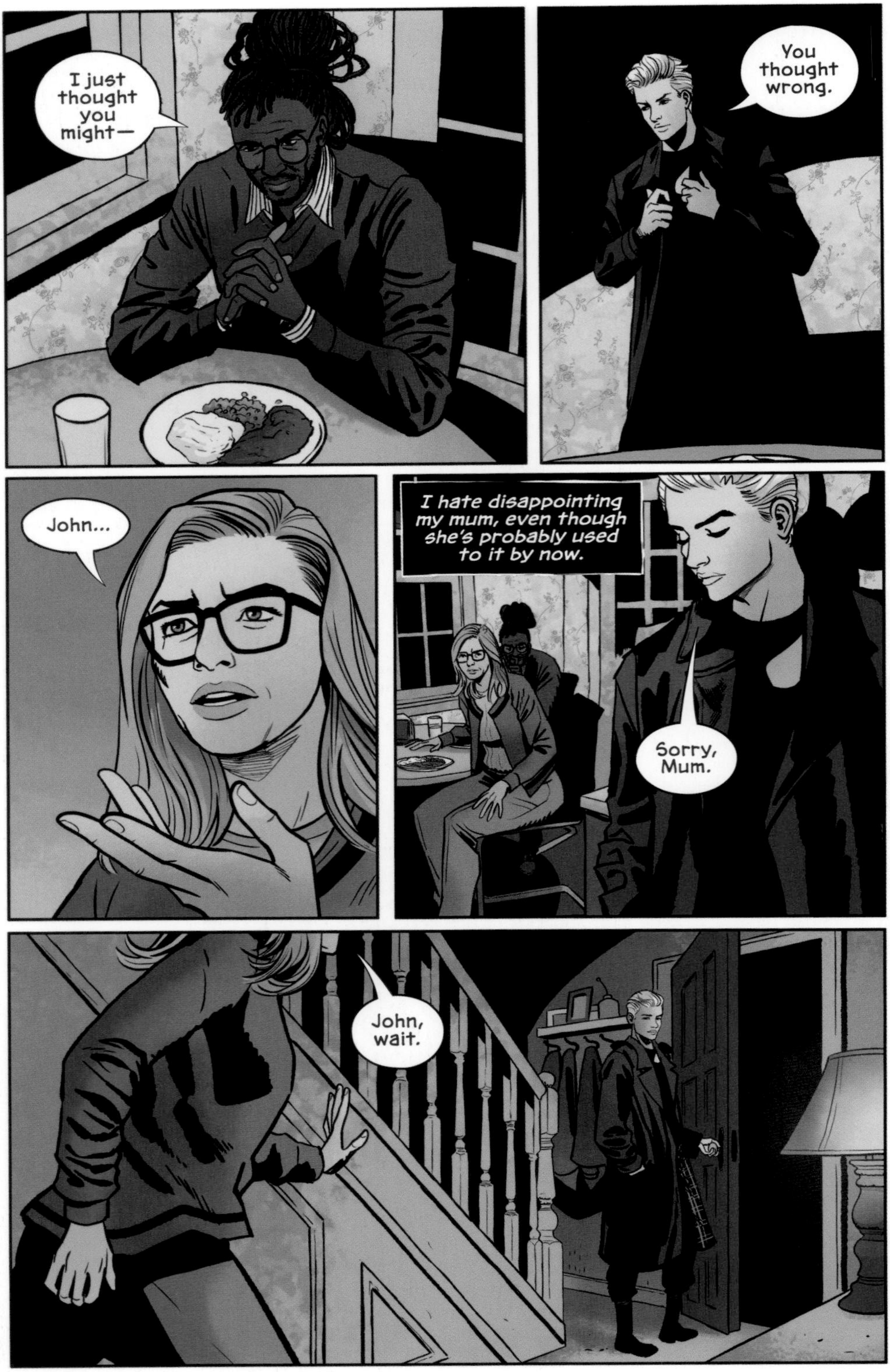
I just thought you might—
You thought wrong.
John...
I hate disappointing my mum, even though she's probably used to it by now.
Sorry, Mum.
John, wait.

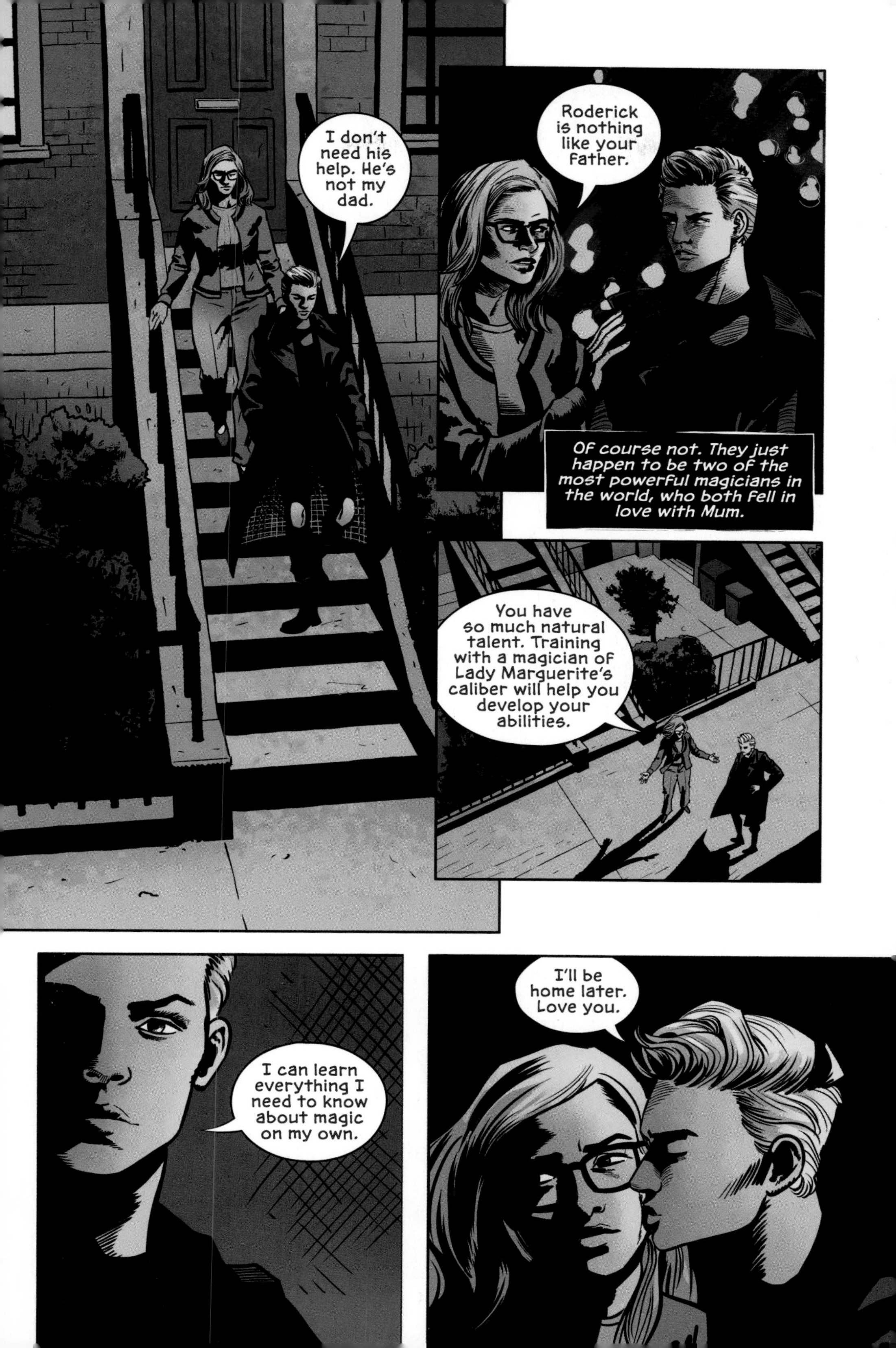
I don't need his help. He's not my dad.
Roderick is nothing like your father.
Of course not. They just happen to be two of the most powerful magicians in the world, who both fell in love with Mum.
You have so much natural talent. Training with a magician of Lady Marguerite's caliber will help you develop your abilities.
I can learn everything I need to know about magic on my own.
I'll be home later. Love you.

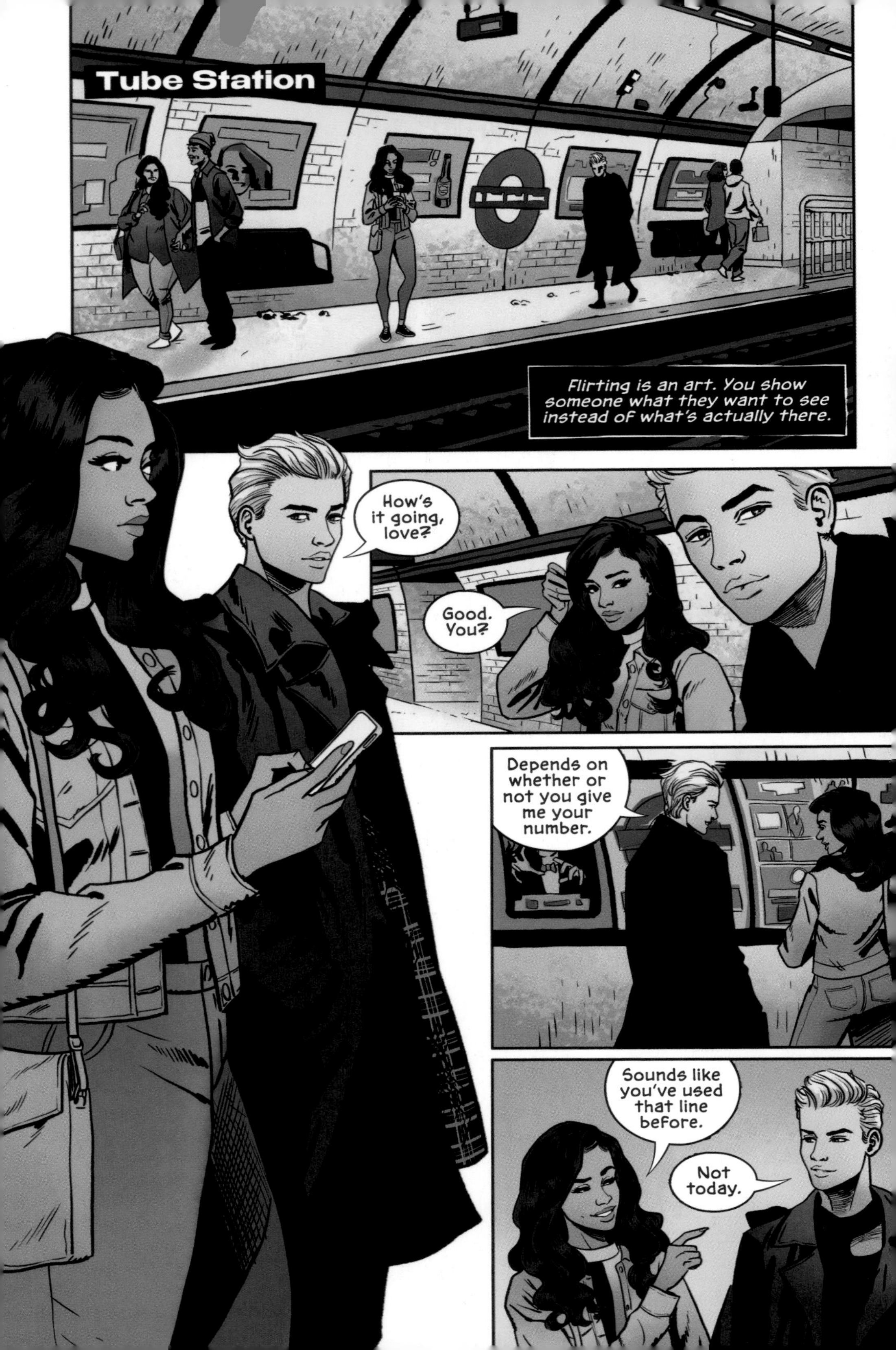
Tube Station
Flirting is an art. You show someone what they want to see instead of what's actually there.
How's it going, love?
Good. You?
Depends on whether or not you give me your number.
Sounds like you've used that line before.
Not today.

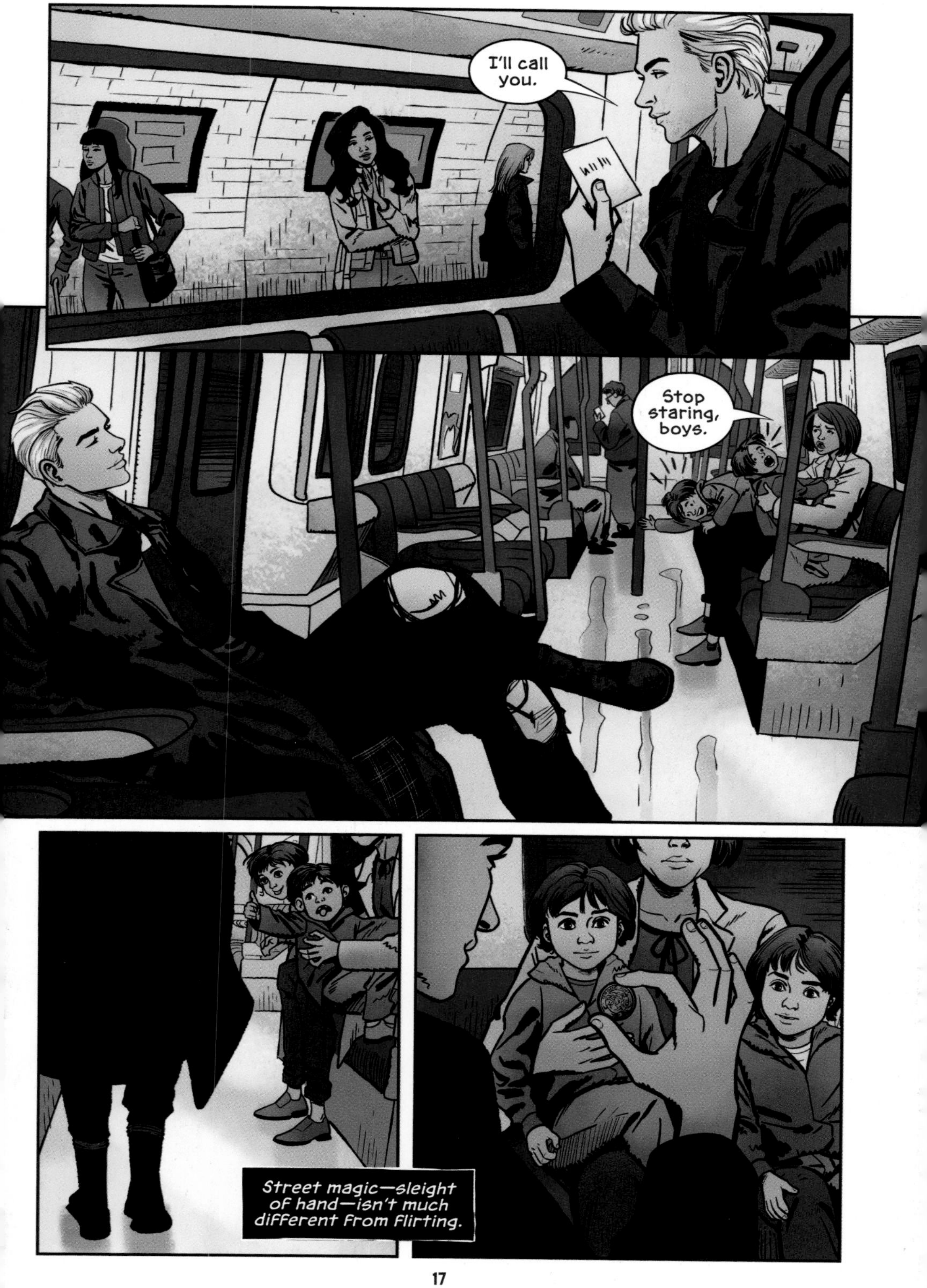
I'll call you.
Stop staring, boys.
Street magic—sleight of hand—isn't much different from flirting.

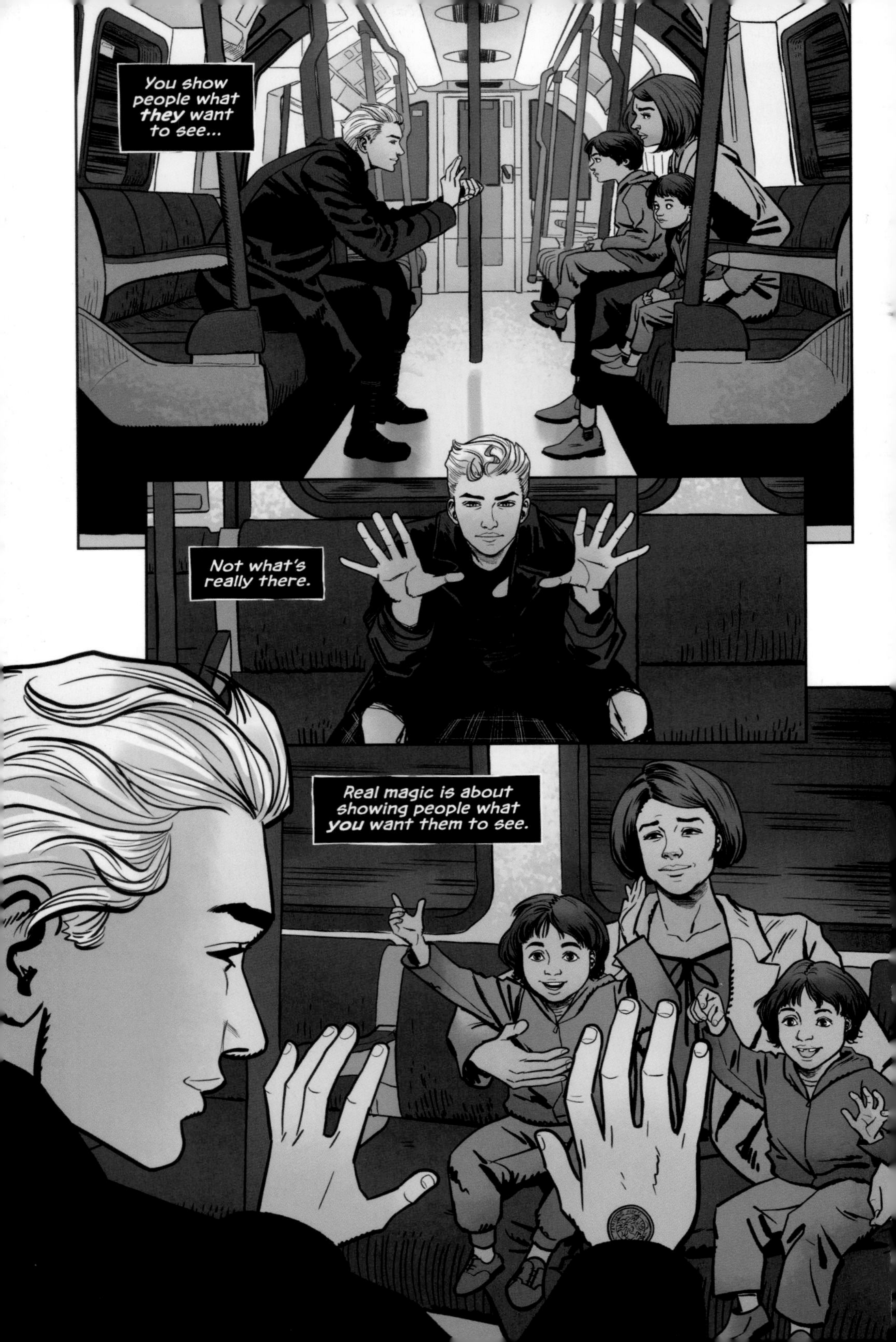
You show people what they want to see...
Not what's really there.
Real magic is about showing people what you want them to see.

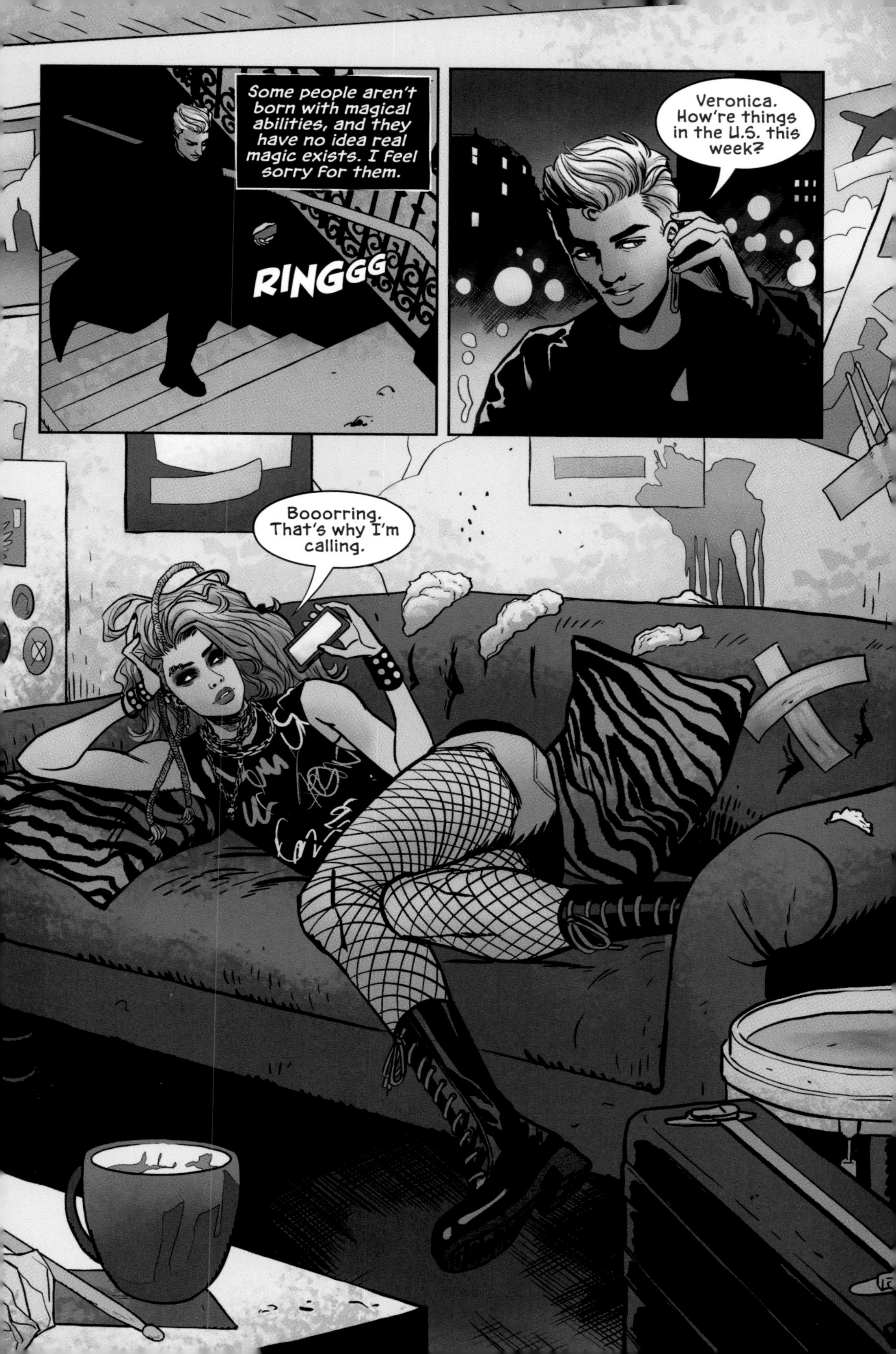

Some people aren't born with magical abilities, and they have no idea real magic exists. I feel sorry for them.
RINGGG
Veronica. How're things in the U.S. this week?
Booorring. That's why I'm calling.

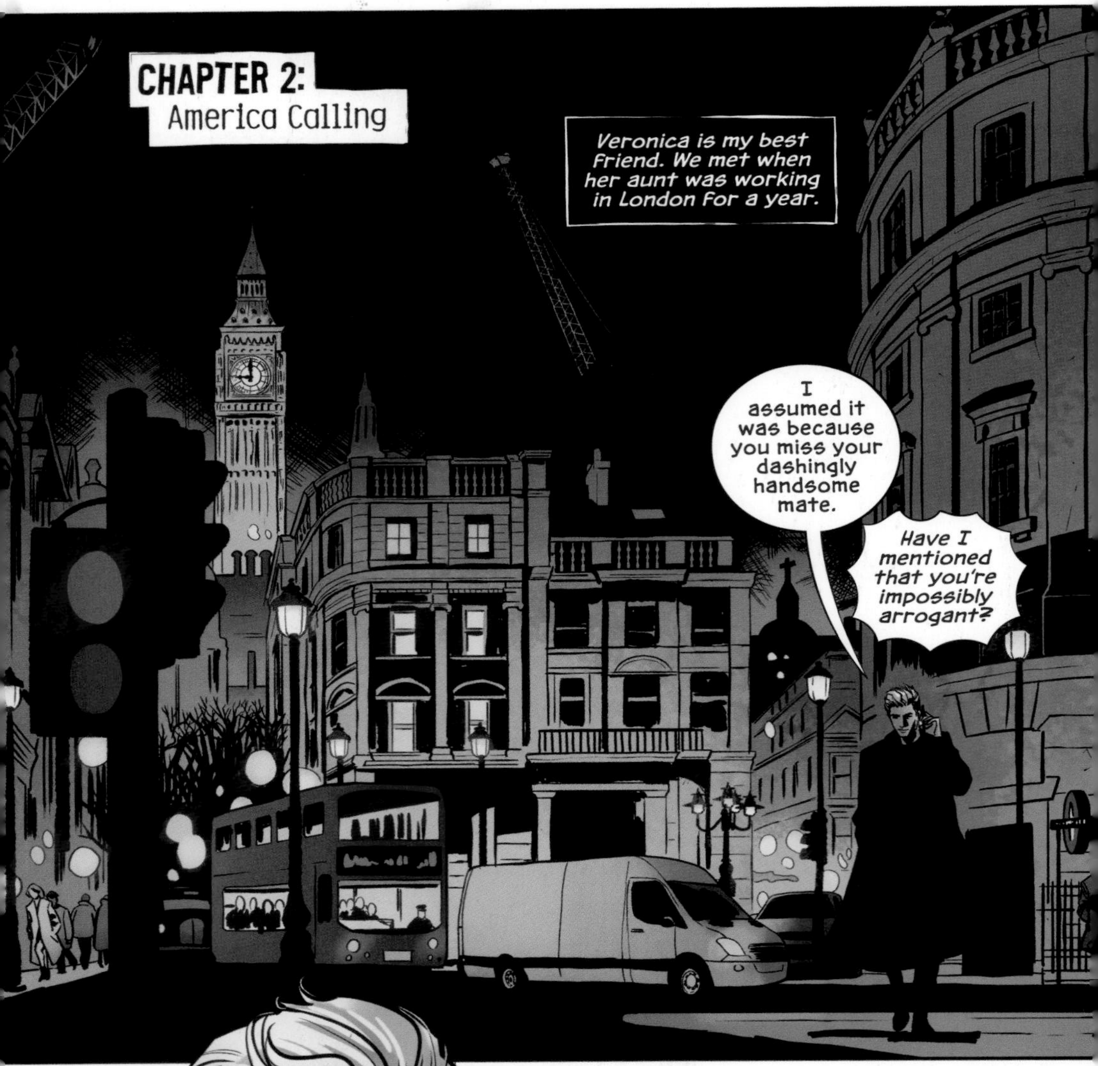
CHAPTER 2:
America Calling
Veronica is my best friend. We met when her aunt was working in London for a year.
I assumed it was because you miss your dashingly handsome mate.
Have I mentioned that you're impossibly arrogant?

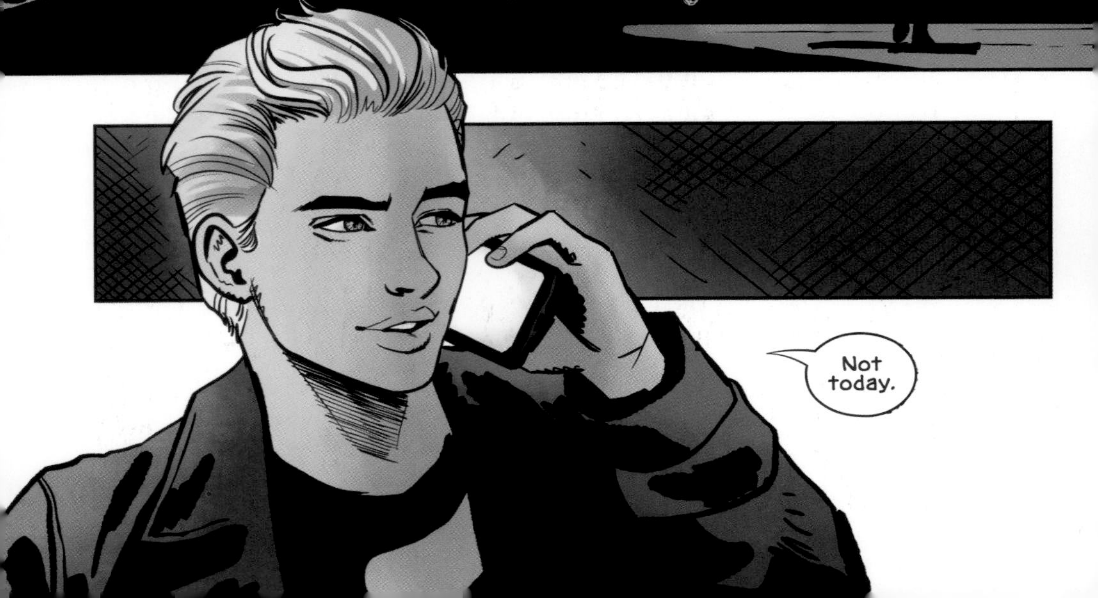
Not today.

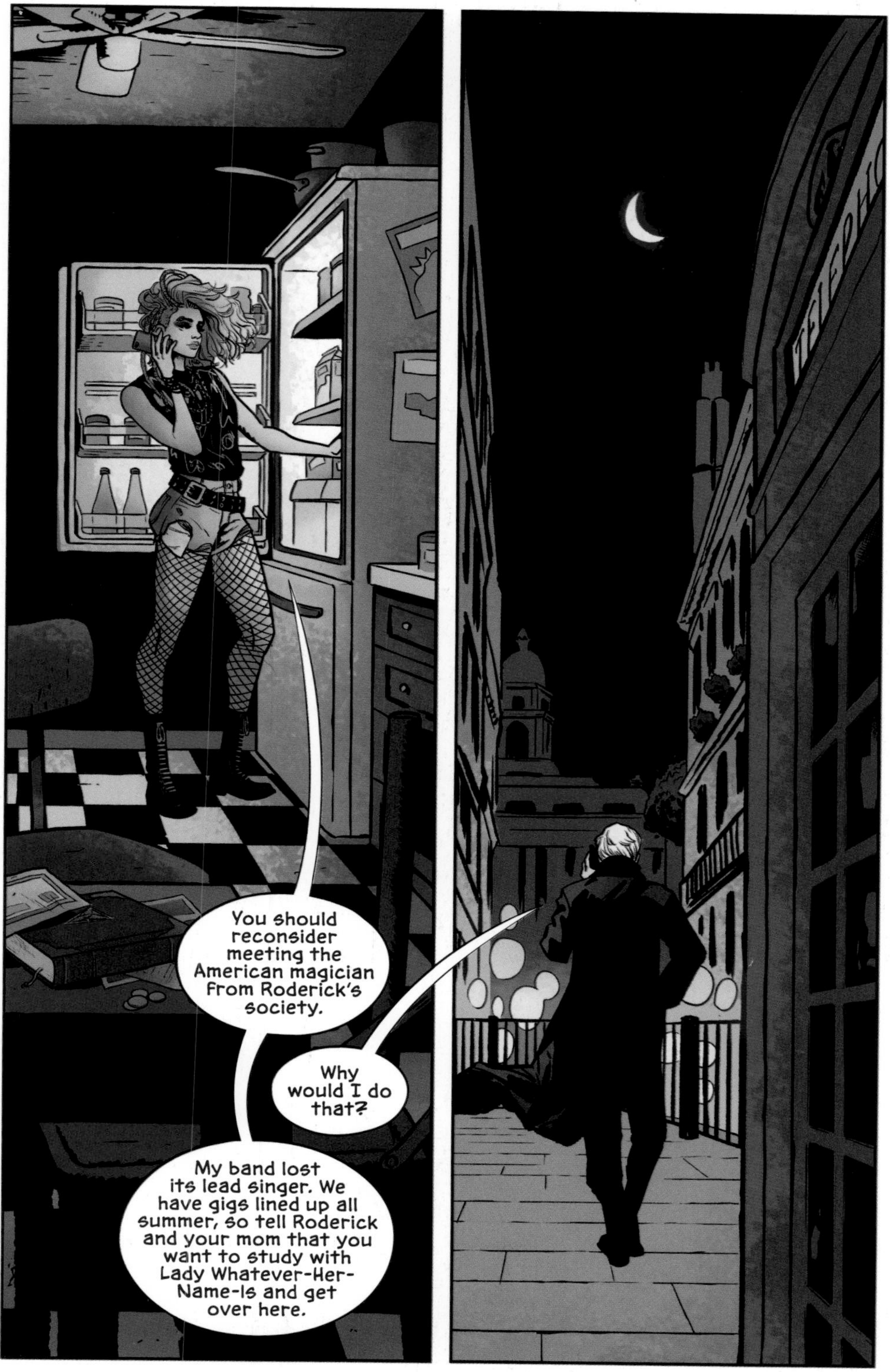
You should reconsider meeting the American magician from Roderick's society.
Why would I do that?
My band lost its lead singer. We have gigs lined up all summer, so tell Roderick and your mom that you want to study with Lady Whatever-Her-Name-Is and get over here.

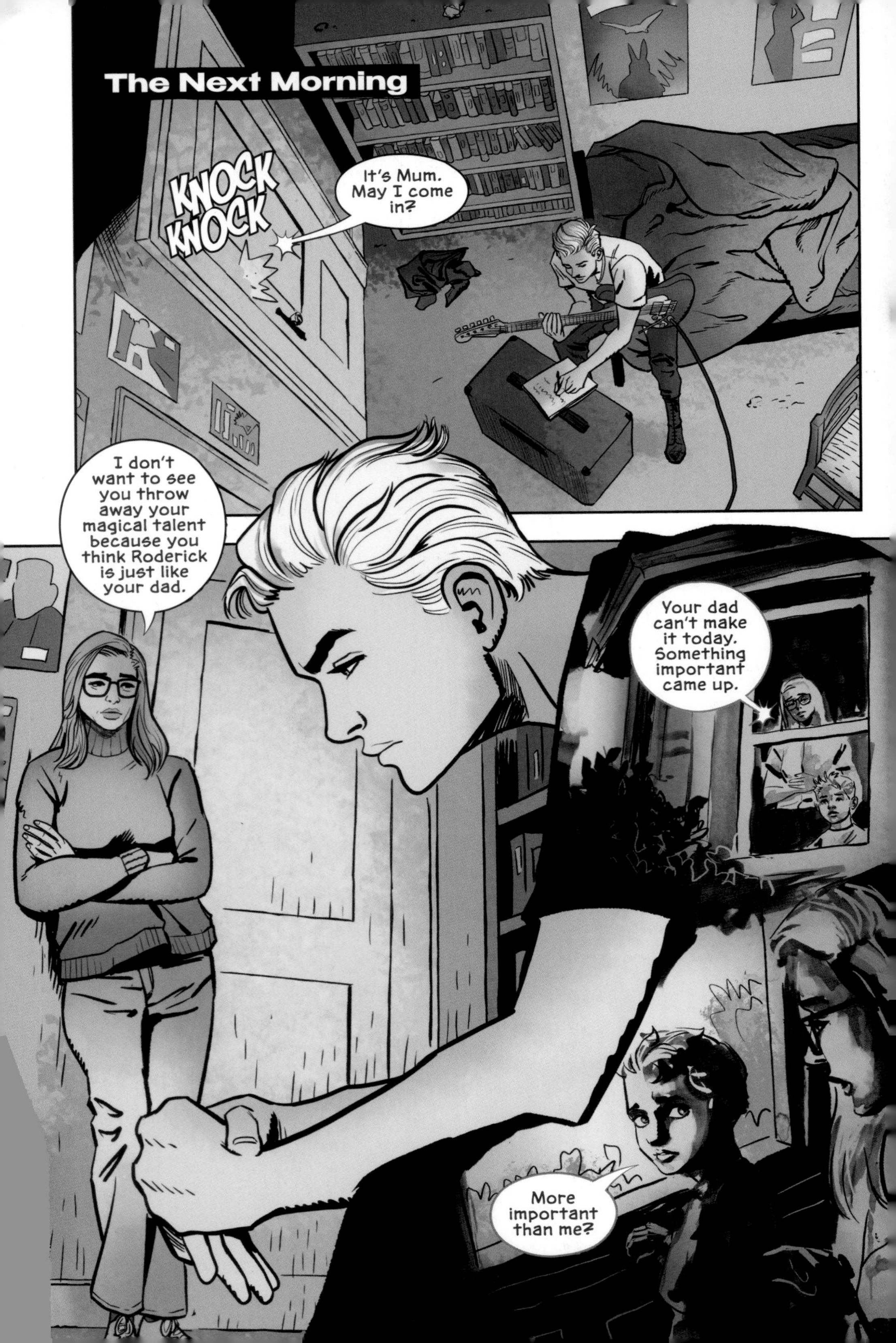
The Next Morning
KNOCK KNOCK
It's Mum. May I come in?
I don't want to see you throw away your magical talent because you think Roderick is just like your dad.
Your dad can't make it today. Something important came up.
More important than me?

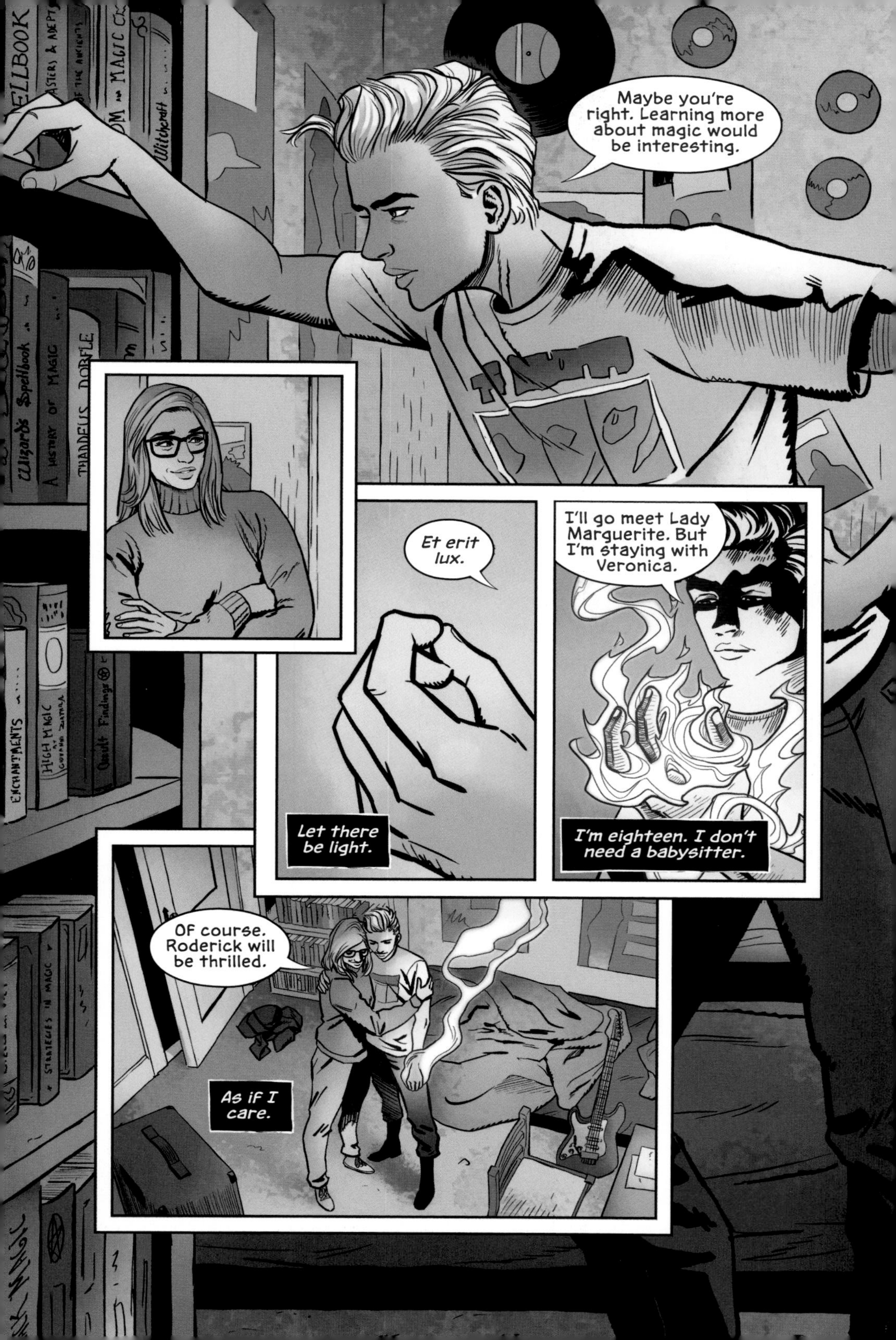
Maybe you're right. Learning more about magic would be interesting.
Et erit lux.
Let there be light.
I'll go meet Lady Marguerite. But I'm staying with Veronica.
I'm eighteen. I don't need a babysitter.
Of course. Roderick will be thrilled.
As if I care.

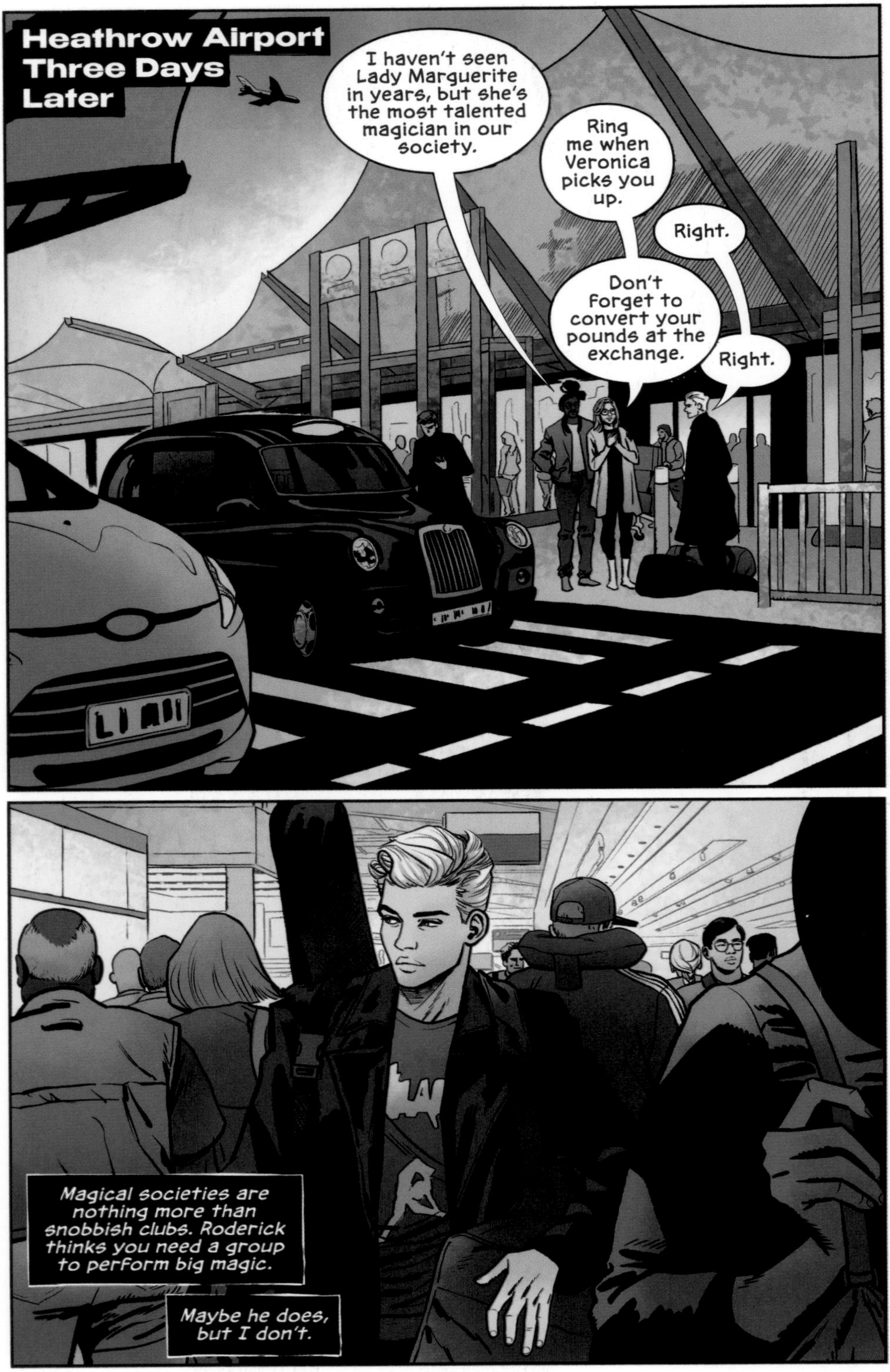
Heathrow Airport
Three Days
Later
I haven't seen Lady Marguerite in years, but she's the most talented magician in our society.
Ring me when Veronica picks you up.
Right.
Don't forget to convert your pounds at the exchange.
Right.
Magical societies are nothing more than snobbish clubs. Roderick thinks you need a group to perform big magic.
Maybe he does, but I don't.

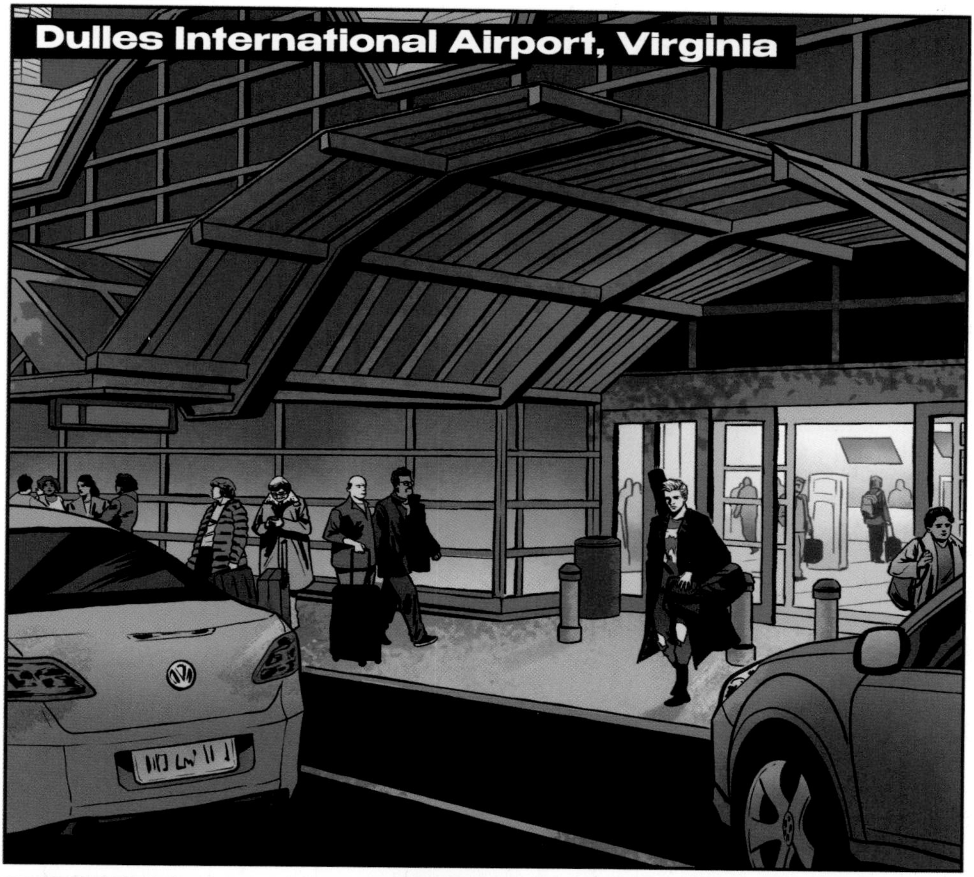
Dulles International Airport, Virginia

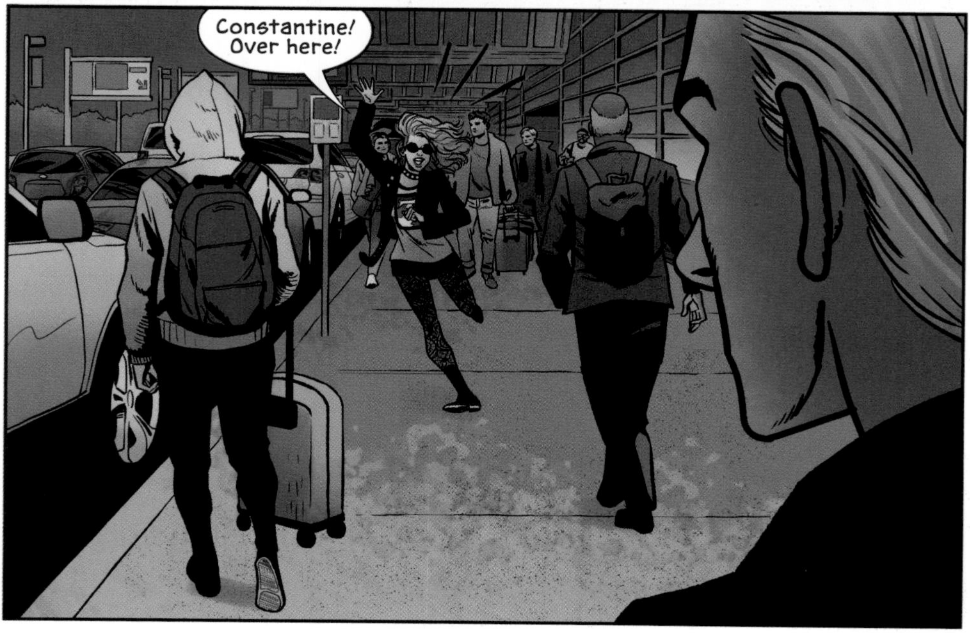
Constantine! Over here!

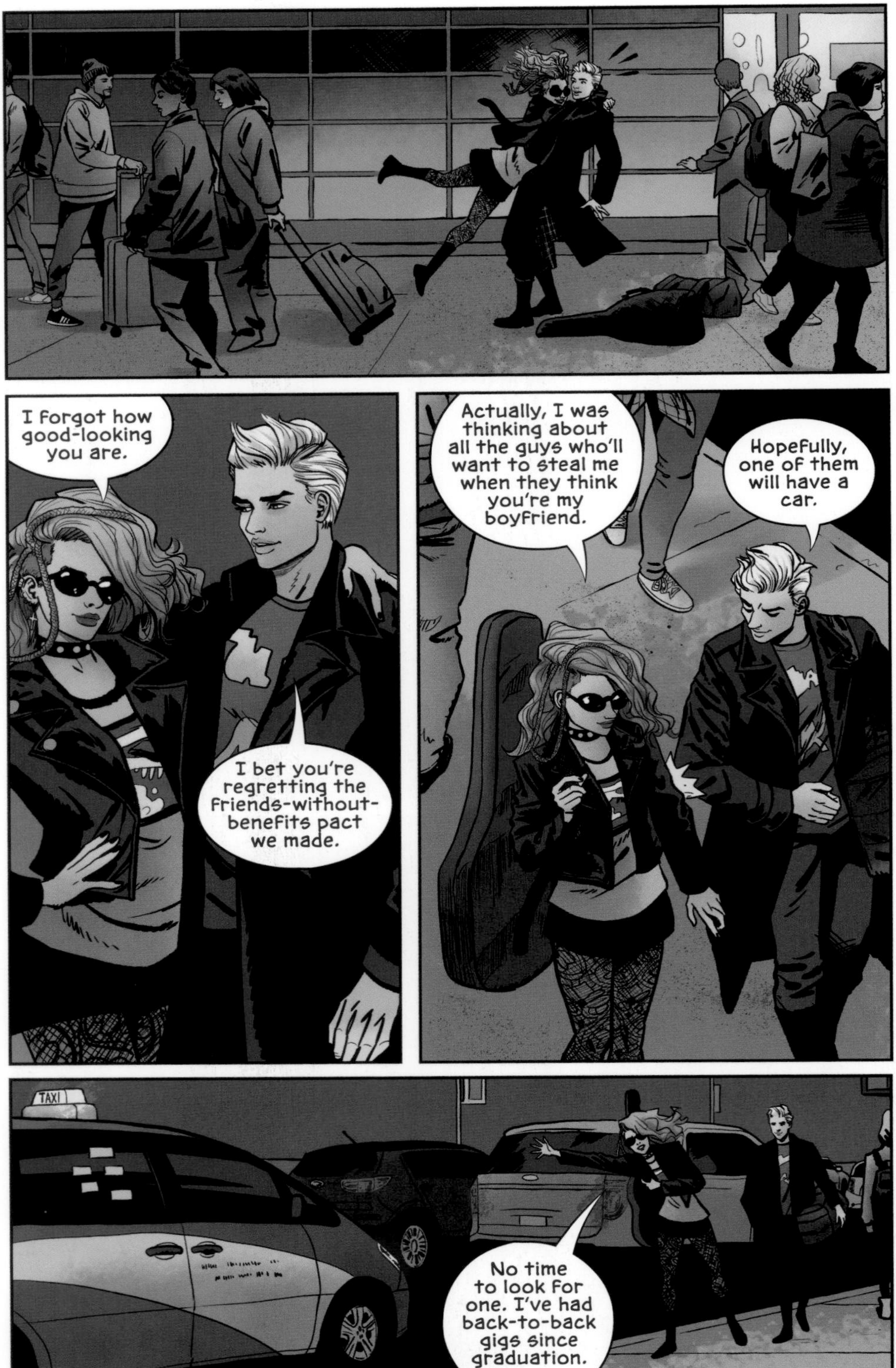
I forgot how good-looking you are.
I bet you're regretting the friends-without-benefits pact we made.
Actually, I was thinking about all the guys who'll want to steal me when they think you're my boyfriend.
Hopefully, one of them will have a car.
TAXI
No time to look for one. I've had back-to-back gigs since graduation.

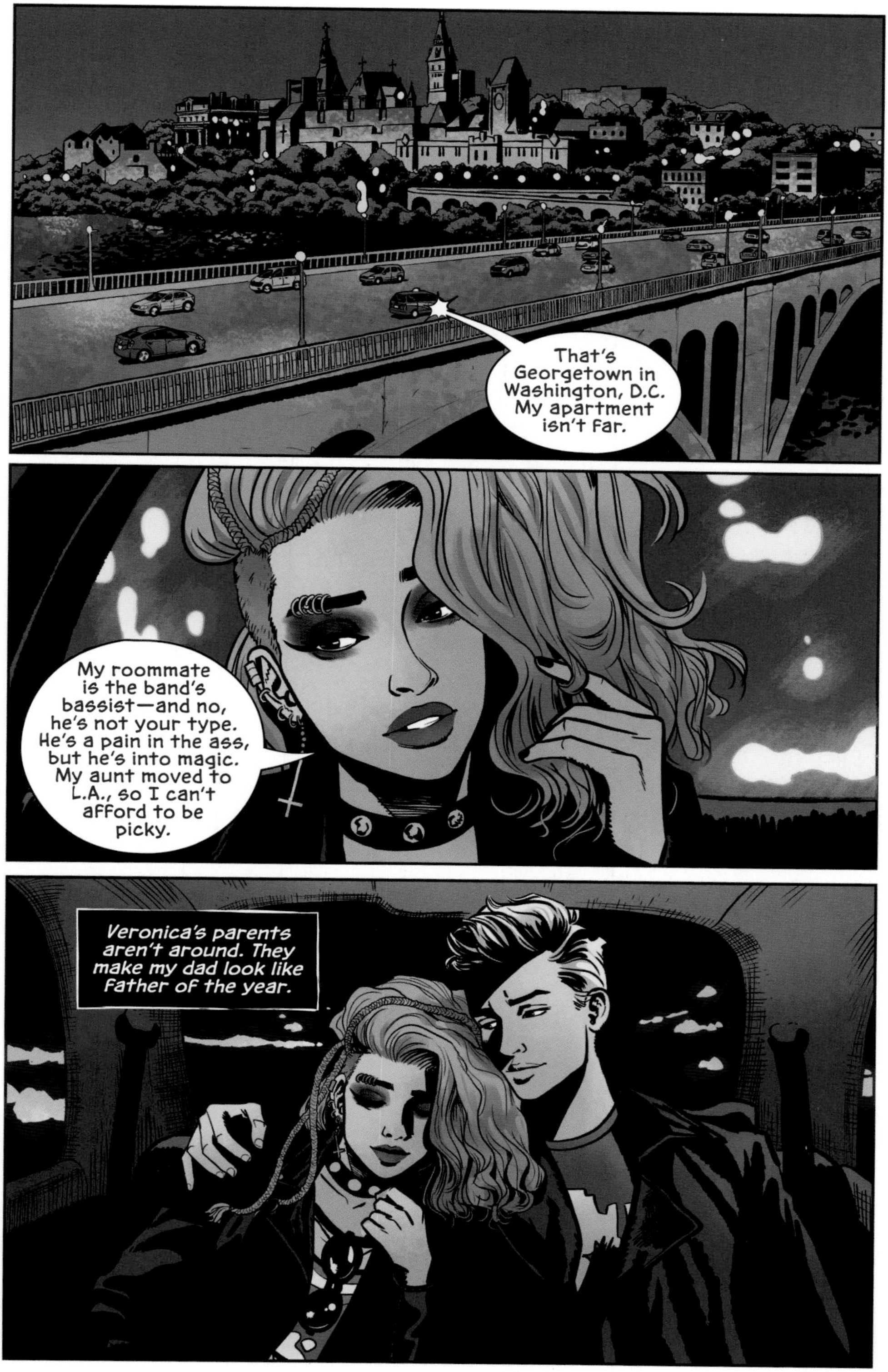

That's Georgetown in Washington, D.C. My apartment isn't far.
My roommate is the band's bassist—and no, he's not your type. He's a pain in the ass, but he's into magic. My aunt moved to L.A., so I can't afford to be picky.
Veronica's parents aren't around. They make my dad look like father of the year.

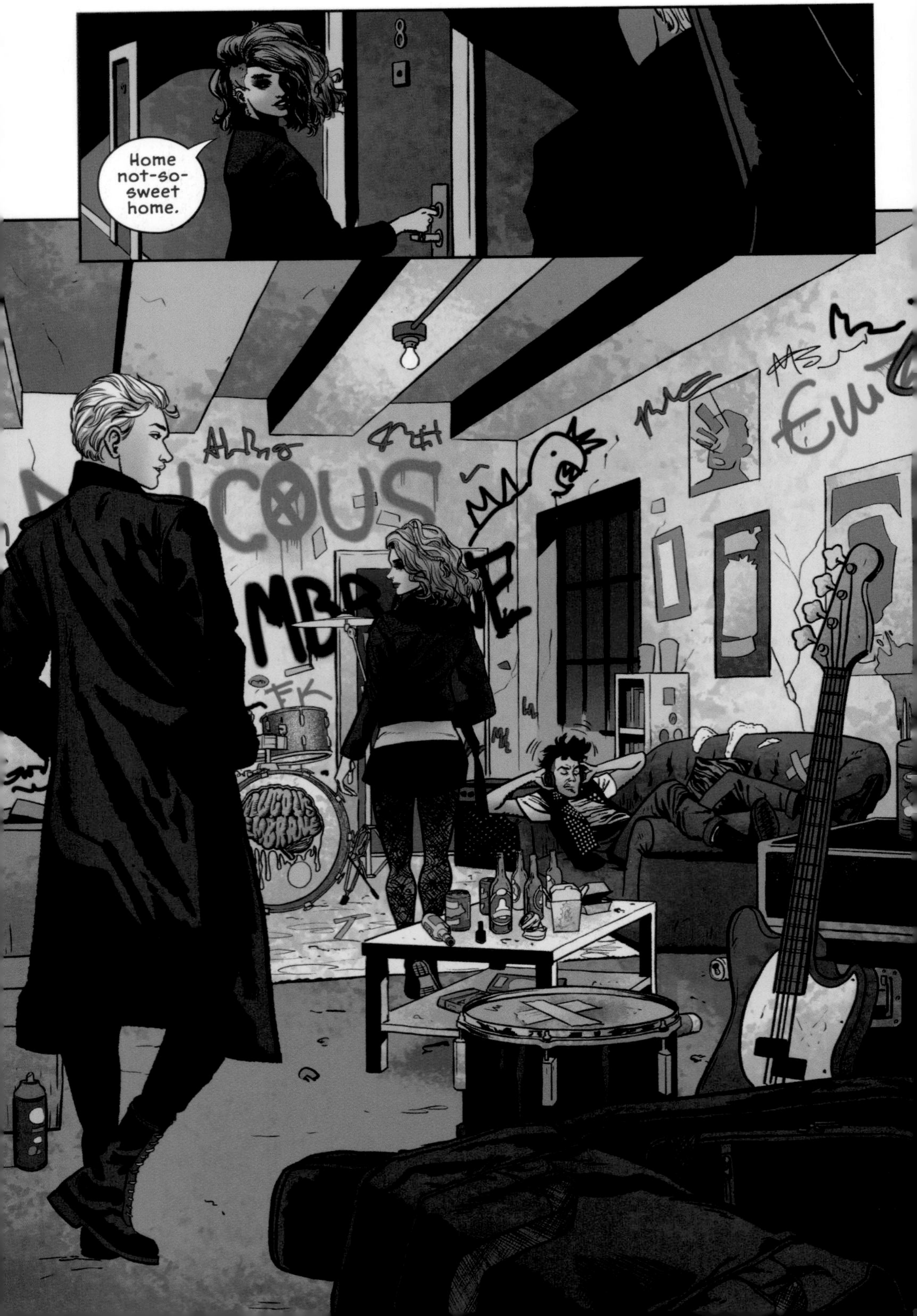
Home not-so-sweet home.

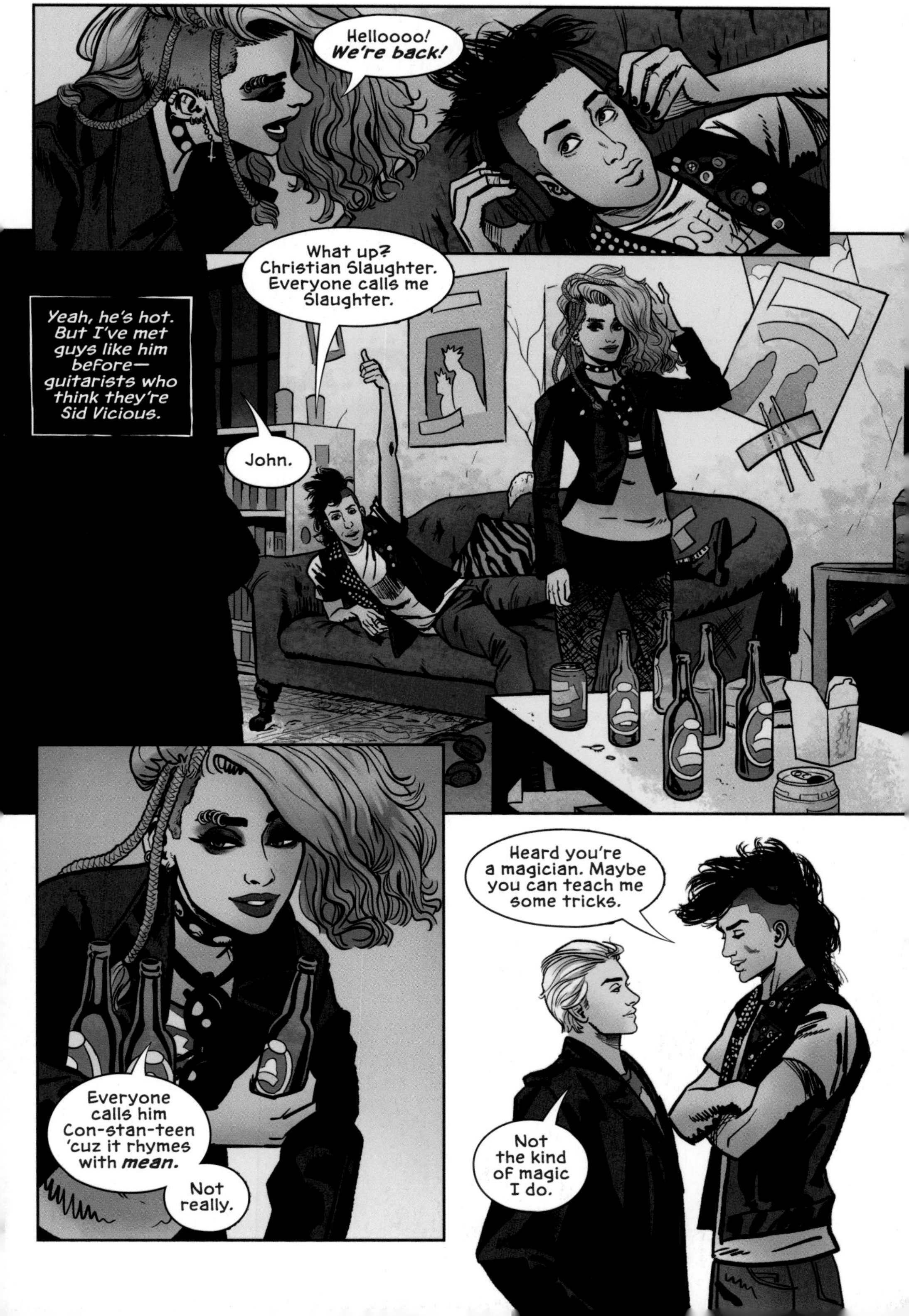
Helloooo! *We're back!*
What up? Christian Slaughter. Everyone calls me Slaughter.
Yeah, he's hot. But I've met guys like him before—guitarists who think they're Sid Vicious.
John.
Everyone calls him Con-stan-teen 'cuz it rhymes with *mean.*
Not really.
Heard you're a magician. Maybe you can teach me some tricks.
Not the kind of magic I do.

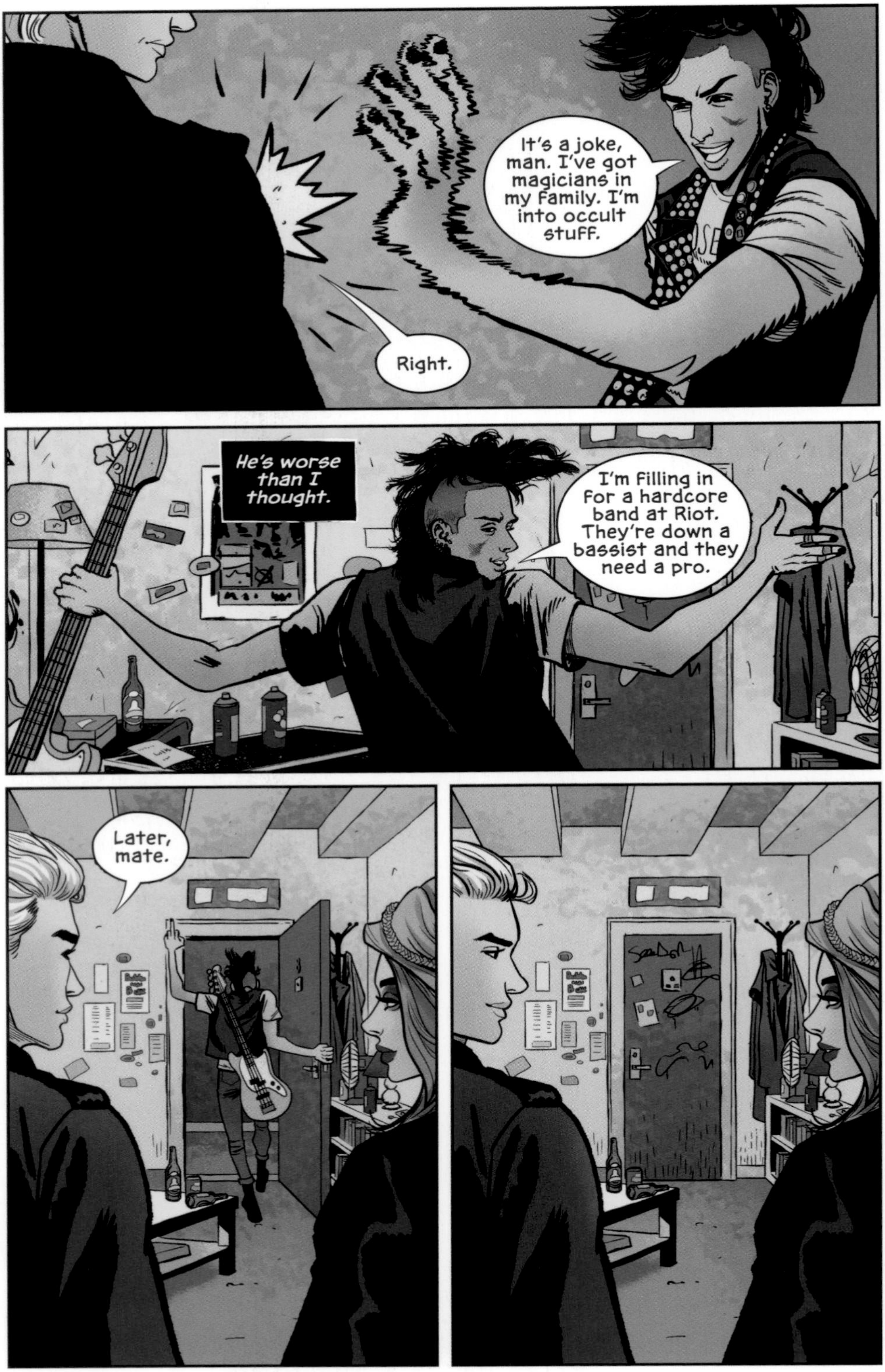
It's a joke, man. I've got magicians in my family. I'm into occult stuff.
Right.
He's worse than I thought.
I'm filling in for a hardcore band at Riot. They're down a bassist and they need a pro.
Later, mate.

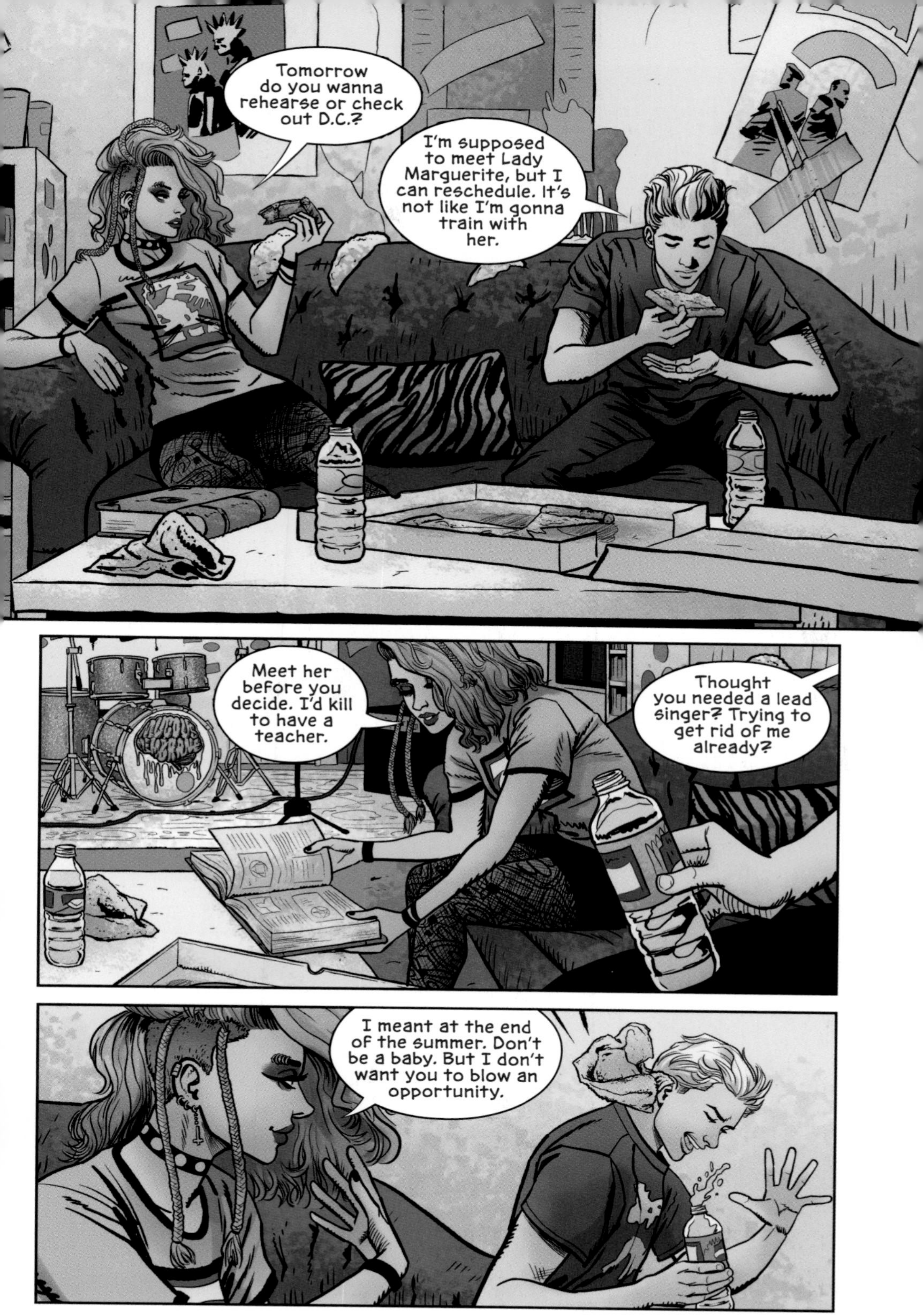
Tomorrow do you wanna rehearse or check out D.C.?
I'm supposed to meet Lady Marguerite, but I can reschedule. It's not like I'm gonna train with her.
Meet her before you decide. I'd kill to have a teacher.
Thought you needed a lead singer? Trying to get rid of me already?
I meant at the end of the summer. Don't be a baby. But I don't want you to blow an opportunity.

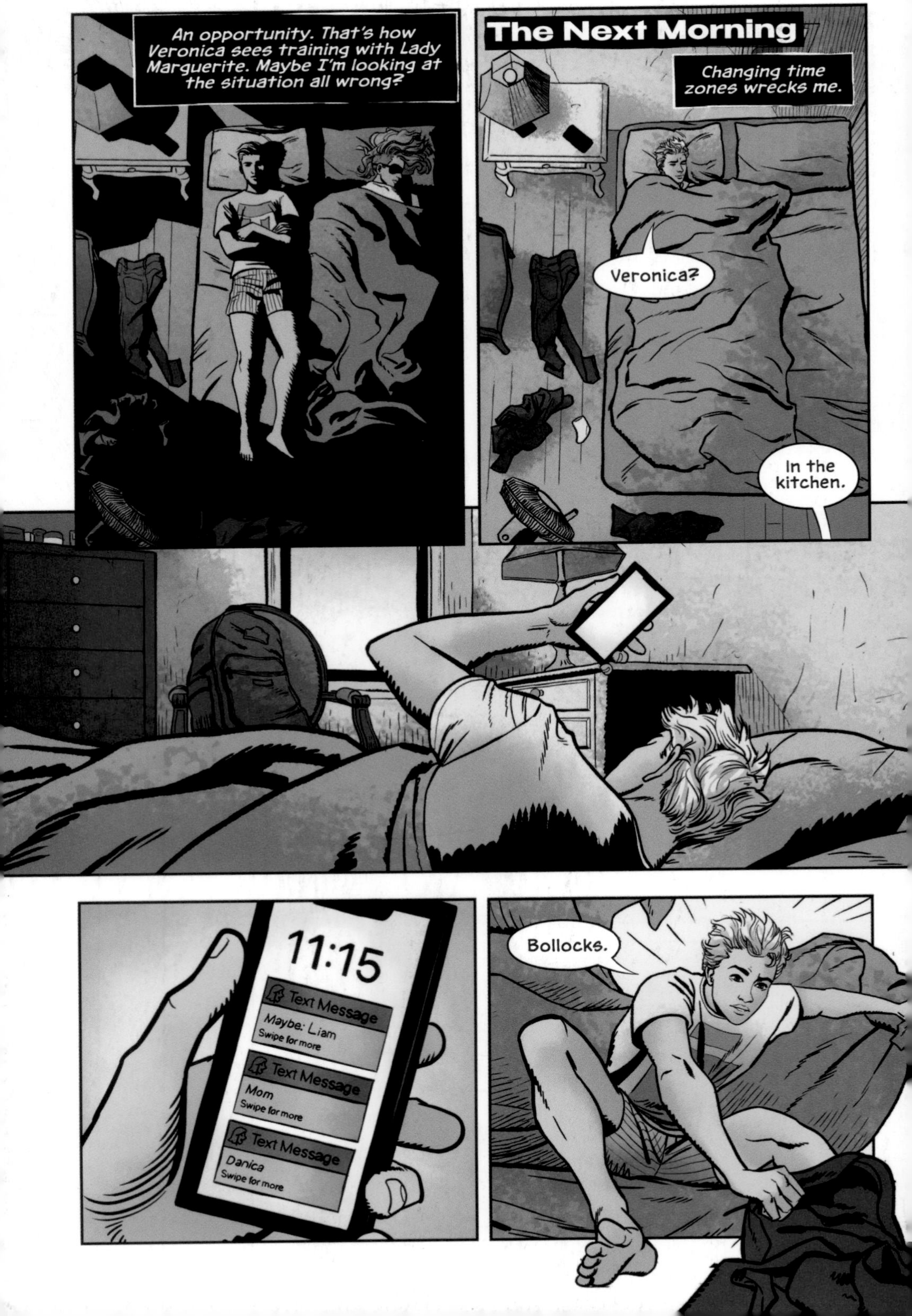

An opportunity. That's how Veronica sees training with Lady Marguerite. Maybe I'm looking at the situation all wrong?
The Next Morning
Changing time zones wrecks me.
Veronica?
In the kitchen.
11:15
Text Message
Maybe: Liam
Swipe for more
Text Message
Mom
Swipe for more
Text Message
Danica
Swipe for more
Bollocks.

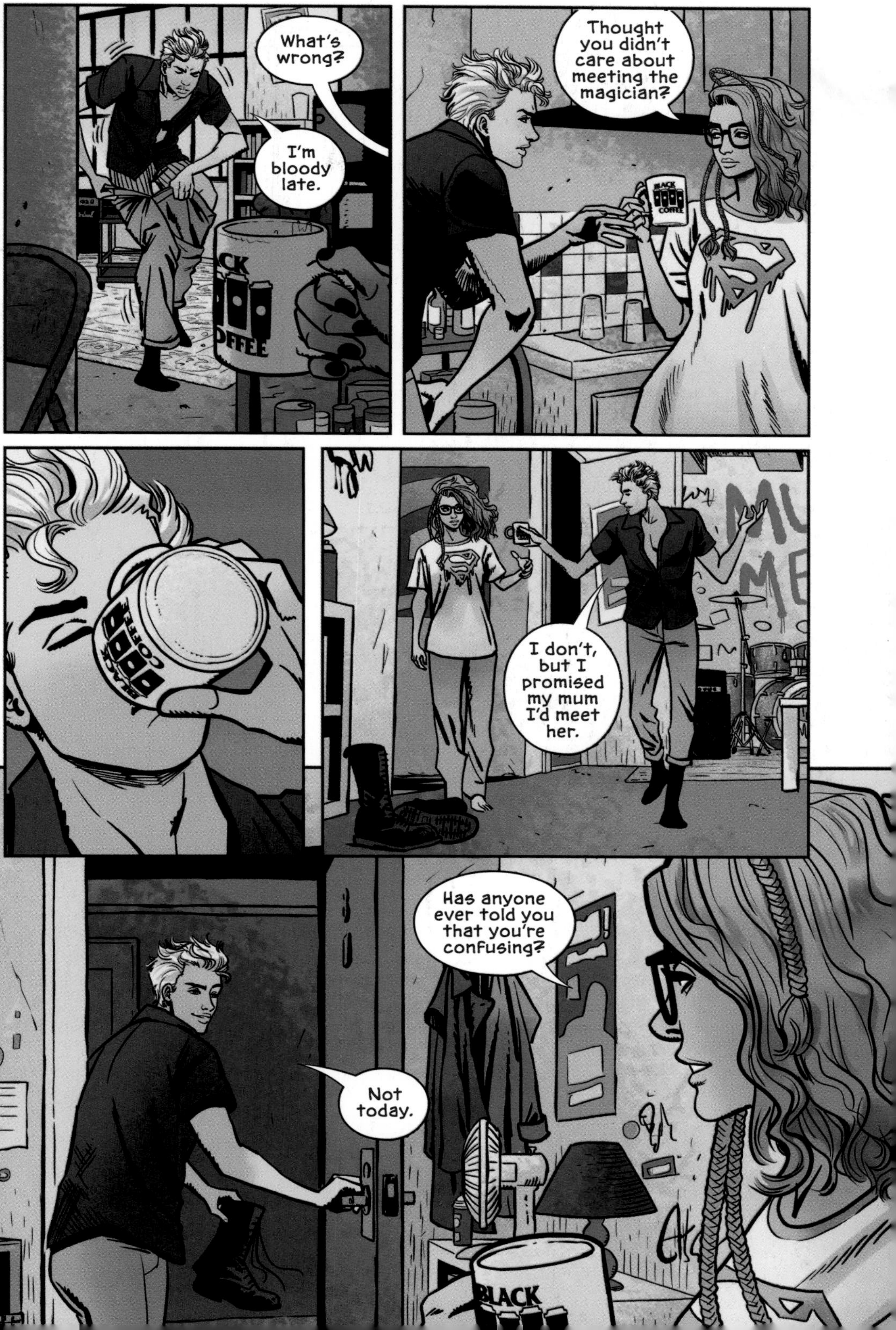
What's wrong?
I'm bloody late.
Thought you didn't care about meeting the magician?
I don't, but I promised my mum I'd meet her.
Has anyone ever told you that you're confusing?
Not today.

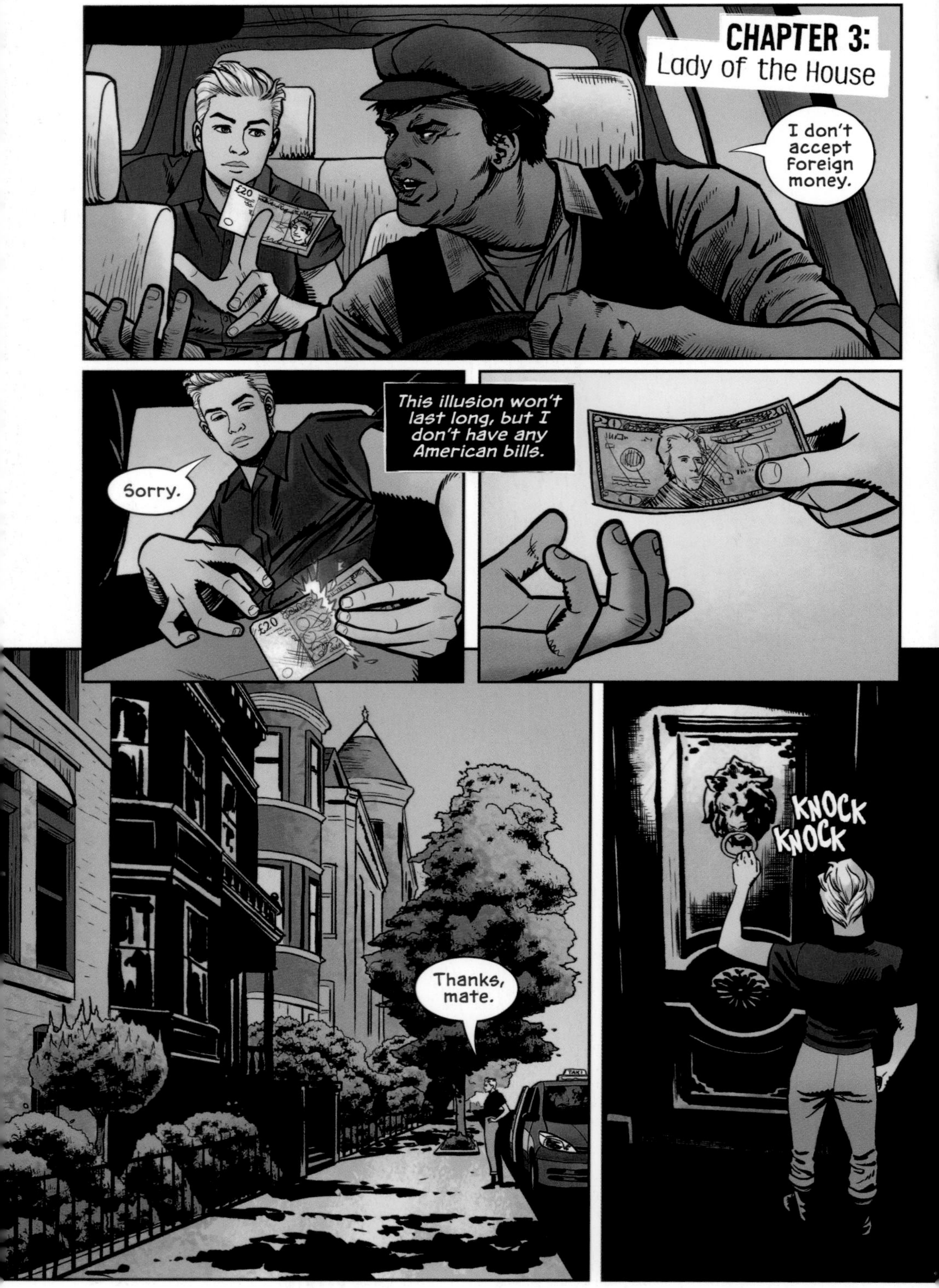
CHAPTER 3:
Lady of the House
I don't accept foreign money.
This illusion won't last long, but I don't have any American bills.
Sorry.
Thanks, mate.
KNOCK
KNOCK

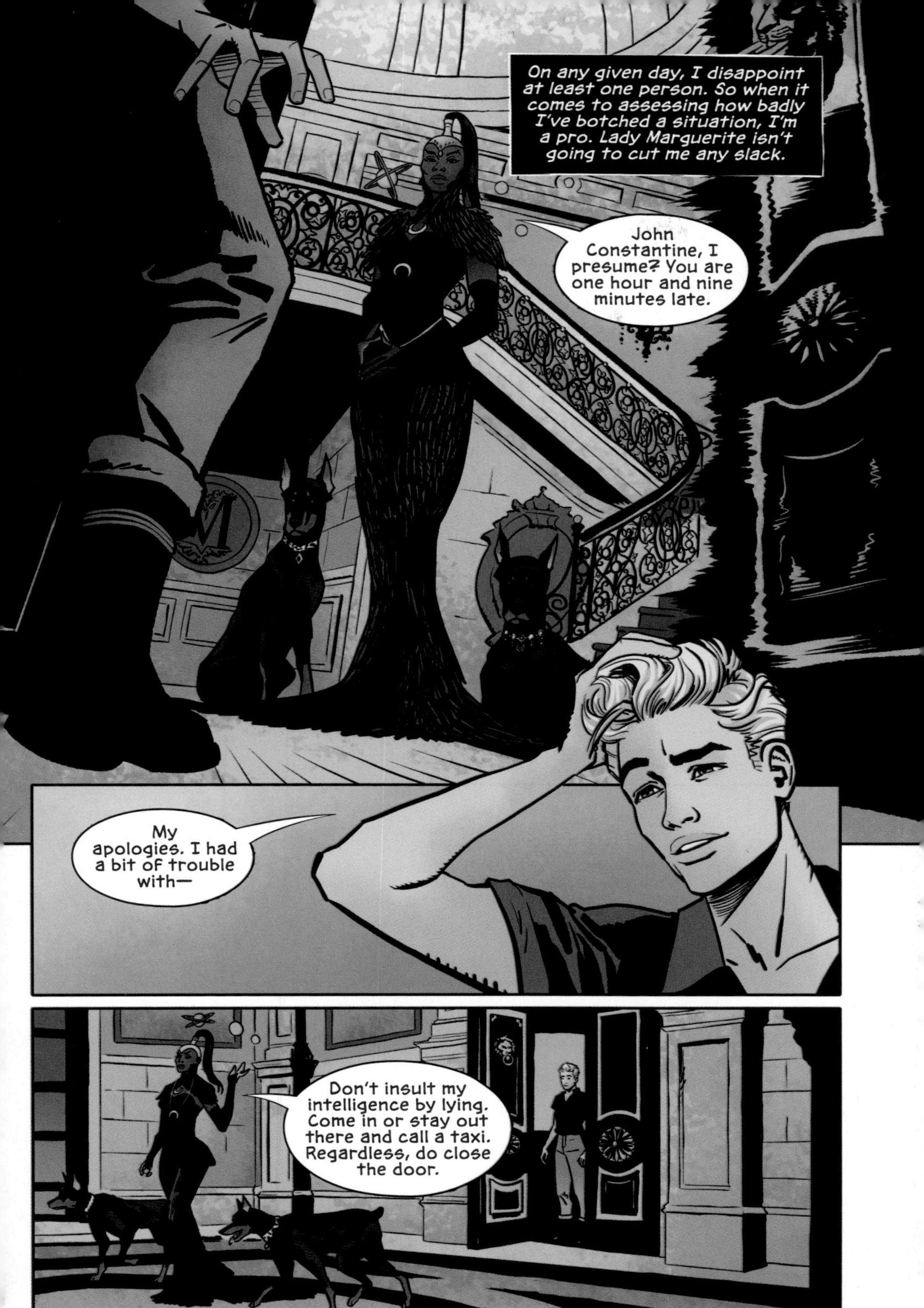
On any given day, I disappoint at least one person. So when it comes to assessing how badly I've botched a situation, I'm a pro. Lady Marguerite isn't going to cut me any slack.
John Constantine, I presume? You are one hour and nine minutes late.
My apologies. I had a bit of trouble with—
Don't insult my intelligence by lying. Come in or stay out there and call a taxi. Regardless, do close the door.

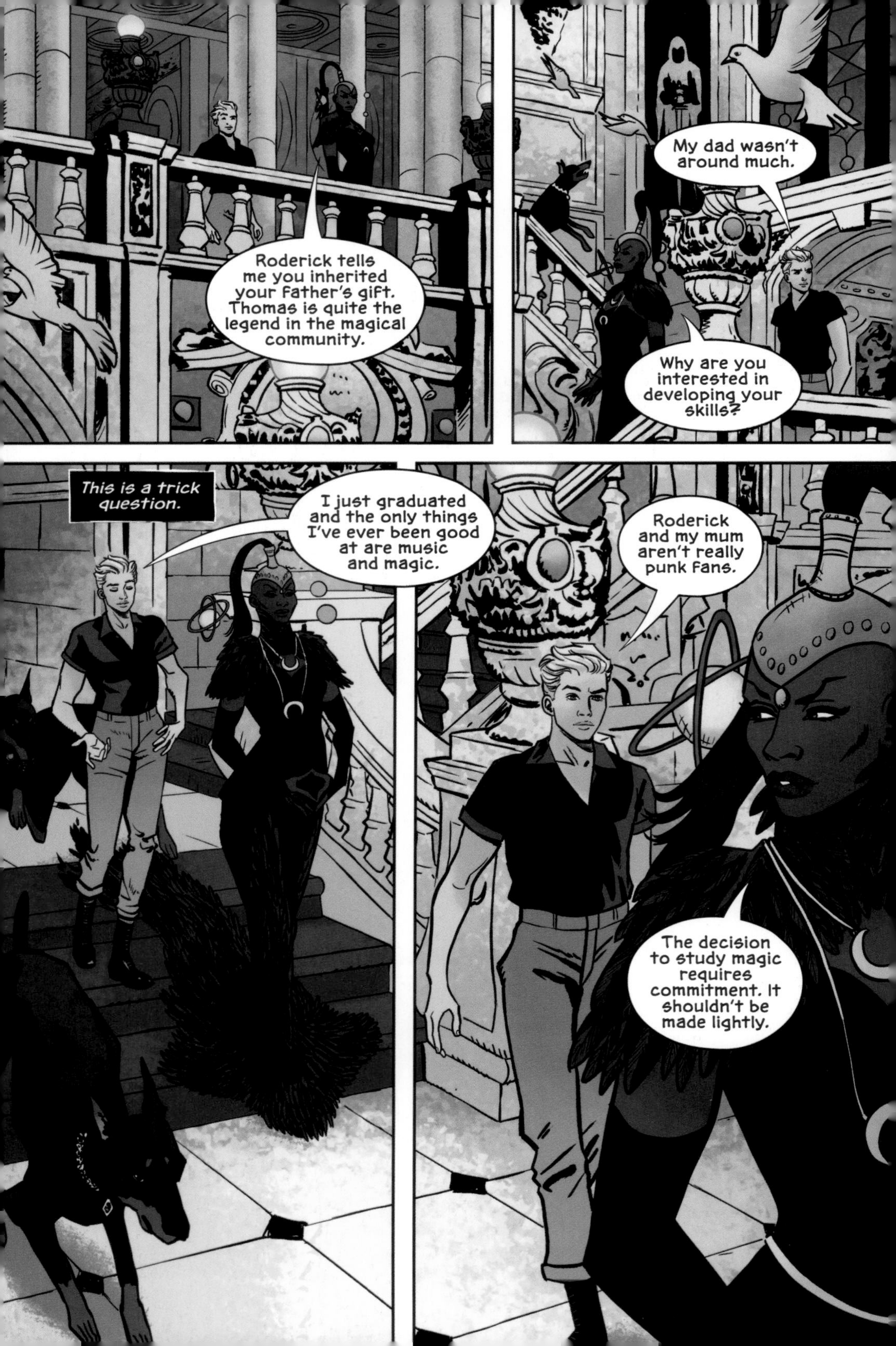
Roderick tells me you inherited your father's gift. Thomas is quite the legend in the magical community.
My dad wasn't around much.
Why are you interested in developing your skills?
This is a trick question.
I just graduated and the only things I've ever been good at are music and magic.
Roderick and my mum aren't really punk fans.
The decision to study magic requires commitment. It shouldn't be made lightly.

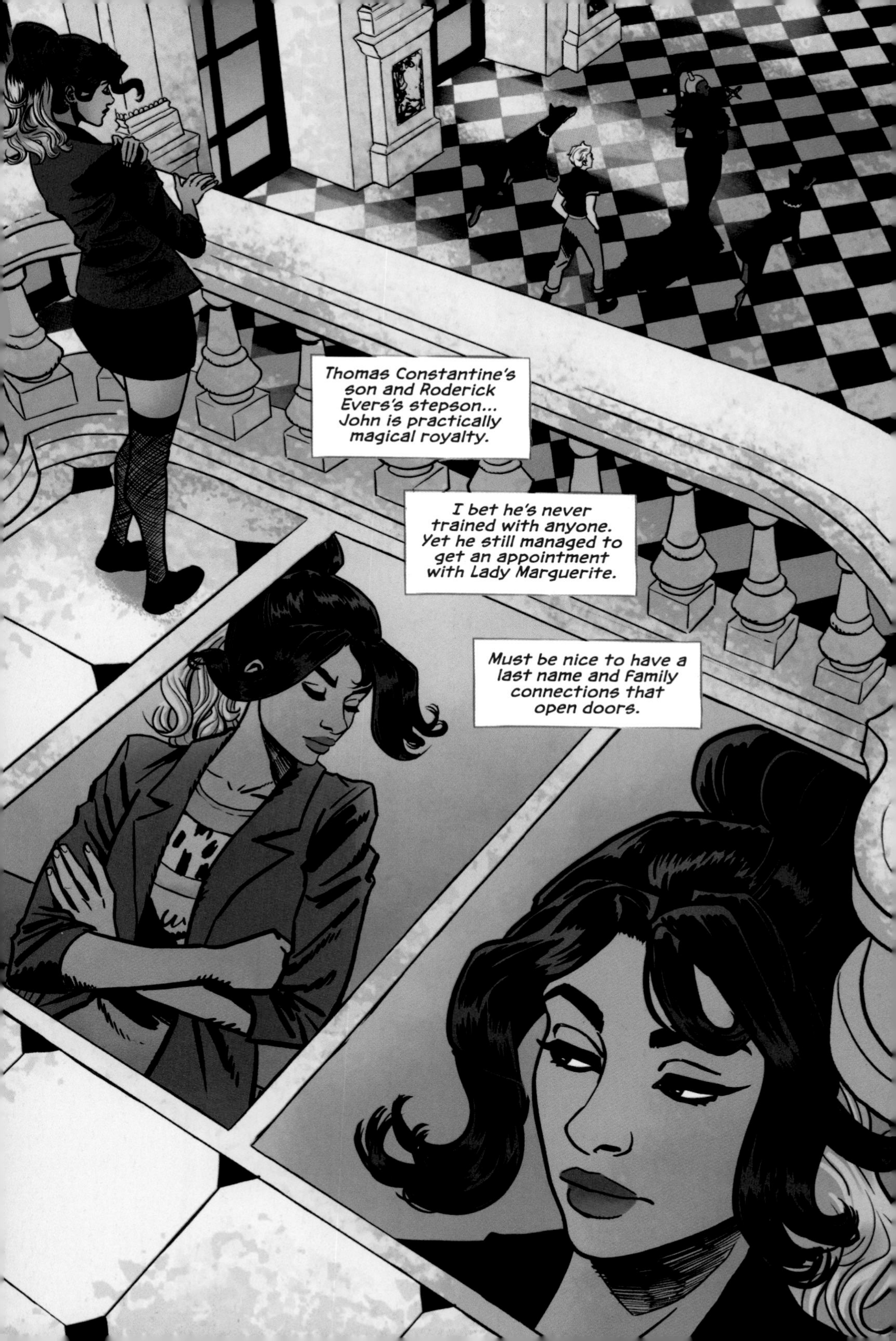
Thomas Constantine's son and Roderick Evers's stepson... John is practically magical royalty.
I bet he's never trained with anyone. Yet he still managed to get an appointment with Lady Marguerite.
Must be nice to have a last name and family connections that open doors.

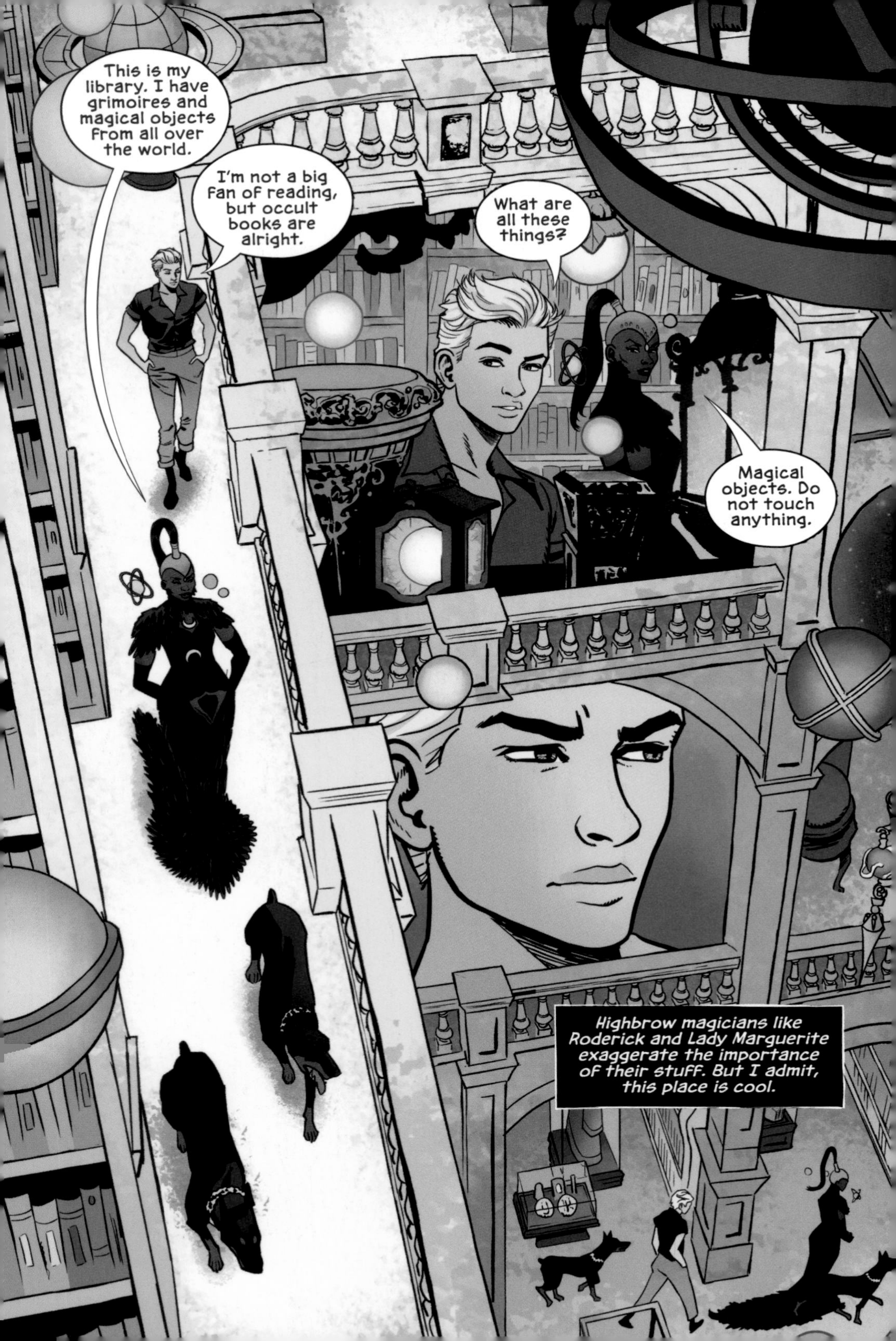
This is my library. I have grimoires and magical objects from all over the world.
I'm not a big fan of reading, but occult books are alright.
What are all these things?
Magical objects. Do not touch anything.
Highbrow magicians like Roderick and Lady Marguerite exaggerate the importance of their stuff. But I admit, this place is cool.

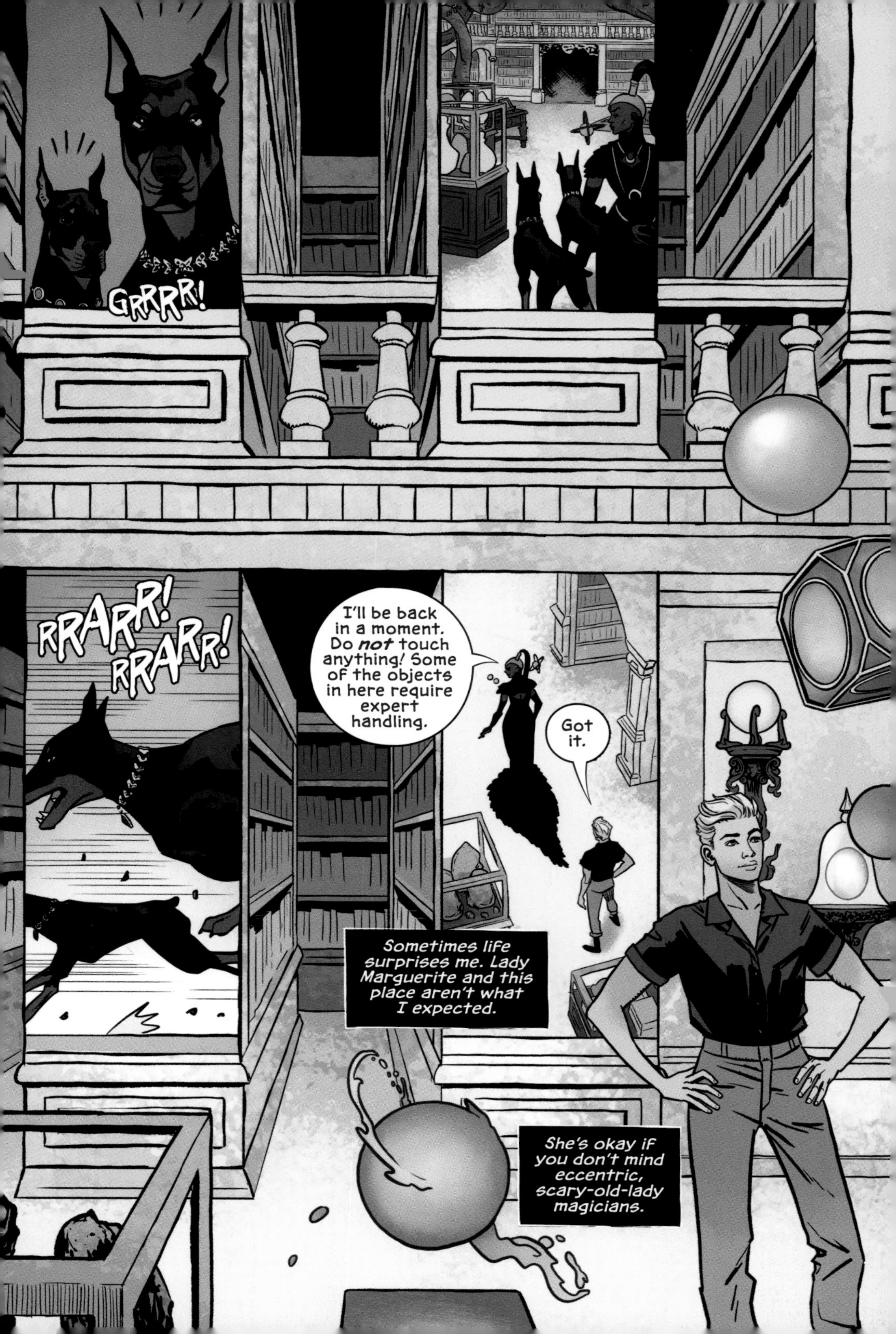
GRRRR!
RRARR! RRARR!
I'll be back in a moment. Do *not* touch anything! Some of the objects in here require expert handling.
Got it.
Sometimes life surprises me. Lady Marguerite and this place aren't what I expected.
She's okay if you don't mind eccentric, scary-old-lady magicians.

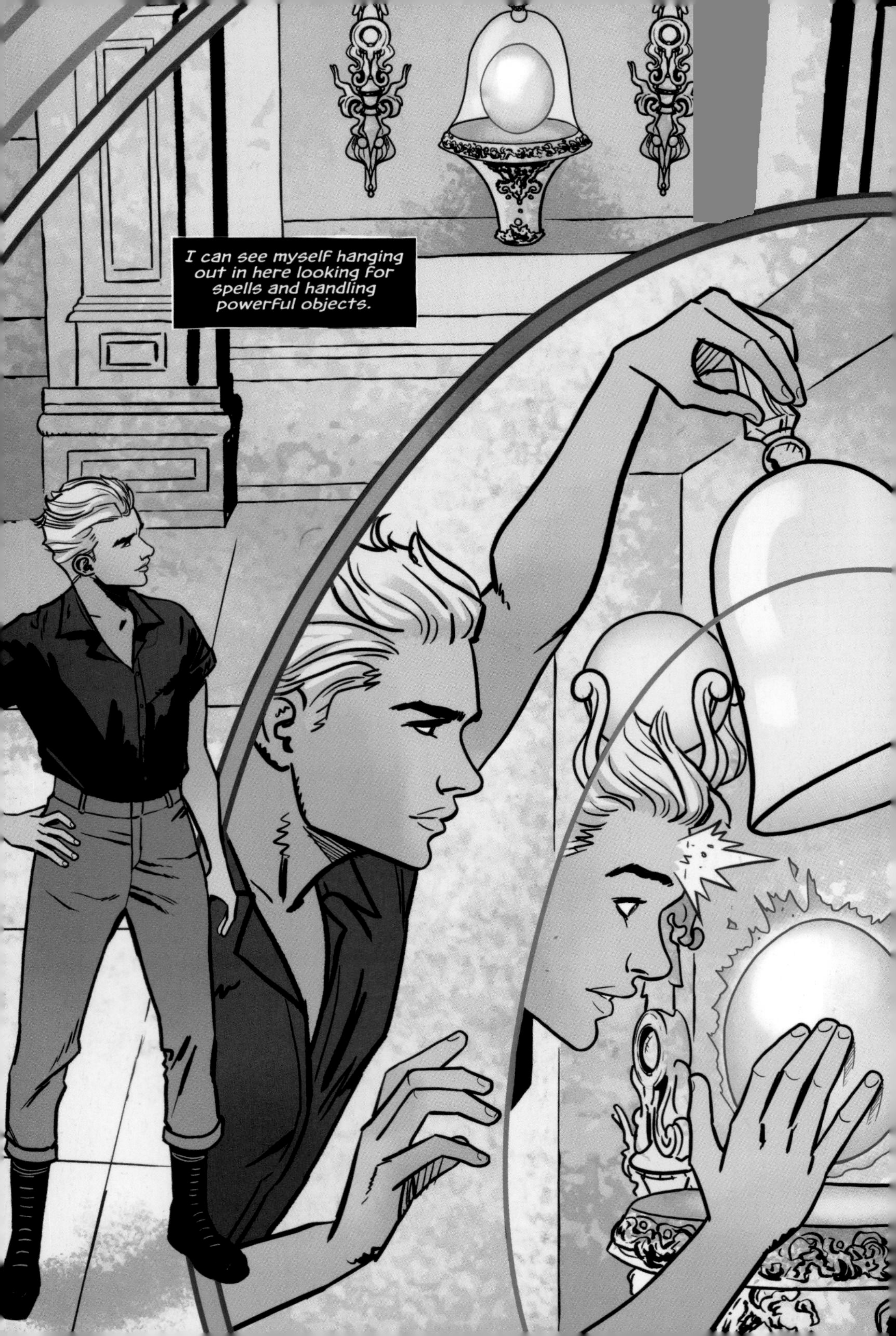
I can see myself hanging out in here looking for spells and handling powerful objects.

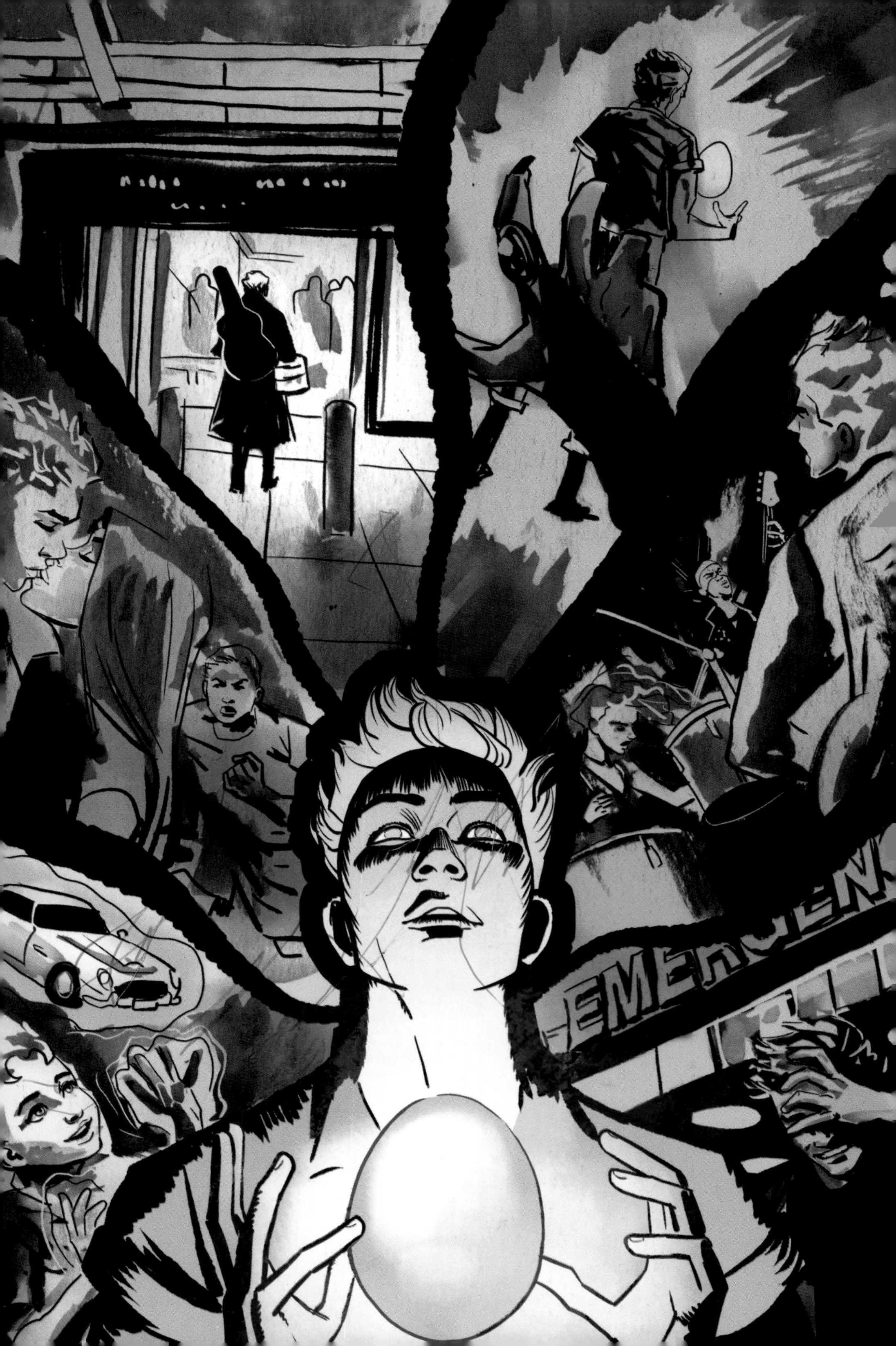
EMERGEN

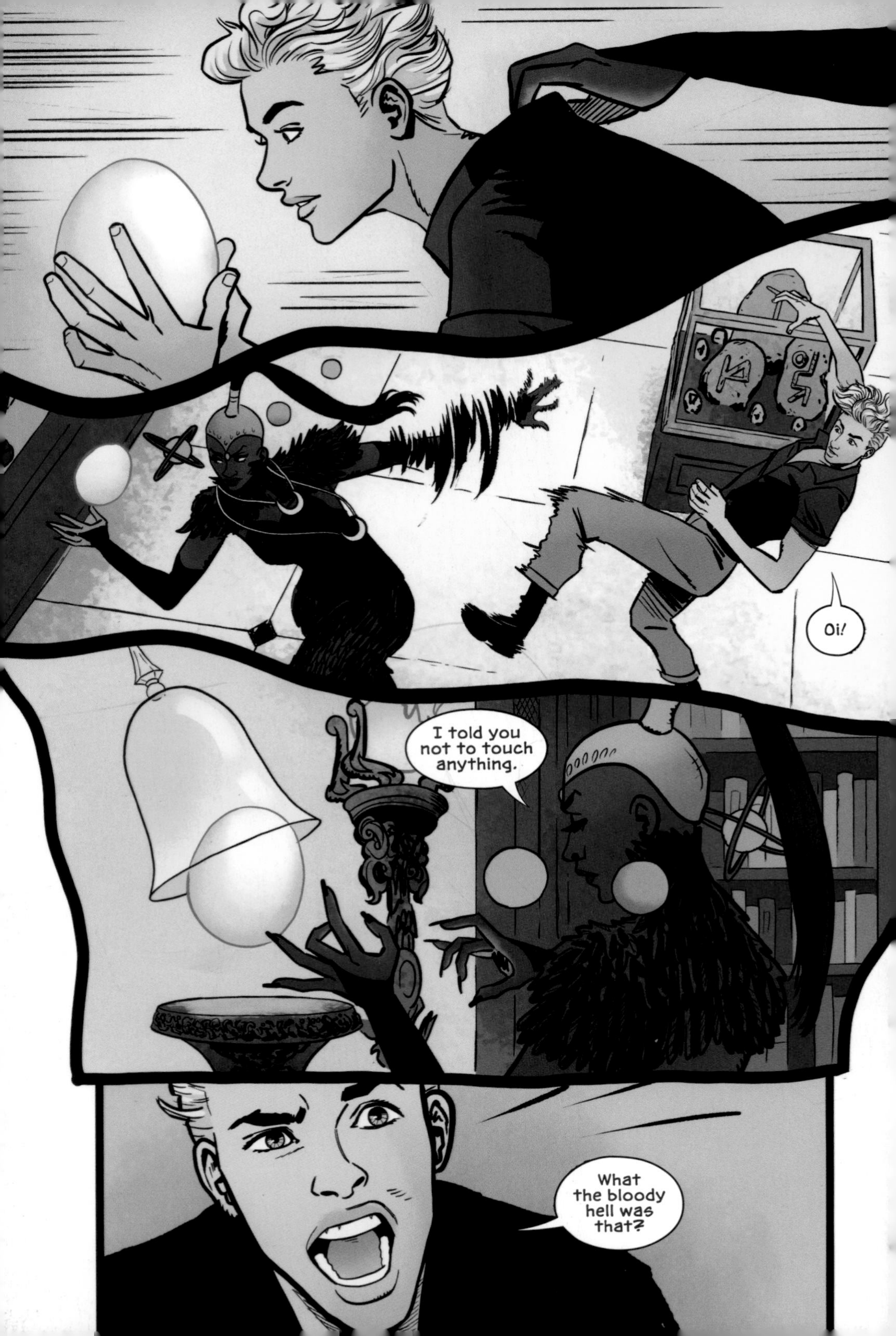
Oi!
I told you not to touch anything.
What the bloody hell was that?

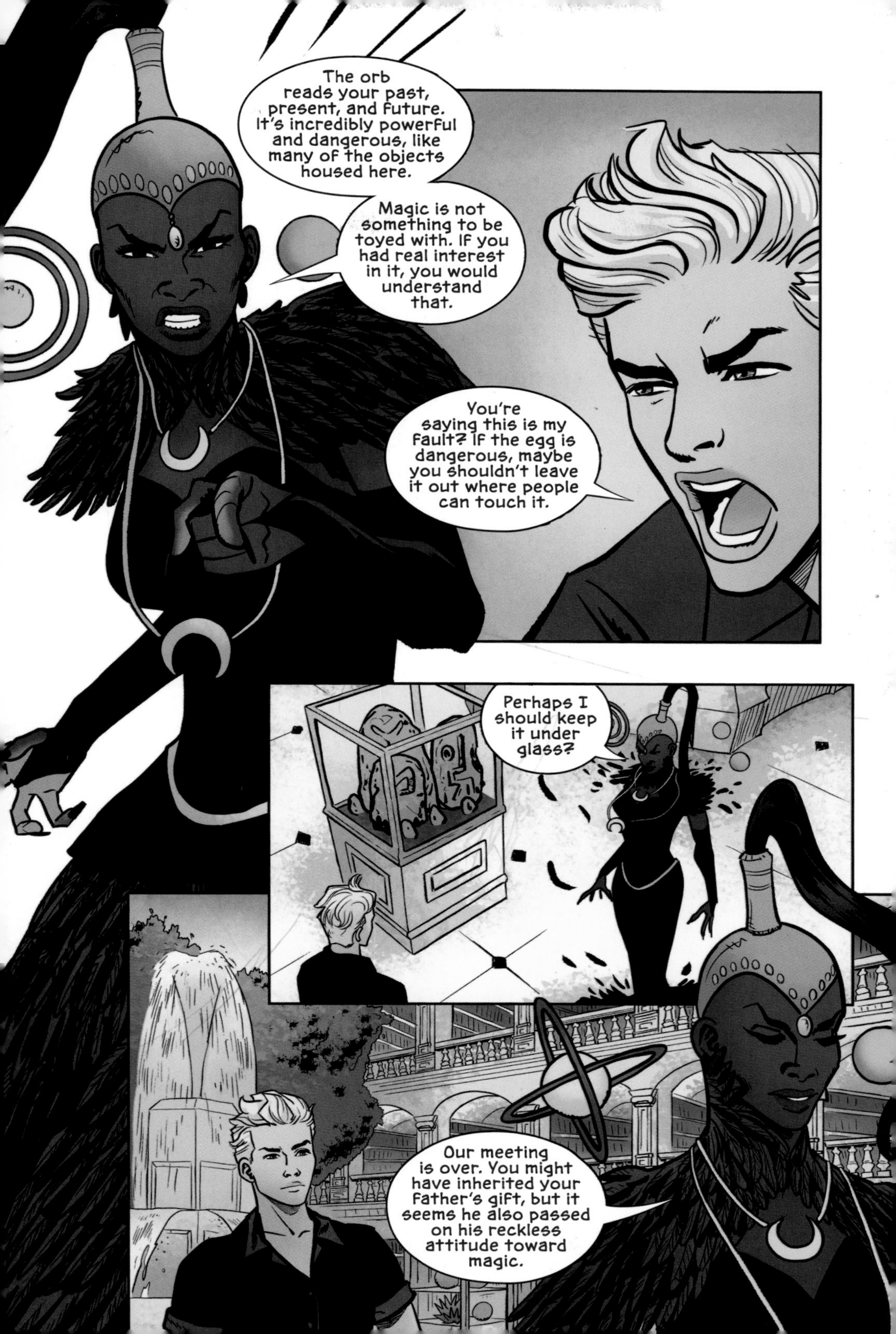
The orb reads your past, present, and future. It's incredibly powerful and dangerous, like many of the objects housed here.
Magic is not something to be toyed with. If you had real interest in it, you would understand that.
You're saying this is my fault? If the egg is dangerous, maybe you shouldn't leave it out where people can touch it.
Perhaps I should keep it under glass?
Our meeting is over. You might have inherited your father's gift, but it seems he also passed on his reckless attitude toward magic.

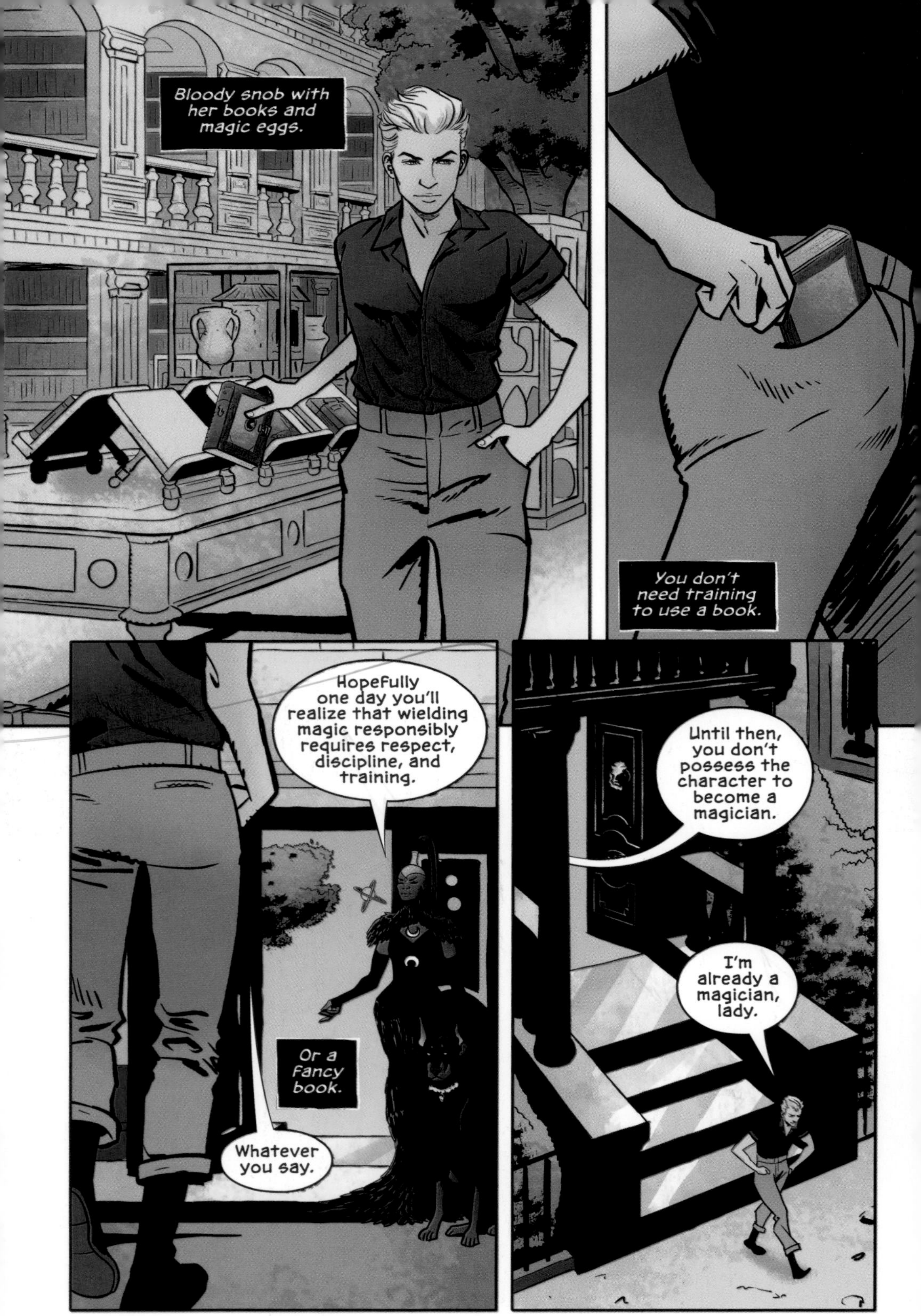
Bloody snob with her books and magic eggs.
You don't need training to use a book.
Hopefully one day you'll realize that wielding magic responsibly requires respect, discipline, and training.
Or a fancy book.
Whatever you say.
Until then, you don't possess the character to become a magician.
I'm already a magician, lady.

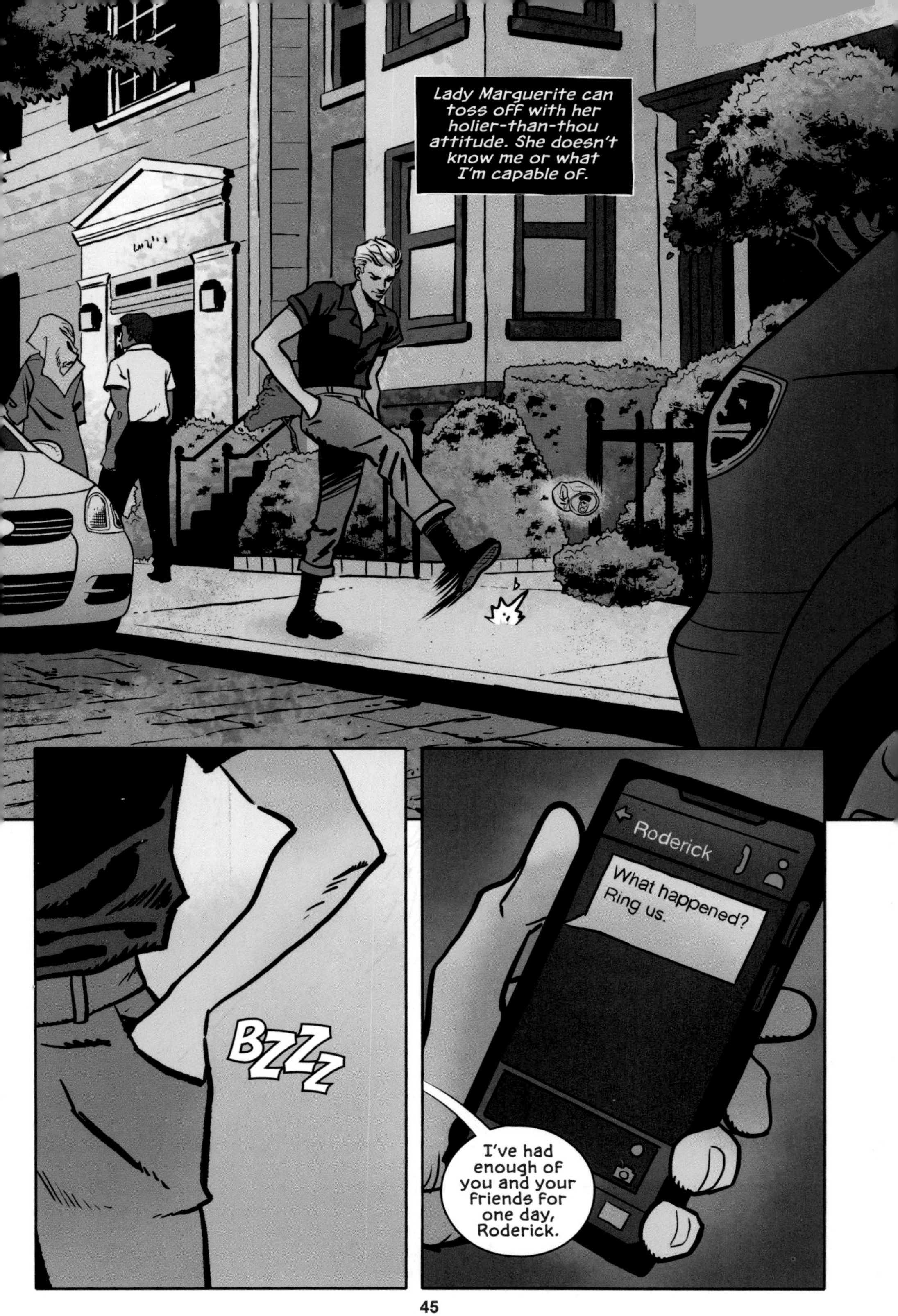
Lady Marguerite can toss off with her holier-than-thou attitude. She doesn't know me or what I'm capable of.
BZZZ
Roderick
What happened? Ring us.
I've had enough of you and your friends for one day, Roderick.

CHAPTER 4: Friends, Fire, and a Fancy Book

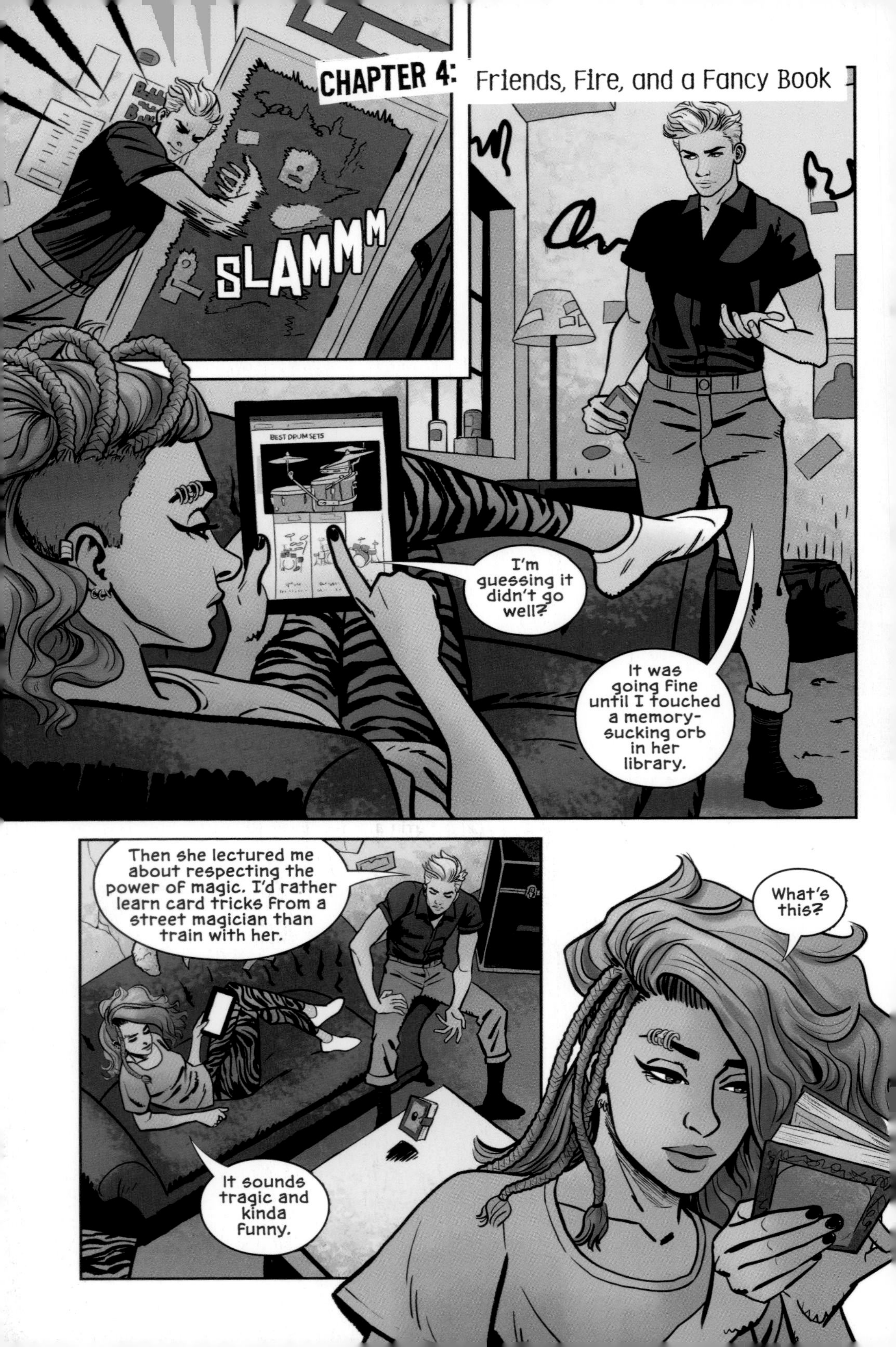

SLAMMM
BEST DRUM SETS
I'm guessing it didn't go well?
It was going fine until I touched a memory-sucking orb in her library.
Then she lectured me about respecting the power of magic. I'd rather learn card tricks from a street magician than train with her.
It sounds tragic and kinda funny.
What's this?

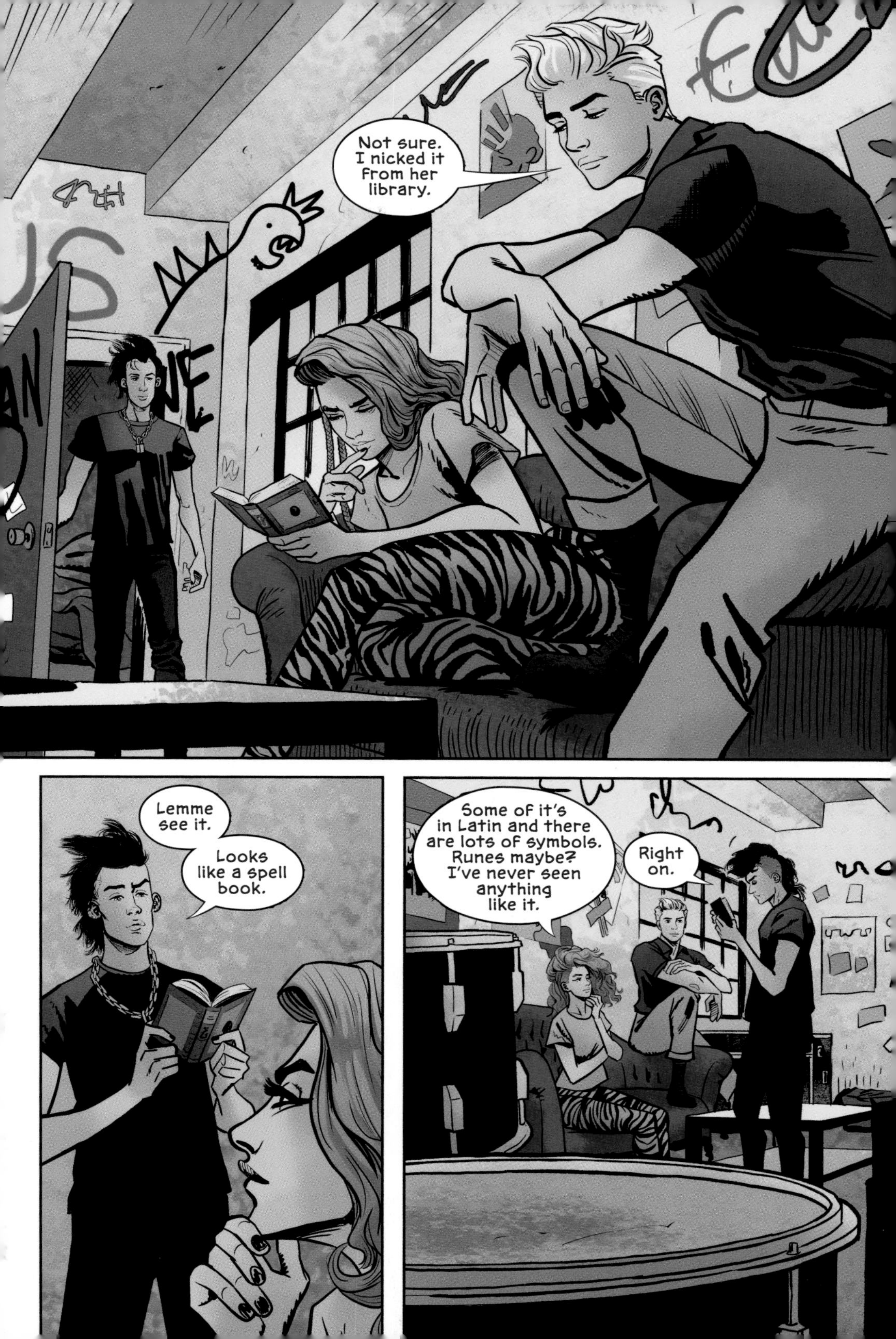
Not sure. I nicked it from her library.
Lemme see it.
Looks like a spell book.
Some of it's in Latin and there are lots of symbols. Runes maybe? I've never seen anything like it.
Right on.

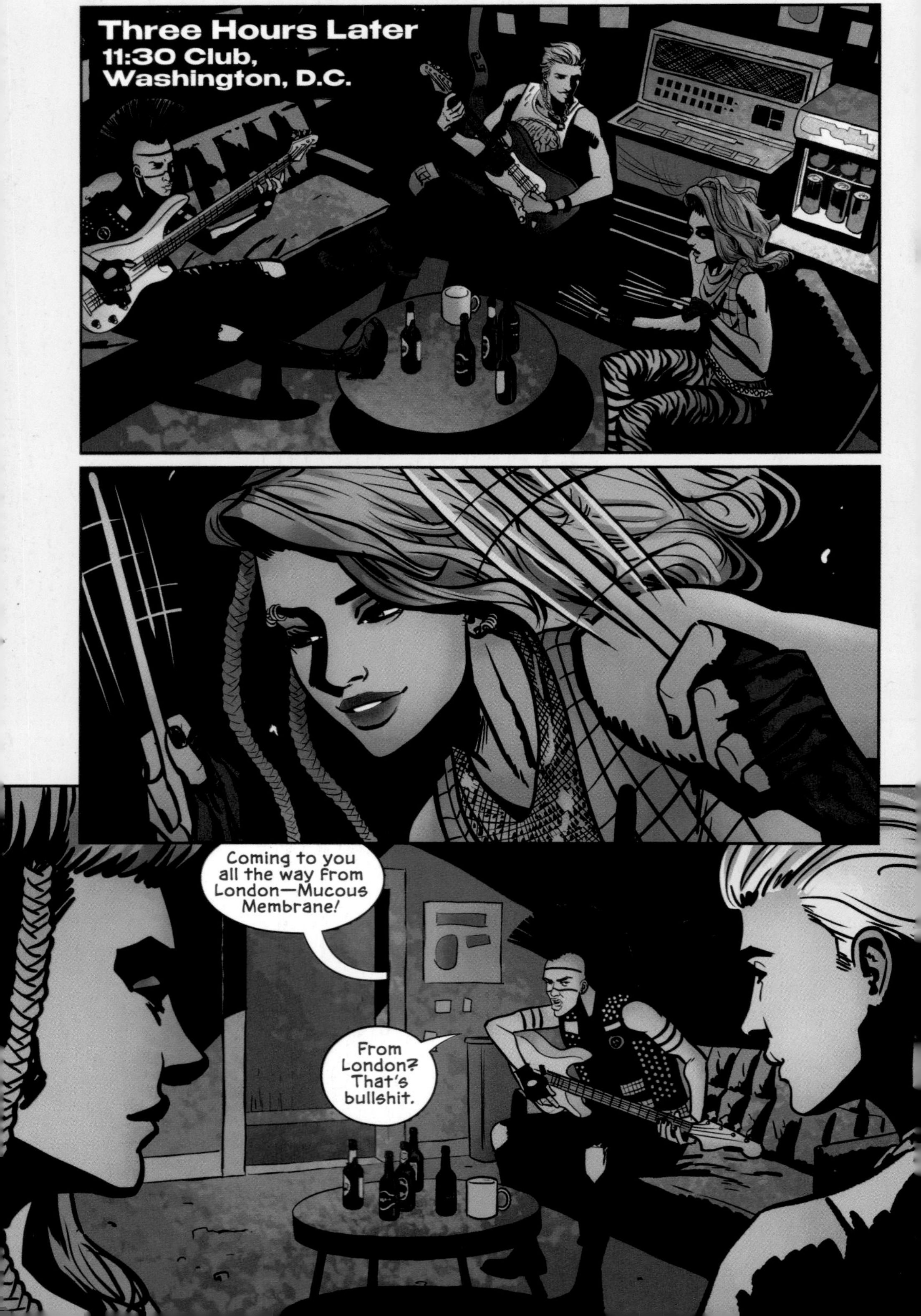
Three Hours Later
11:30 Club,
Washington, D.C.
Coming to you all the way from London—Mucous Membrane!
From London? That's bullshit.

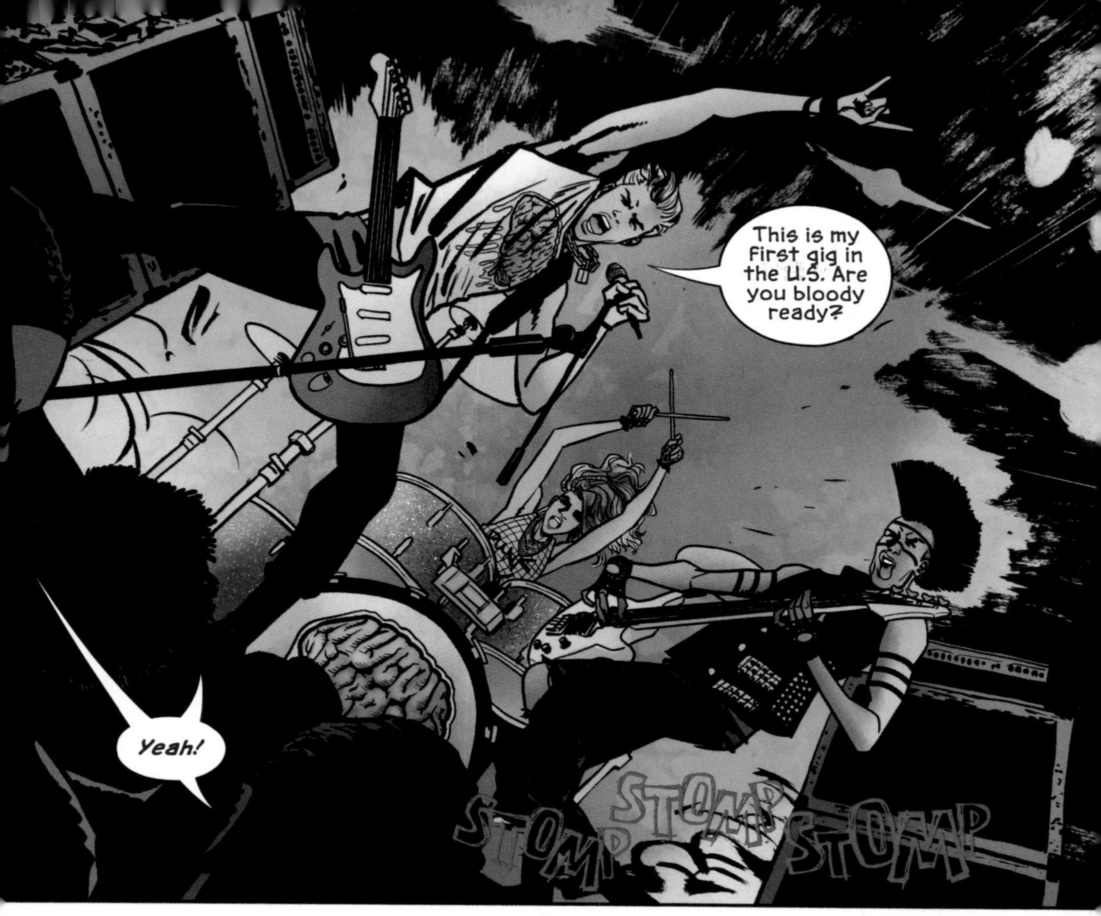
This is my first gig in the U.S. Are you bloody ready?
Yeah!
STOMP STOMP STOMP

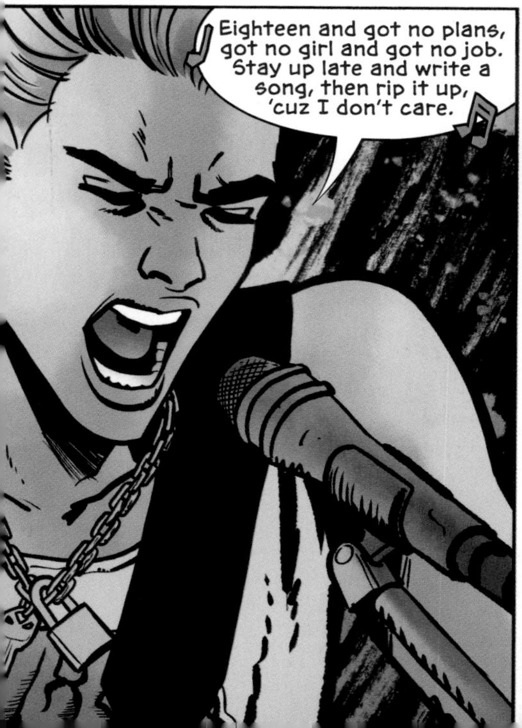
Eighteen and got no plans, got no girl and got no job. Stay up late and write a song, then rip it up, 'cuz I don't care.

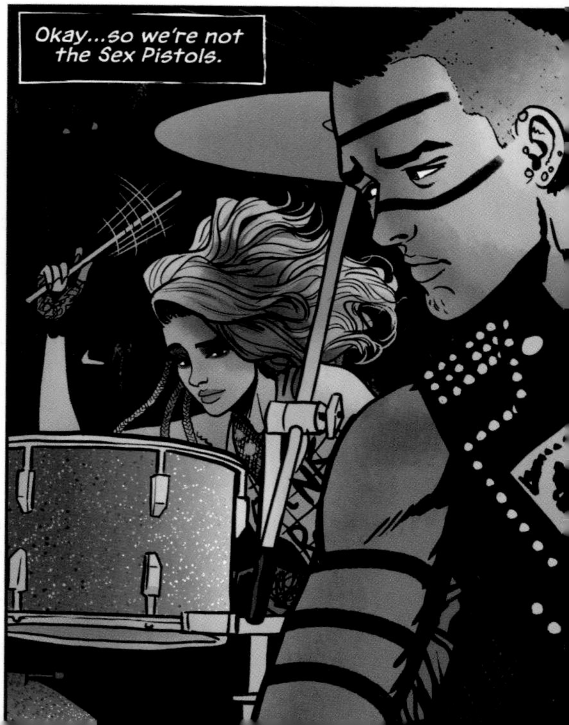
Okay...so we're not the Sex Pistols.

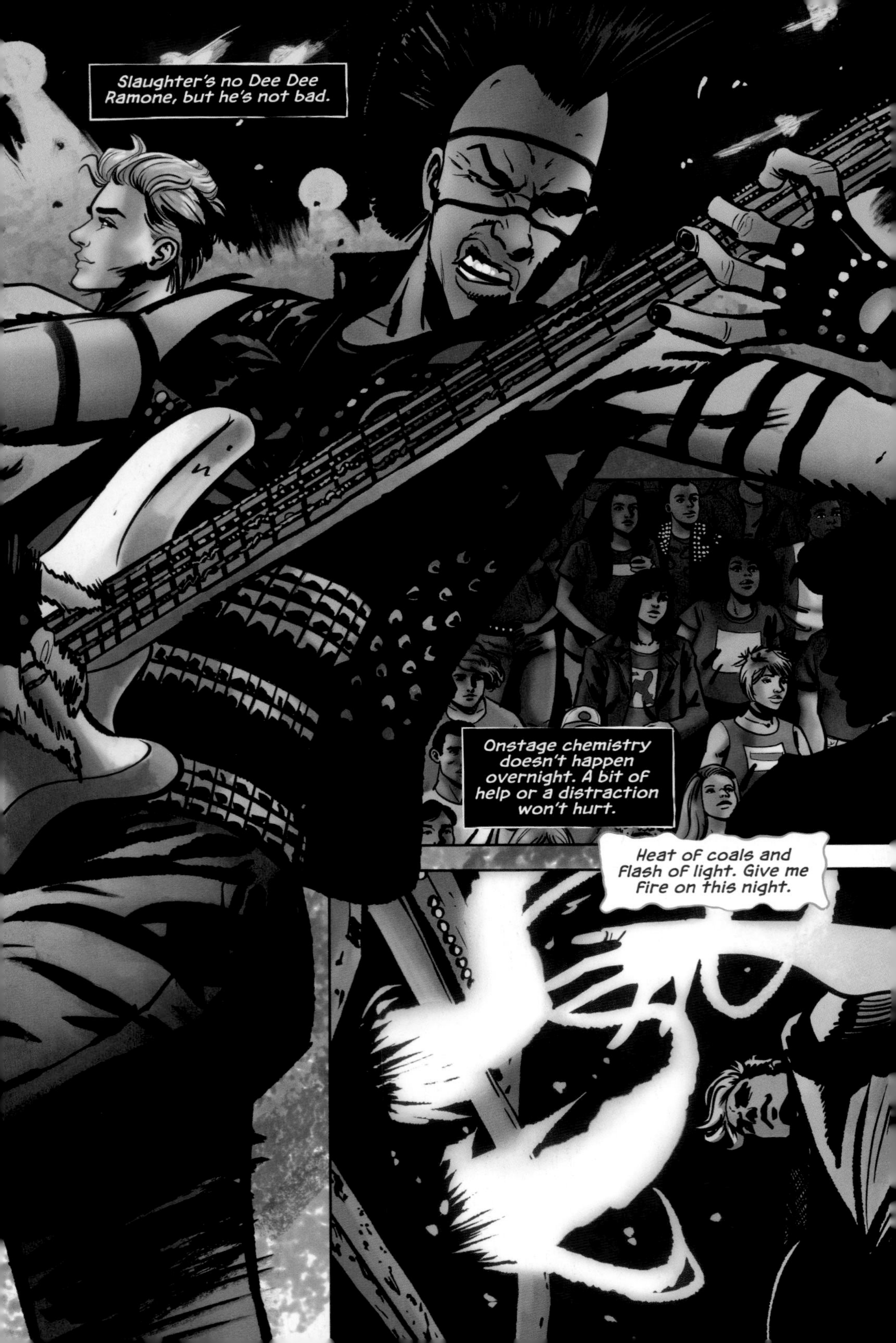
Slaughter's no Dee Dee Ramone, but he's not bad.
Onstage chemistry doesn't happen overnight. A bit of help or a distraction won't hurt.
Heat of coals and flash of light. Give me fire on this night.

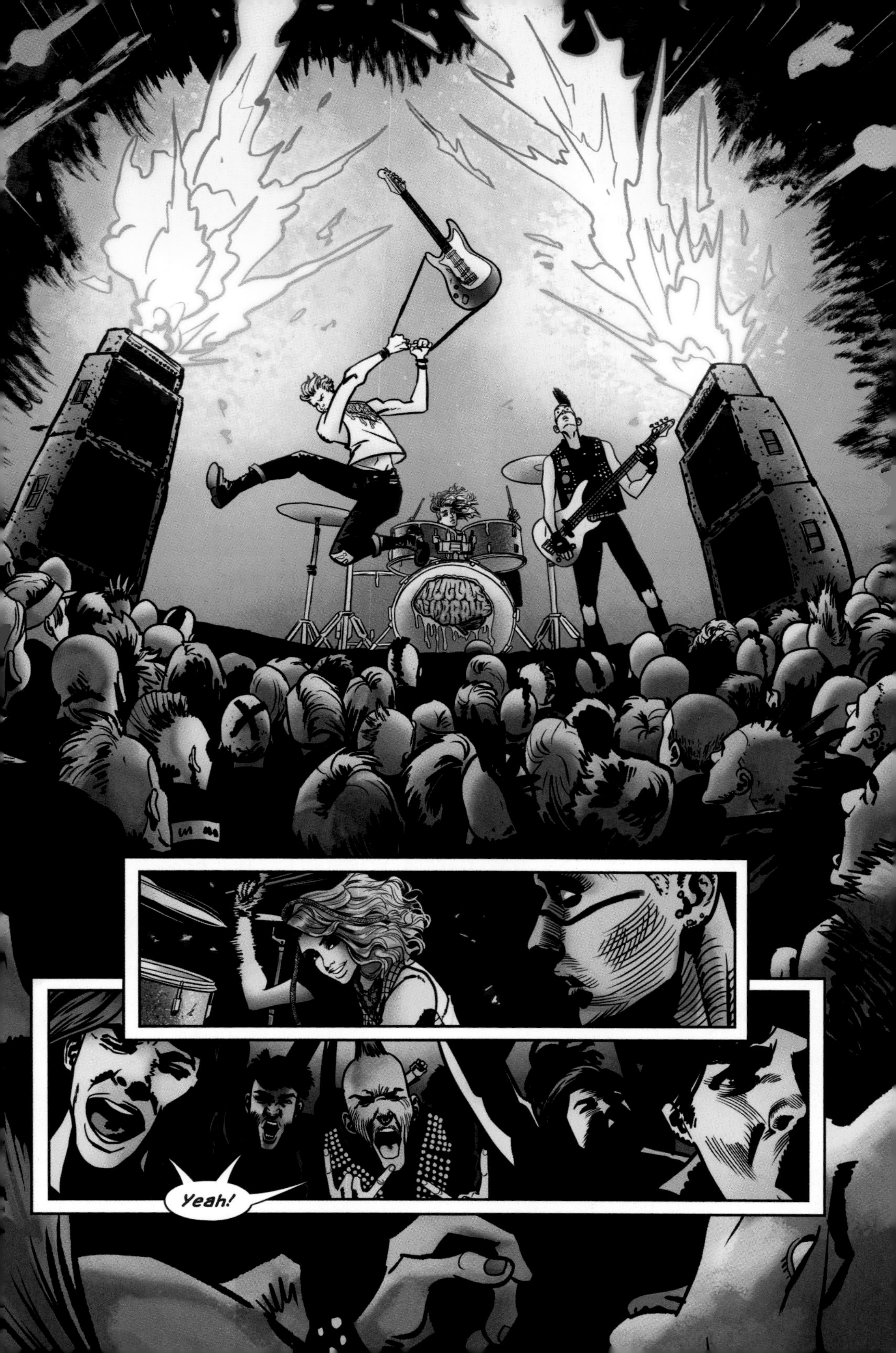
Yeah!

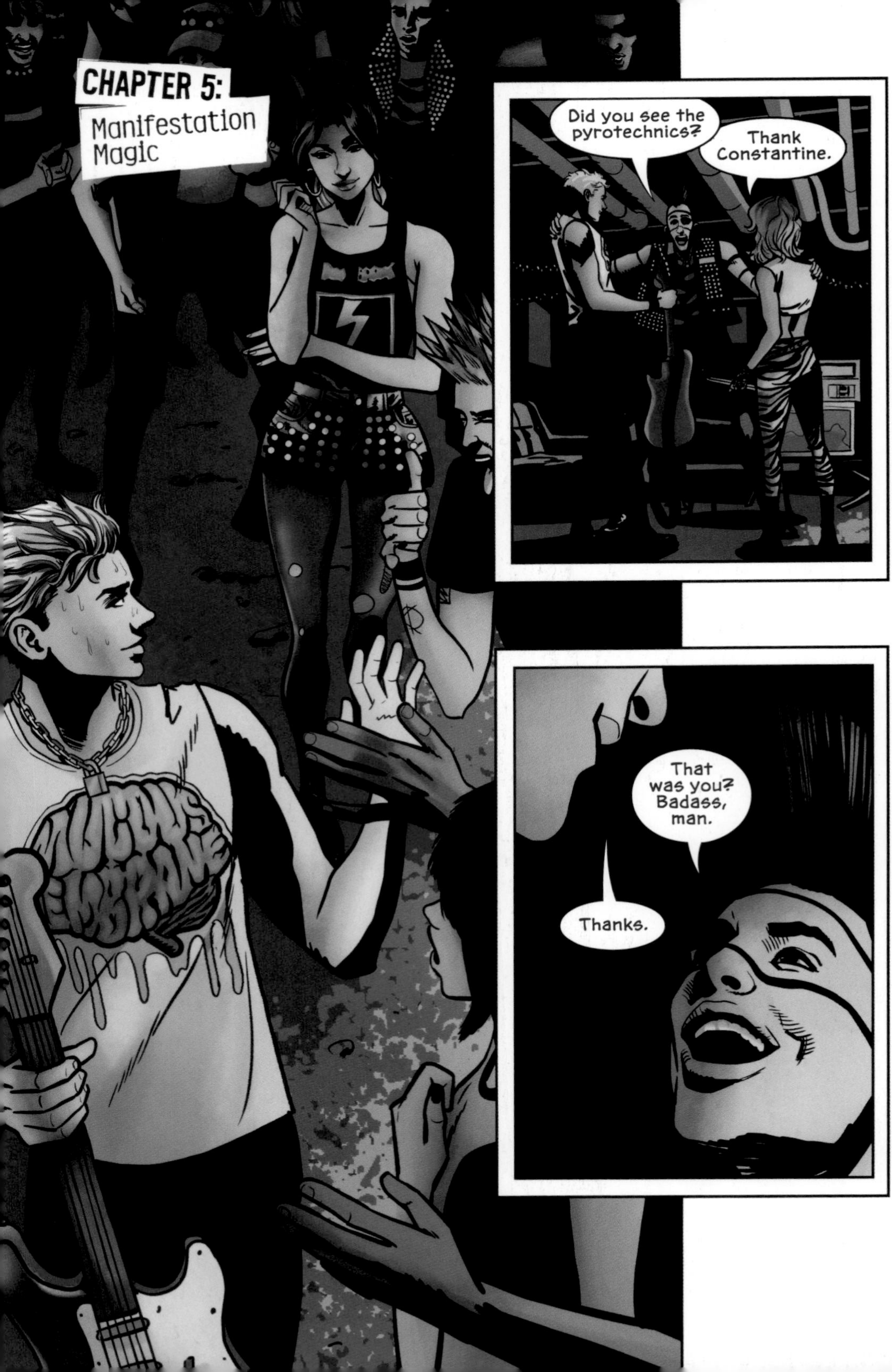
CHAPTER 5:
Manifestation Magic
Did you see the pyrotechnics?
Thank Constantine.
That was you? Badass, man.
Thanks.

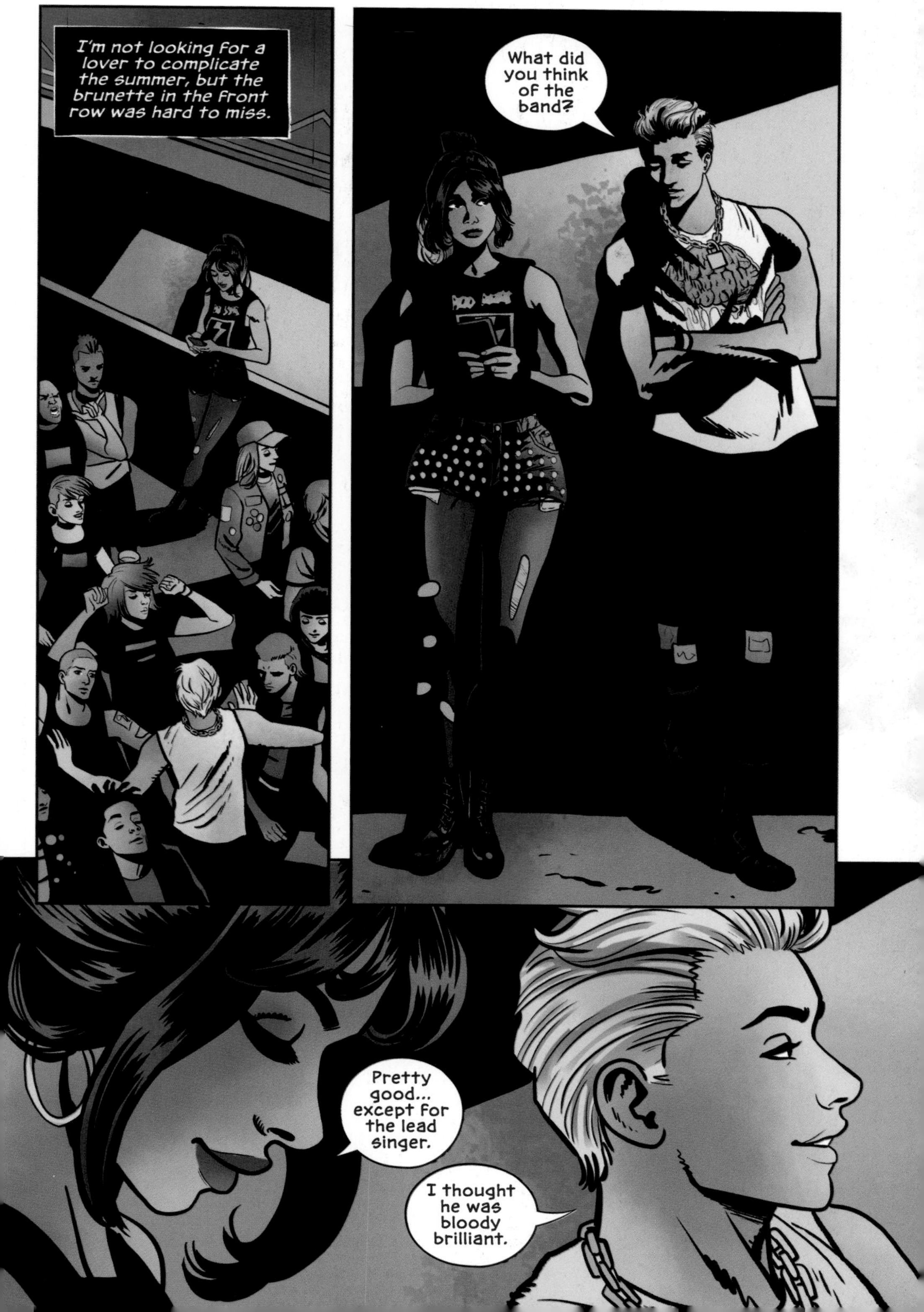
I'm not looking for a lover to complicate the summer, but the brunette in the front row was hard to miss.
What did you think of the band?
Pretty good... except for the lead singer.
I thought he was bloody brilliant.

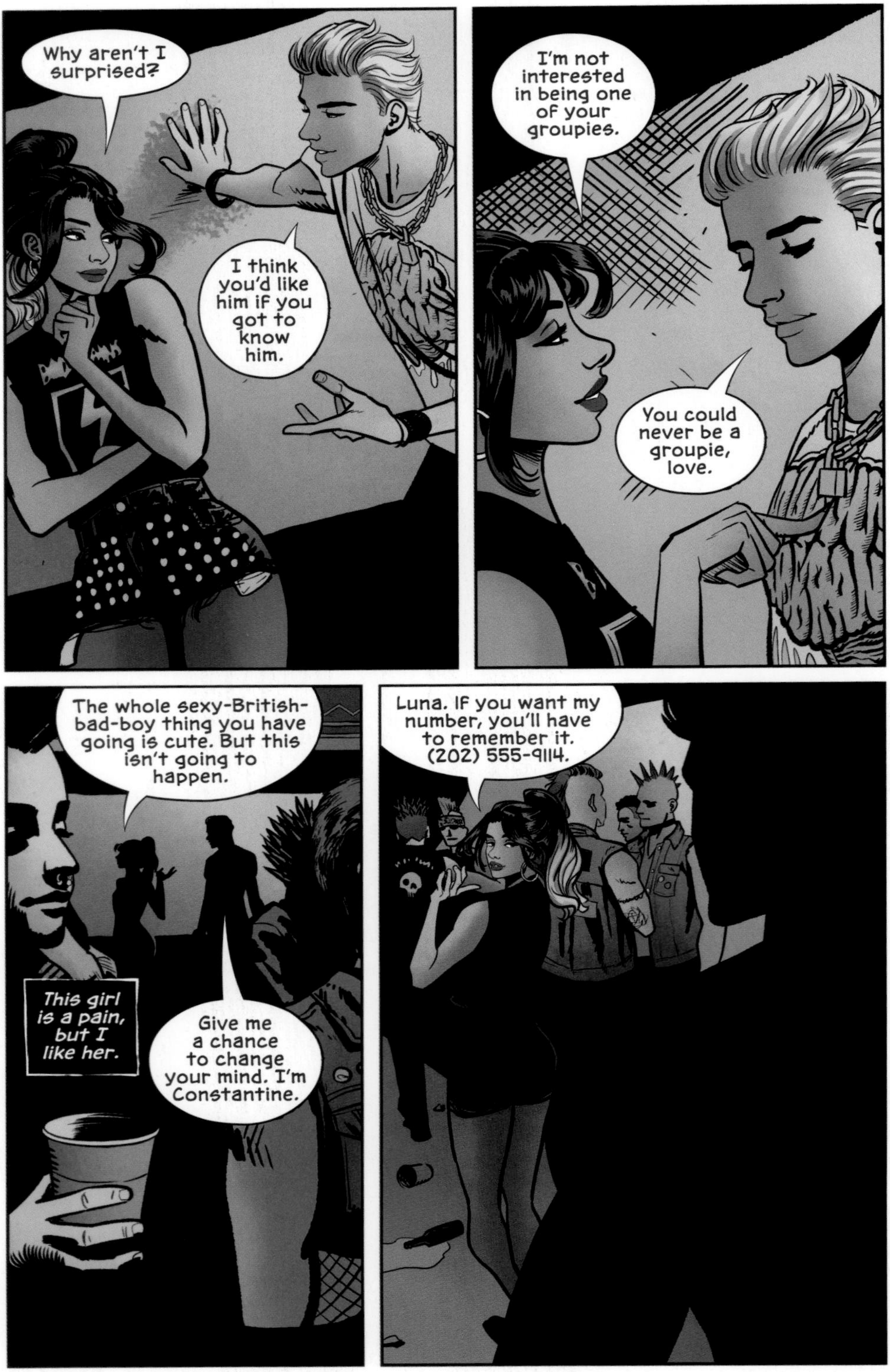
Why aren't I surprised?
I think you'd like him if you got to know him.
I'm not interested in being one of your groupies.
You could never be a groupie, love.
The whole sexy-British-bad-boy thing you have going is cute. But this isn't going to happen.
This girl is a pain, but I like her.
Give me a chance to change your mind. I'm Constantine.
Luna. If you want my number, you'll have to remember it. (202) 555-9114.

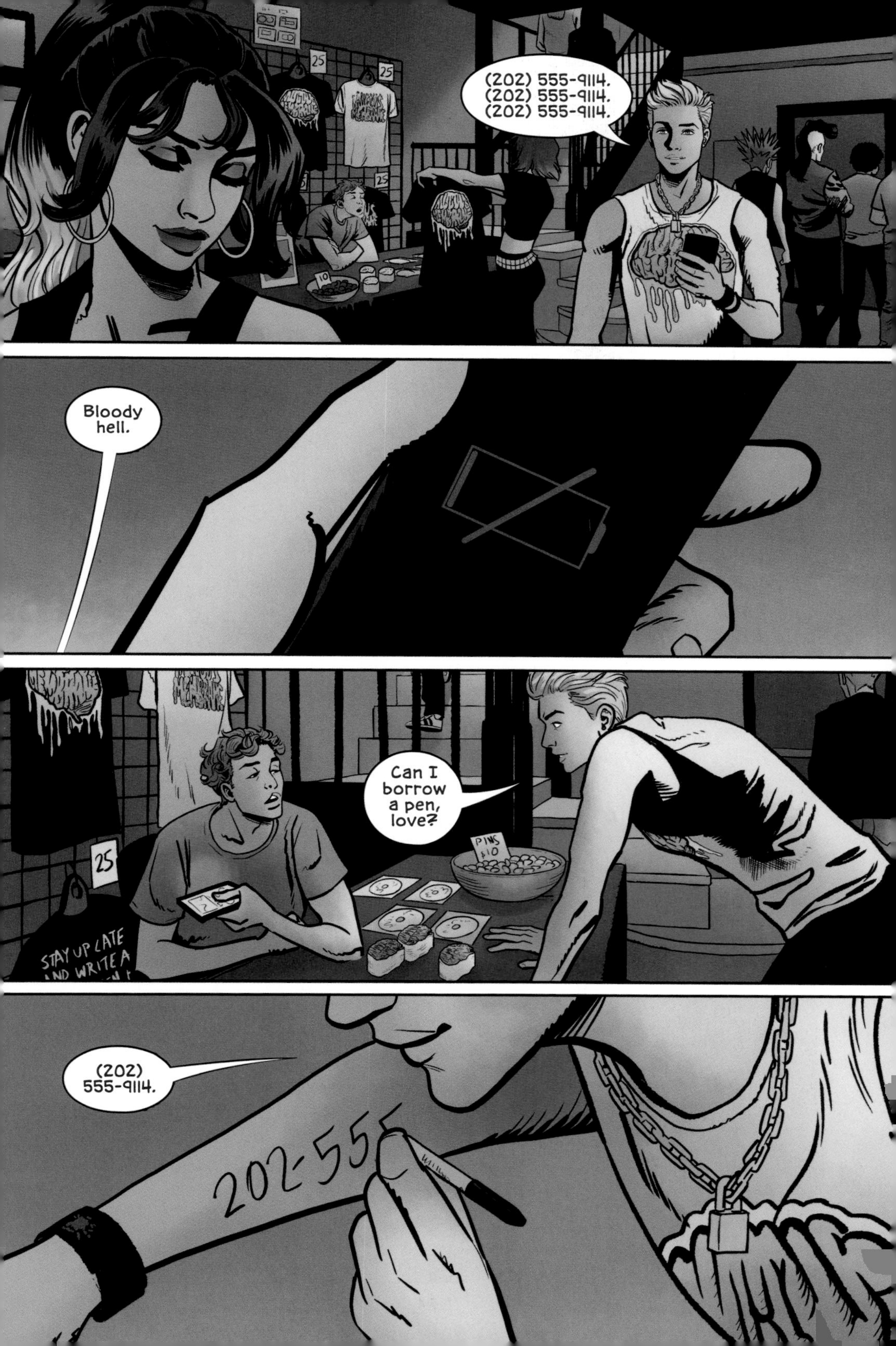

(202) 555-9114.
(202) 555-9114.
(202) 555-9114.
Bloody hell.
Can I borrow a pen, love?
PINS $10
25
STAY UP LATE
AND WRITE A
(202) 555-9114.
202-555

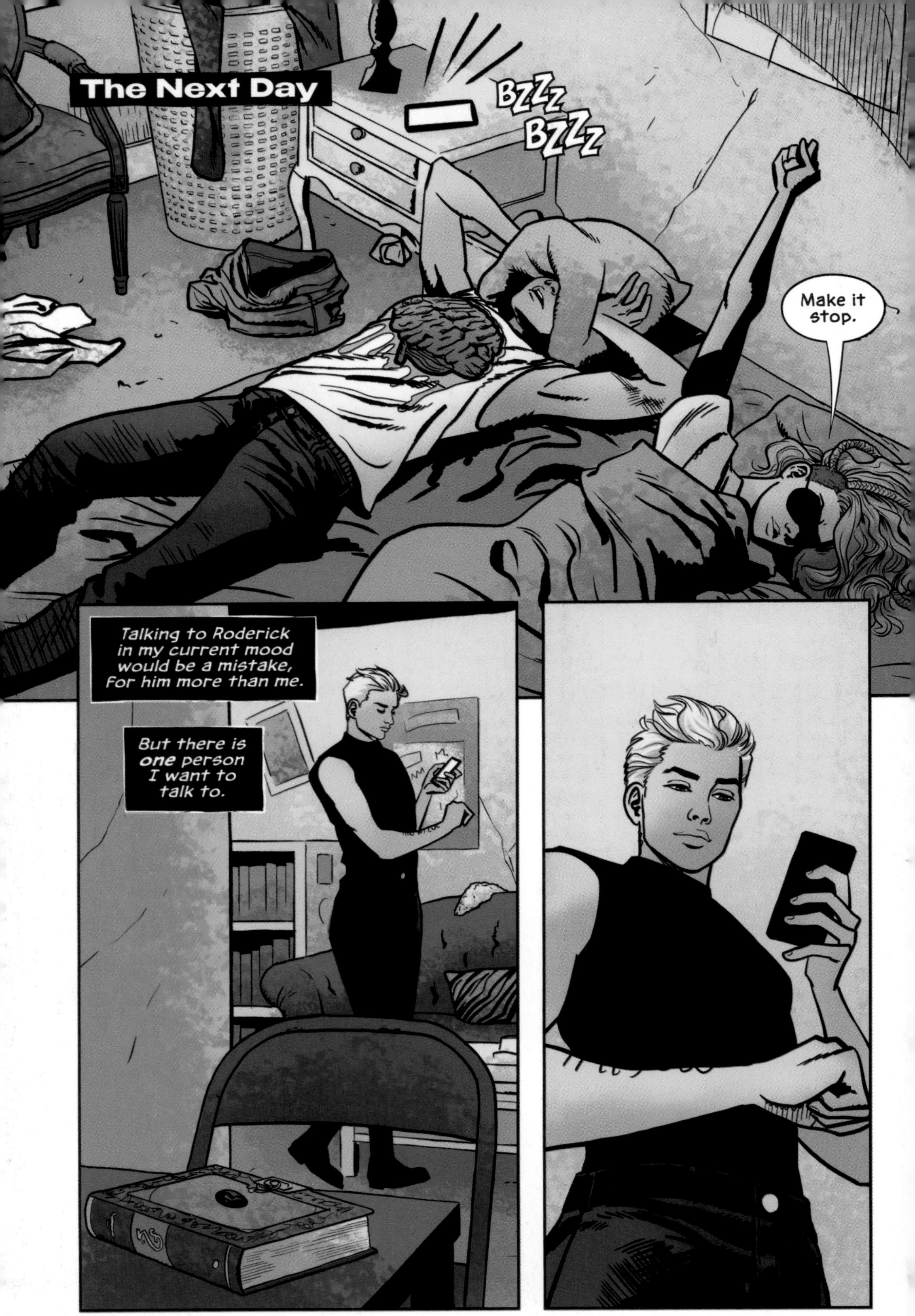
The Next Day
BZZZ
BZZZ
Make it stop.
Talking to Roderick in my current mood would be a mistake, for him more than me.
But there is one person I want to talk to.

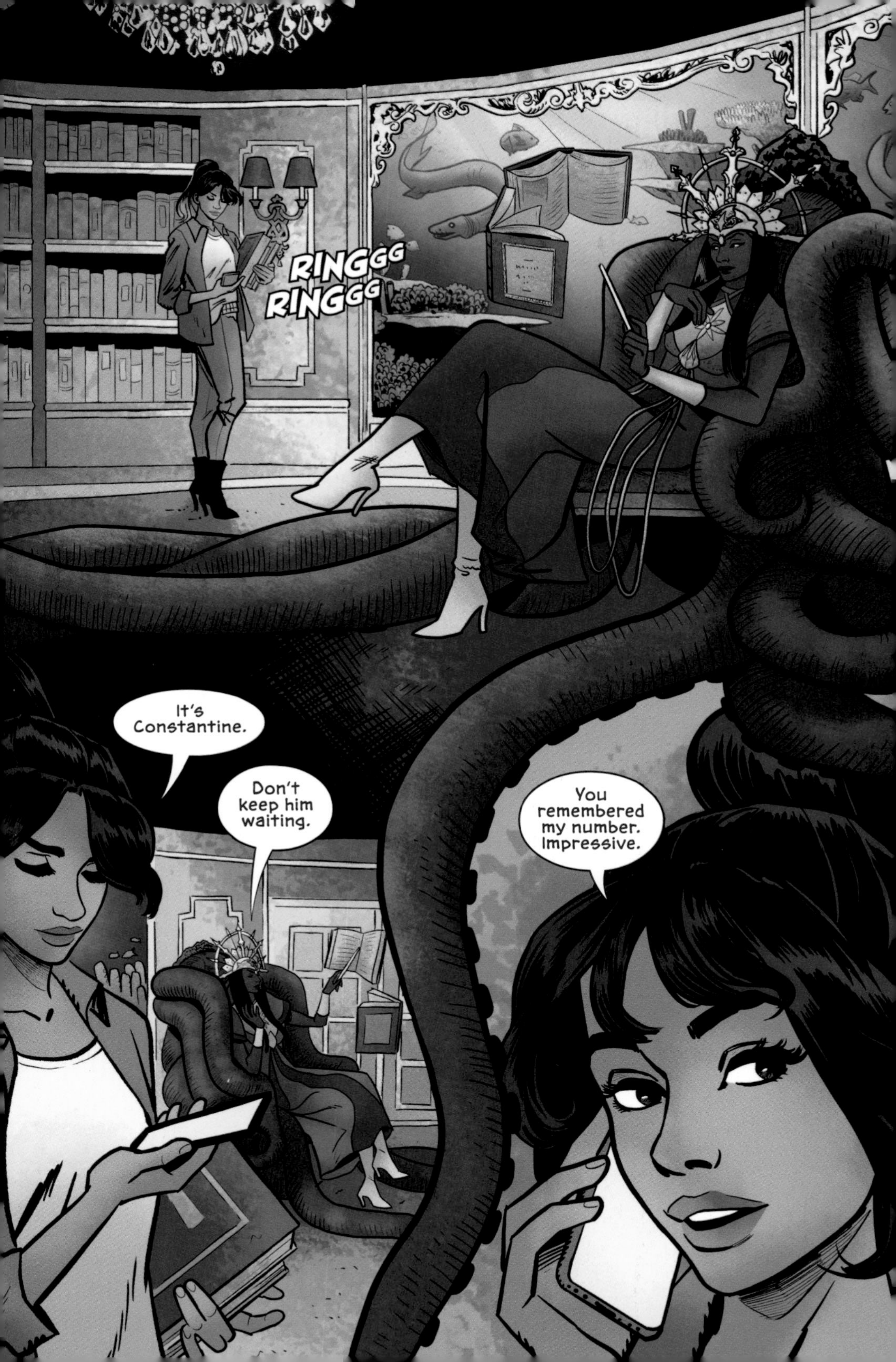
RINGGG
RINGGG
It's Constantine.
Don't keep him waiting.
You remembered my number. Impressive.

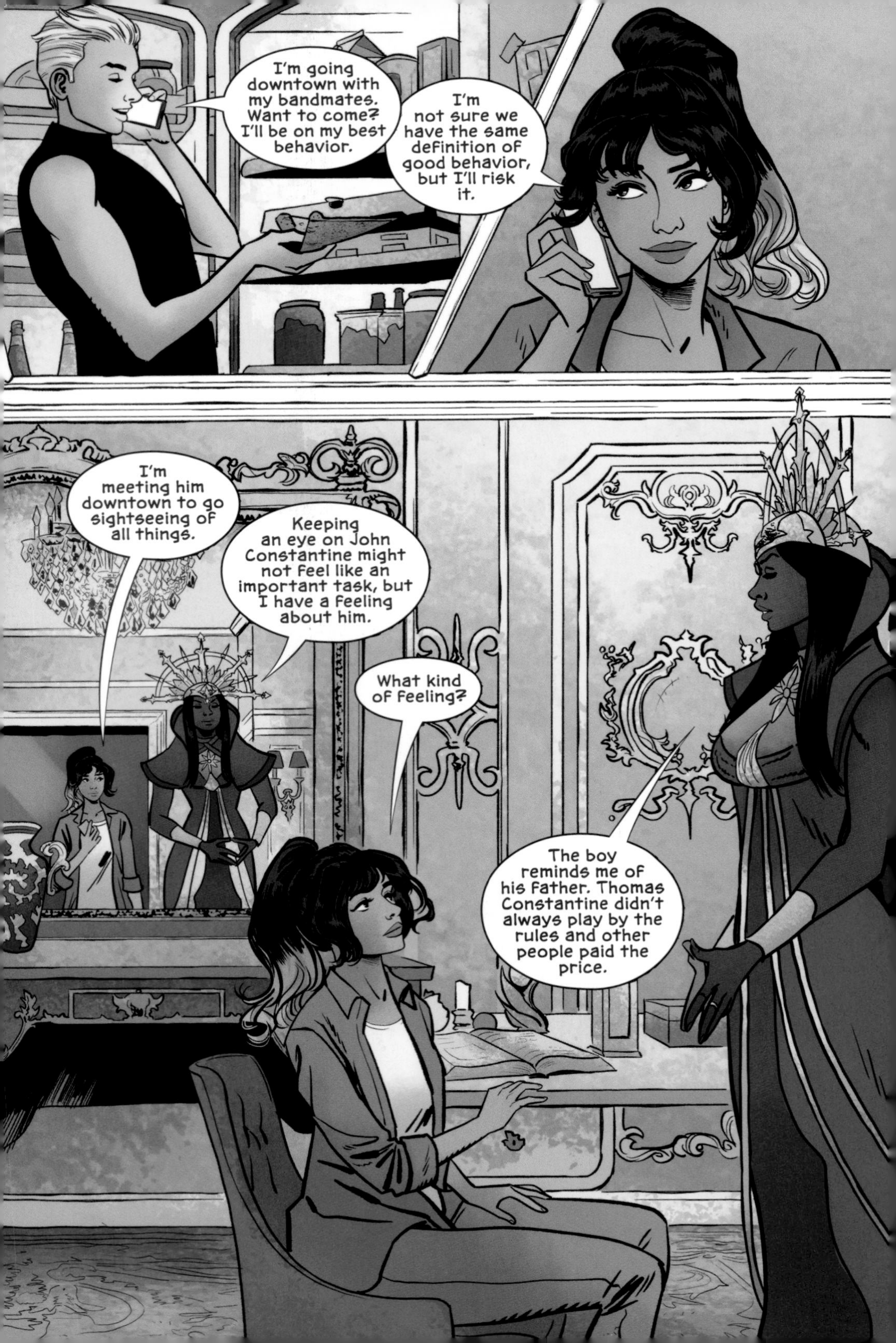
I'm going downtown with my bandmates. Want to come? I'll be on my best behavior.
I'm not sure we have the same definition of good behavior, but I'll risk it.
I'm meeting him downtown to go sightseeing of all things.
Keeping an eye on John Constantine might not feel like an important task, but I have a feeling about him.
What kind of feeling?
The boy reminds me of his father. Thomas Constantine didn't always play by the rules and other people paid the price.

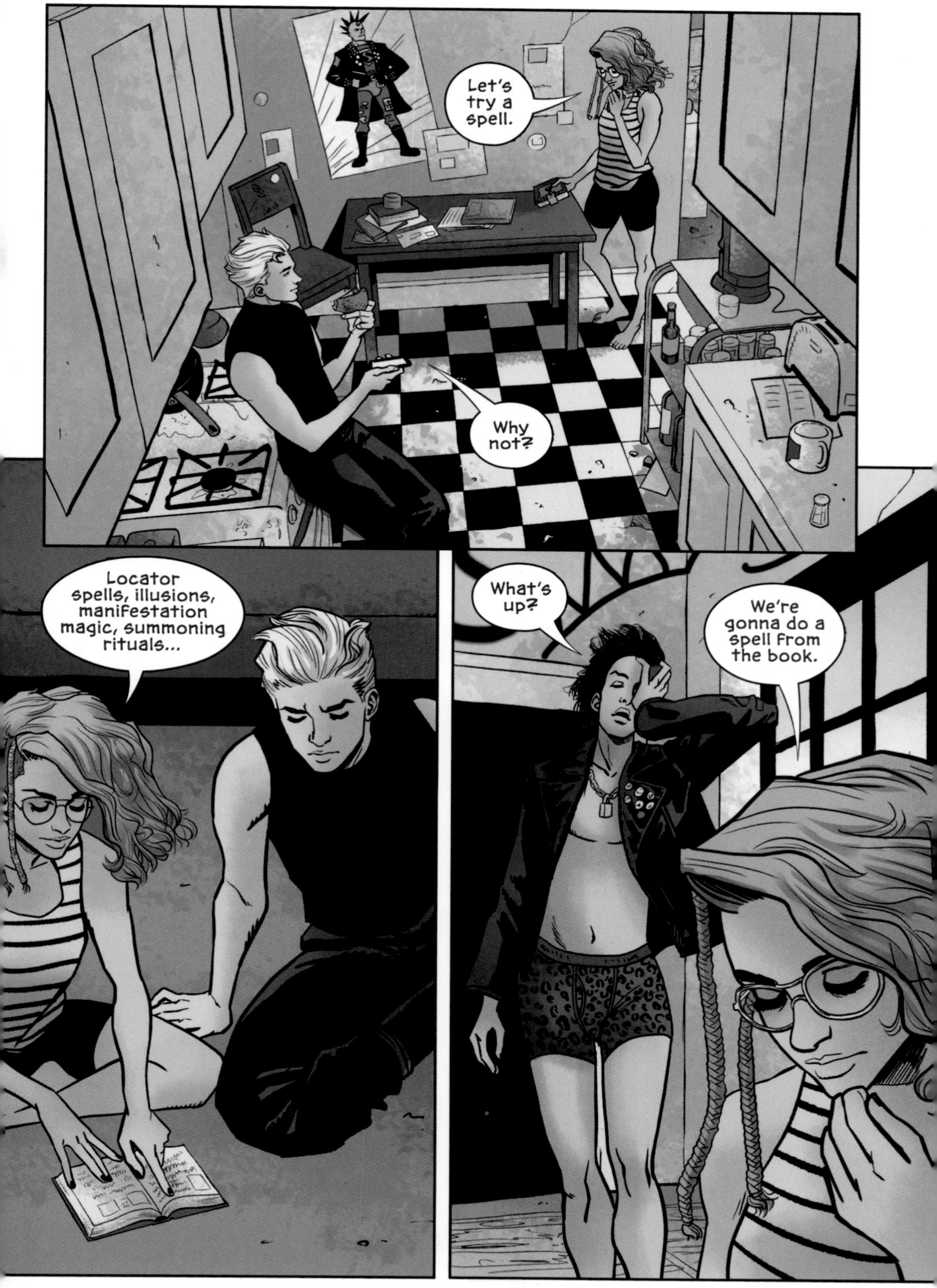

Let's try a spell.
Why not?
Locator spells, illusions, manifestation magic, summoning rituals...
What's up?
We're gonna do a spell from the book.

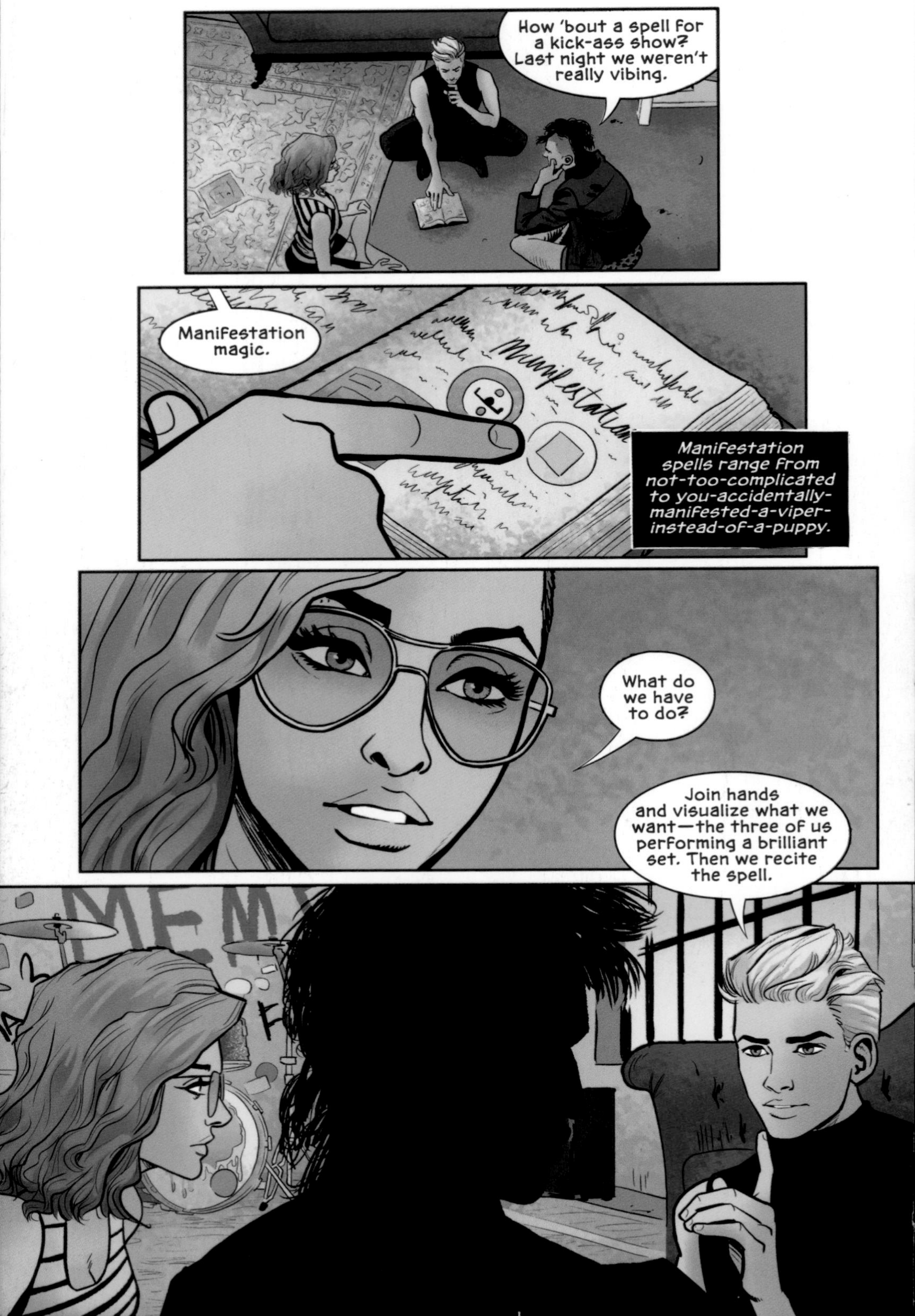
How 'bout a spell for a kick-ass show? Last night we weren't really vibing.
Manifestation magic.
Manifestation spells range from not-too-complicated to you-accidentally-manifested-a-viper-instead-of-a-puppy.
What do we have to do?
Join hands and visualize what we want—the three of us performing a brilliant set. Then we recite the spell.

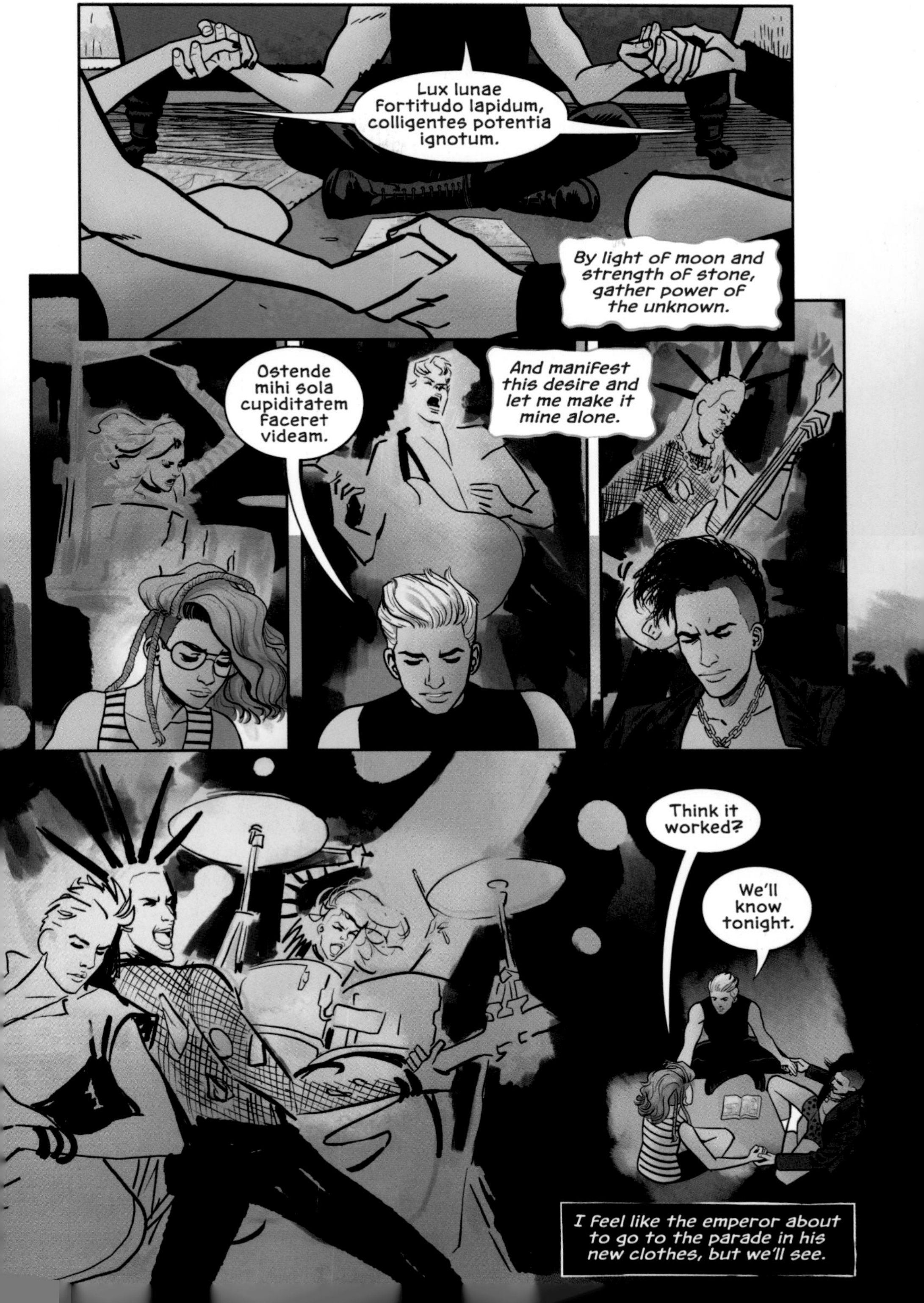
Lux lunae fortitudo lapidum, colligentes potentia ignotum.
By light of moon and strength of stone, gather power of the unknown.
Ostende mihi sola cupiditatem faceret videam.
And manifest this desire and let me make it mine alone.
Think it worked?
We'll know tonight.
I feel like the emperor about to go to the parade in his new clothes, but we'll see.

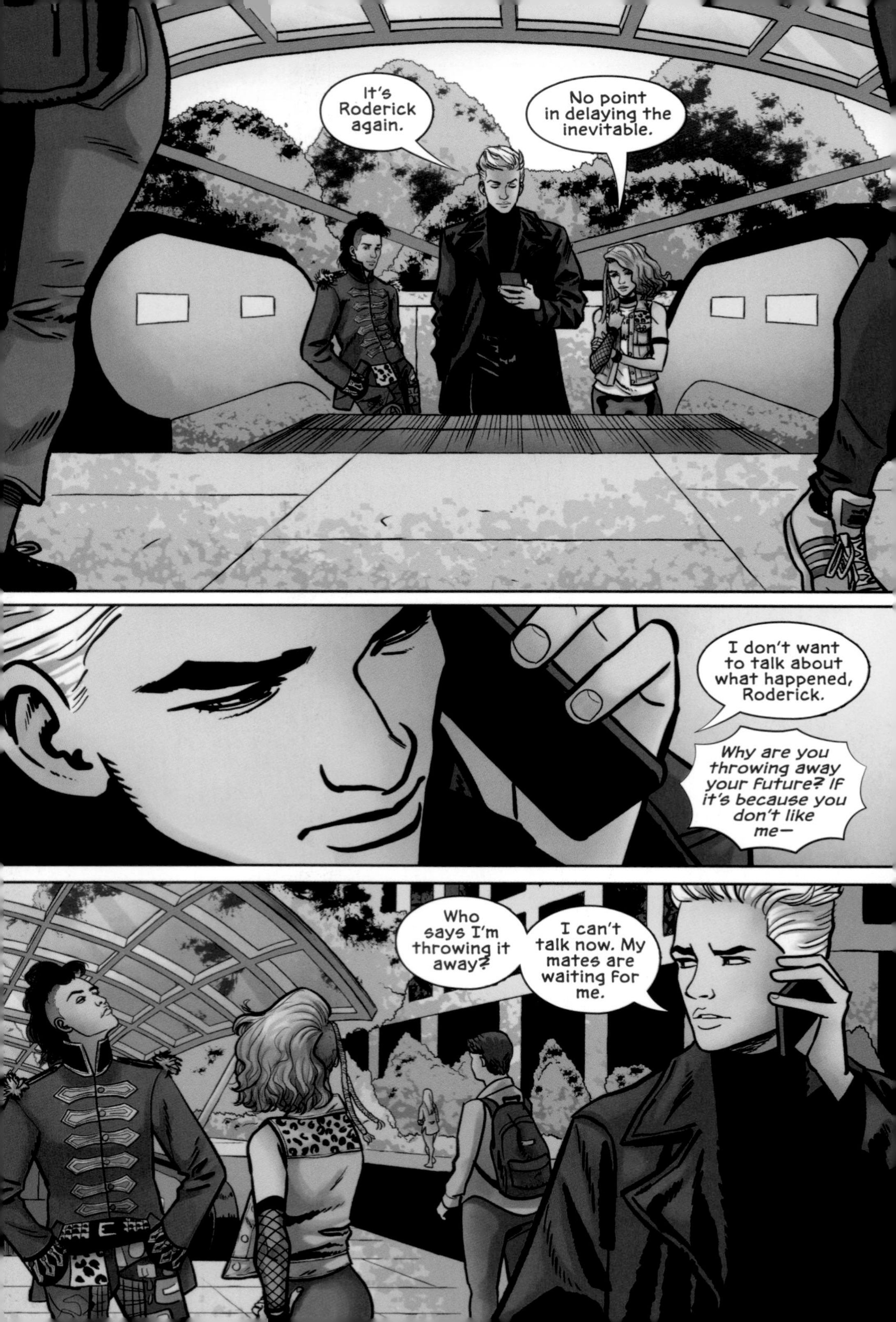
It's Roderick again.
No point in delaying the inevitable.
I don't want to talk about what happened, Roderick.
Why are you throwing away your future? If it's because you don't like me—
Who says I'm throwing it away?
I can't talk now. My mates are waiting for me.

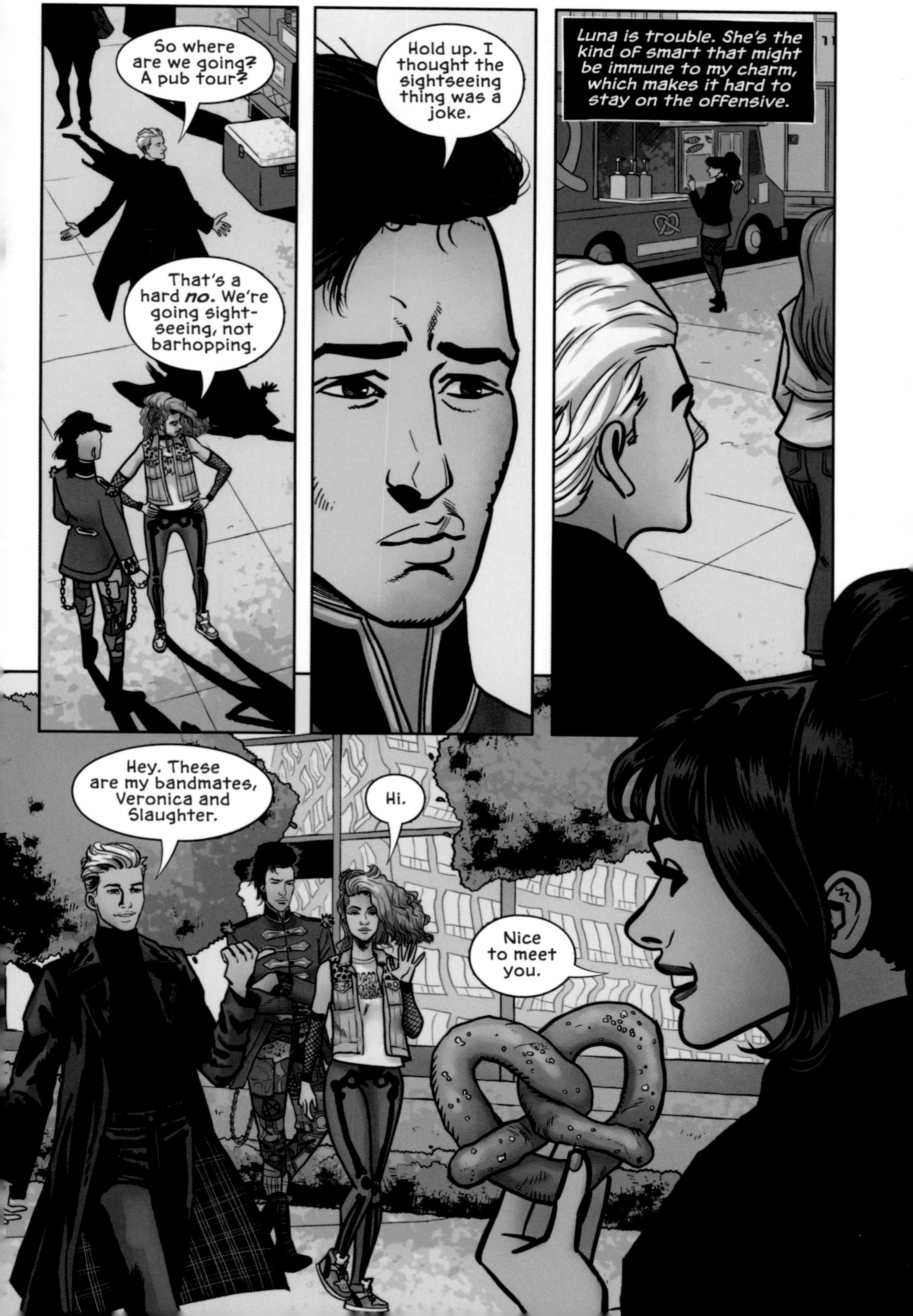
So where are we going? A pub tour?
That's a hard *no.* We're going sight-seeing, not barhopping.
Hold up. I thought the sightseeing thing was a joke.
Luna is trouble. She's the kind of smart that might be immune to my charm, which makes it hard to stay on the offensive.
Hey. These are my bandmates, Veronica and Slaughter.
Hi.
Nice to meet you.

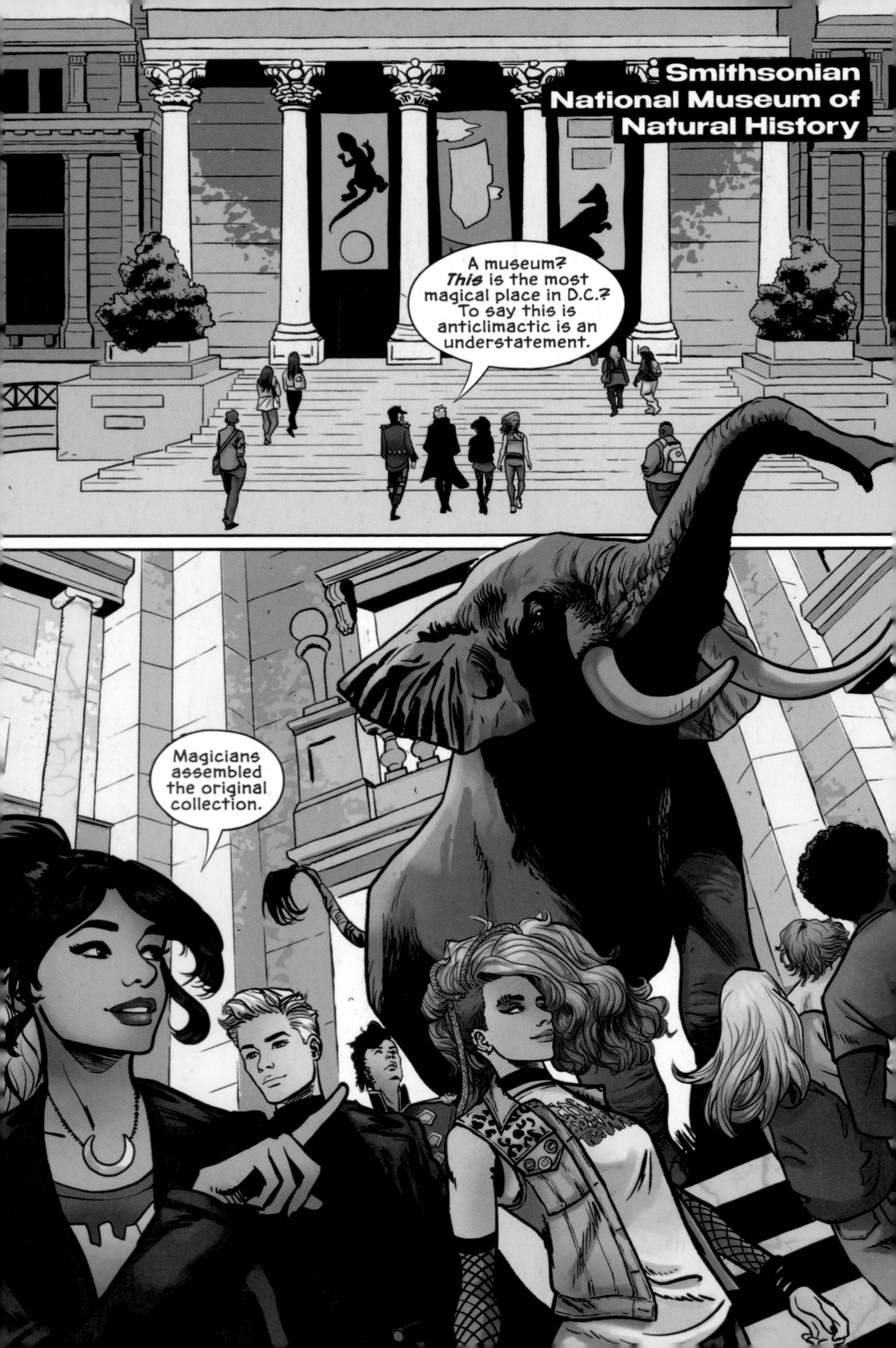

Smithsonian National Museum of Natural History
A museum? This is the most magical place in D.C.? To say this is anticlimactic is an understatement.
Magicians assembled the original collection.

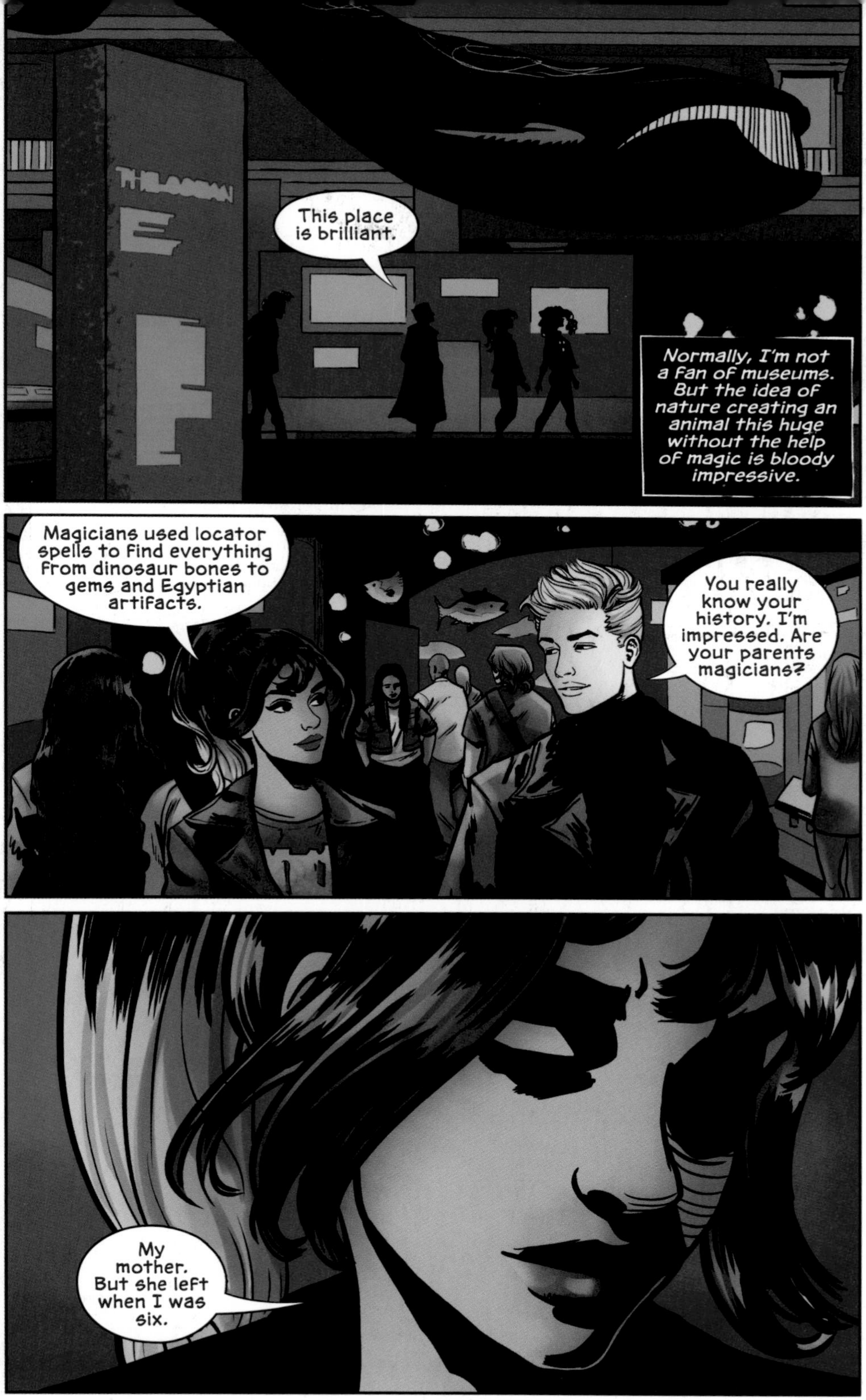
This place is brilliant.
Normally, I'm not a fan of museums. But the idea of nature creating an animal this huge without the help of magic is bloody impressive.
Magicians used locator spells to find everything from dinosaur bones to gems and Egyptian artifacts.
You really know your history. I'm impressed. Are your parents magicians?
My mother. But she left when I was six.

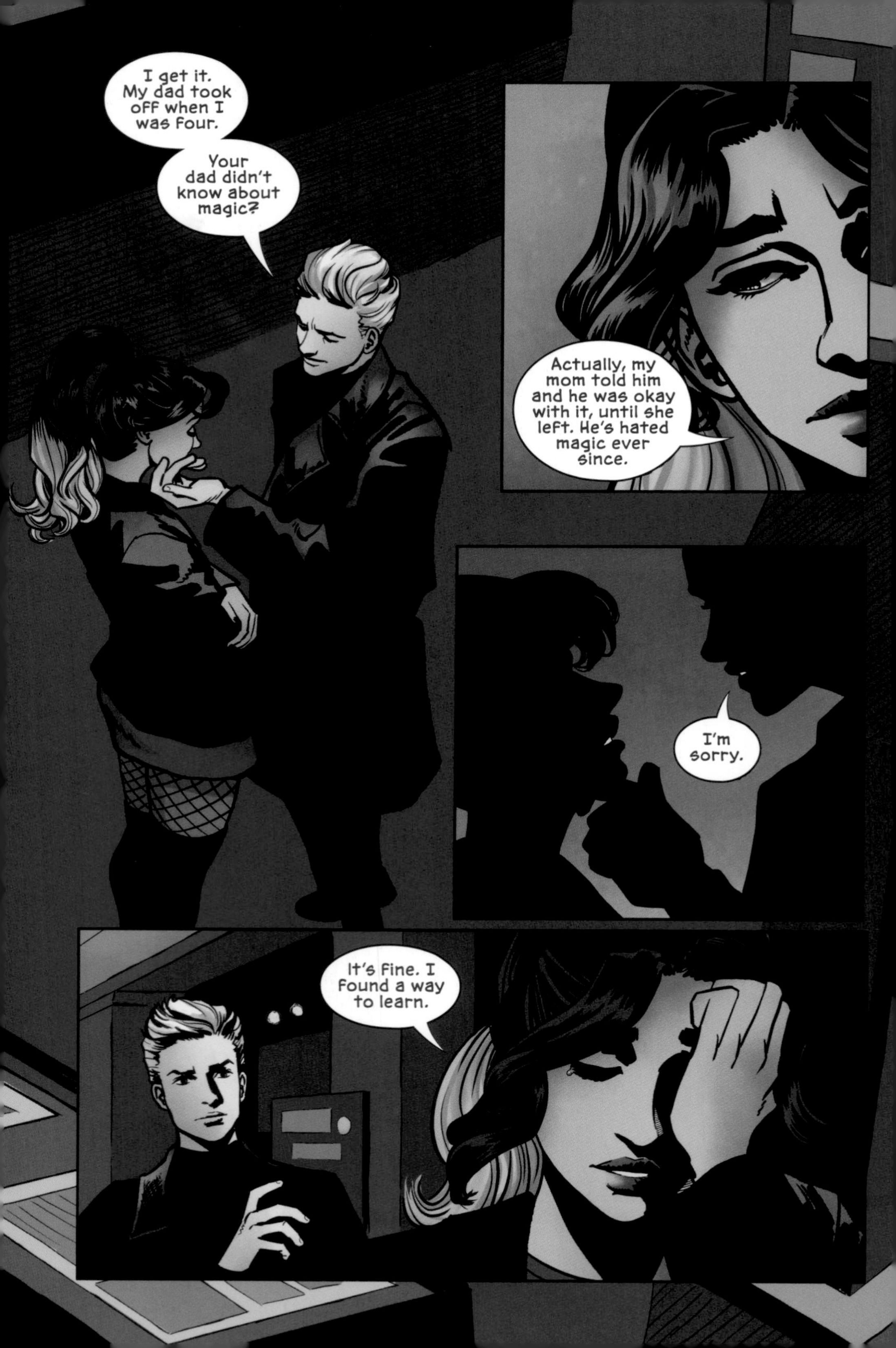
I get it. My dad took off when I was four.
Your dad didn't know about magic?
Actually, my mom told him and he was okay with it, until she left. He's hated magic ever since.
I'm sorry.
It's fine. I found a way to learn.

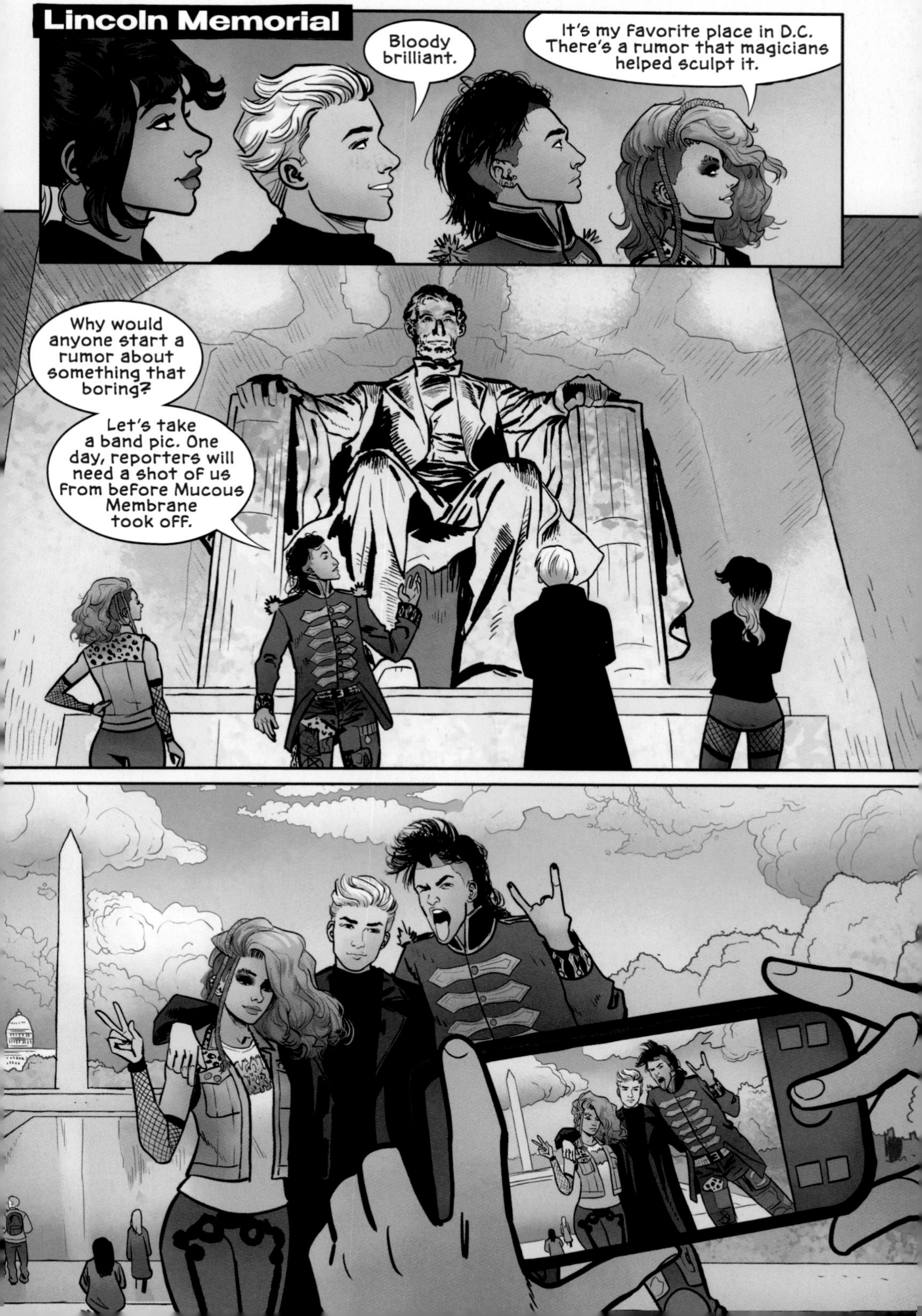
Lincoln Memorial
Bloody brilliant.
It's my favorite place in D.C. There's a rumor that magicians helped sculpt it.
Why would anyone start a rumor about something that boring?
Let's take a band pic. One day, reporters will need a shot of us from before Mucous Membrane took off.

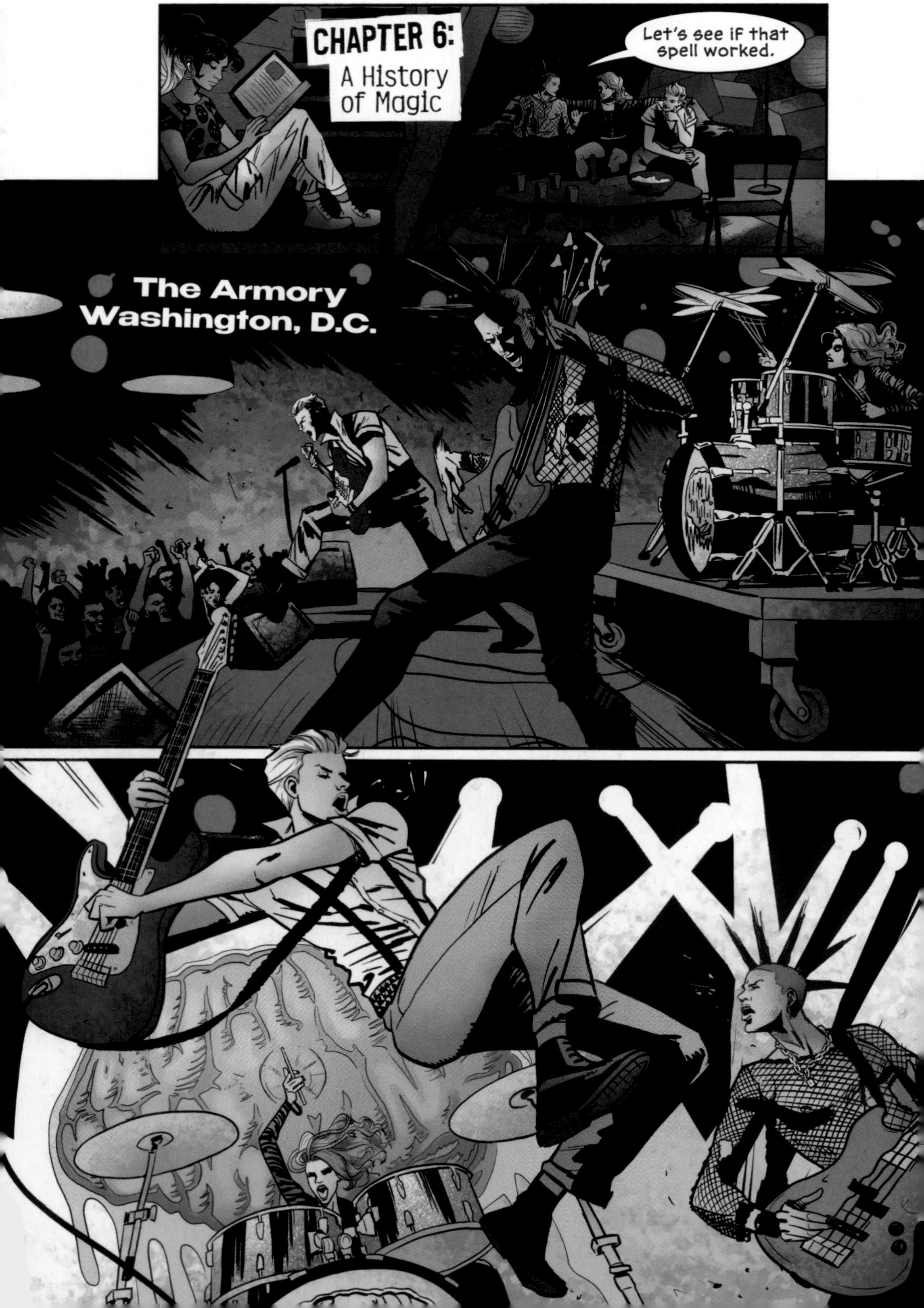
CHAPTER 6:
A History of Magic
Let's see if that spell worked.
The Armory
Washington, D.C.

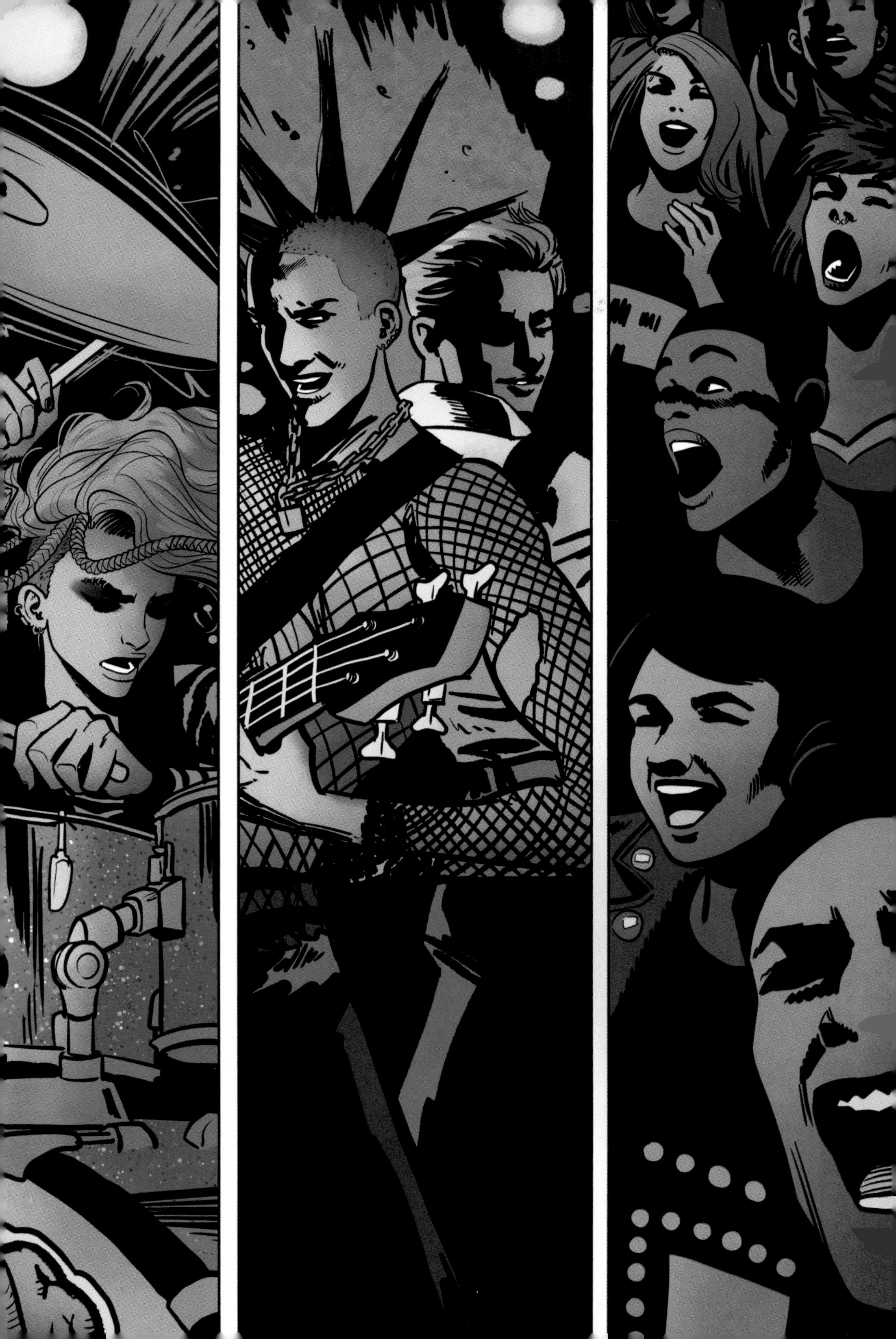

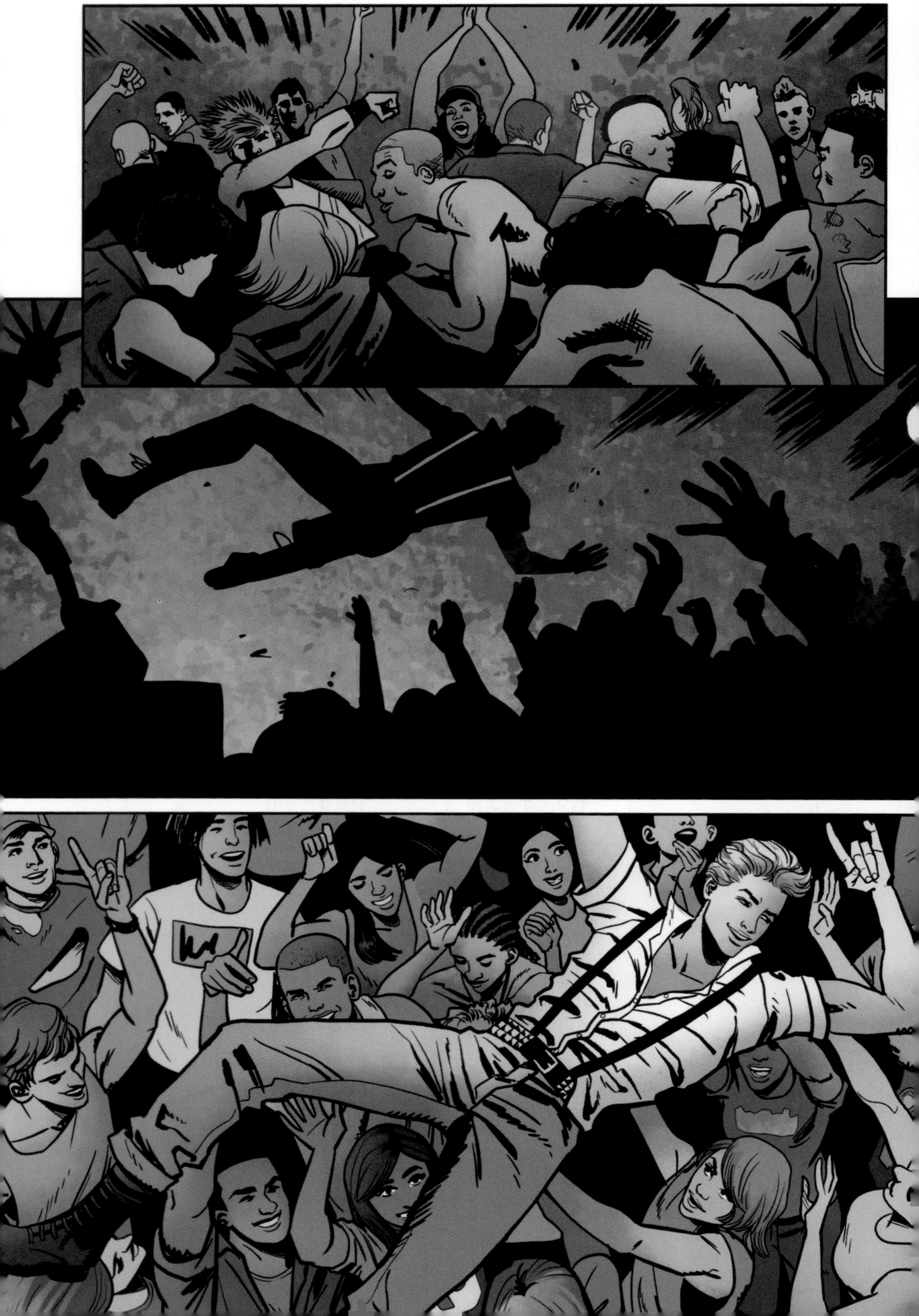

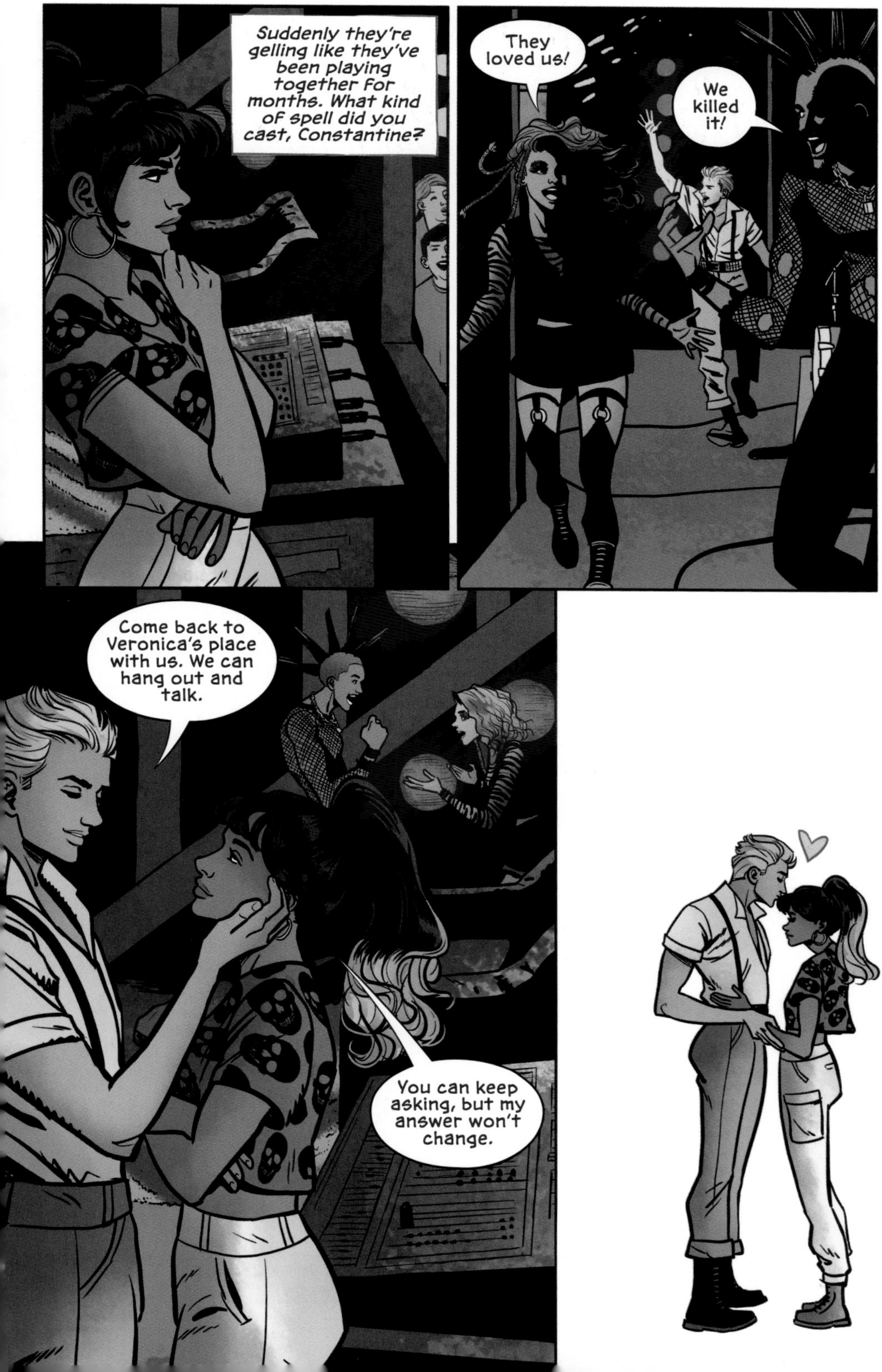
Suddenly they're gelling like they've been playing together for months. What kind of spell did you cast, Constantine?
They loved us!
We killed it!
Come back to Veronica's place with us. We can hang out and talk.
You can keep asking, but my answer won't change.

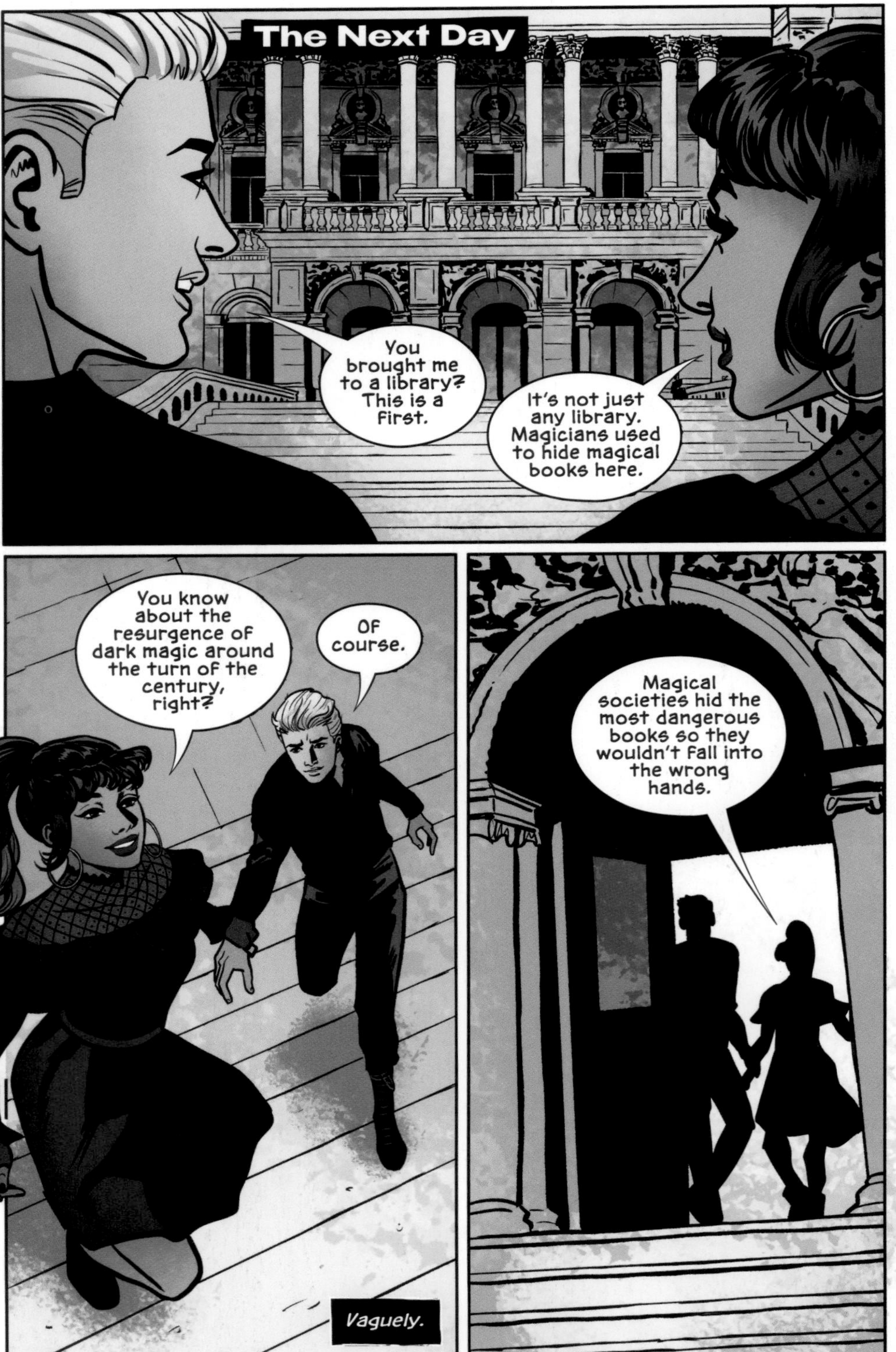
The Next Day
You brought me to a library? This is a first.
It's not just any library. Magicians used to hide magical books here.
You know about the resurgence of dark magic around the turn of the century, right?
Of course.
Vaguely.
Magical societies hid the most dangerous books so they wouldn't fall into the wrong hands.

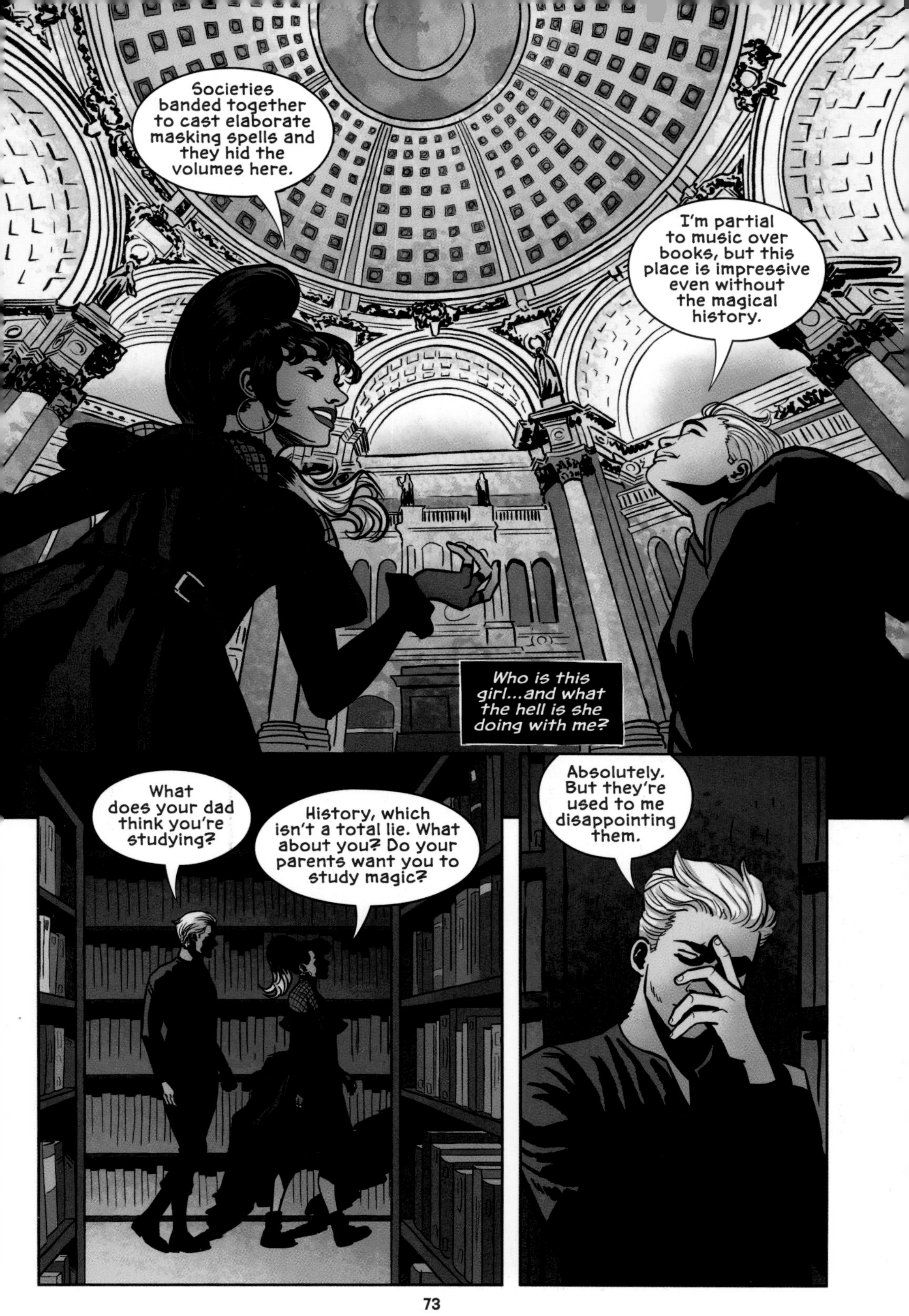
Societies banded together to cast elaborate masking spells and they hid the volumes here.
I'm partial to music over books, but this place is impressive even without the magical history.
Who is this girl...and what the hell is she doing with me?
What does your dad think you're studying?
History, which isn't a total lie. What about you? Do your parents want you to study magic?
Absolutely. But they're used to me disappointing them.

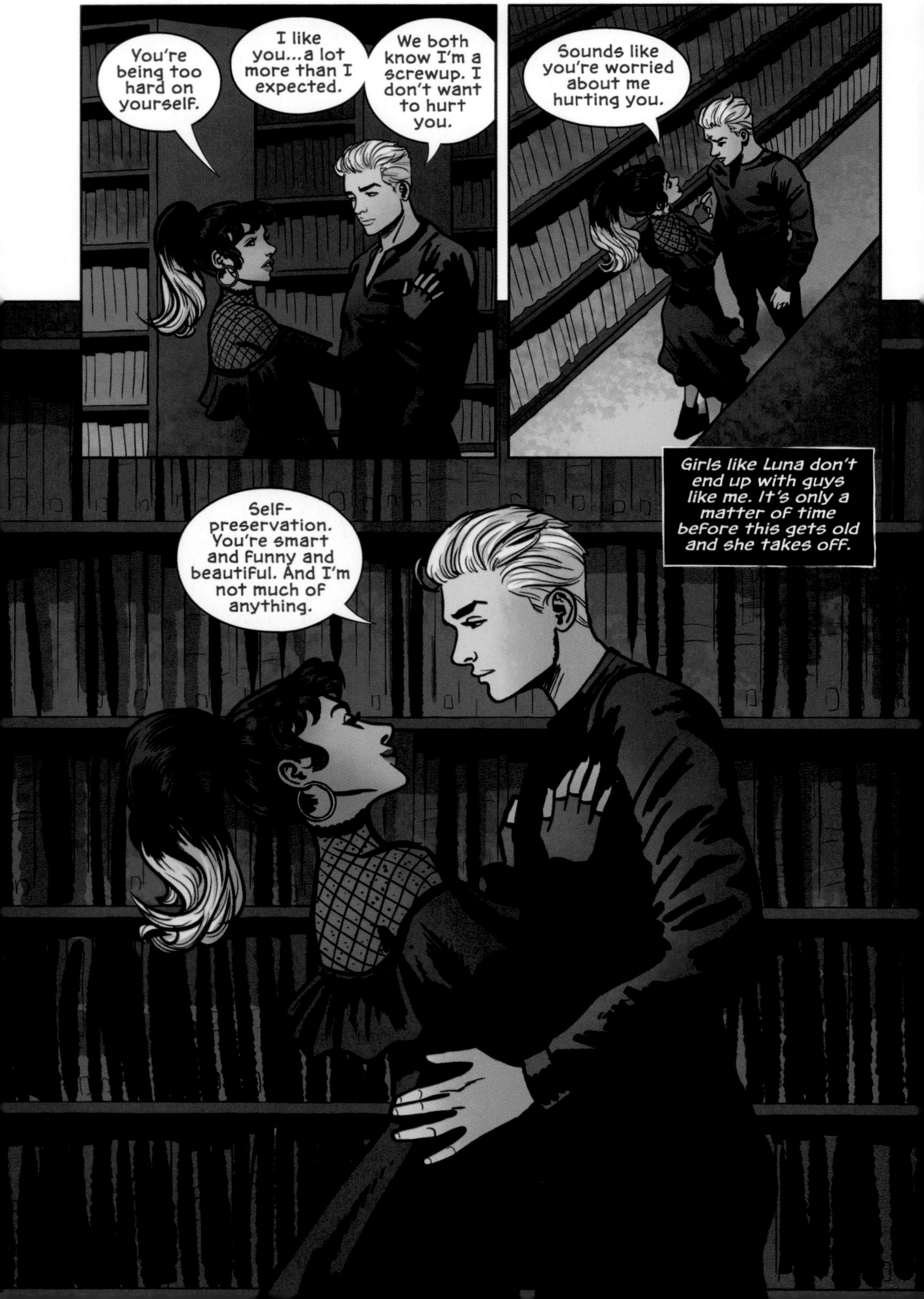
You're being too hard on yourself.
I like you...a lot more than I expected.
We both know I'm a screwup. I don't want to hurt you.
Sounds like you're worried about me hurting you.
Girls like Luna don't end up with guys like me. It's only a matter of time before this gets old and she takes off.
Self-preservation. You're smart and funny and beautiful. And I'm not much of anything.

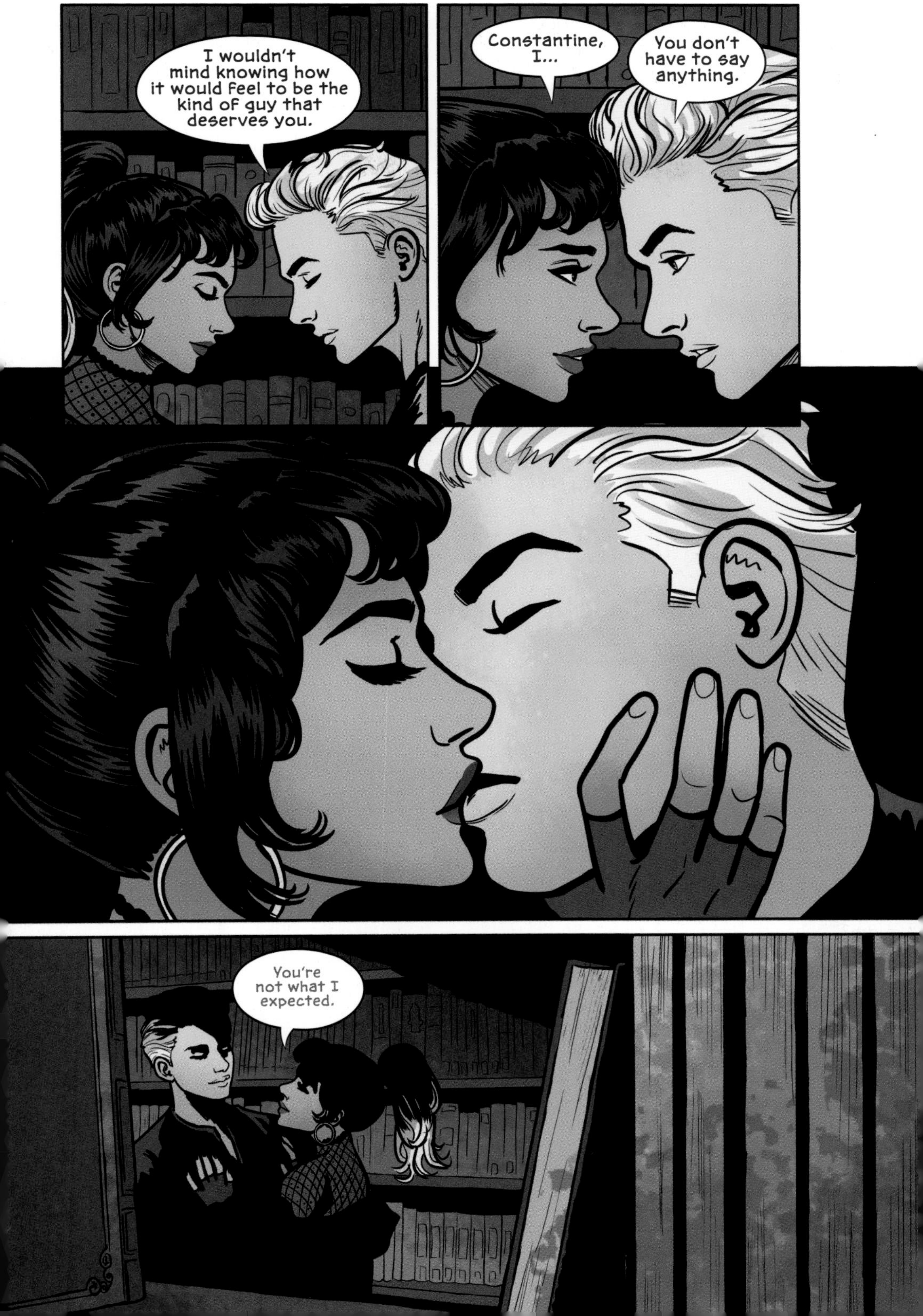

I wouldn't mind knowing how it would feel to be the kind of guy that deserves you.
Constantine, I...
You don't have to say anything.
You're not what I expected.

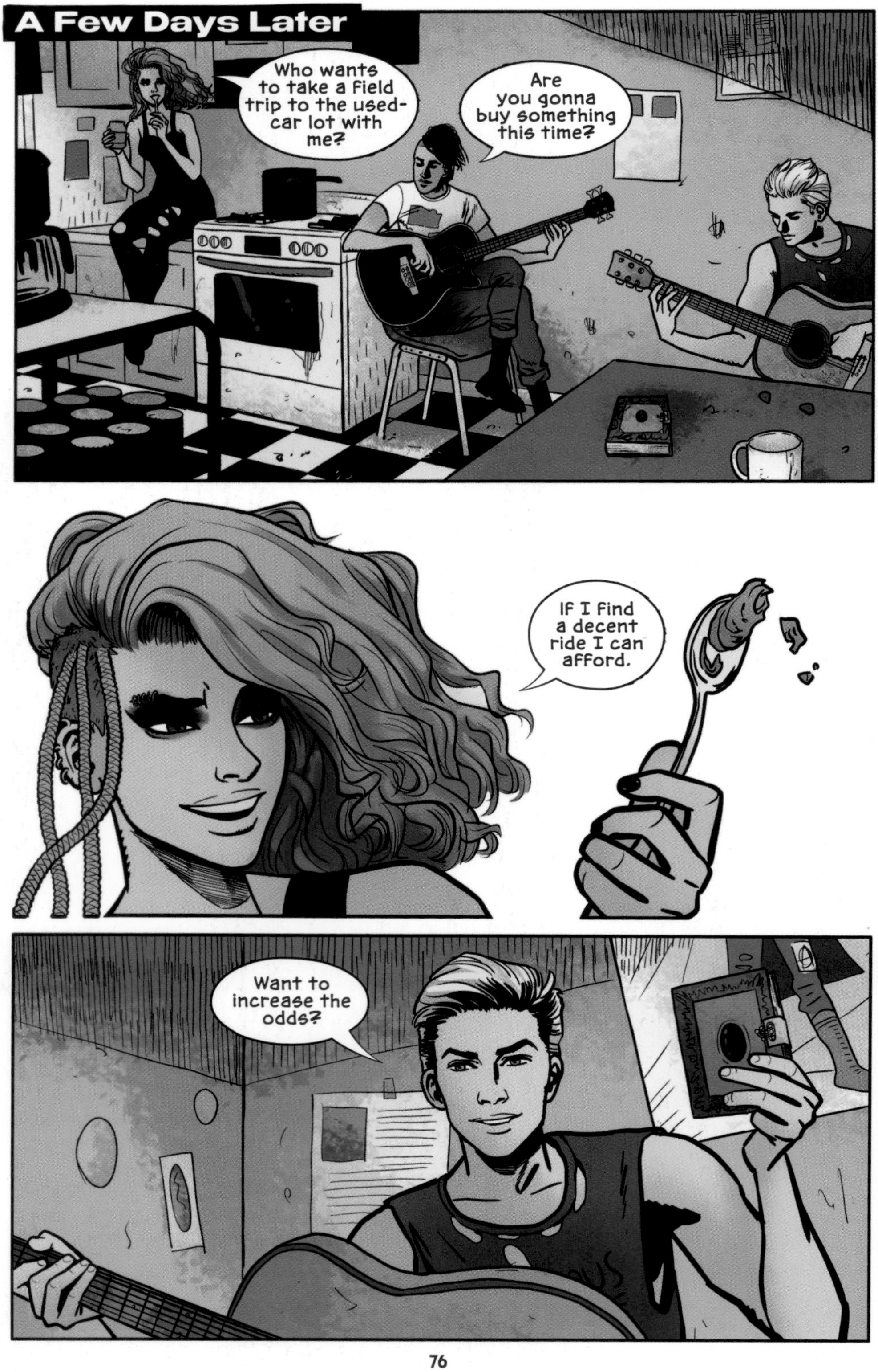
A Few Days Later
Who wants to take a field trip to the used-car lot with me?
Are you gonna buy something this time?
If I find a decent ride I can afford.
Want to increase the odds?

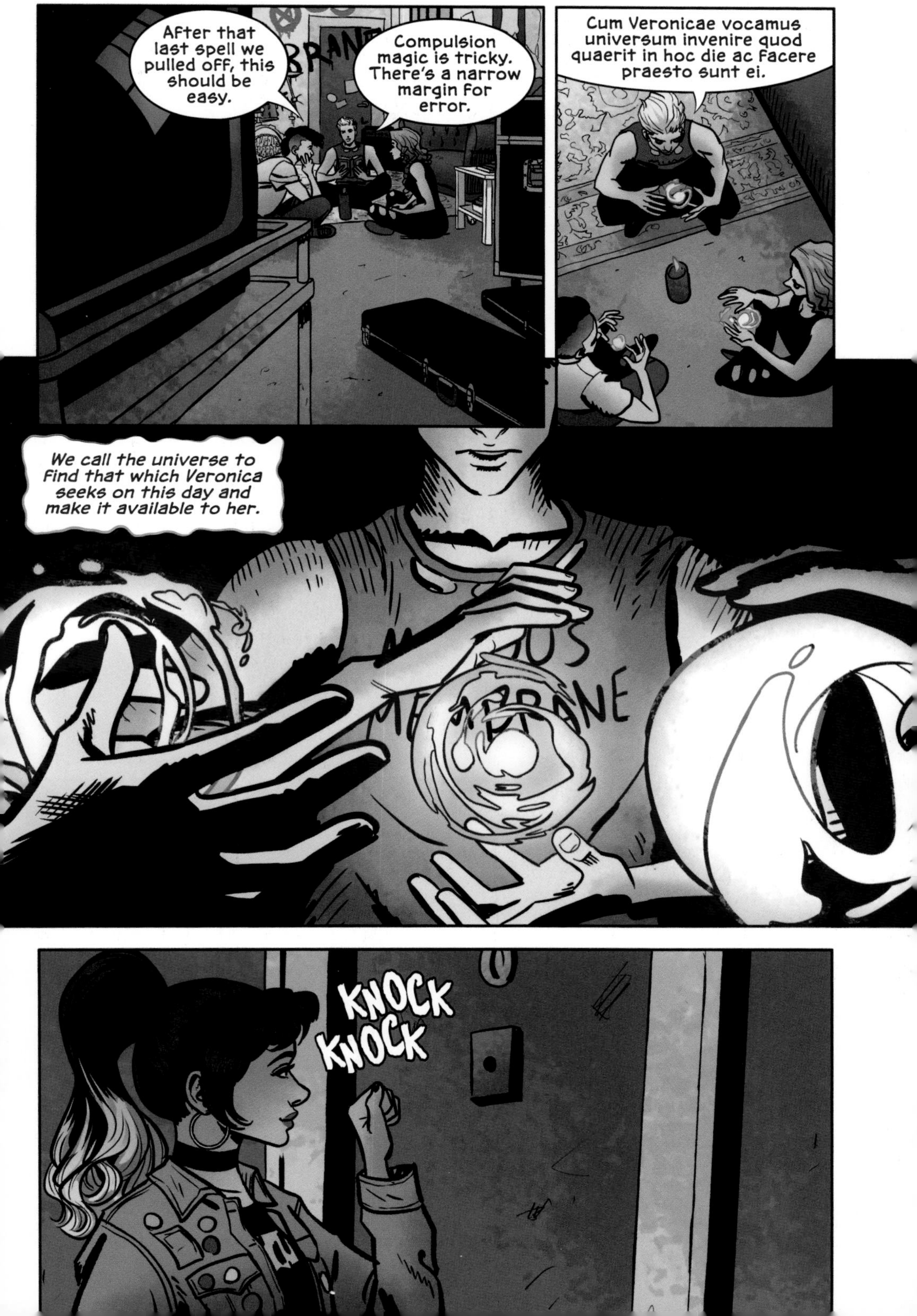
After that last spell we pulled off, this should be easy.
Compulsion magic is tricky. There's a narrow margin for error.
Cum Veronicae vocamus universum invenire quod quaerit in hoc die ac facere praesto sunt ei.
We call the universe to find that which Veronica seeks on this day and make it available to her.
KNOCK KNOCK

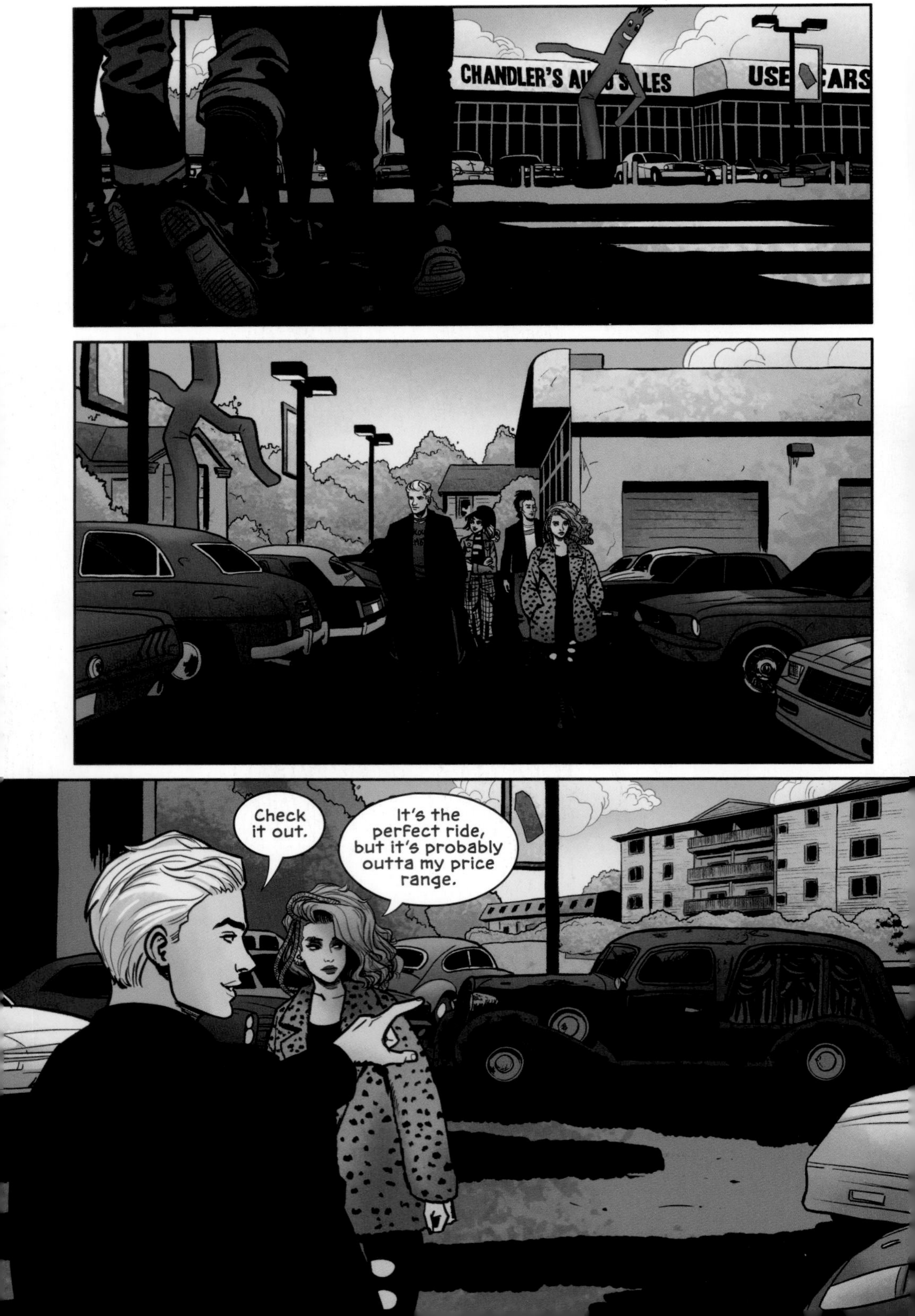
CHANDLER'S AU S LES
USE CARS
Check it out.
It's the perfect ride, but it's probably outta my price range.

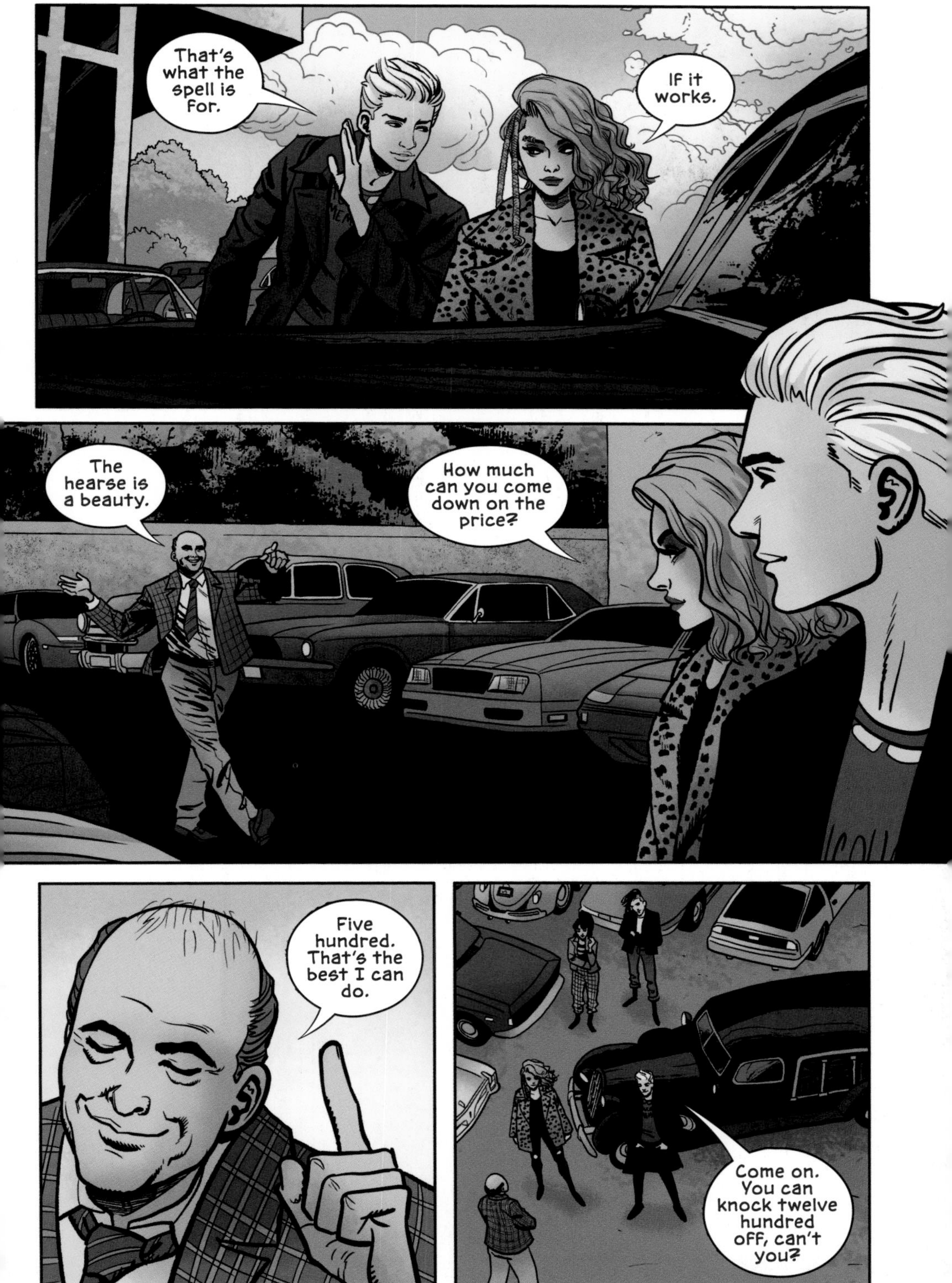
That's what the spell is for.
If it works.
The hearse is a beauty.
How much can you come down on the price?
Five hundred. That's the best I can do.
Come on. You can knock twelve hundred off, can't you?

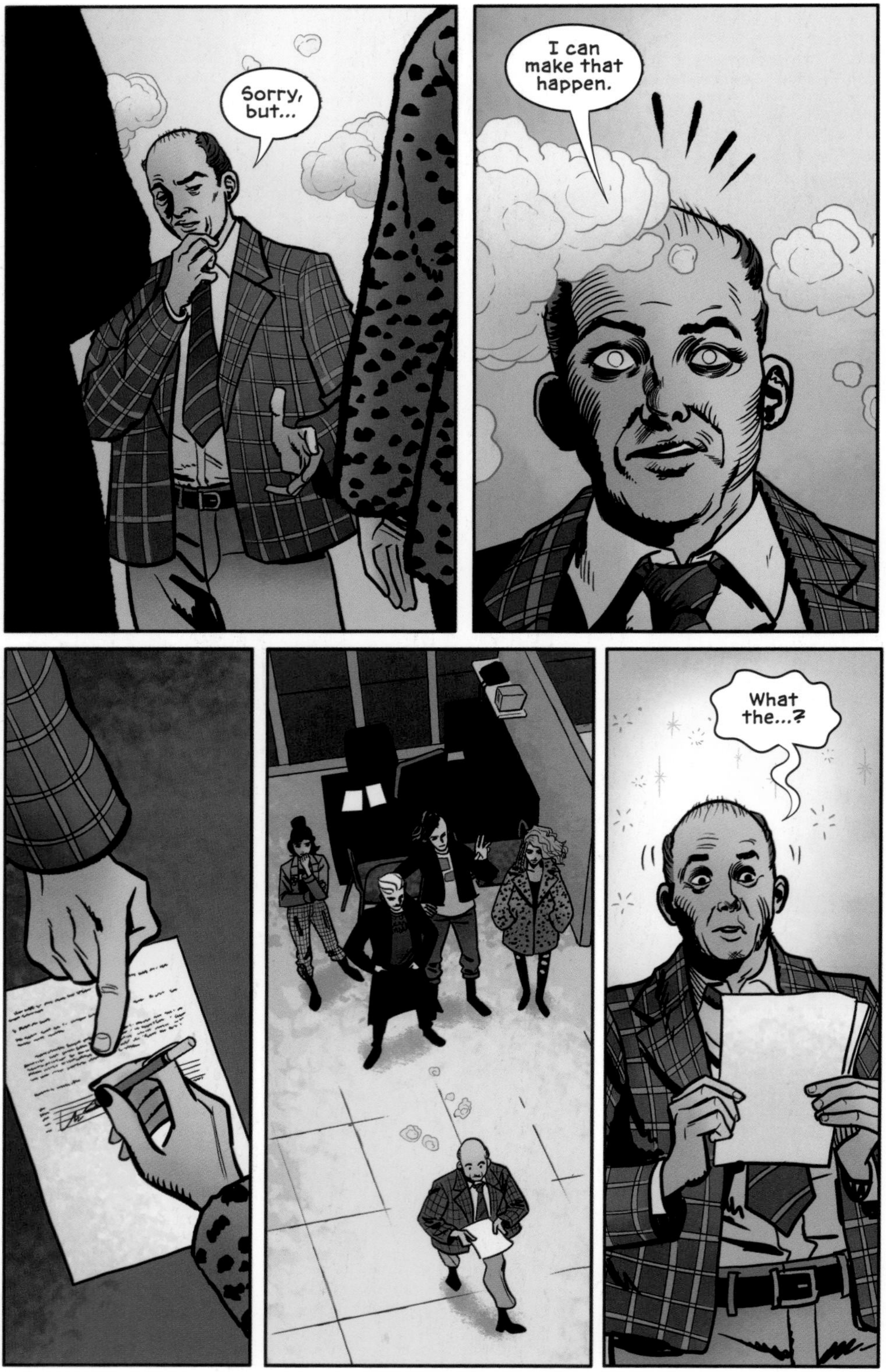
Sorry, but...
I can make that happen.
What the...?

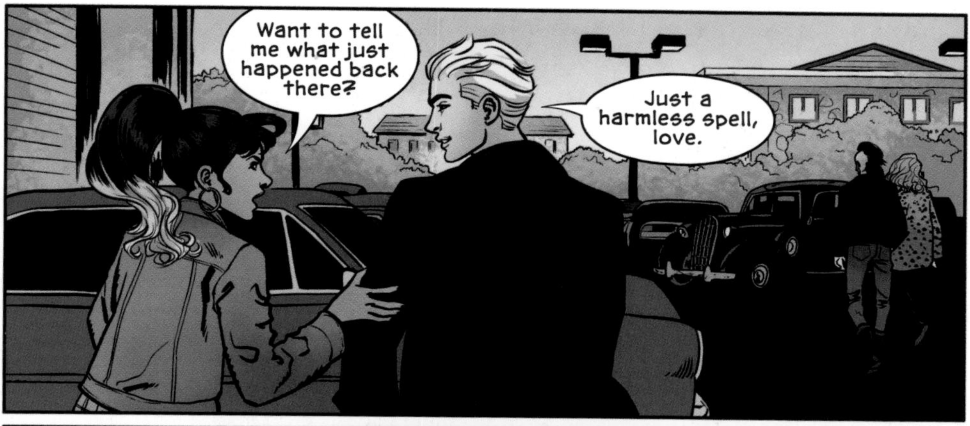
Want to tell me what just happened back there?
Just a harmless spell, love.

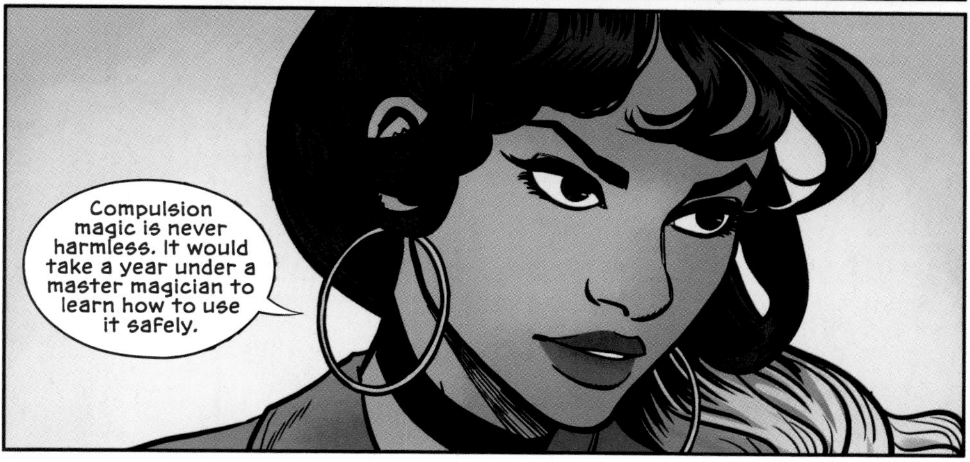
Compulsion magic is never harmless. It would take a year under a master magician to learn how to use it safely.

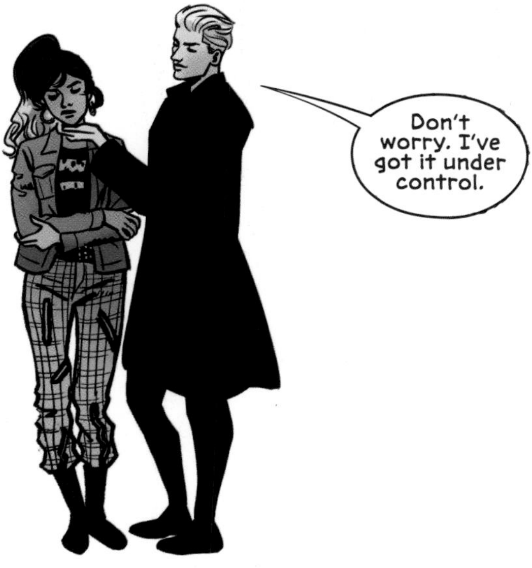
Don't worry. I've got it under control.

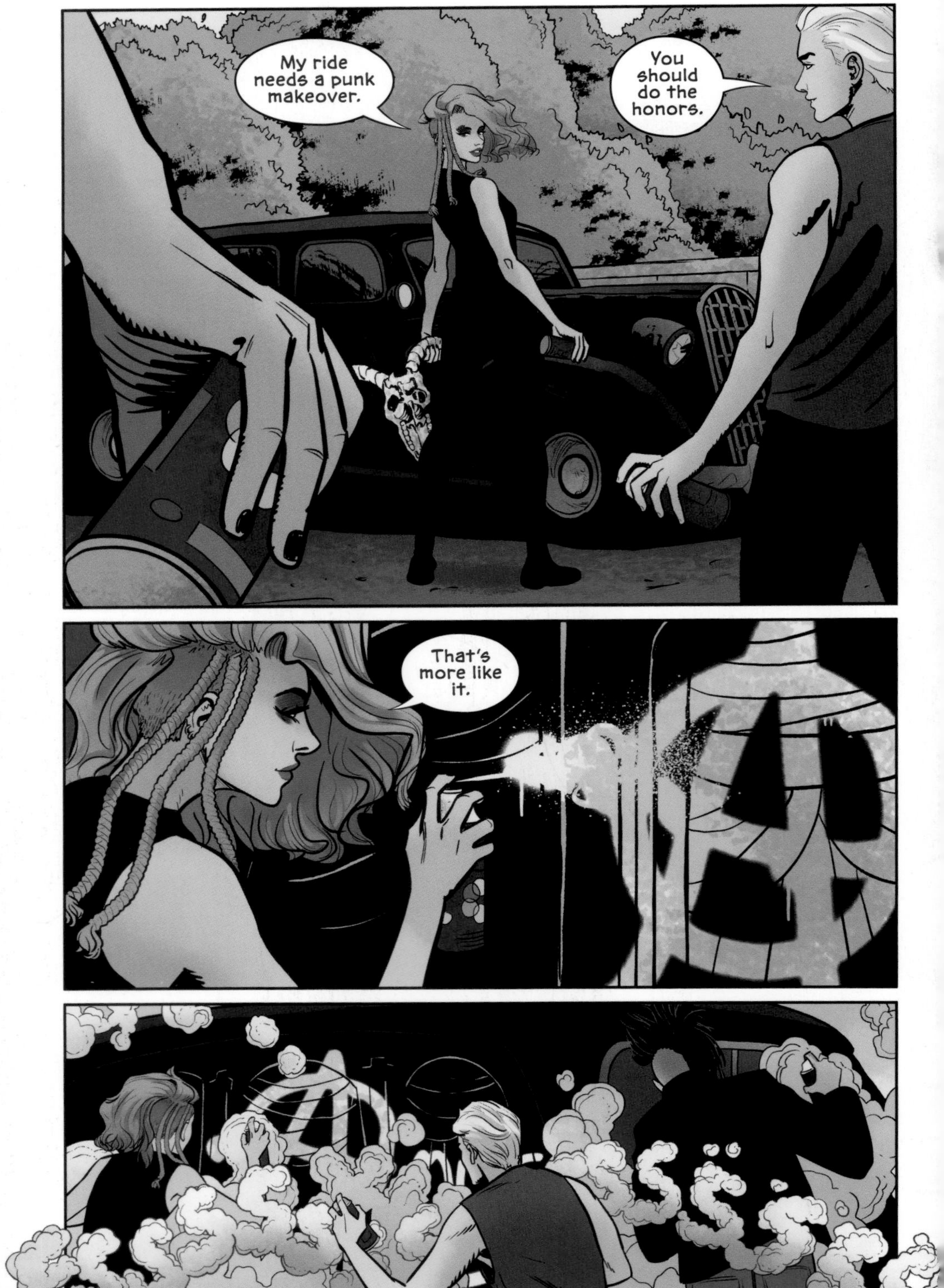
My ride needs a punk makeover.
You should do the honors.
That's more like it.

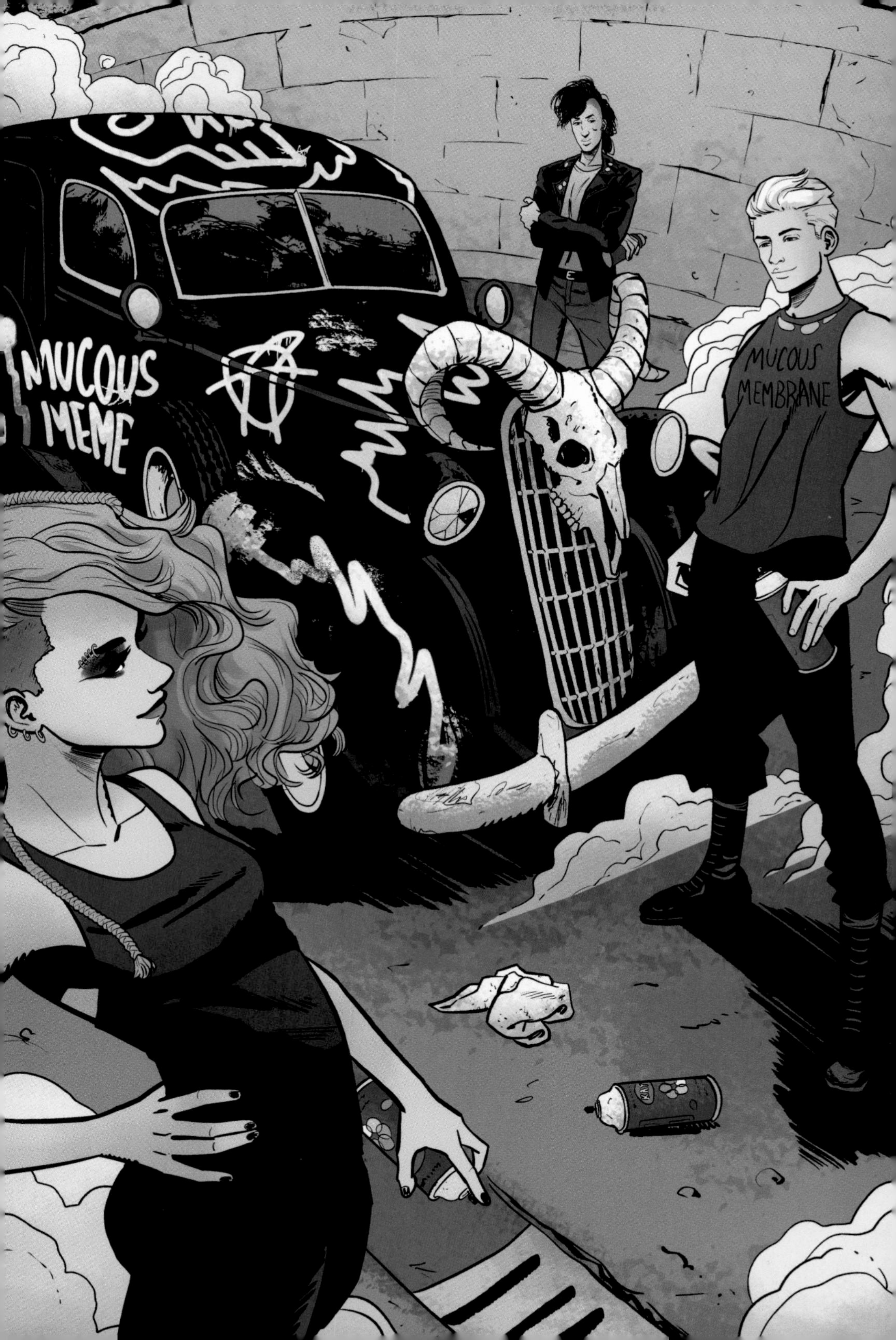
MUCOUS
MEME
MUCOUS
MEMBRANE

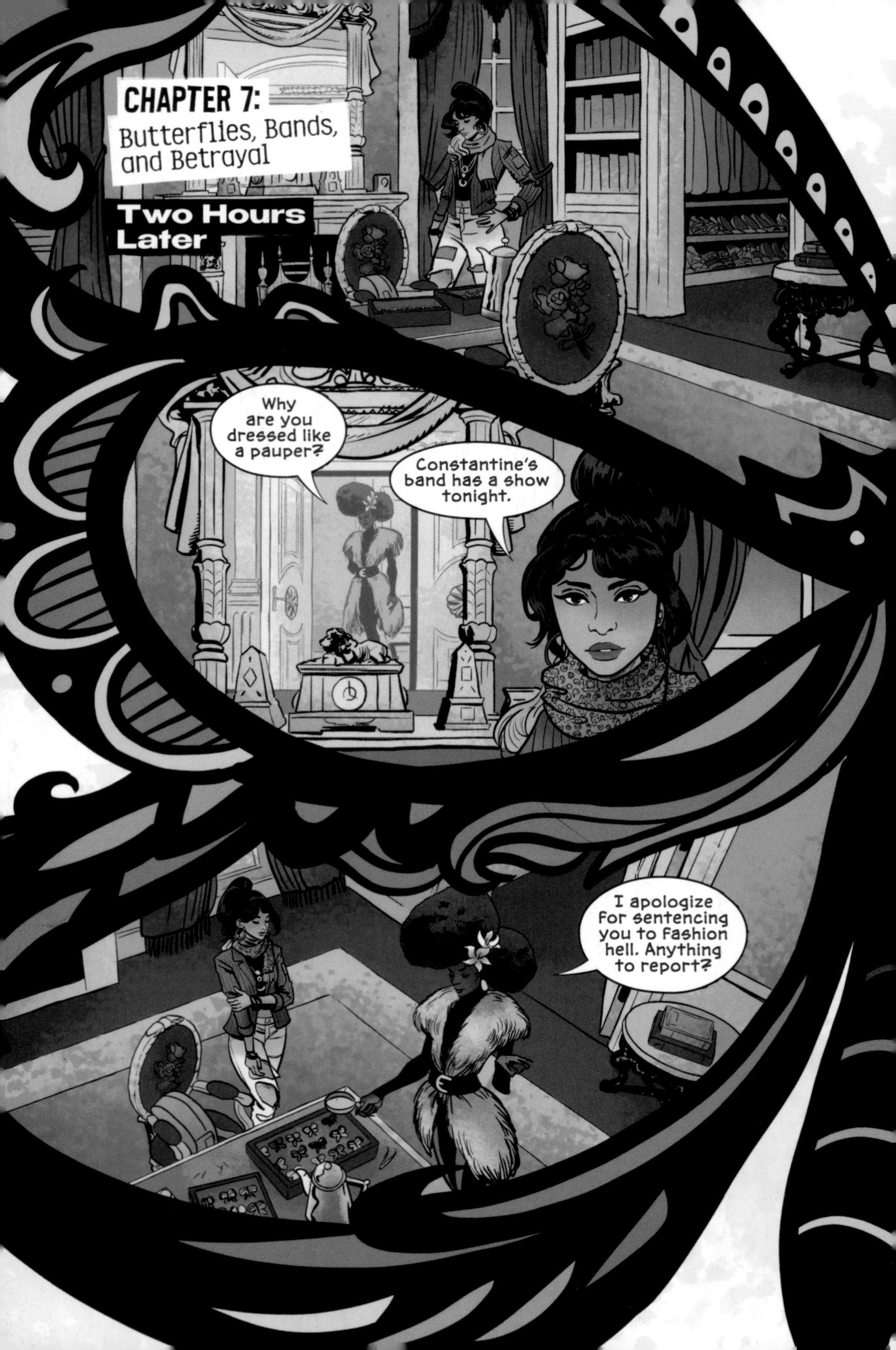
CHAPTER 7:
Butterflies, Bands, and Betrayal
Two Hours Later
Why are you dressed like a pauper?
Constantine's band has a show tonight.
I apologize for sentencing you to fashion hell. Anything to report?

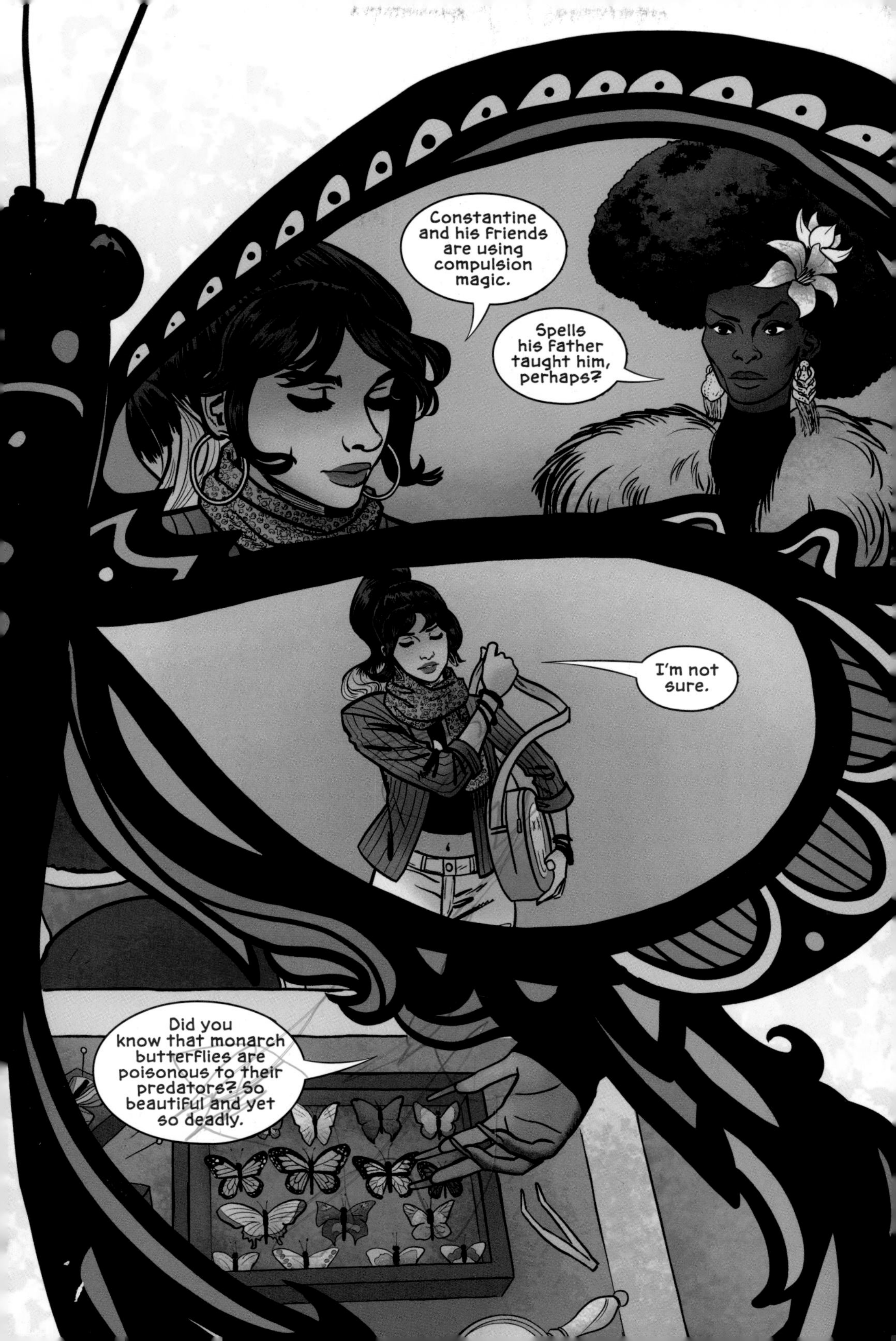
Constantine and his friends are using compulsion magic.
Spells his father taught him, perhaps?
I'm not sure.
Did you know that monarch butterflies are poisonous to their predators? So beautiful and yet so deadly.

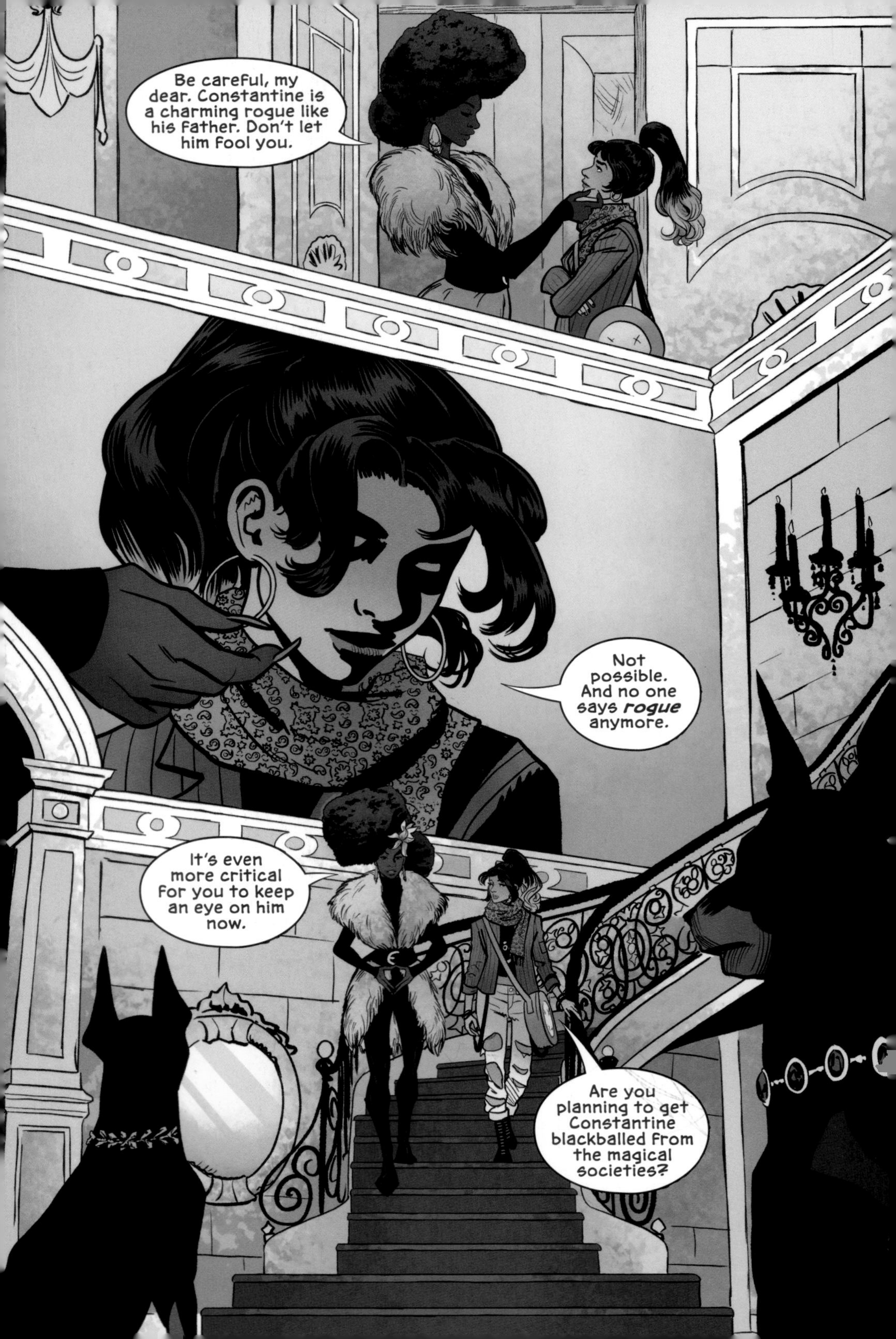
Be careful, my dear. Constantine is a charming rogue like his father. Don't let him fool you.
Not possible. And no one says *rogue* anymore.
It's even more critical for you to keep an eye on him now.
Are you planning to get Constantine blackballed from the magical societies?

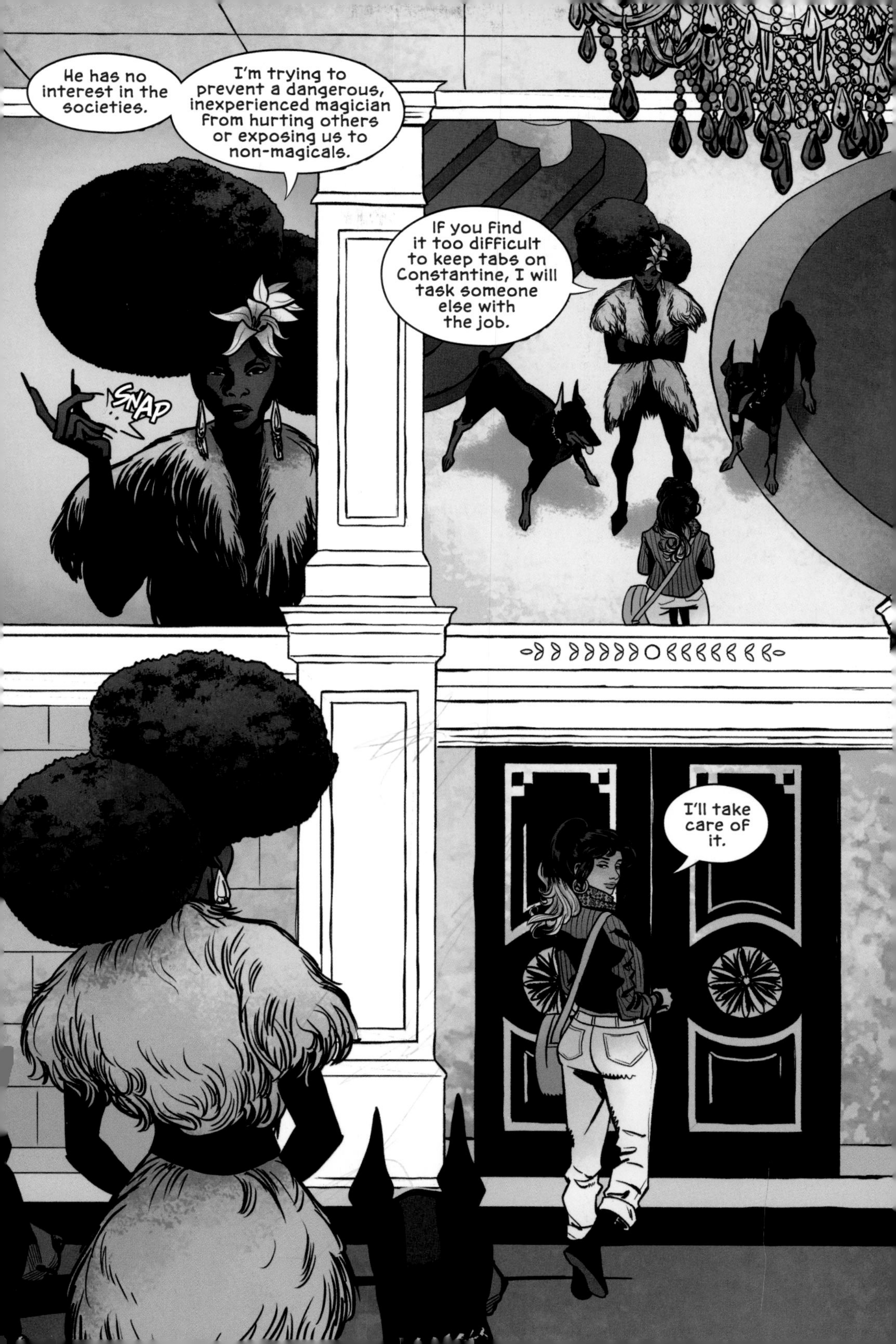
He has no interest in the societies.
I'm trying to prevent a dangerous, inexperienced magician from hurting others or exposing us to non-magicals.
SNAP
If you find it too difficult to keep tabs on Constantine, I will task someone else with the job.
I'll take care of it.

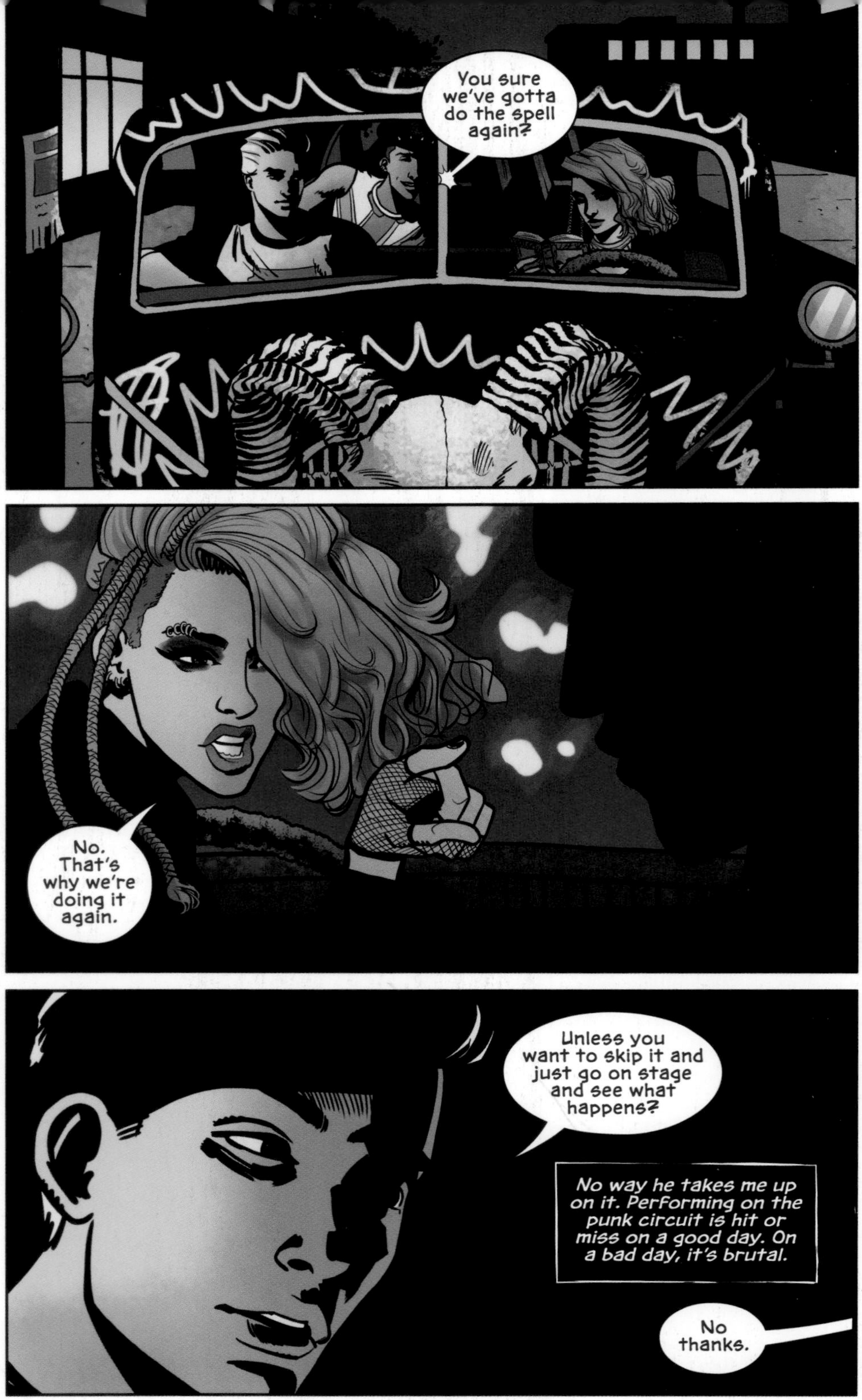
You sure we've gotta do the spell again?
No. That's why we're doing it again.
Unless you want to skip it and just go on stage and see what happens?
No way he takes me up on it. Performing on the punk circuit is hit or miss on a good day. On a bad day, it's brutal.
No thanks.

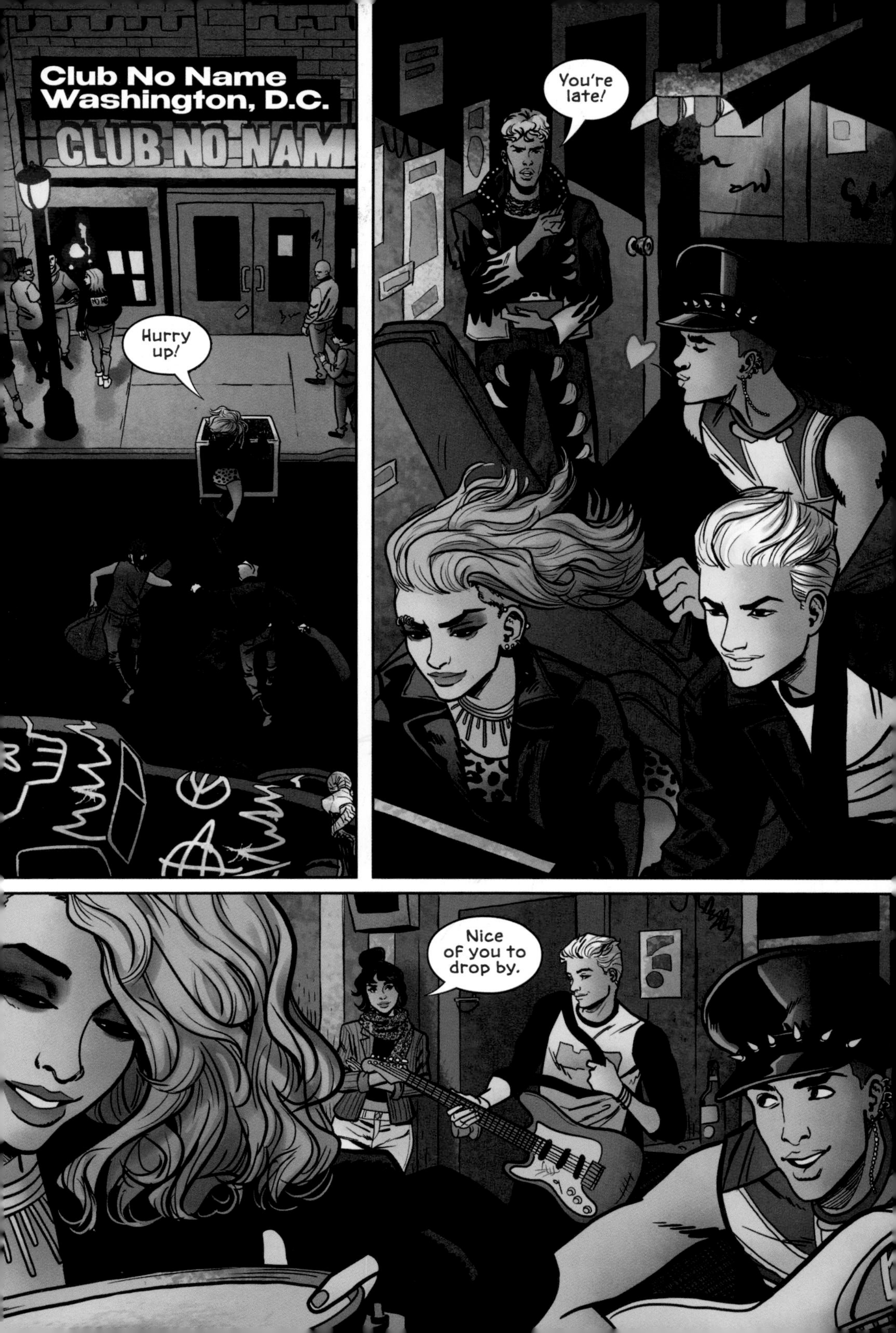
Club No Name
Washington, D.C.
CLUB NO NAM
Hurry up!
You're late!
Nice of you to drop by.

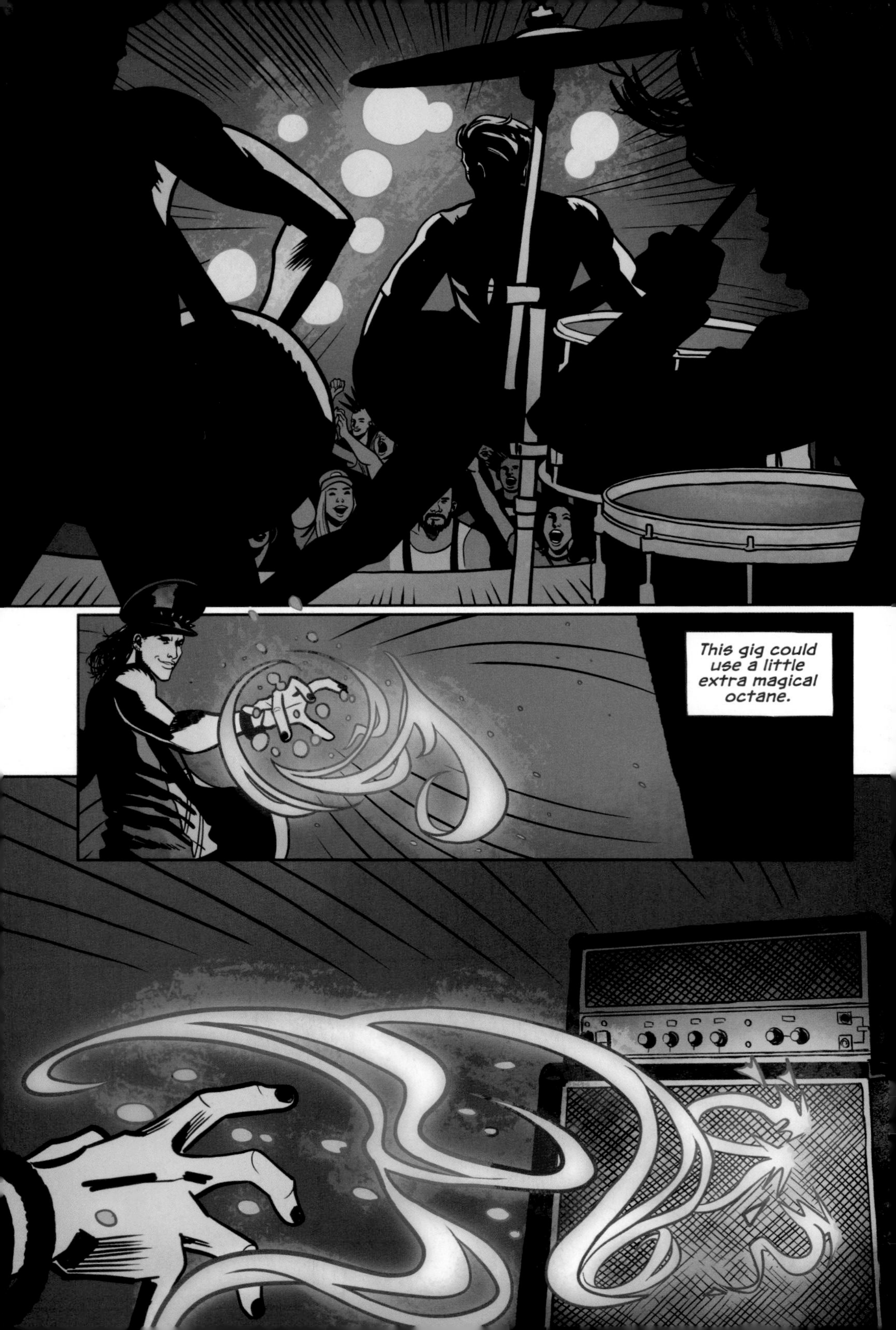
This gig could use a little extra magical octane.

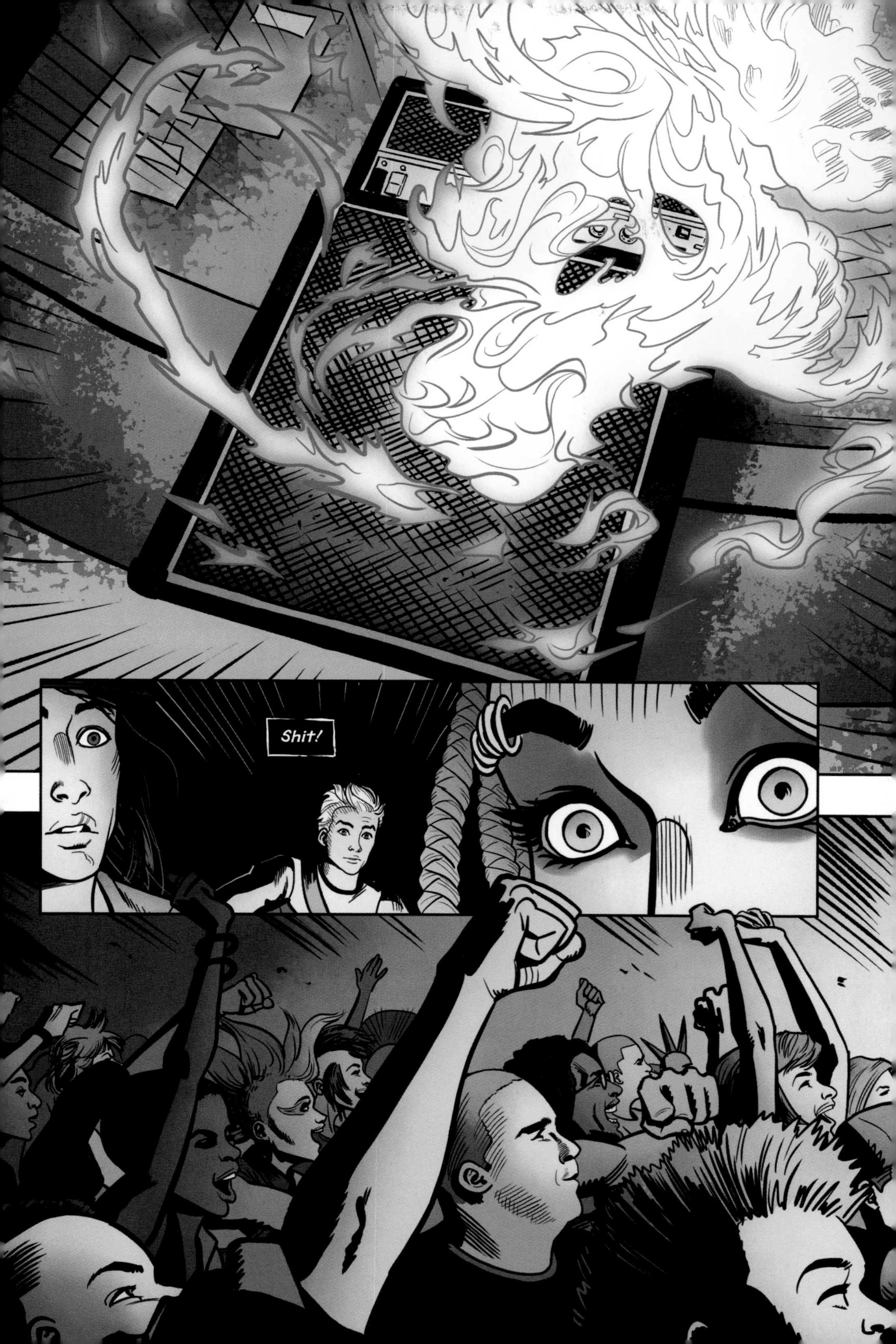
Shit!

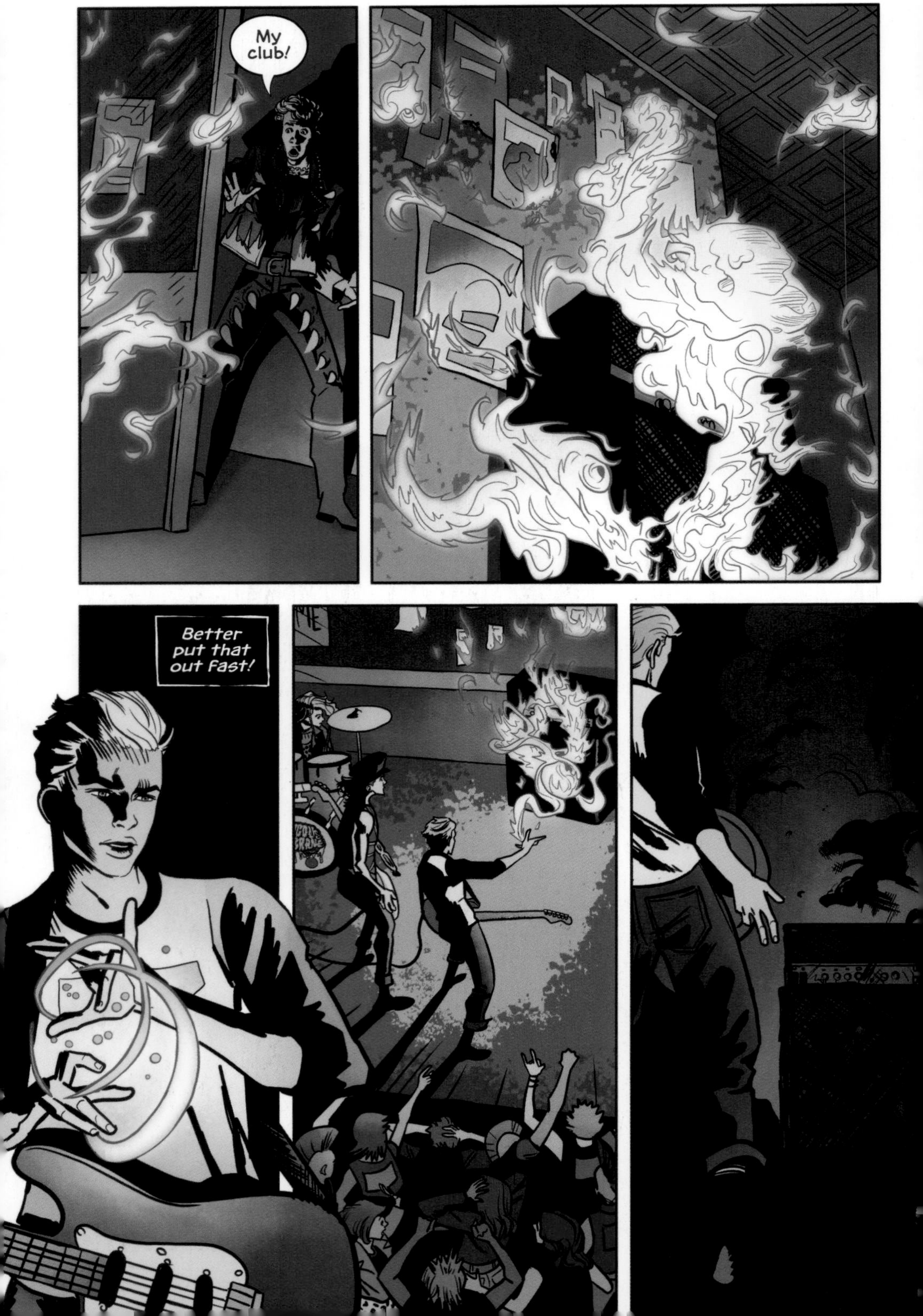
My club!
Better put that out fast!

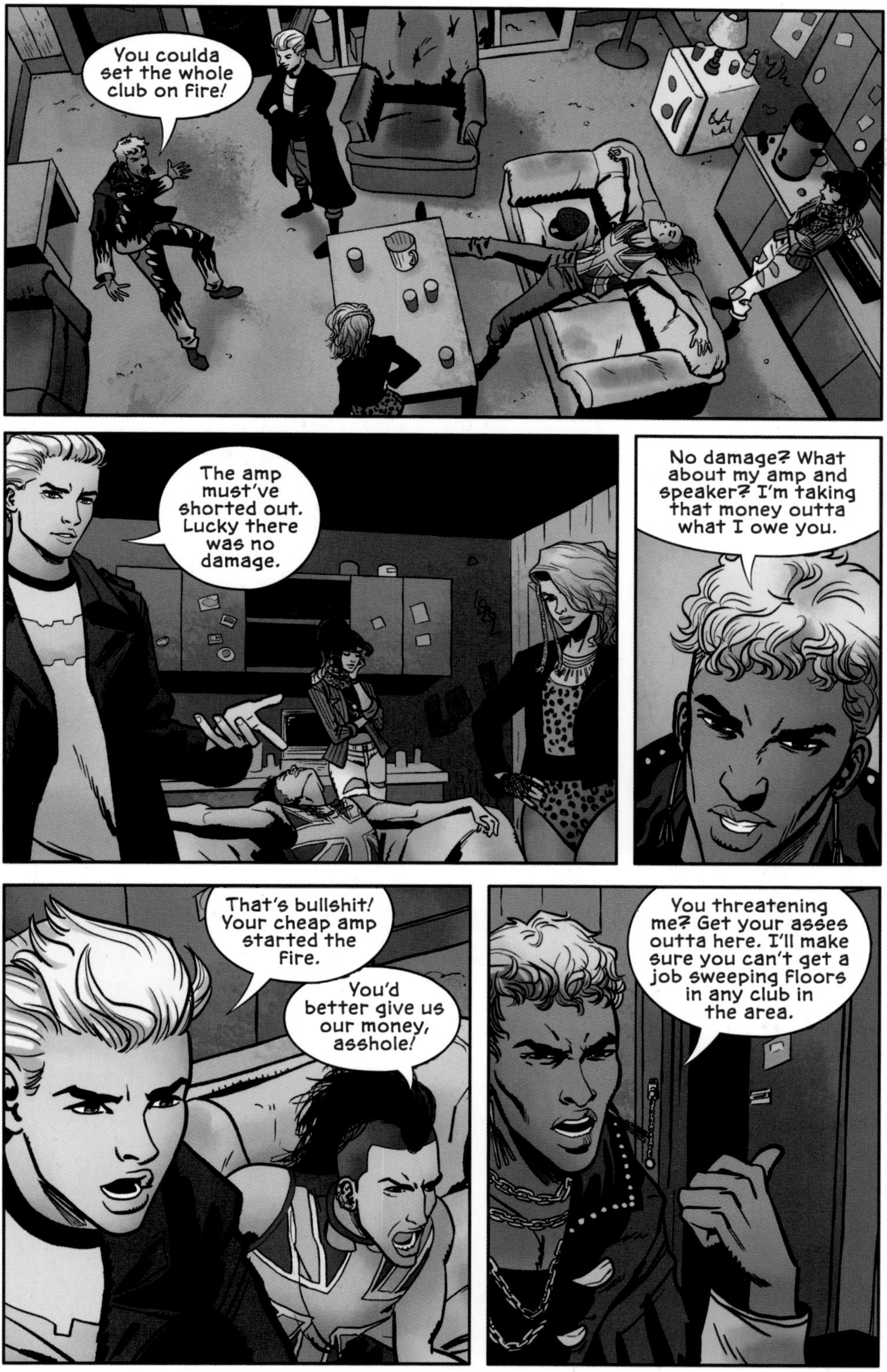
You coulda set the whole club on fire!
The amp must've shorted out. Lucky there was no damage.
No damage? What about my amp and speaker? I'm taking that money outta what I owe you.
That's bullshit! Your cheap amp started the fire.
You'd better give us our money, asshole!
You threatening me? Get your asses outta here. I'll make sure you can't get a job sweeping floors in any club in the area.

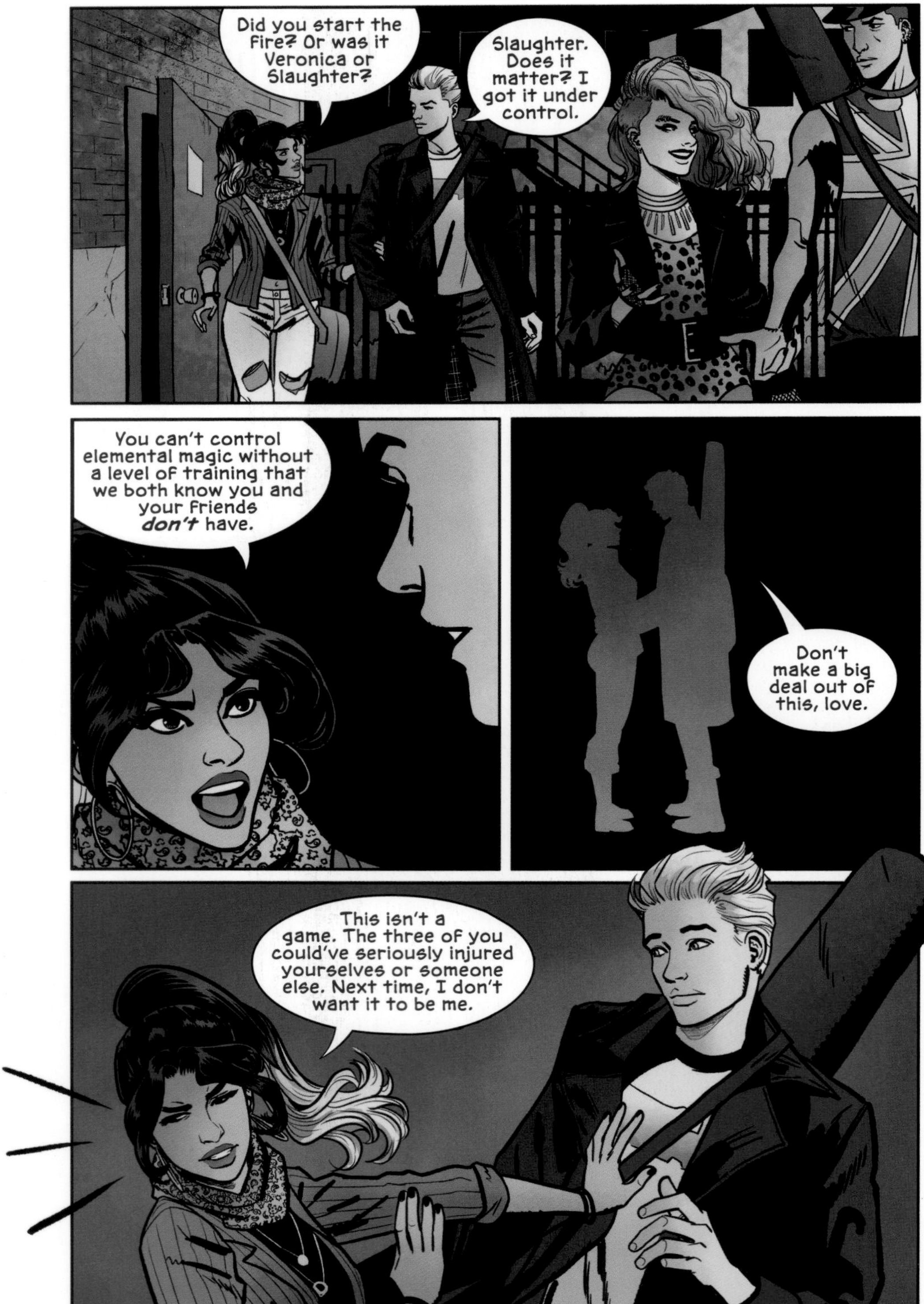
Did you start the fire? Or was it Veronica or Slaughter?
Slaughter. Does it matter? I got it under control.
You can't control elemental magic without a level of training that we both know you and your friends *don't* have.
Don't make a big deal out of this, love.
This isn't a game. The three of you could've seriously injured yourselves or someone else. Next time, I don't want it to be me.

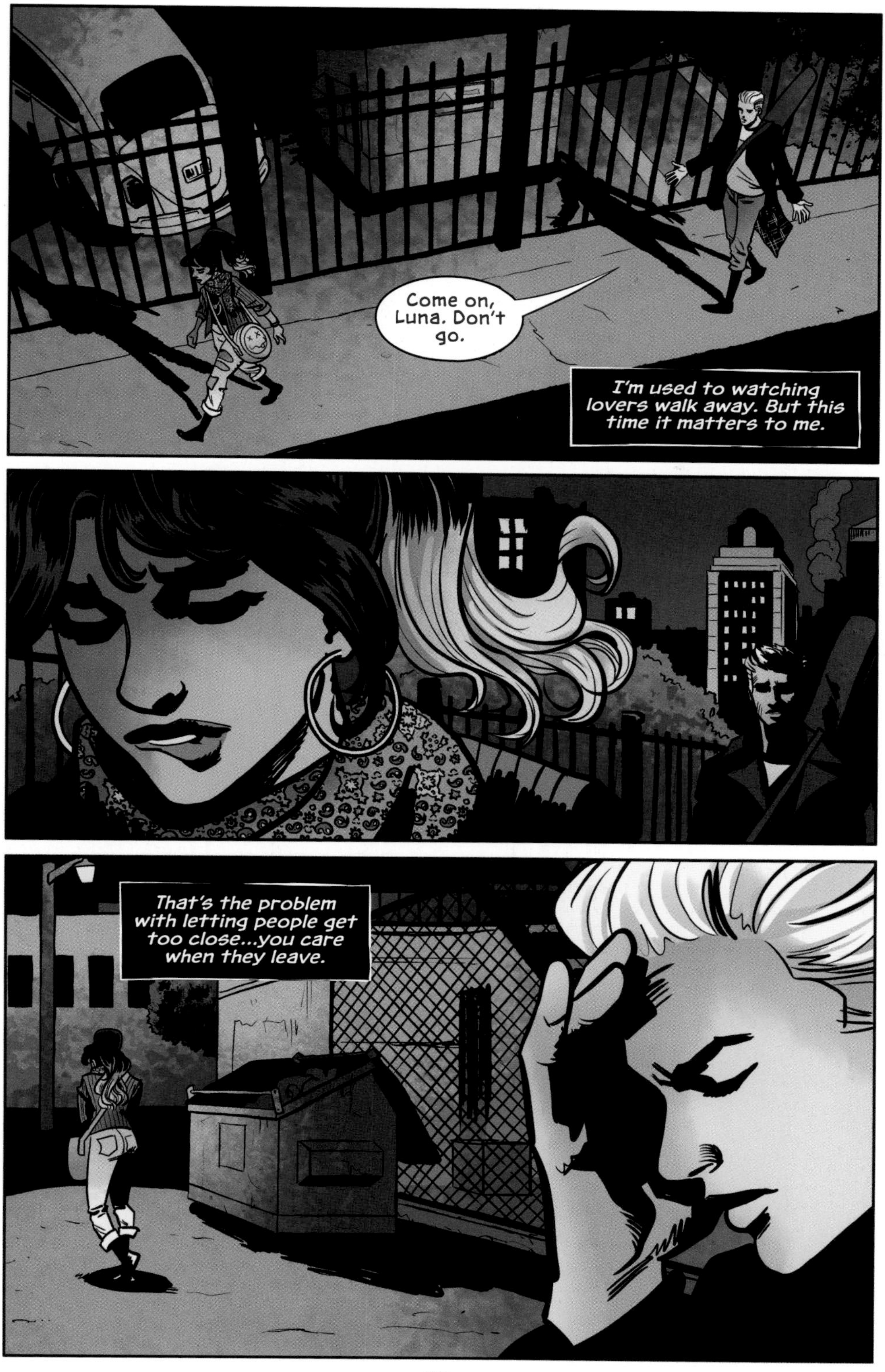
Come on, Luna. Don't go.
I'm used to watching lovers walk away. But this time it matters to me.
That's the problem with letting people get too close...you care when they leave.

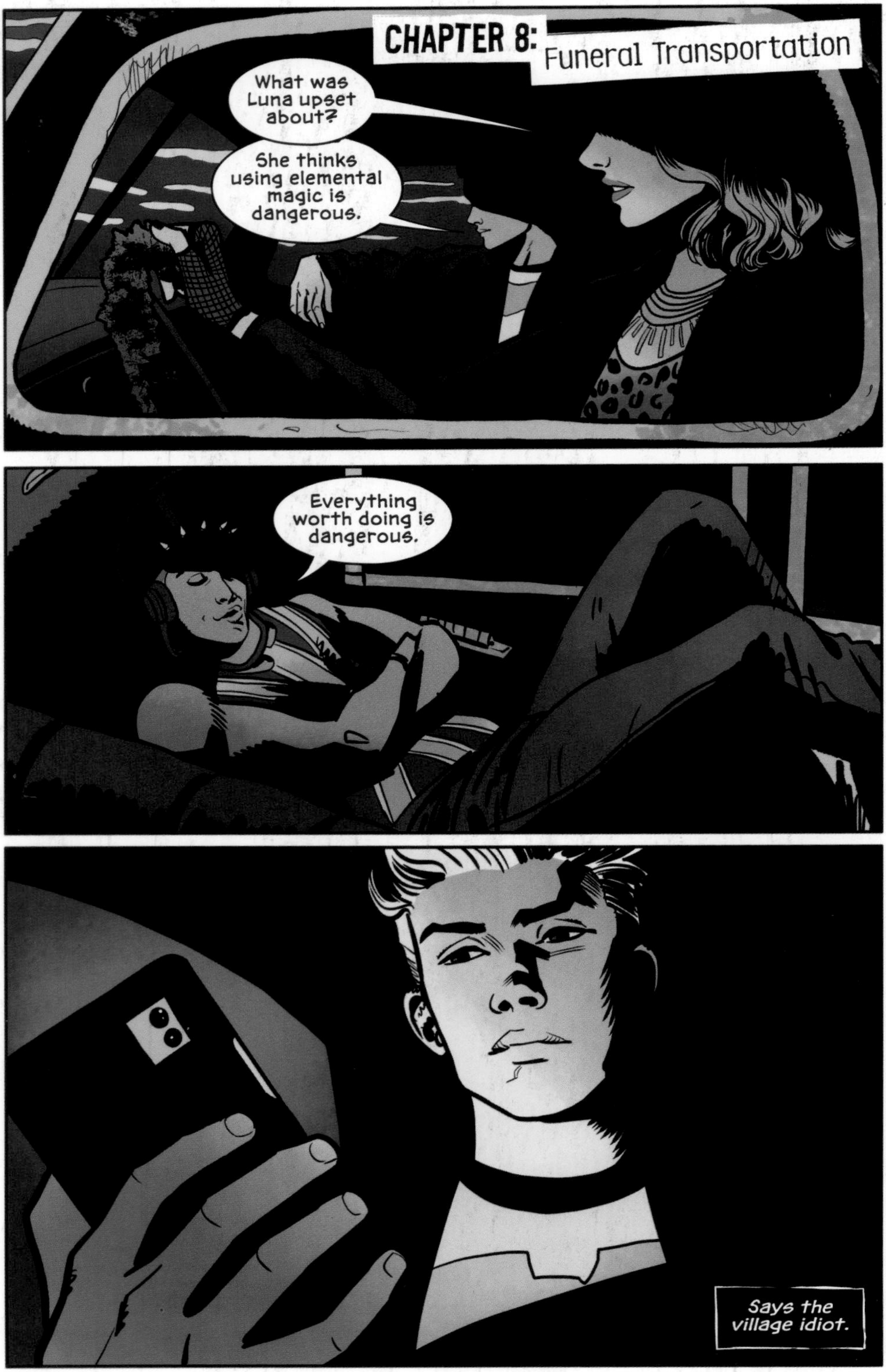
CHAPTER 8: Funeral Transportation
What was Luna upset about?
She thinks using elemental magic is dangerous.
Everything worth doing is dangerous.
Says the village idiot.

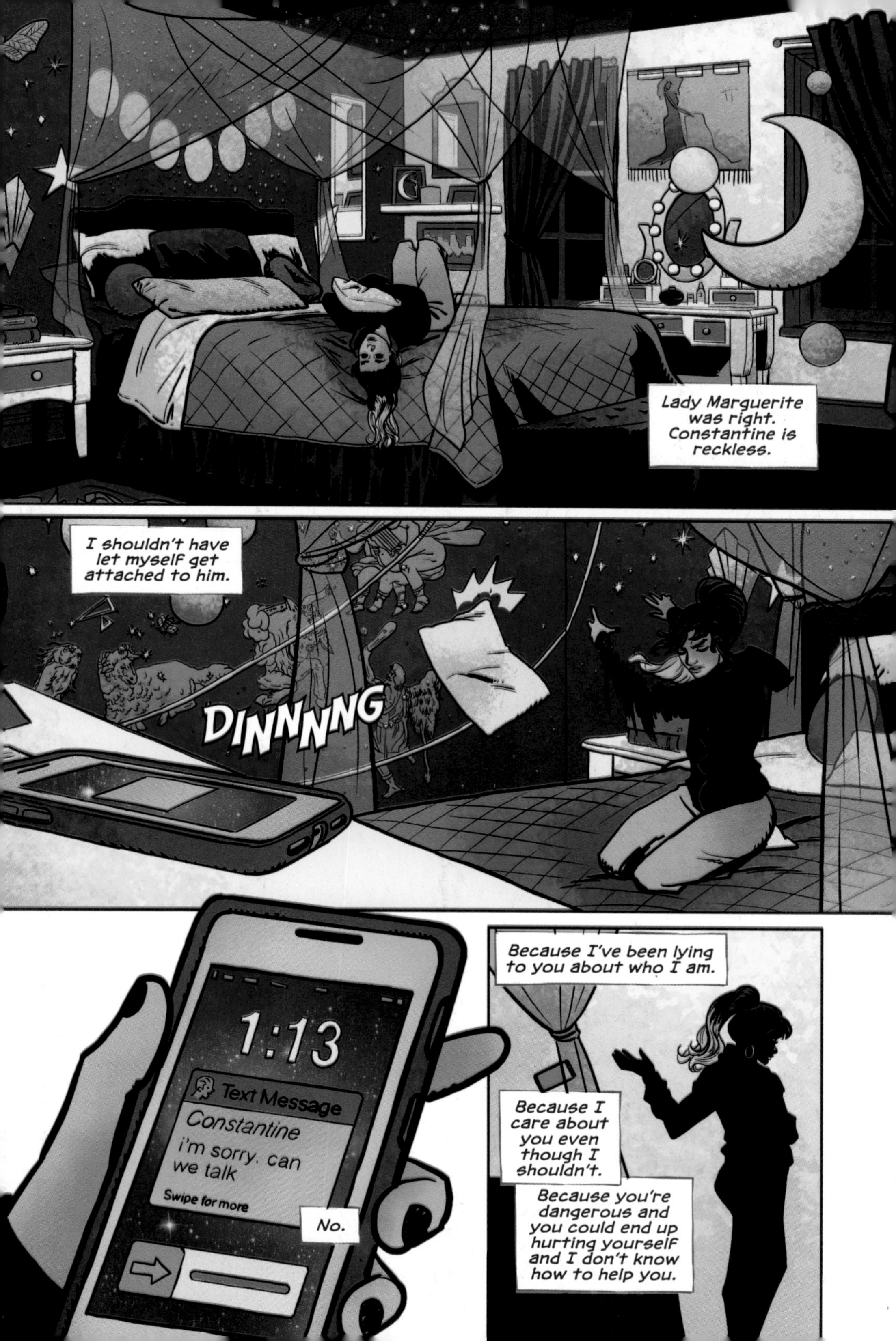
Lady Marguerite was right. Constantine is reckless.
I shouldn't have let myself get attached to him.
DINNNNG
1:13
Text Message
Constantine
i'm sorry. can we talk
Swipe for more
No.
Because I've been lying to you about who I am.
Because I care about you even though I shouldn't.
Because you're dangerous and you could end up hurting yourself and I don't know how to help you.

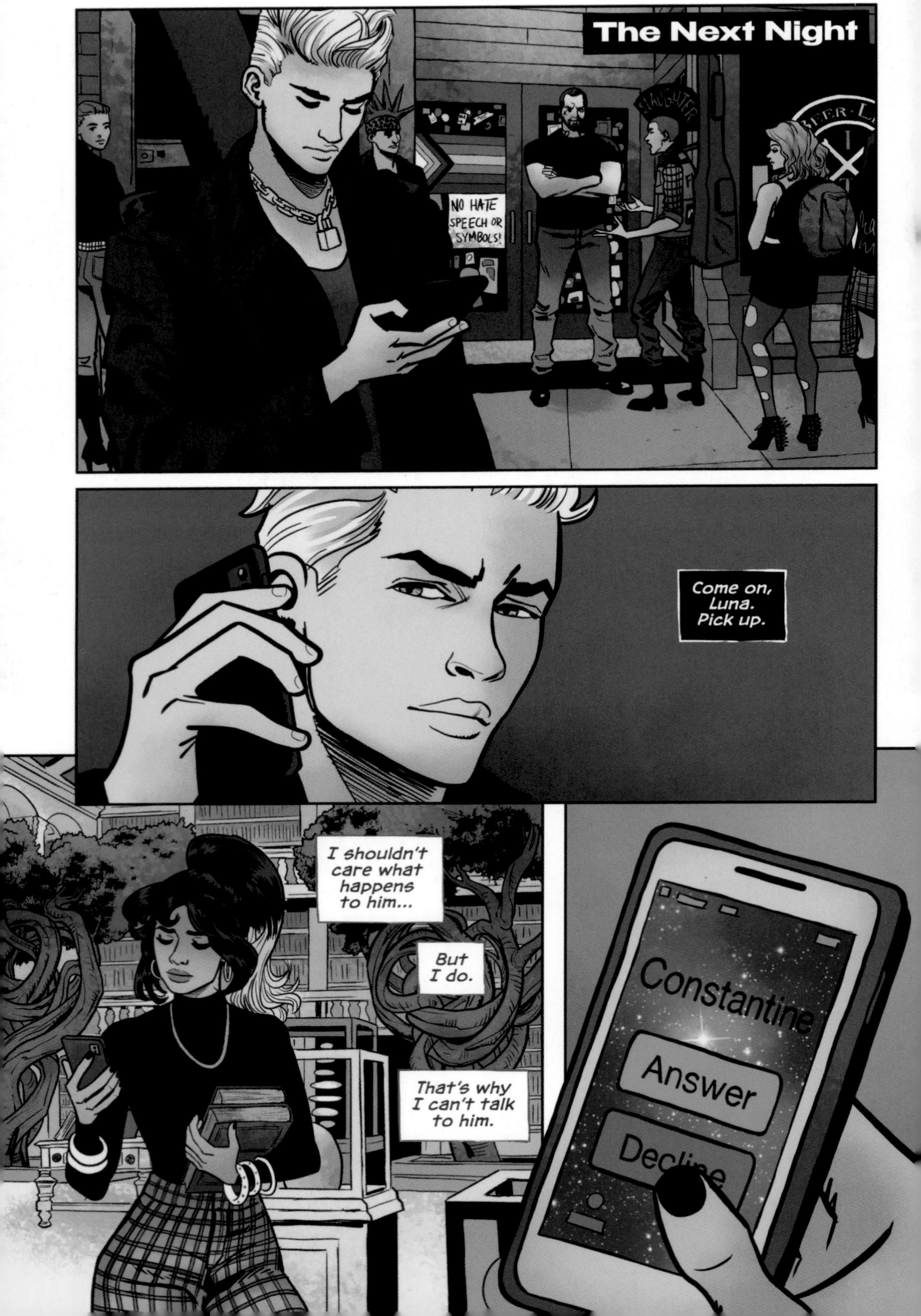
The Next Night
NO HATE SPEECH OR SYMBOLS!
Come on, Luna. Pick up.
I shouldn't care what happens to him...
But I do.
That's why I can't talk to him.
Constantine
Answer
Decline

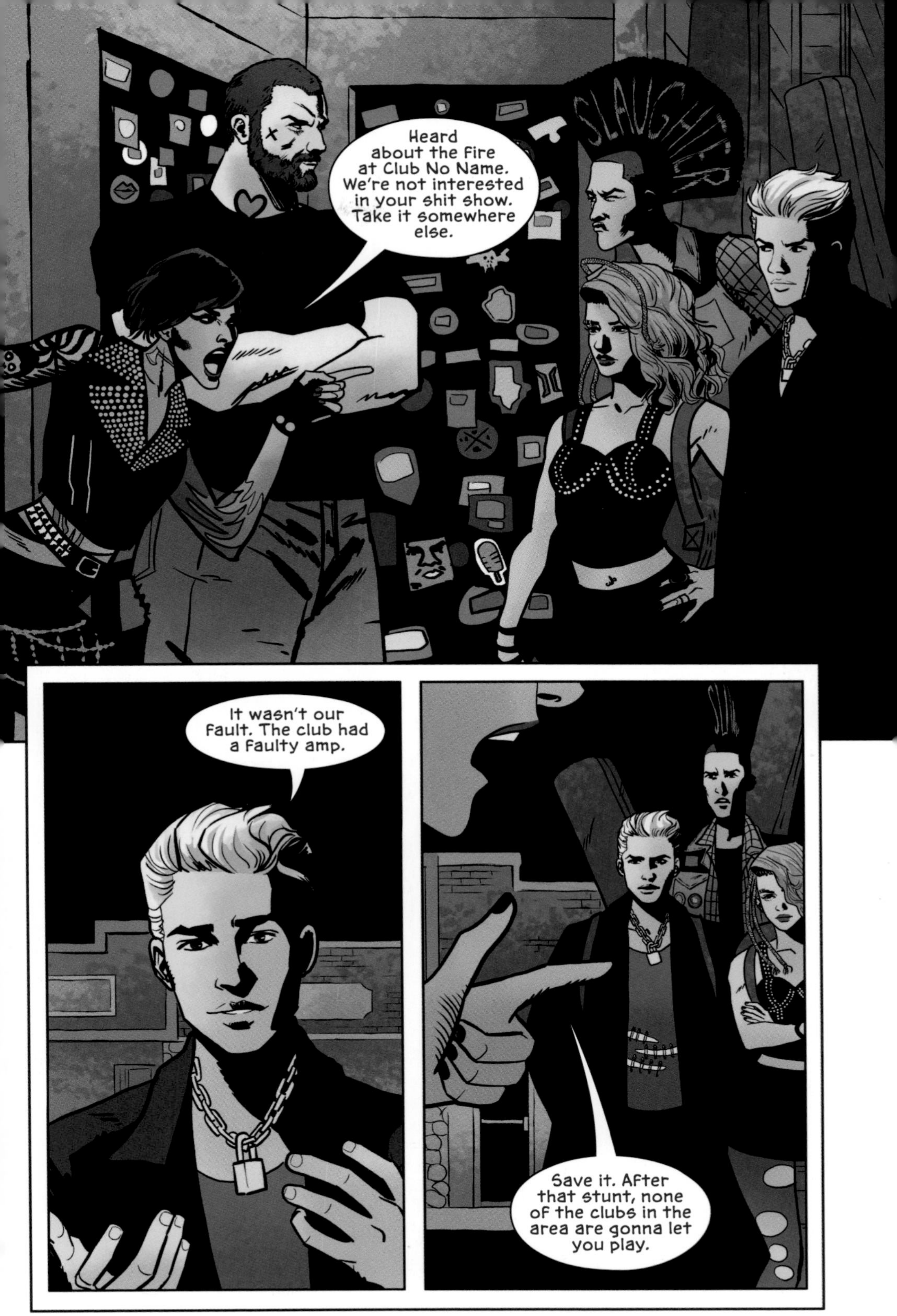
SLAUGHTER
Heard about the fire at Club No Name. We're not interested in your shit show. Take it somewhere else.
It wasn't our fault. The club had a faulty amp.
Save it. After that stunt, none of the clubs in the area are gonna let you play.

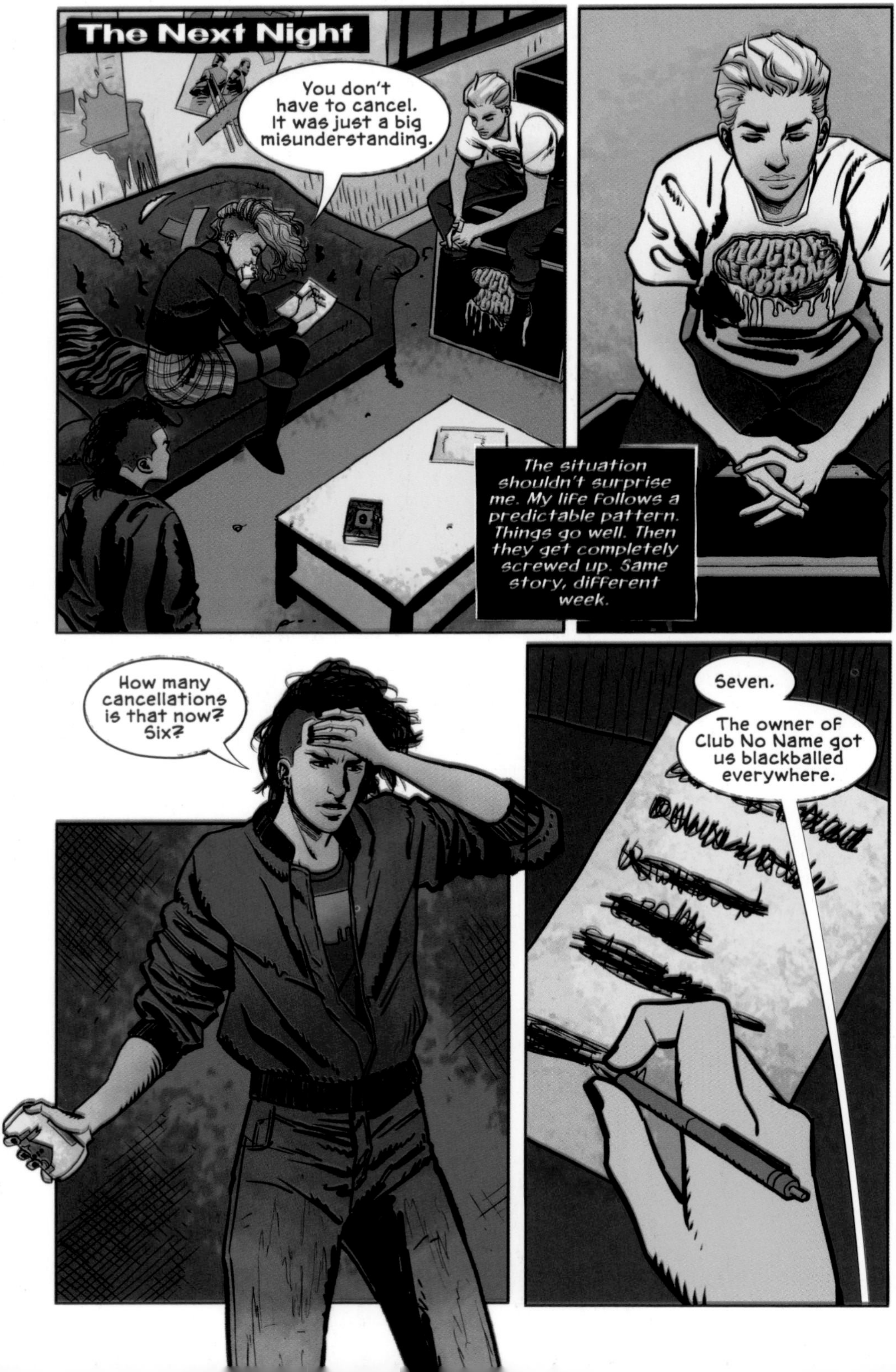
The Next Night
You don't have to cancel. It was just a big misunderstanding.
The situation shouldn't surprise me. My life follows a predictable pattern. Things go well. Then they get completely screwed up. Same story, different week.
How many cancellations is that now? Six?
Seven.
The owner of Club No Name got us blackballed everywhere.

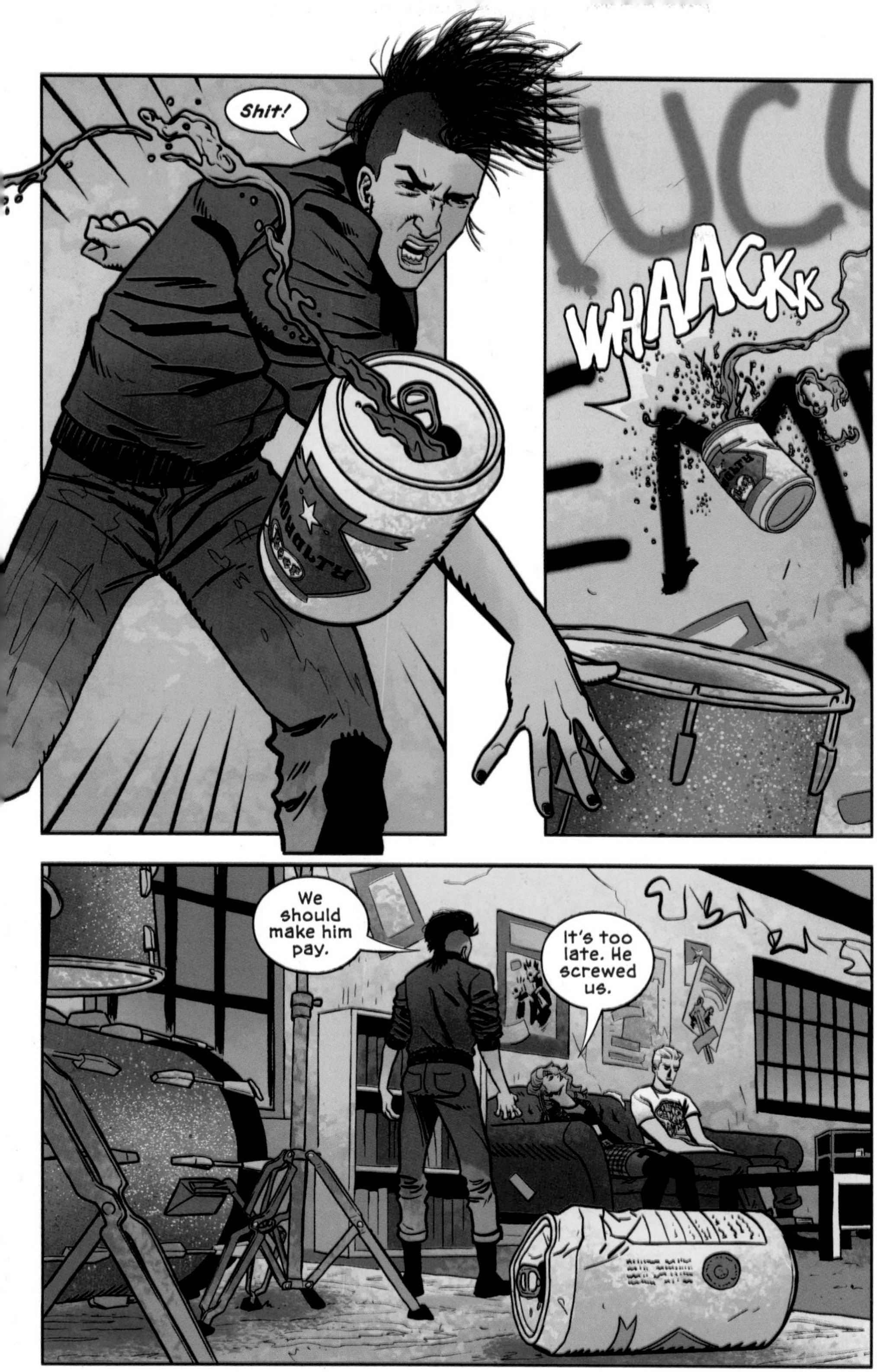
Shit!
WHAACKk
We should make him pay.
It's too late. He screwed us.

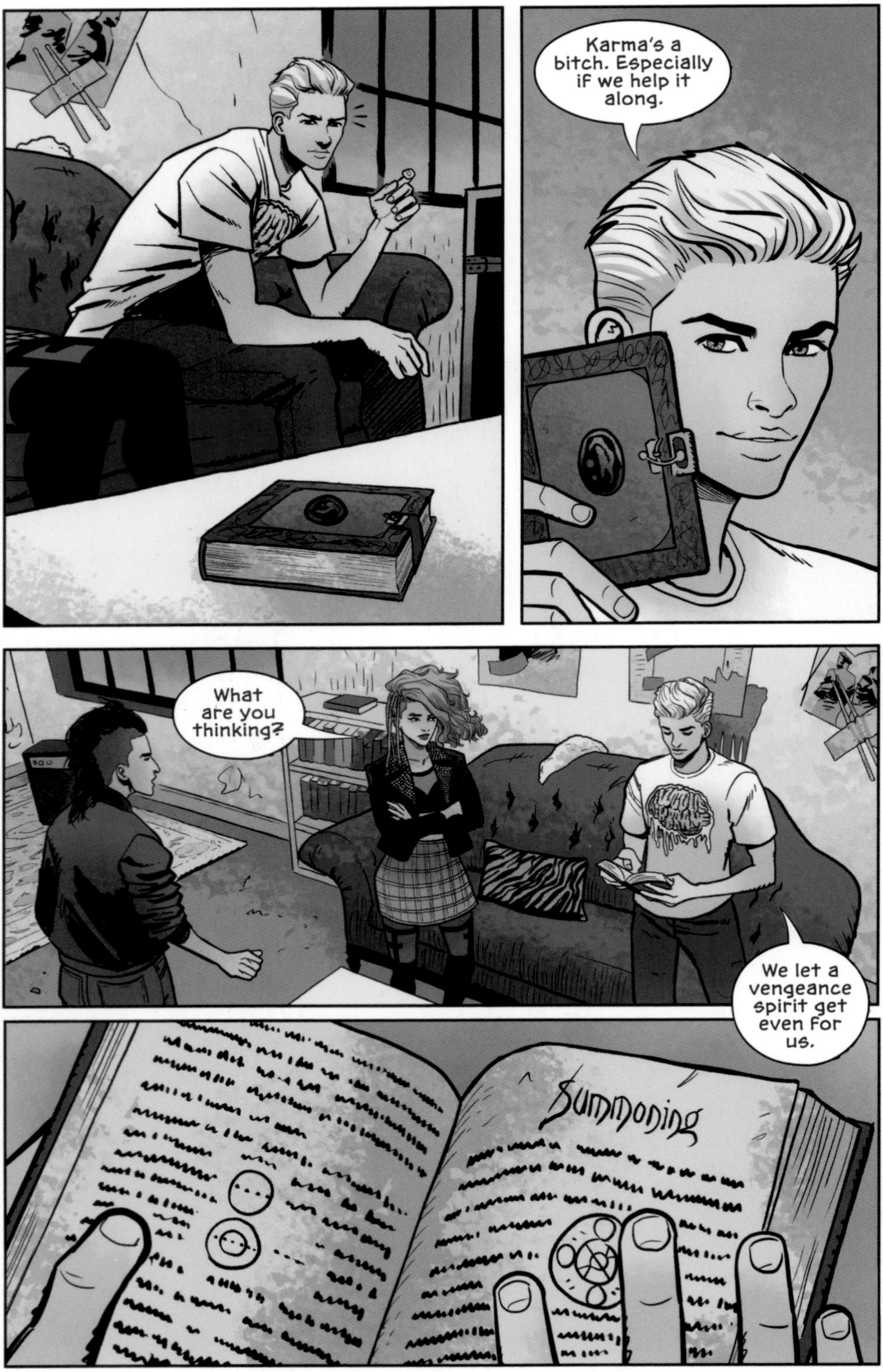
Karma's a bitch. Especially if we help it along.
What are you thinking?
We let a vengeance spirit get even for us.
Summoning

CHAPTER 9:
Bad Magic

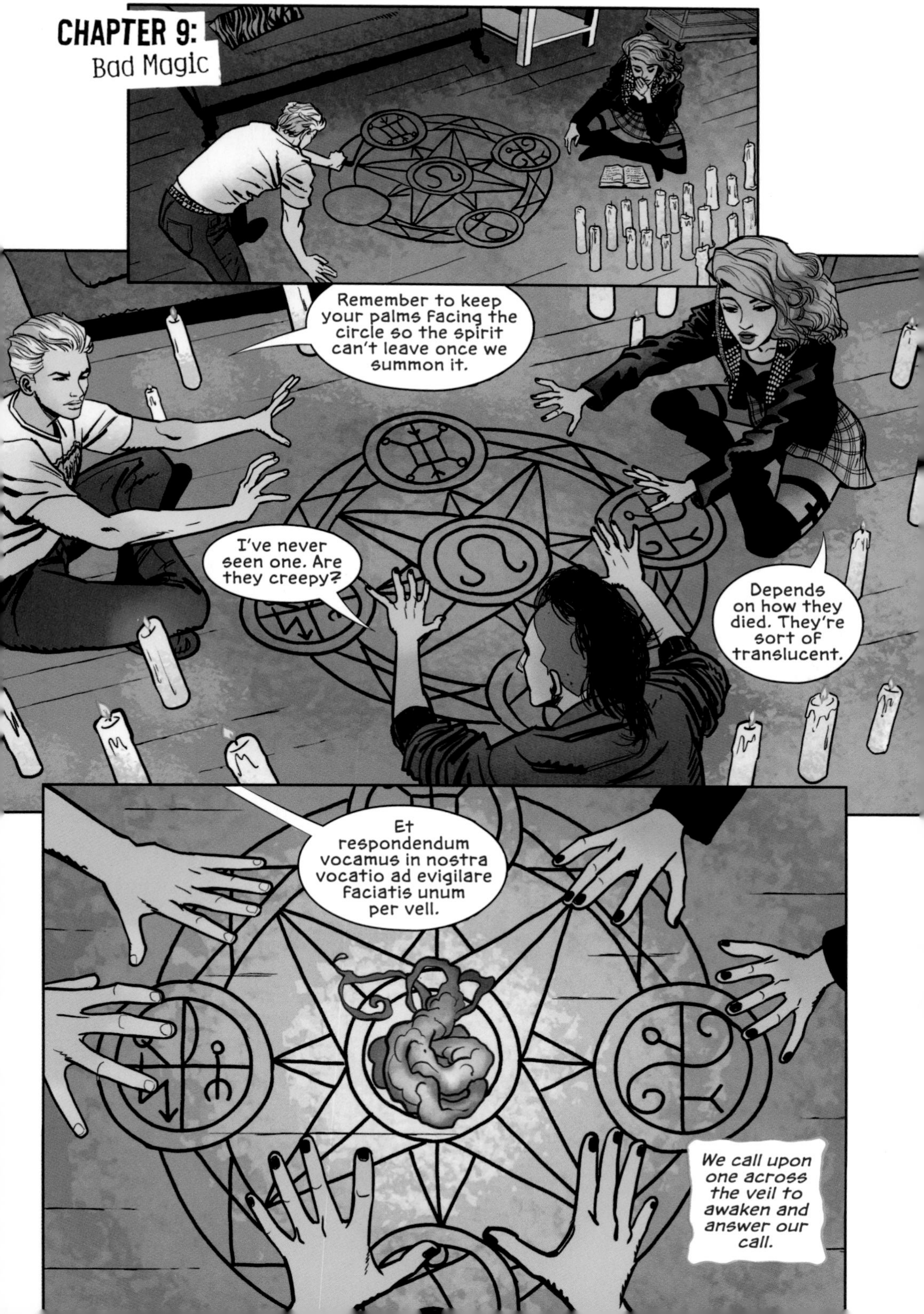

Remember to keep your palms facing the circle so the spirit can't leave once we summon it.
I've never seen one. Are they creepy?
Depends on how they died. They're sort of translucent.
Et respondendum vocamus in nostra vocatio ad evigilare faciatis unum per vell.
We call upon one across the veil to awaken and answer our call.

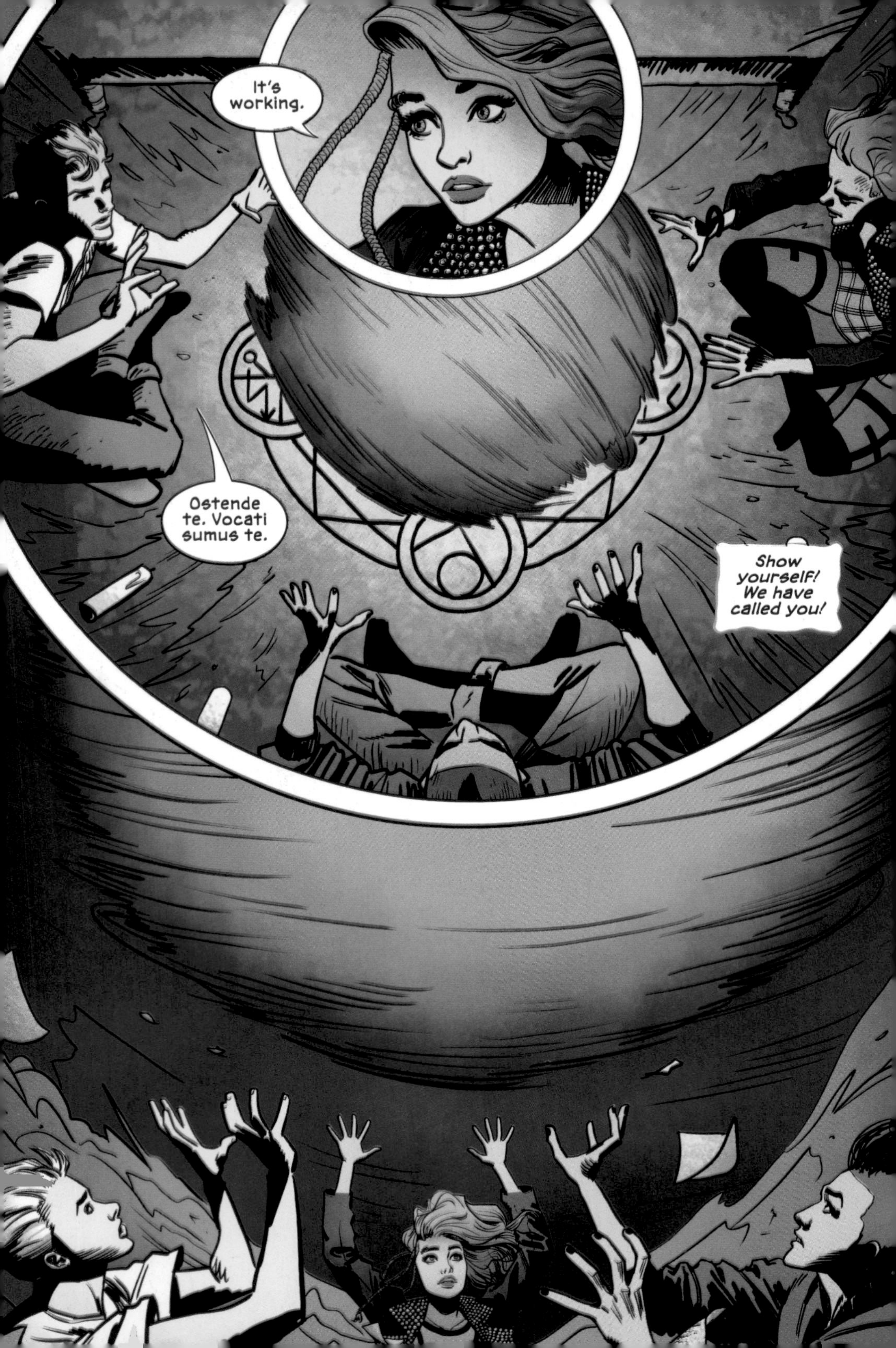
It's working.
Ostende te. Vocati sumus te.
Show yourself! We have called you!

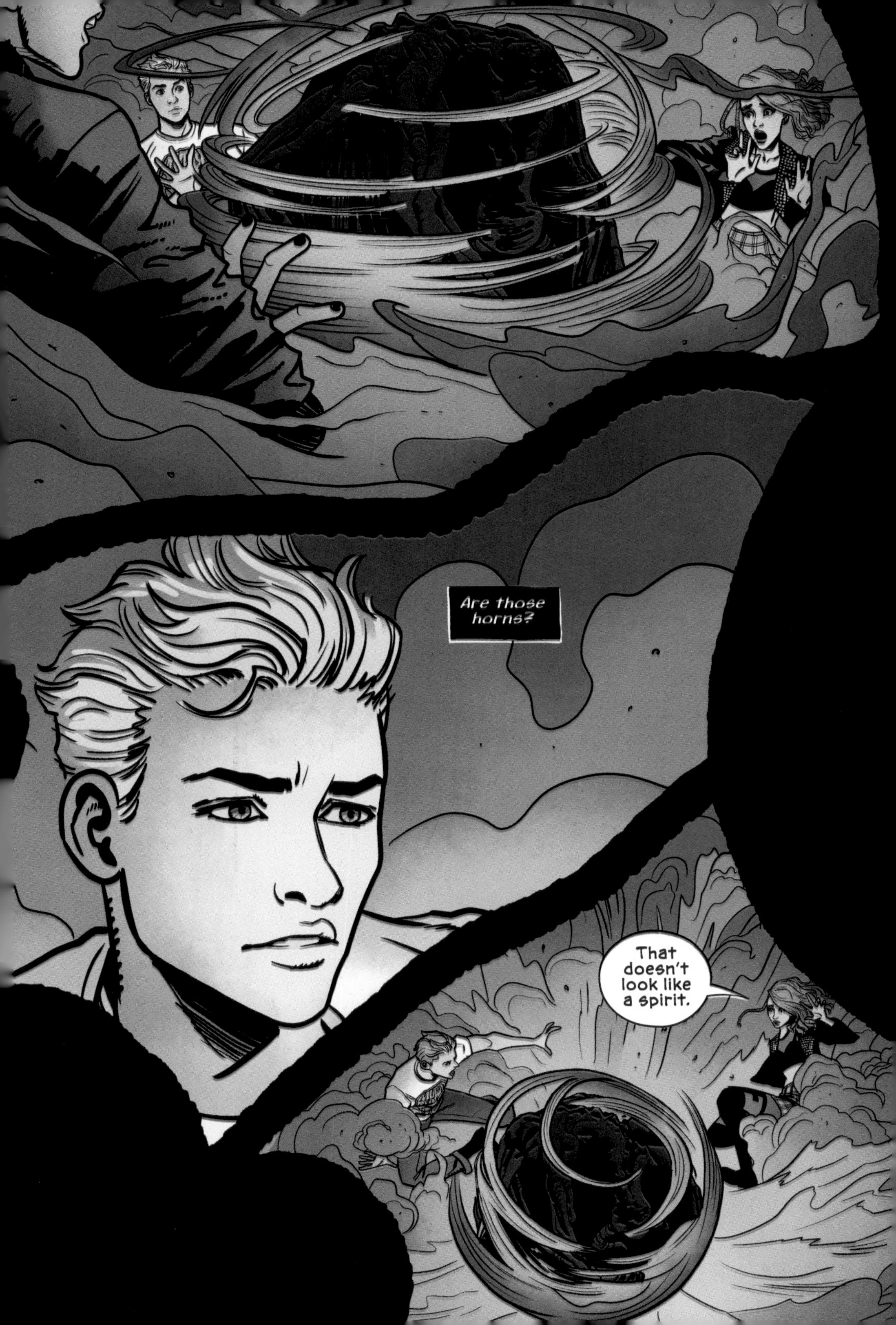
Are those horns?
That doesn't look like a spirit.

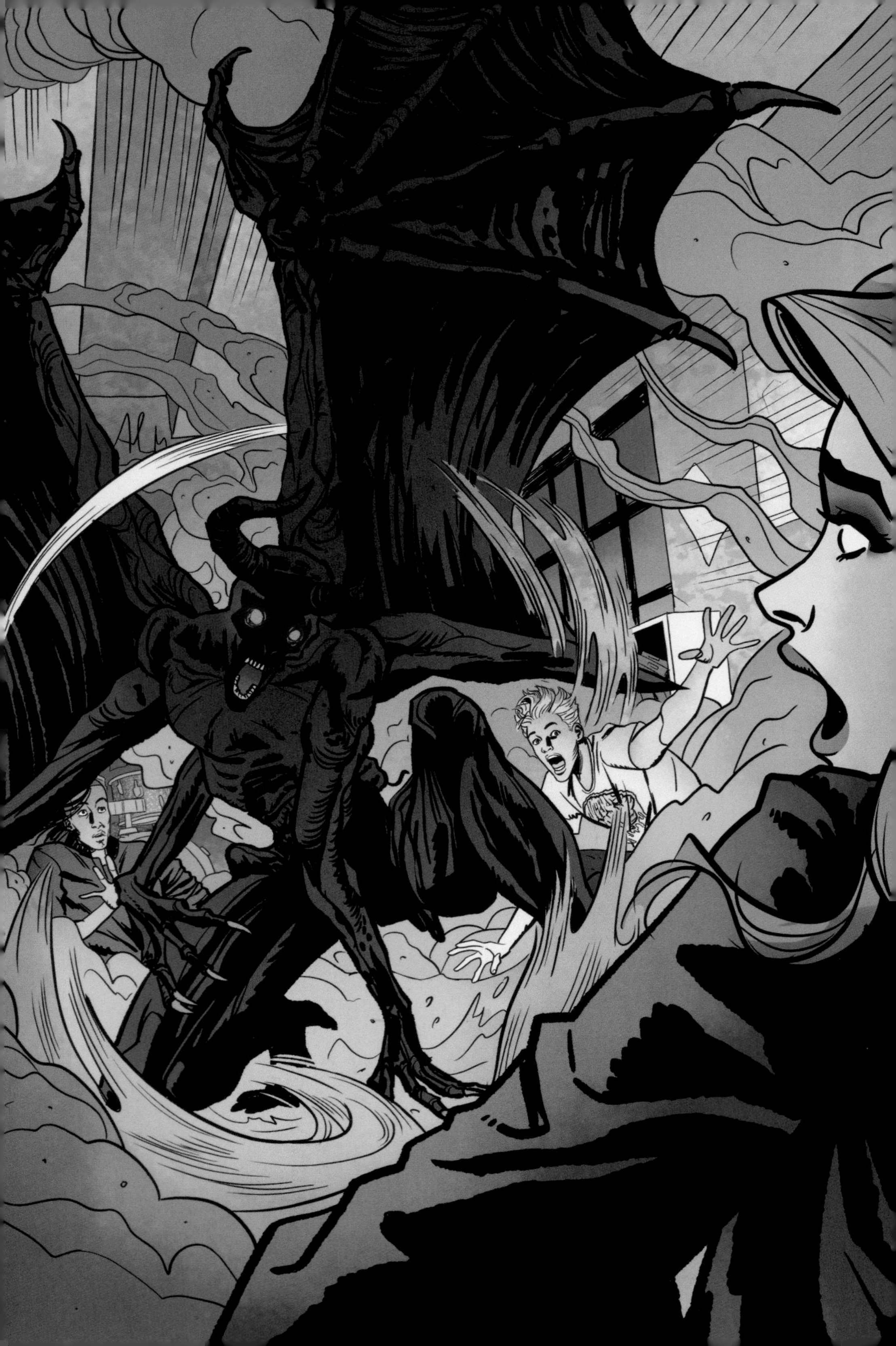

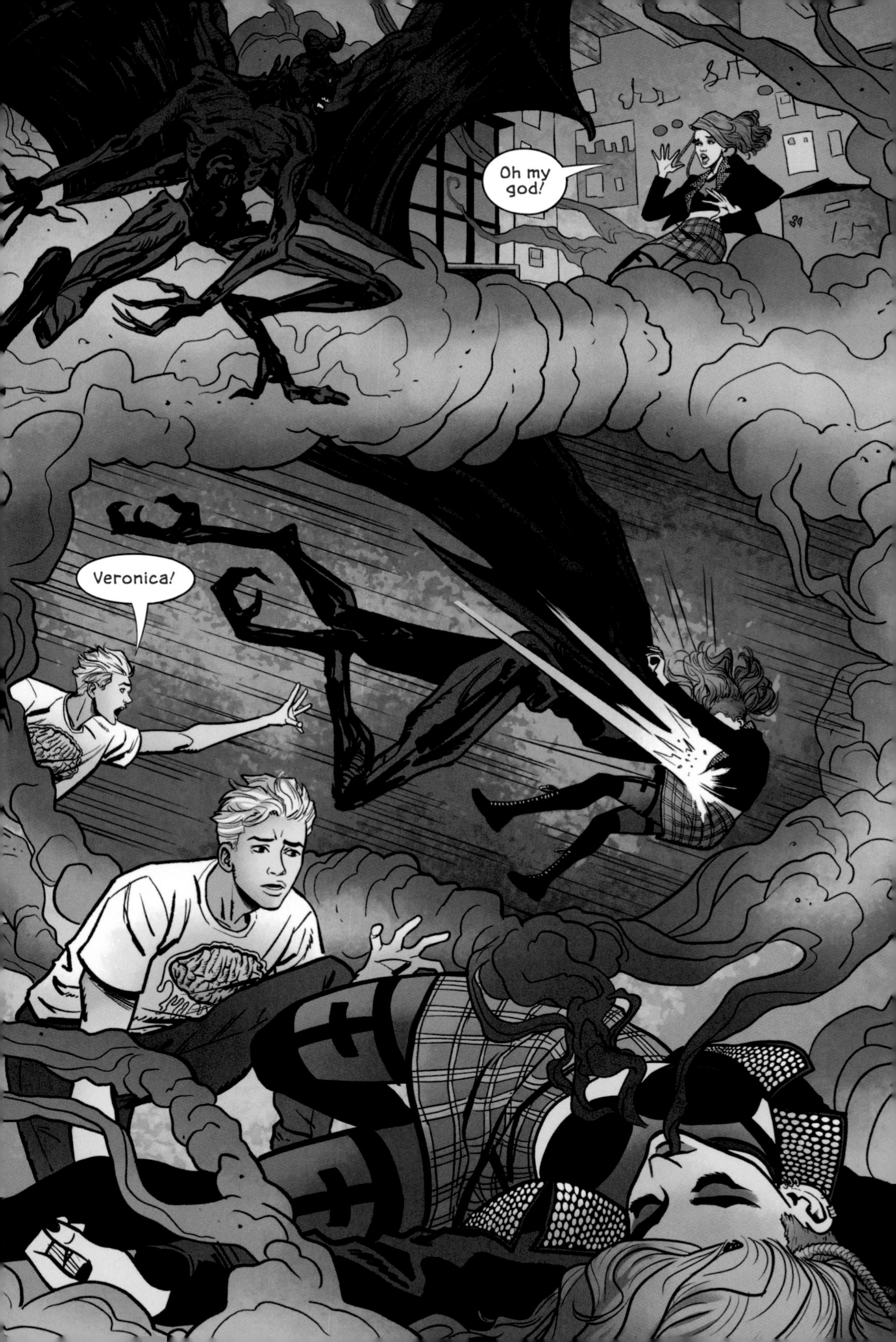
Oh my god!
Veronica!

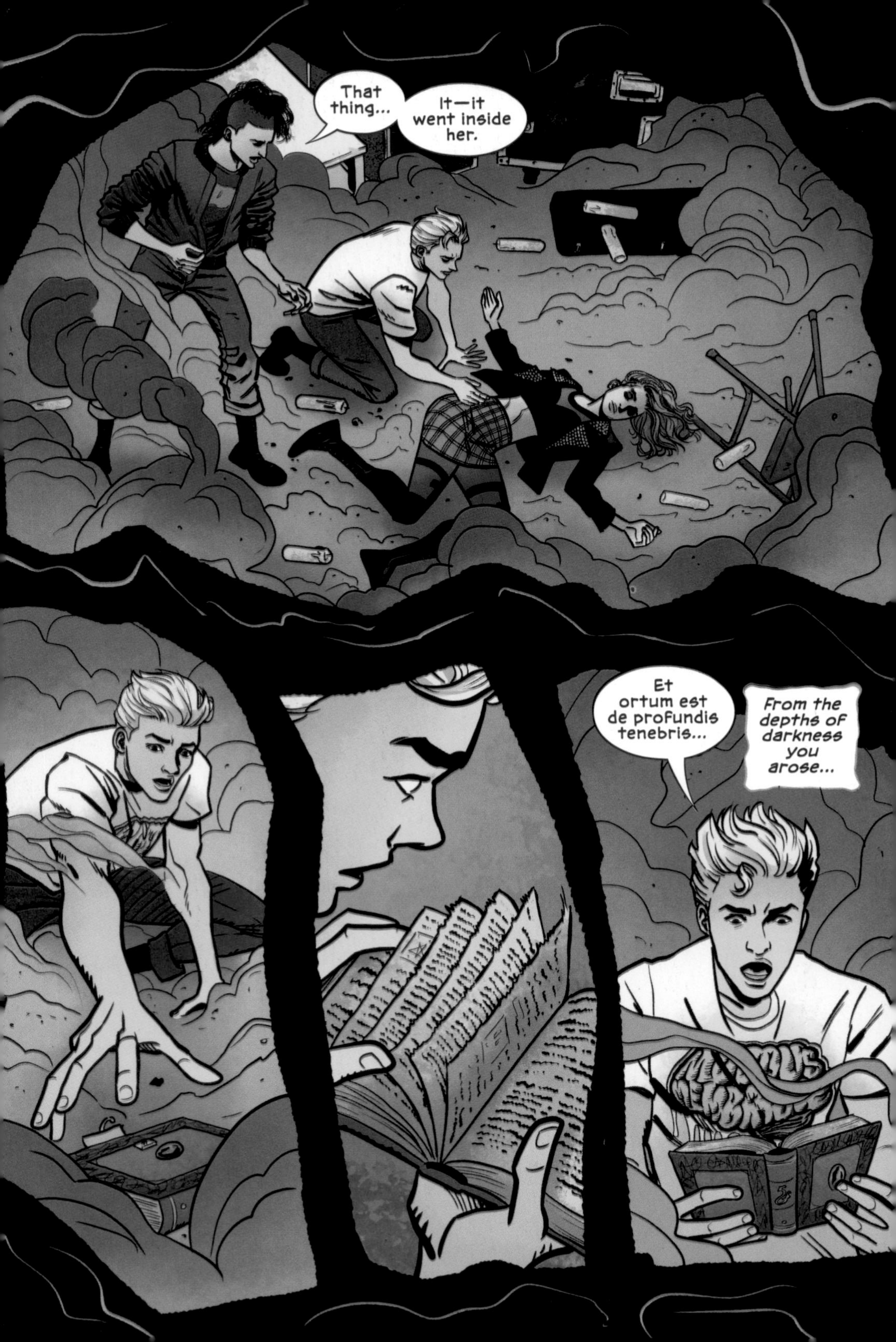
That thing...
It—it went inside her.
Et ortum est de profundis tenebris...
From the depths of darkness you arose...

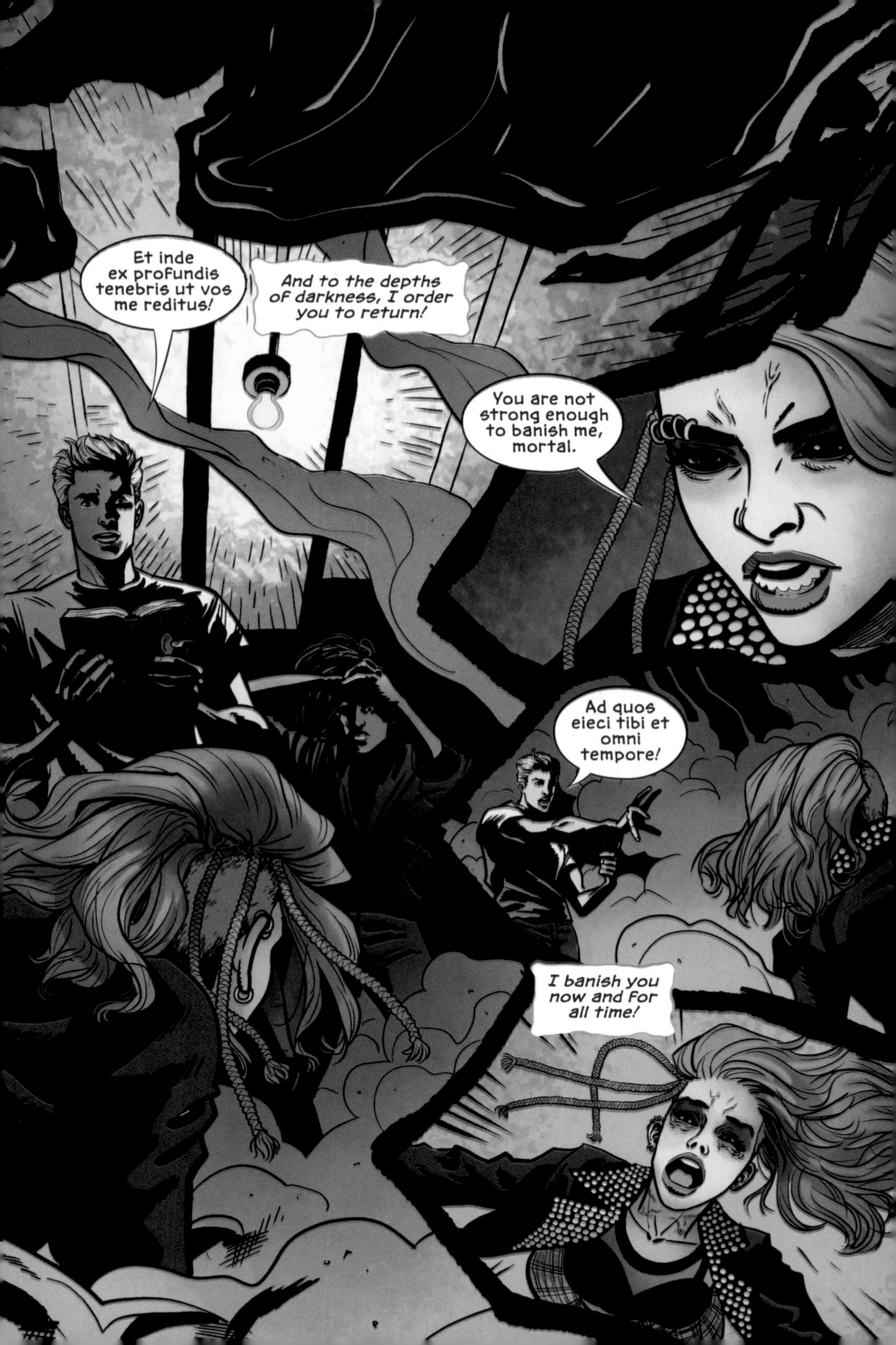

Et inde ex profundis tenebris ut vos me reditus!
And to the depths of darkness, I order you to return!
You are not strong enough to banish me, mortal.
Ad quos eieci tibi et omni tempore!
I banish you now and for all time!

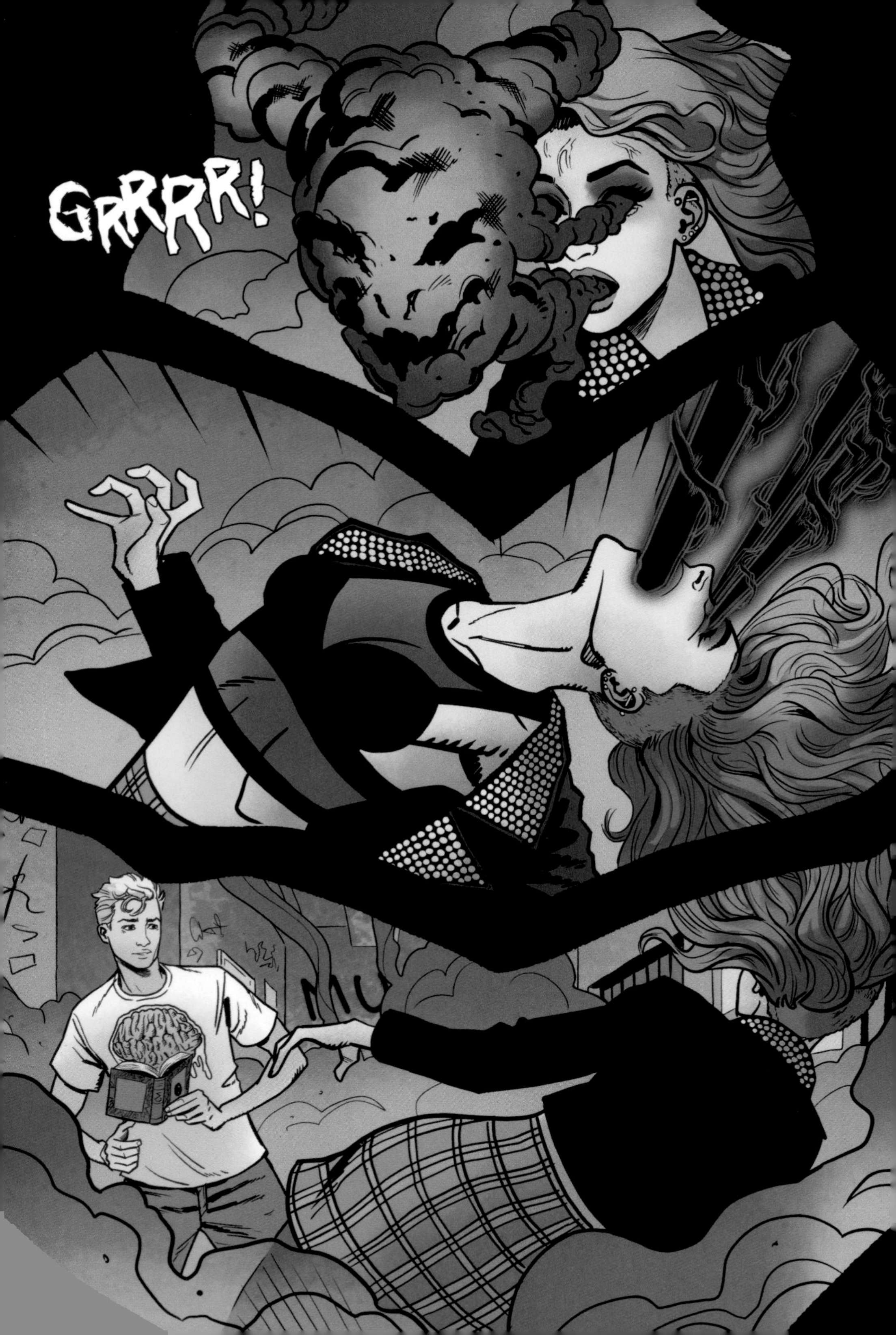
GRRRR!

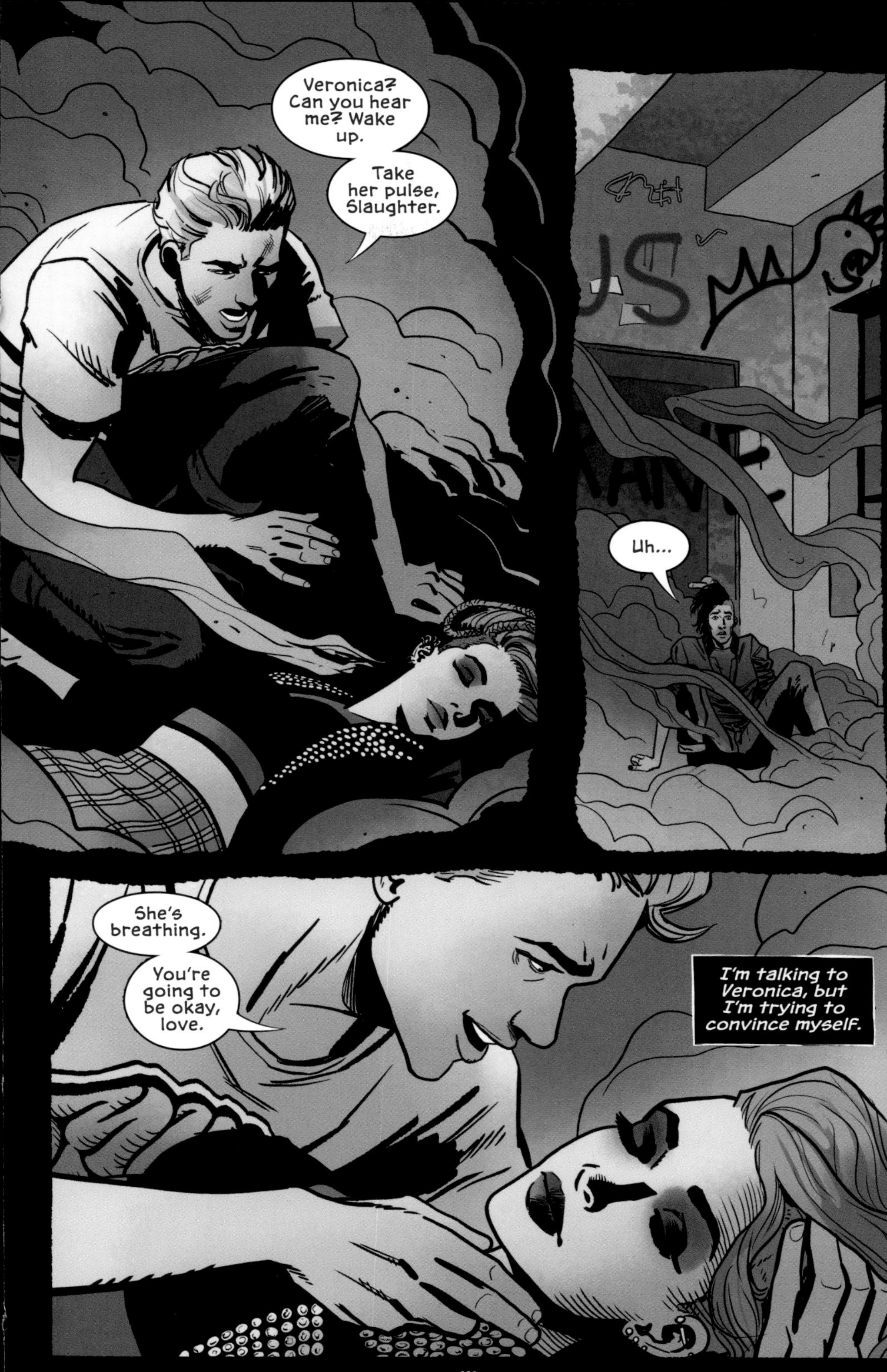
Veronica? Can you hear me? Wake up.
Take her pulse, Slaughter.
Uh...
She's breathing.
You're going to be okay, love.
I'm talking to Veronica, but I'm trying to convince myself.

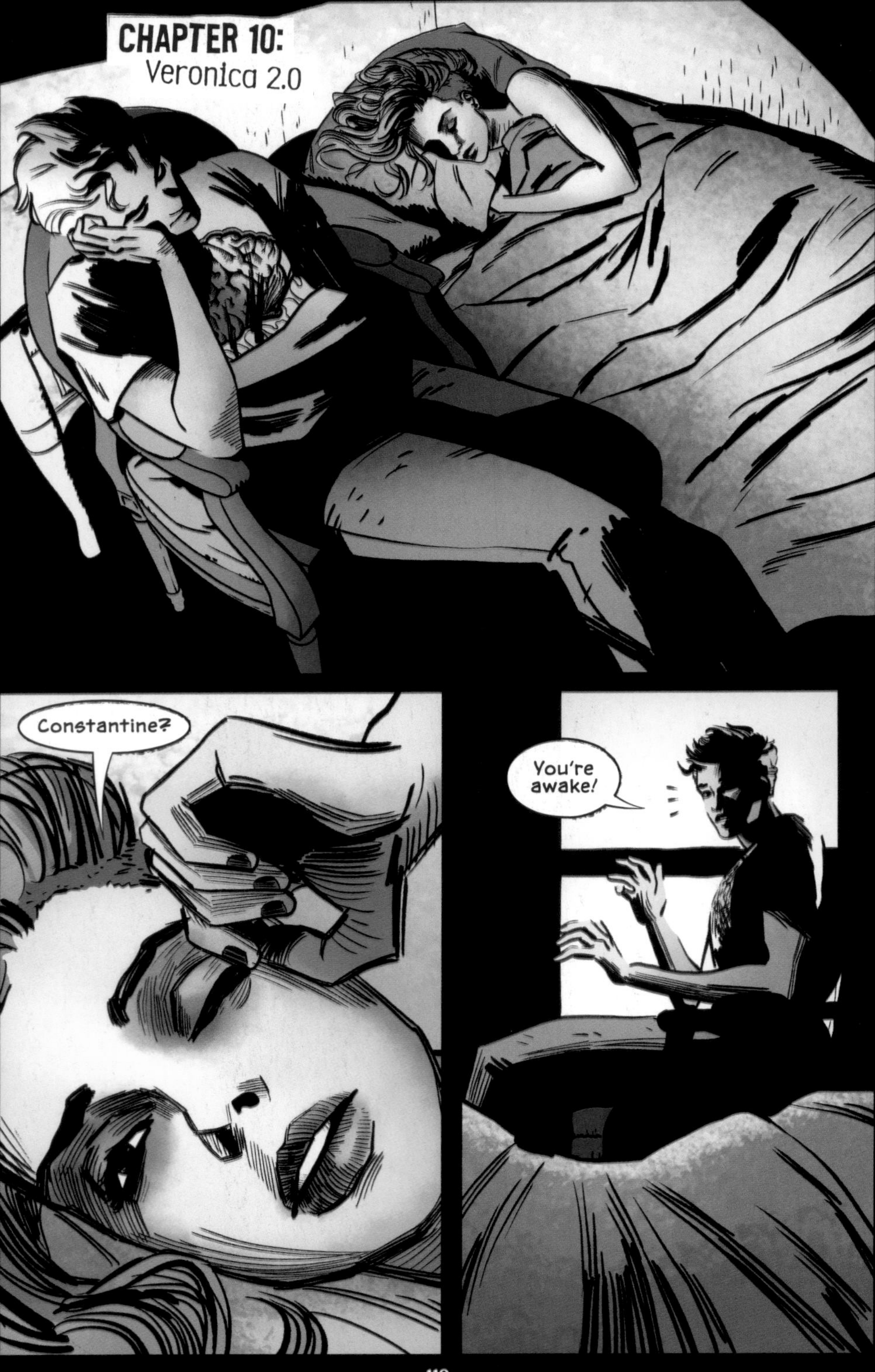
CHAPTER 10:
Veronica 2.0
Constantine?
You're awake!

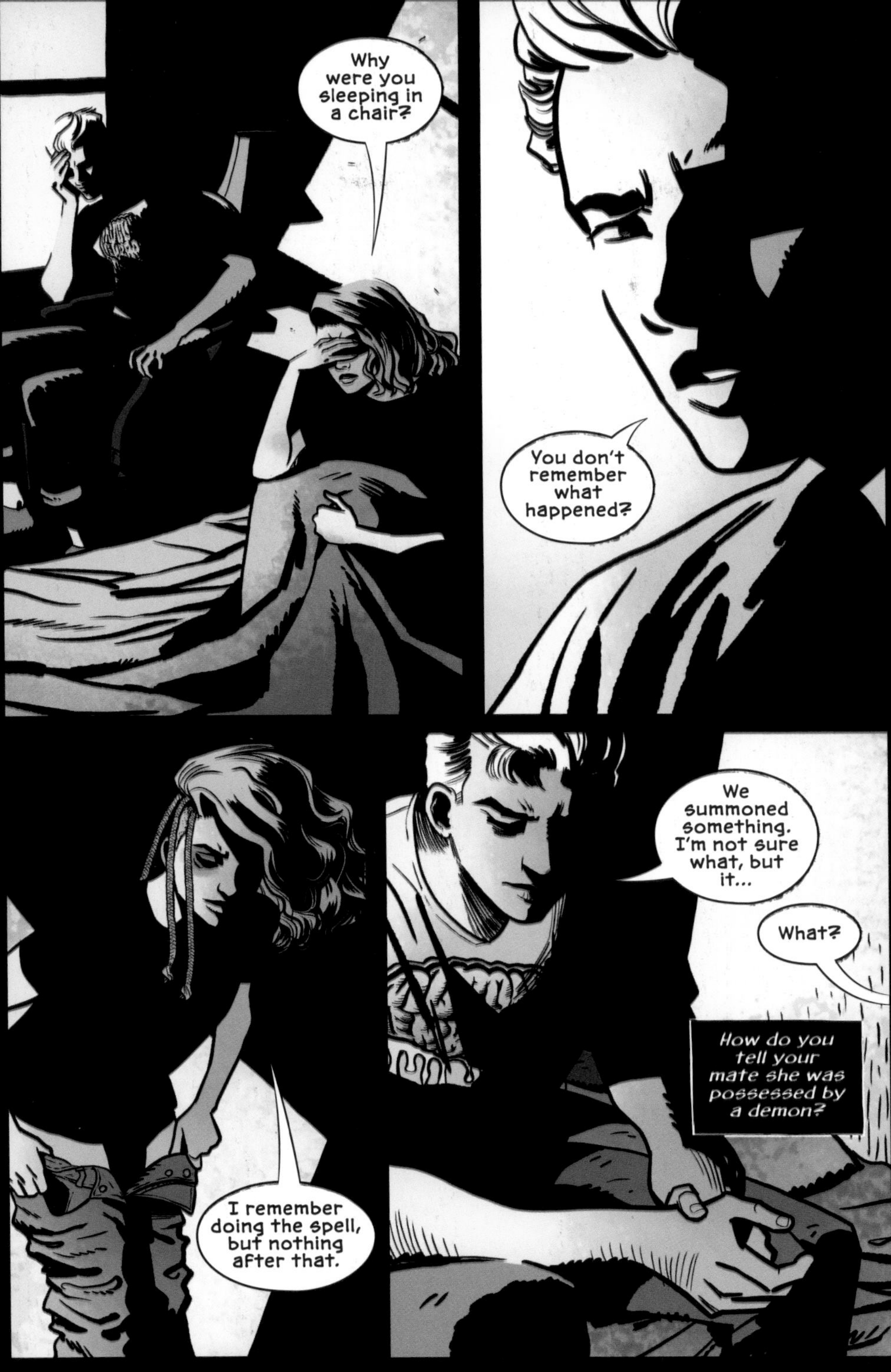
Why were you sleeping in a chair?
You don't remember what happened?
I remember doing the spell, but nothing after that.
We summoned something. I'm not sure what, but it...
What?
How do you tell your mate she was possessed by a demon?

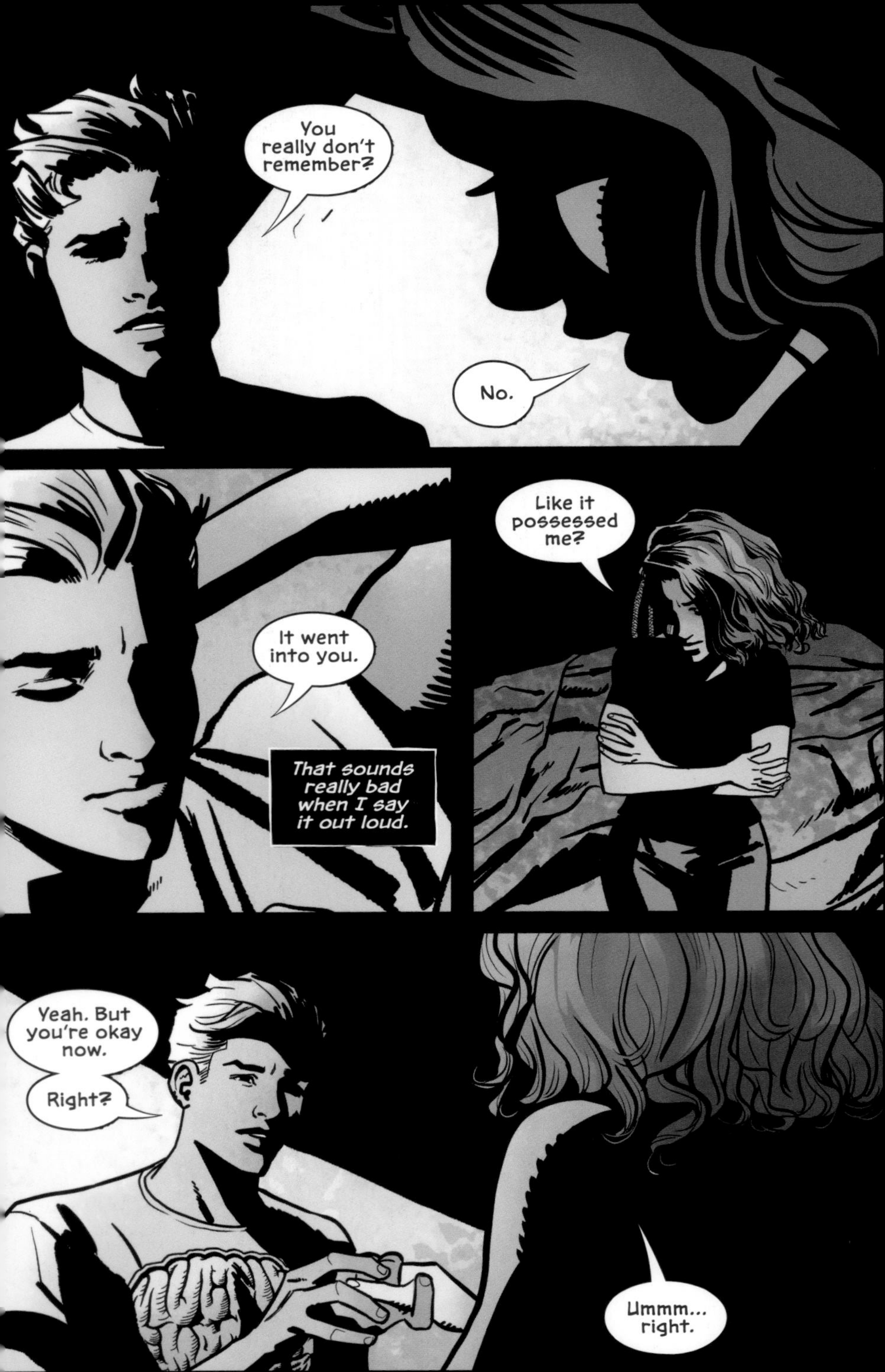
You really don't remember?
No.
It went into you.
That sounds really bad when I say it out loud.
Like it possessed me?
Yeah. But you're okay now.
Right?
Ummm... right.

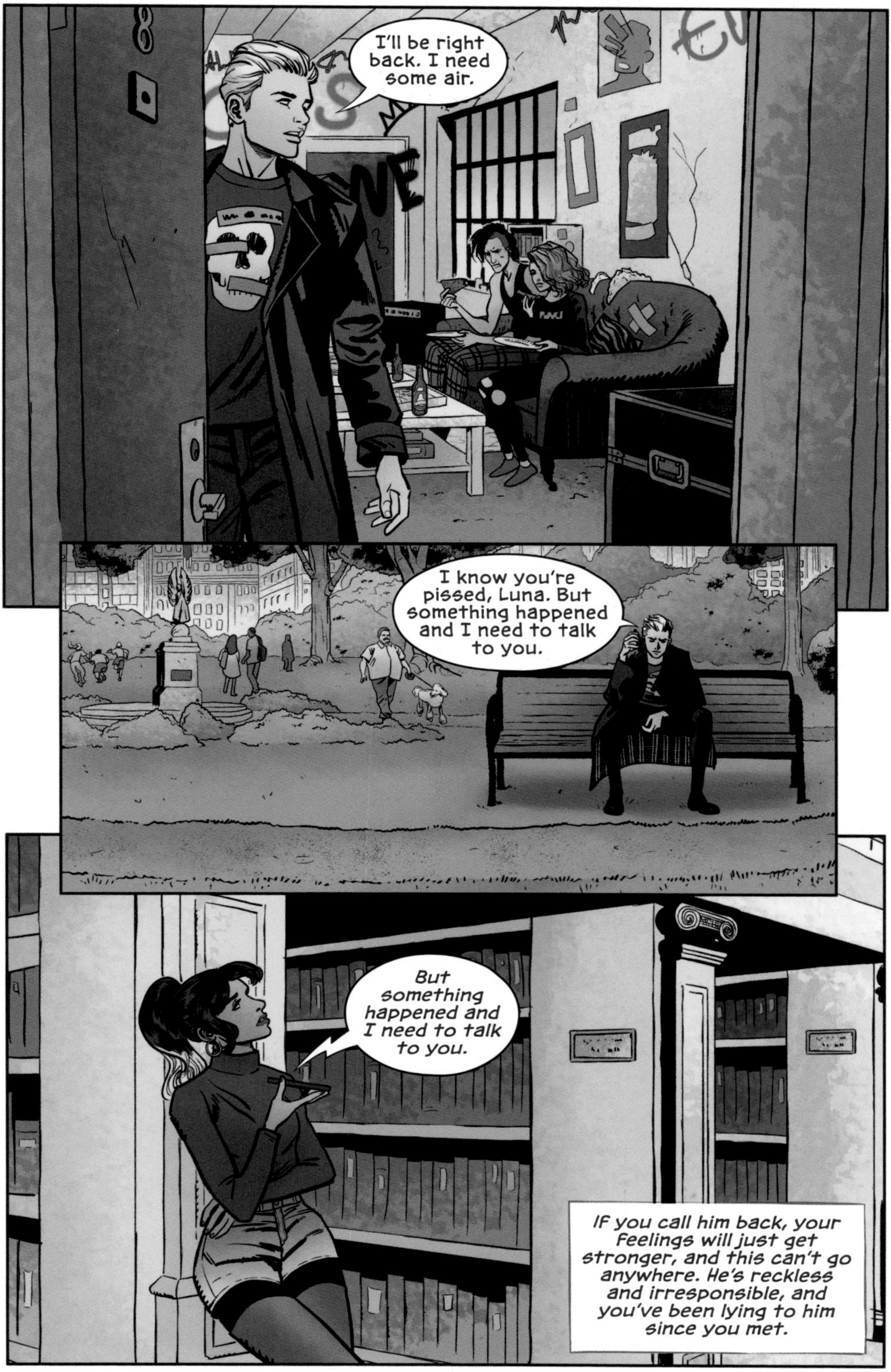
I'll be right back. I need some air.
I know you're pissed, Luna. But something happened and I need to talk to you.
But something happened and I need to talk to you.
If you call him back, your feelings will just get stronger, and this can't go anywhere. He's reckless and irresponsible, and you've been lying to him since you met.

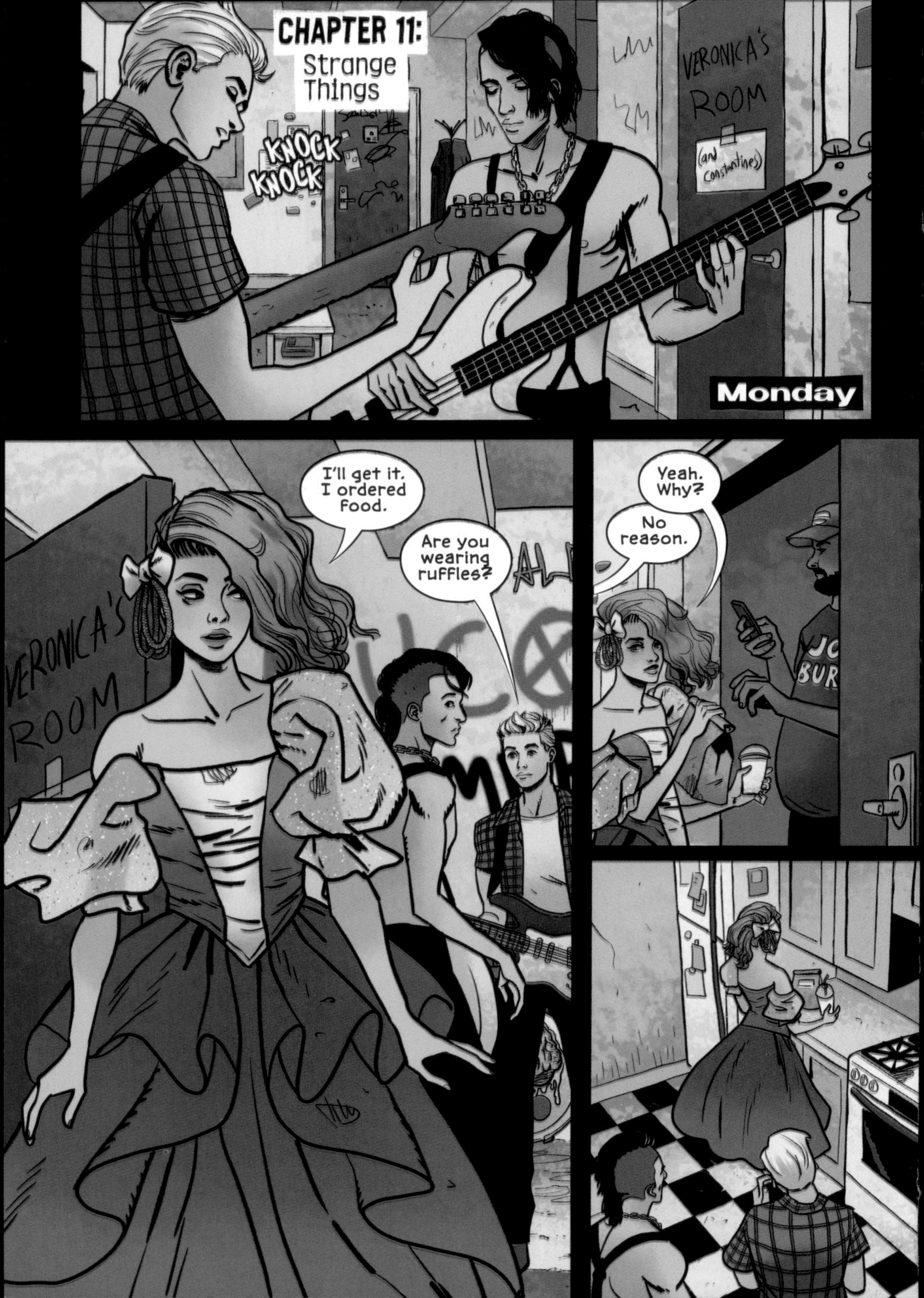
CHAPTER 11:
Strange Things
KNOCK KNOCK
VERONICA'S ROOM
(and constantines)
Monday
I'll get it. I ordered food.
Are you wearing ruffles?
VERONICA'S ROOM
Yeah. Why?
No reason.

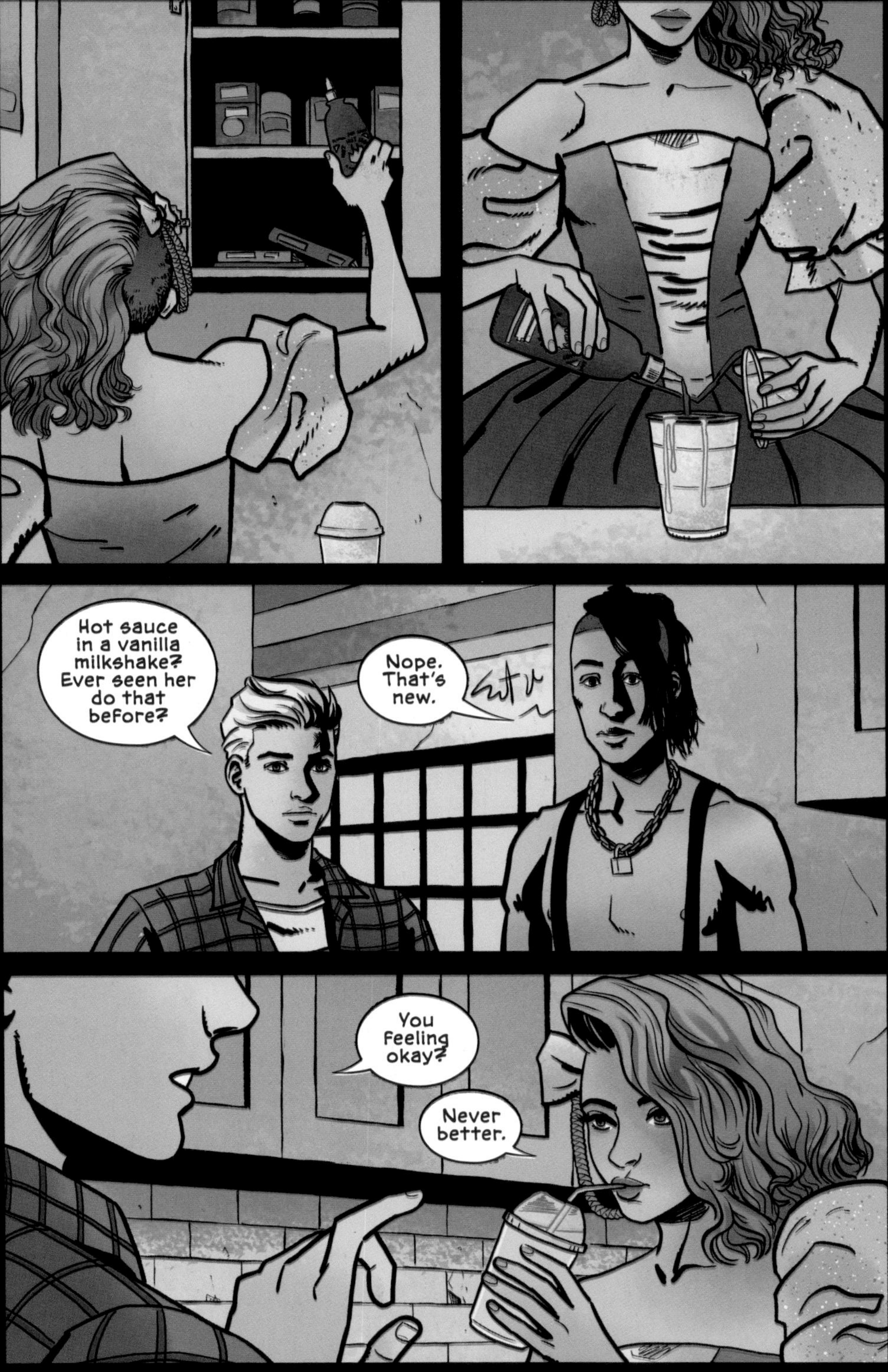
Hot sauce in a vanilla milkshake? Ever seen her do that before?
Nope. That's new.
You feeling okay?
Never better.

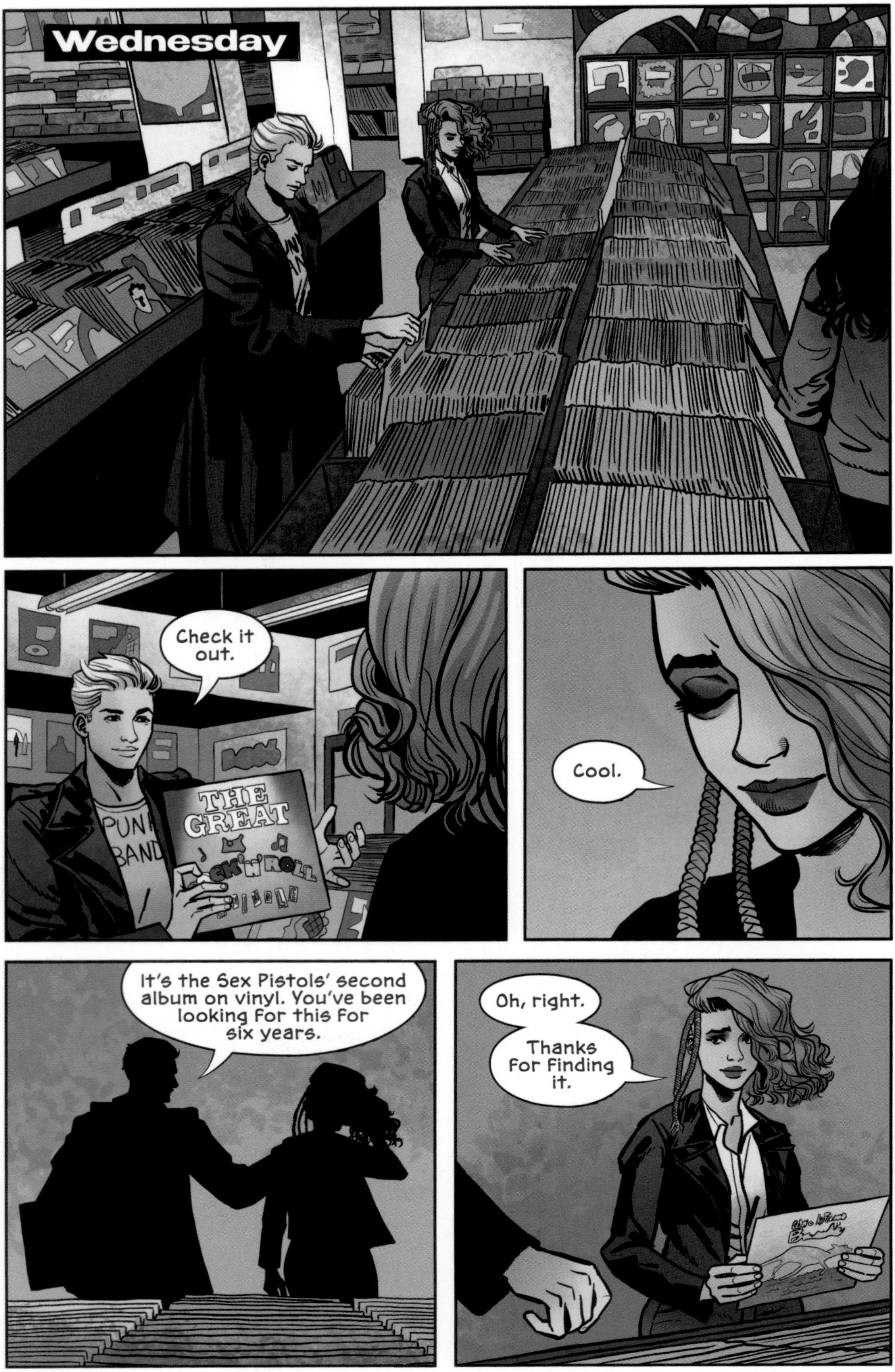
Wednesday
Check it out.
PUNK BAND
THE GREAT
Cool.
It's the Sex Pistols' second album on vinyl. You've been looking for this for six years.
Oh, right.
Thanks for finding it.

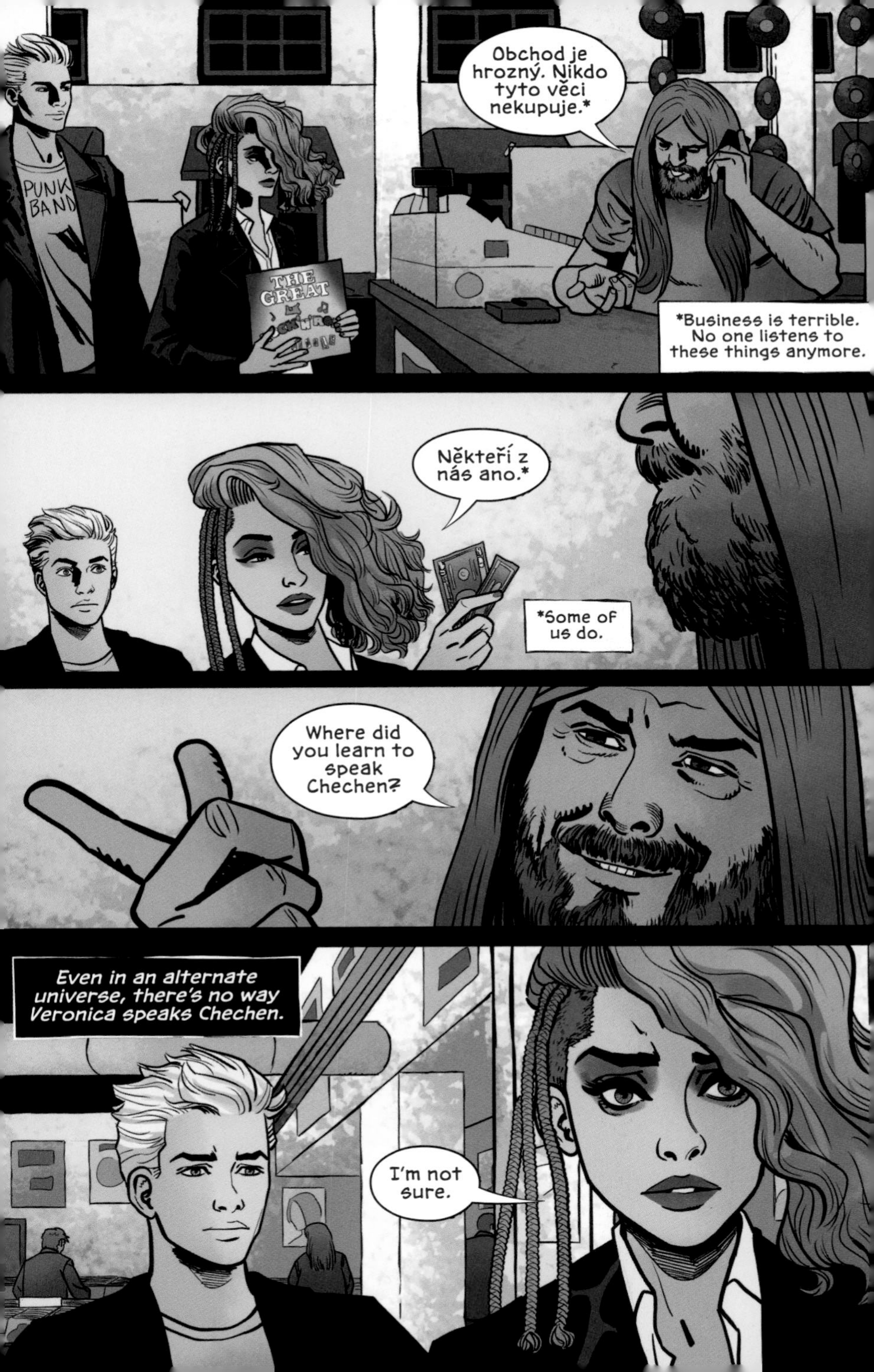
Obchod je hrozný. Nikdo tyto věci nekupuje.*
*Business is terrible. No one listens to these things anymore.
Někteří z nás ano.*
*Some of us do.
Where did you learn to speak Chechen?
Even in an alternate universe, there's no way Veronica speaks Chechen.
I'm not sure.

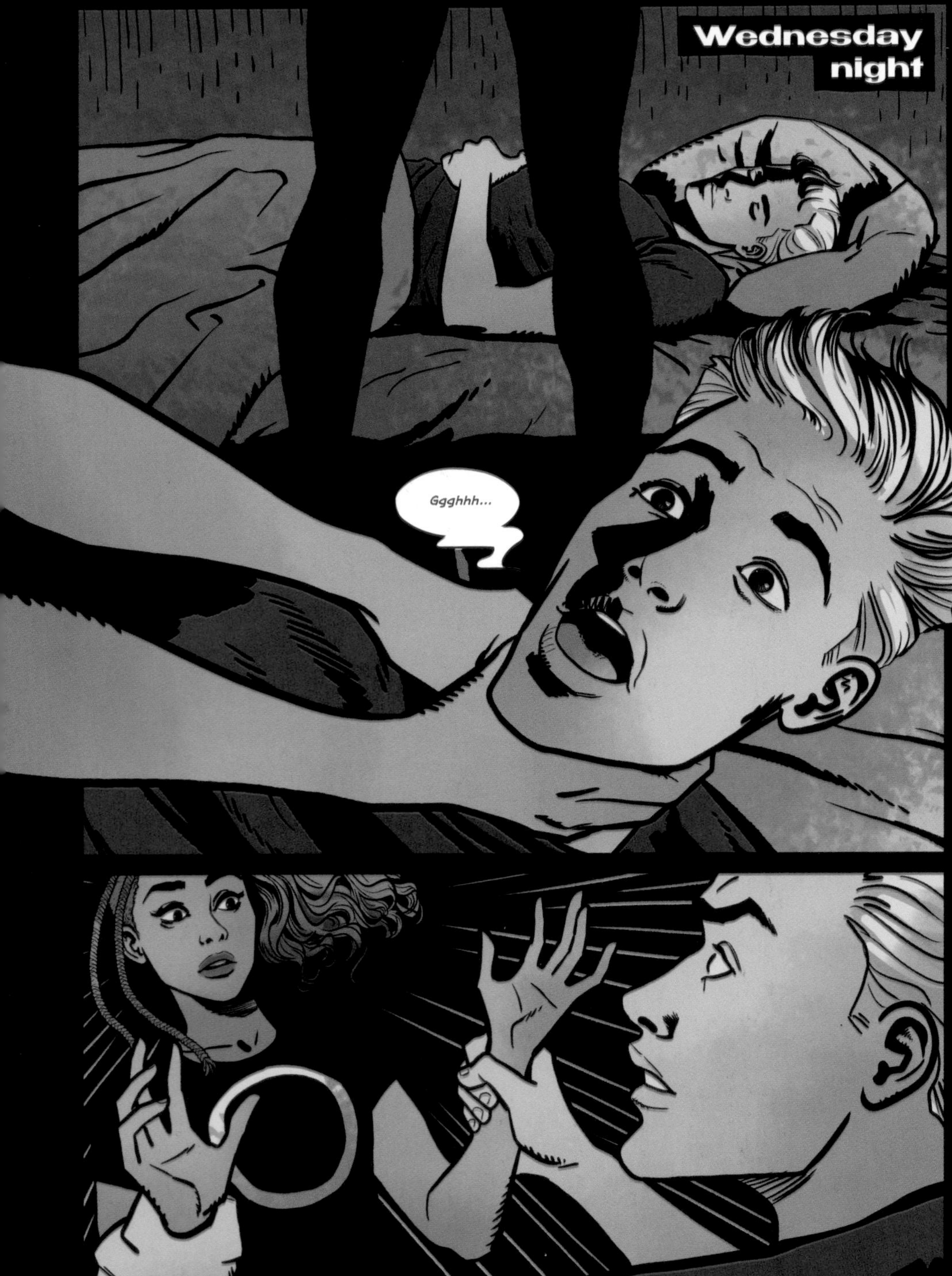
Wednesday night
Ggghhh...
Bloody hell!

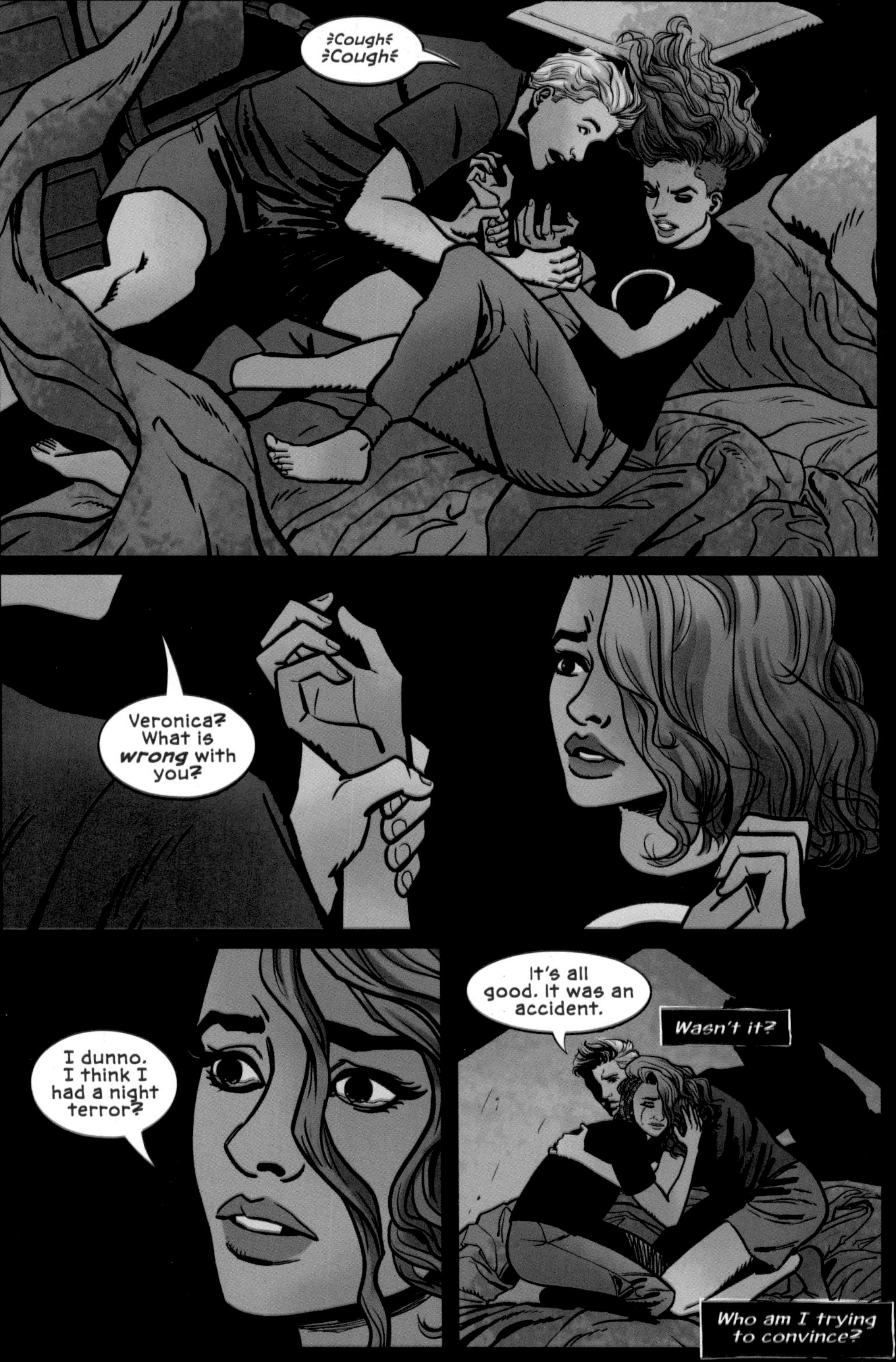

Cough
Cough
Veronica? What is **wrong** with you?
I dunno. I think I had a night terror?
It's all good. It was an accident.
Wasn't it?
Who am I trying to convince?

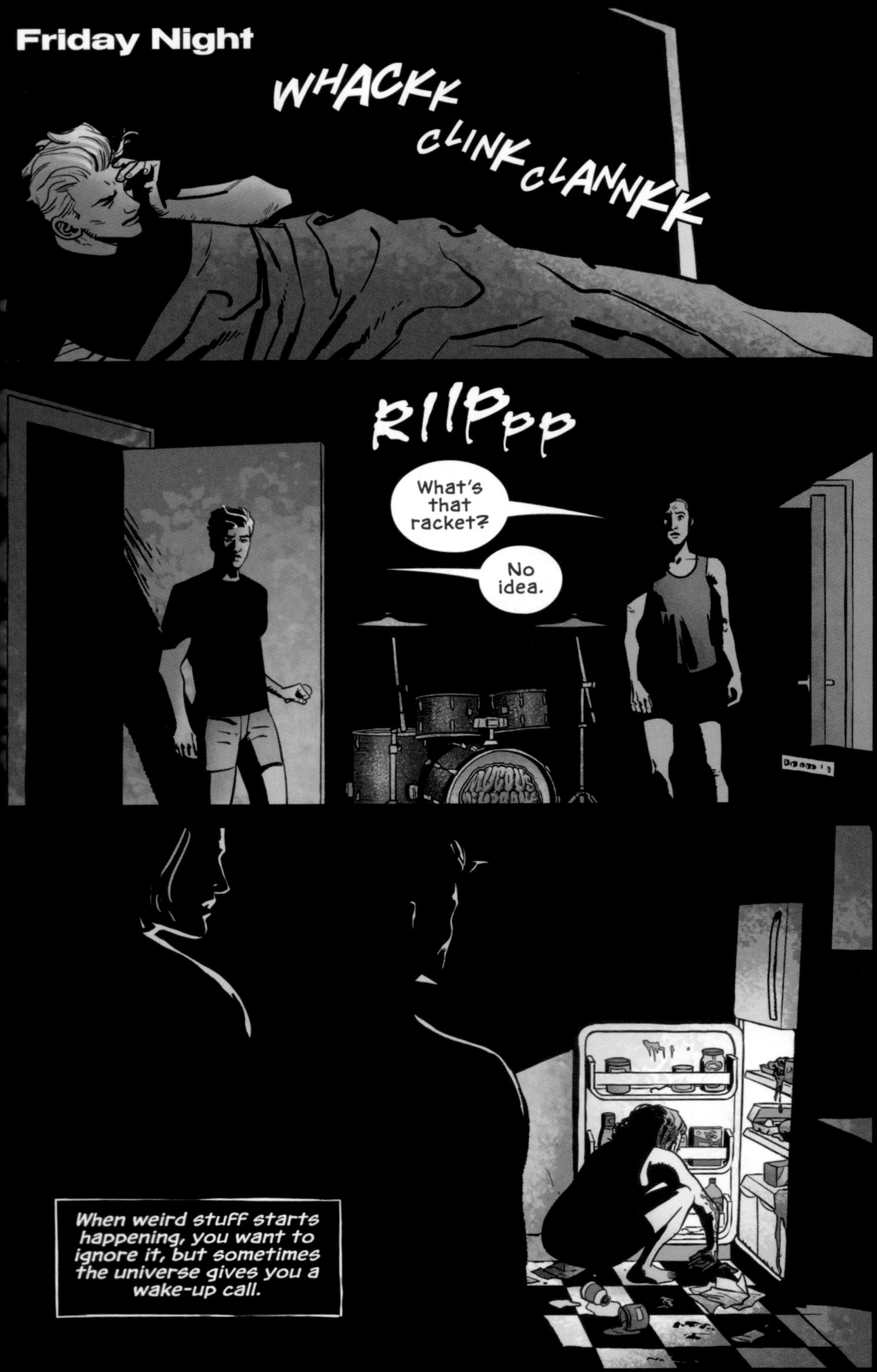
Friday Night
WHACKK
CLINK CLANNKK
RIIPpp
What's that racket?
No idea.
When weird stuff starts happening, you want to ignore it, but sometimes the universe gives you a wake-up call.

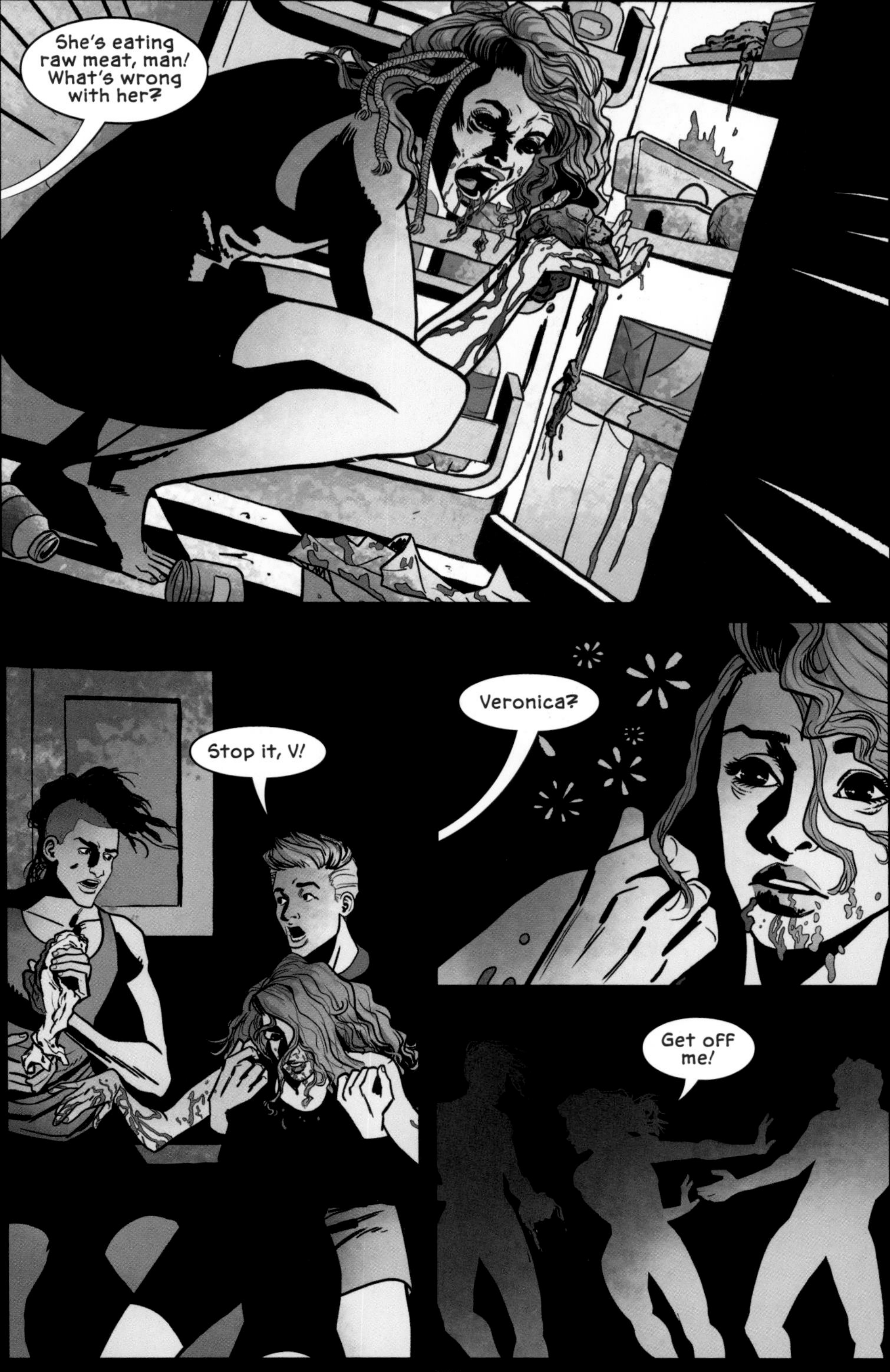
She's eating raw meat, man! What's wrong with her?
Stop it, V!
Veronica?
Get off me!

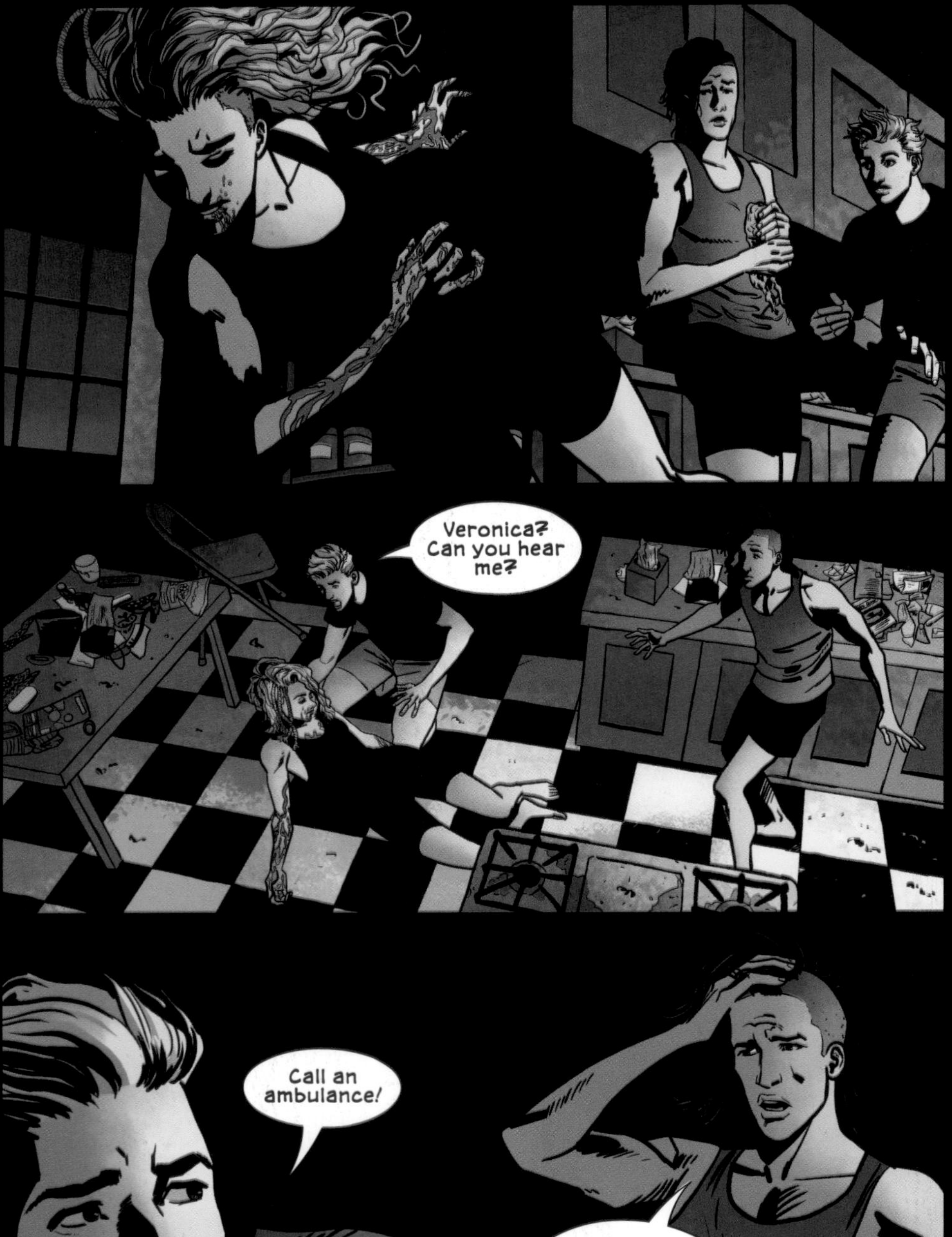
Veronica? Can you hear me?
Call an ambulance!
What if the paramedics call the cops? They'll think we did something to her.

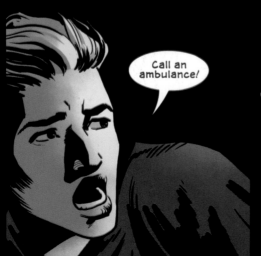

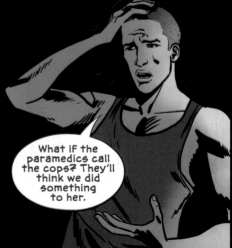

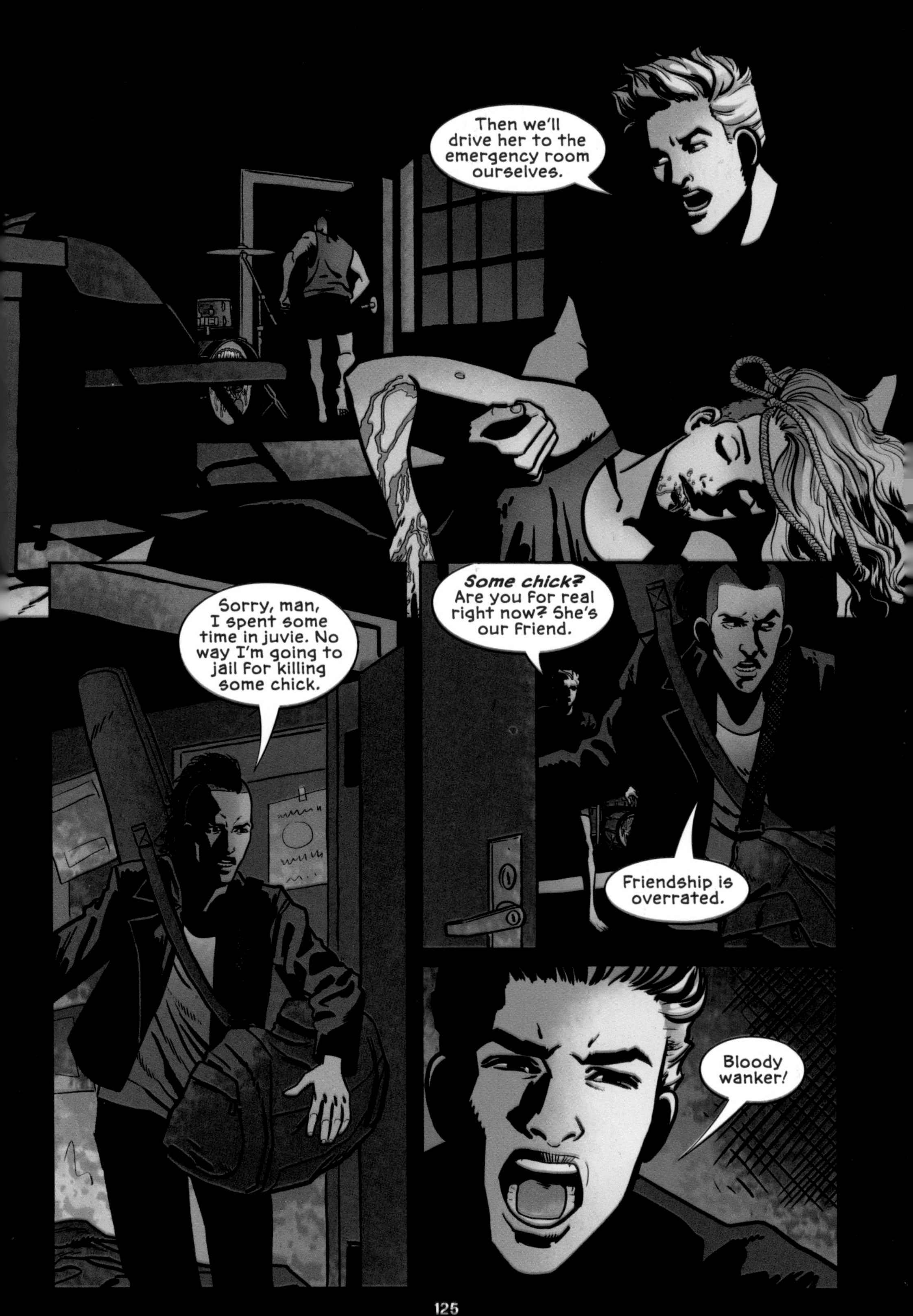
Then we'll drive her to the emergency room ourselves.
Sorry, man, I spent some time in juvie. No way I'm going to jail for killing some chick.
Some chick? Are you for real right now? She's our friend.
Friendship is overrated.
Bloody wanker!

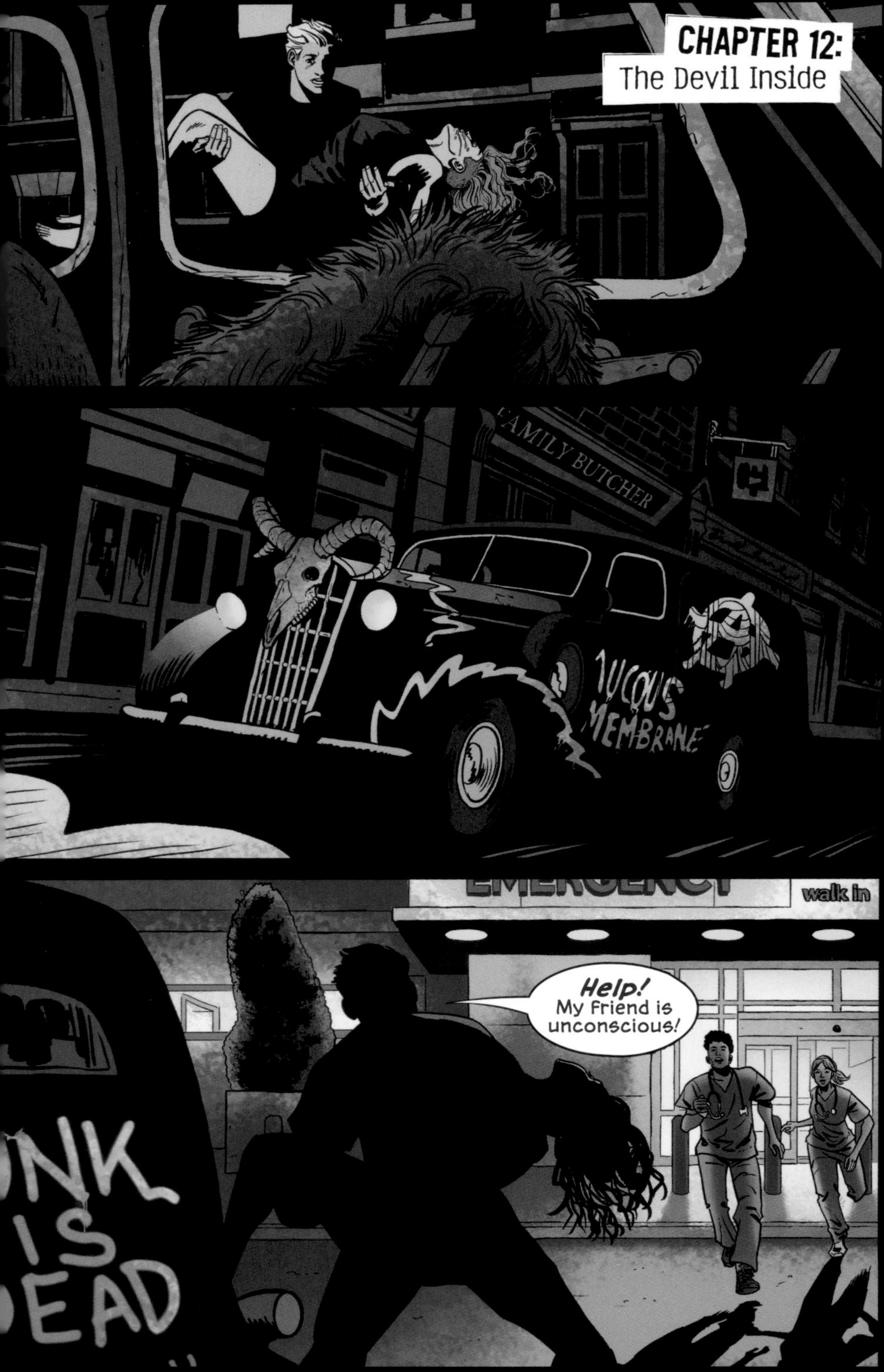
CHAPTER 12:
The Devil Inside
FAMILY BUTCHER
walk in
Help! My friend is unconscious!

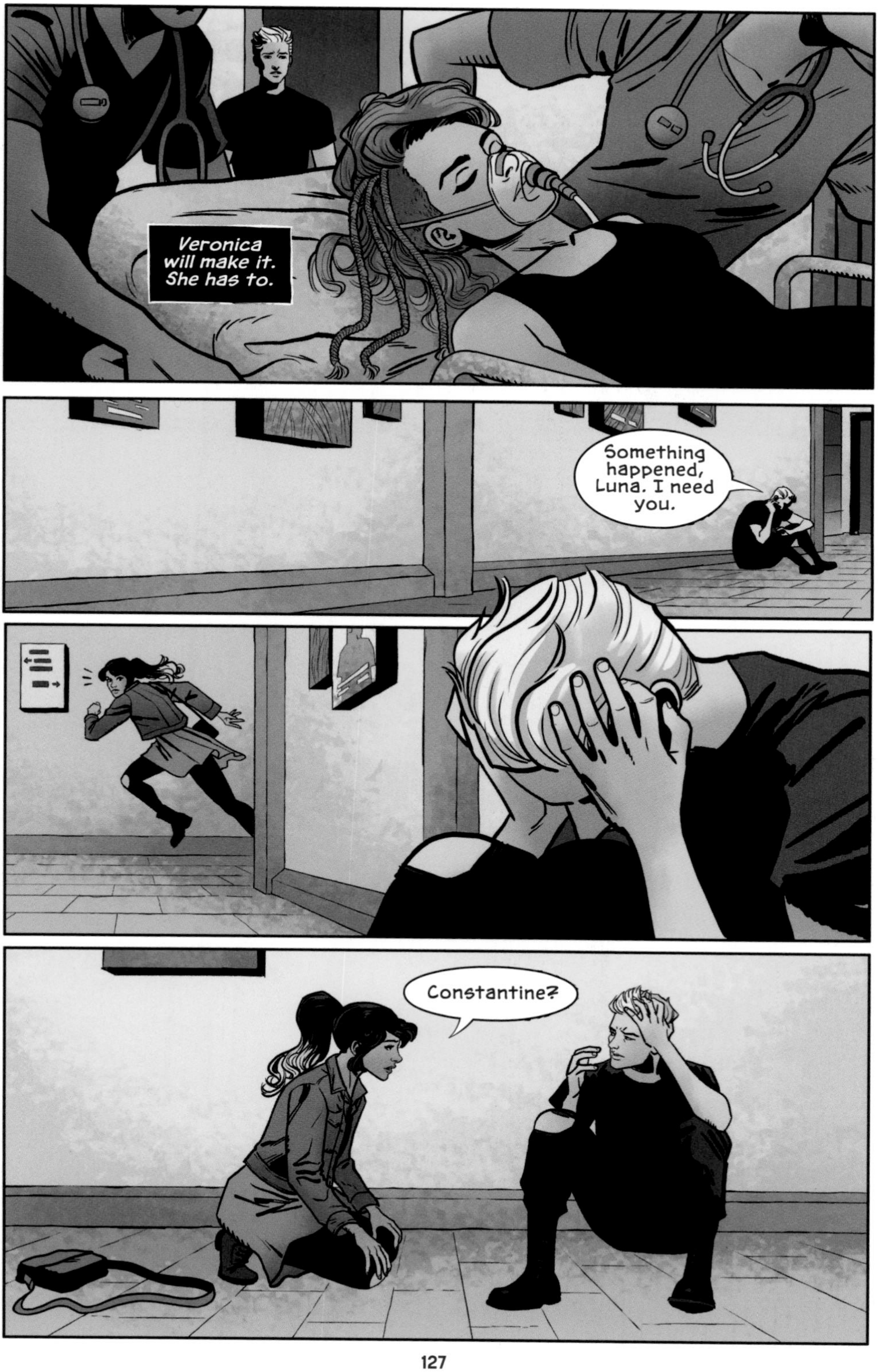

Veronica will make it. She has to.
Something happened, Luna. I need you.
Constantine?

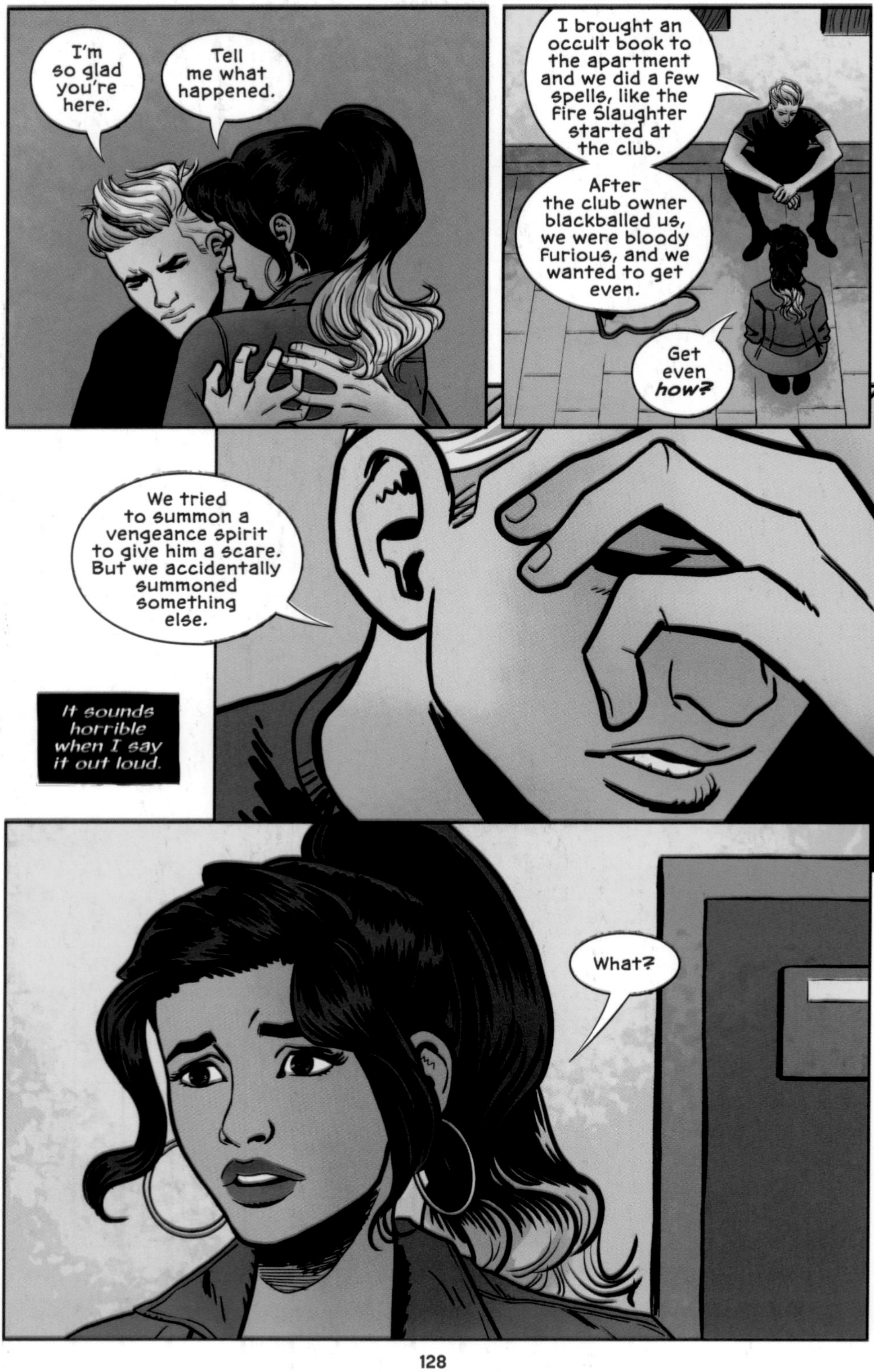
I'm so glad you're here.
Tell me what happened.
I brought an occult book to the apartment and we did a few spells, like the Fire Slaughter started at the club.
After the club owner blackballed us, we were bloody furious, and we wanted to get even.
Get even *how?*
We tried to summon a vengeance spirit to give him a scare. But we accidentally summoned something else.
It sounds horrible when I say it out loud.
What?

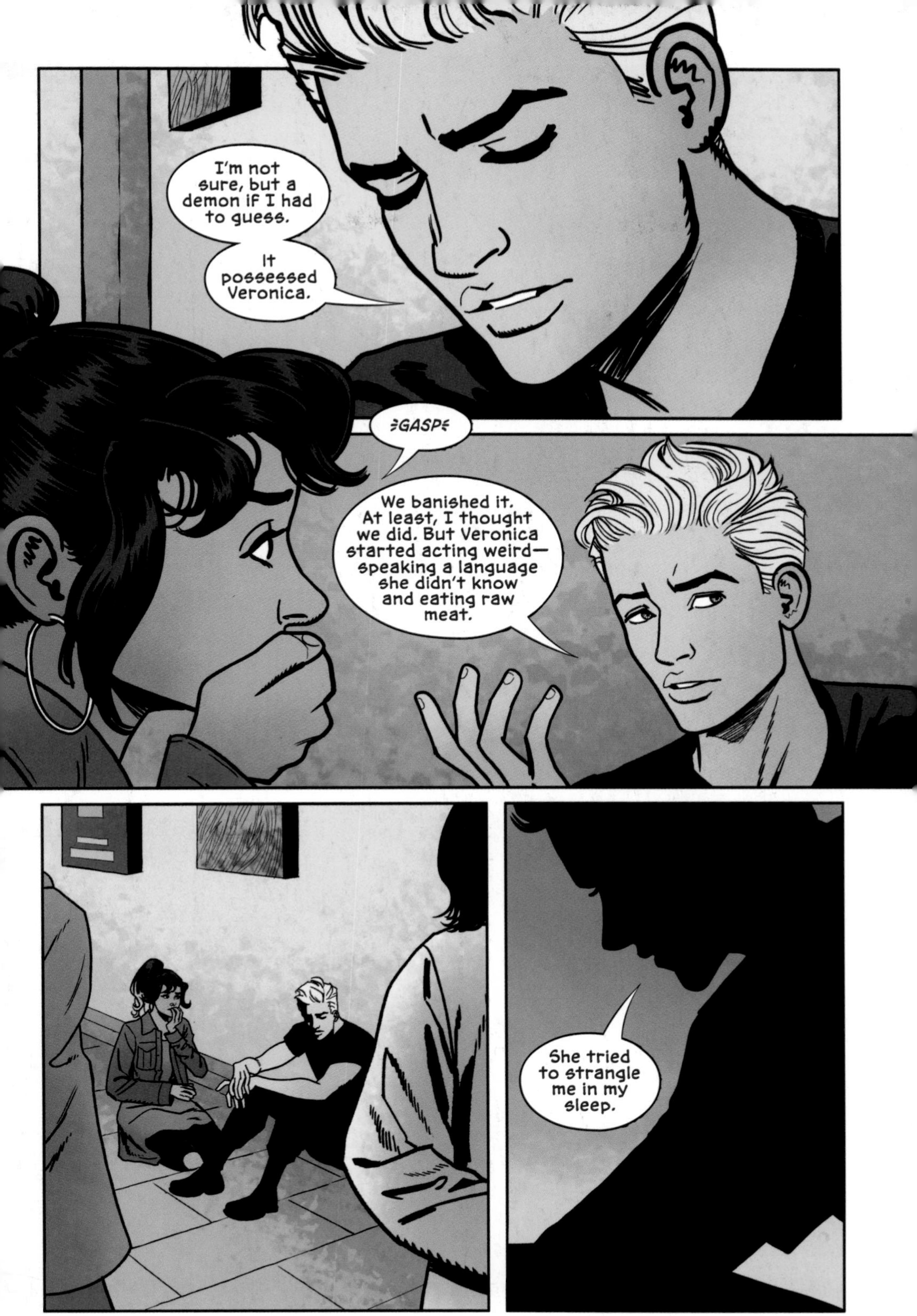
I'm not sure, but a demon if I had to guess.
It possessed Veronica.
GASP
We banished it. At least, I thought we did. But Veronica started acting weird—speaking a language she didn't know and eating raw meat.
She tried to strangle me in my sleep.

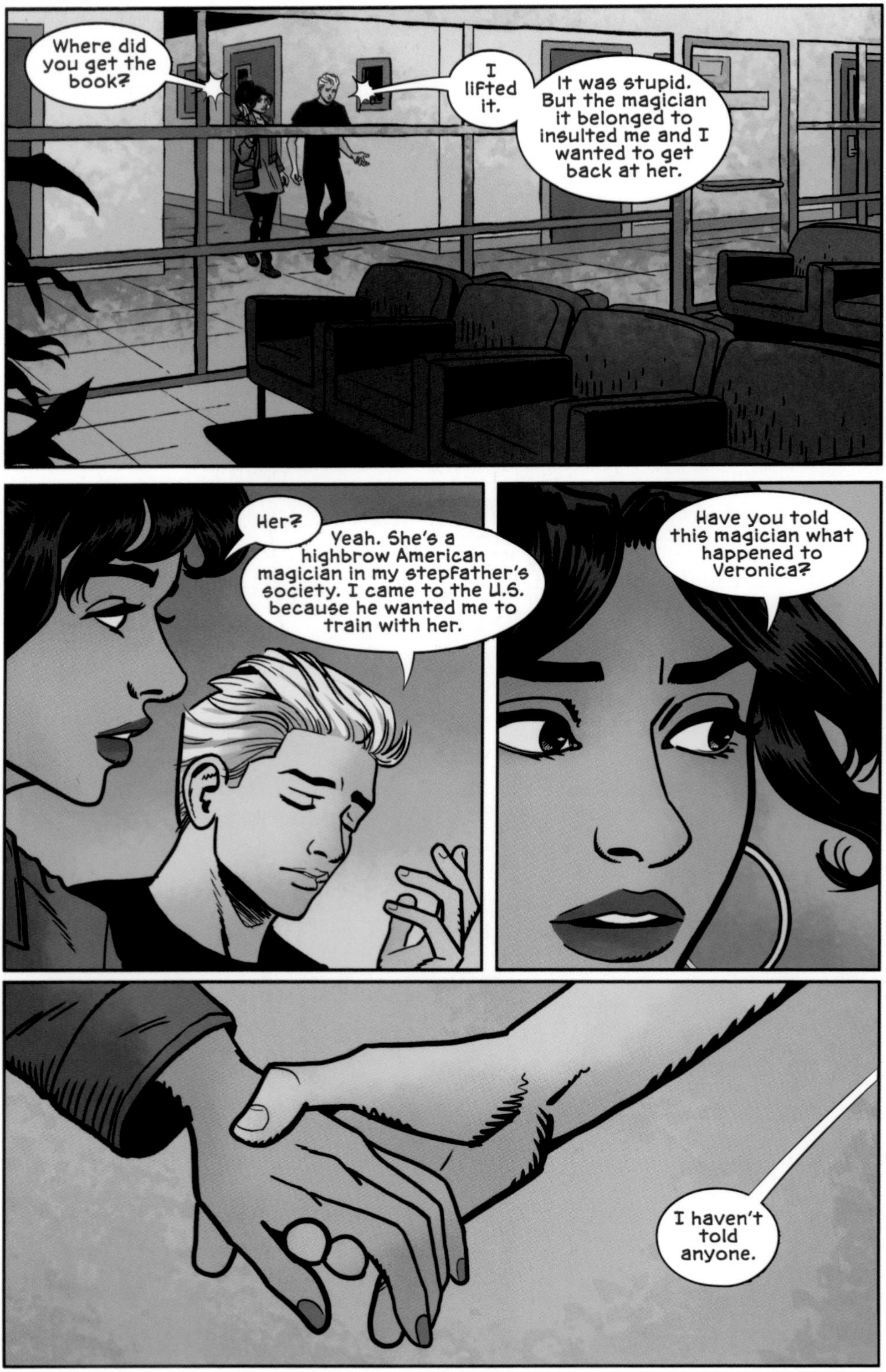
Where did you get the book?
I lifted it.
It was stupid. But the magician it belonged to insulted me and I wanted to get back at her.
Her?
Yeah. She's a highbrow American magician in my stepfather's society. I came to the U.S. because he wanted me to train with her.
Have you told this magician what happened to Veronica?
I haven't told anyone.

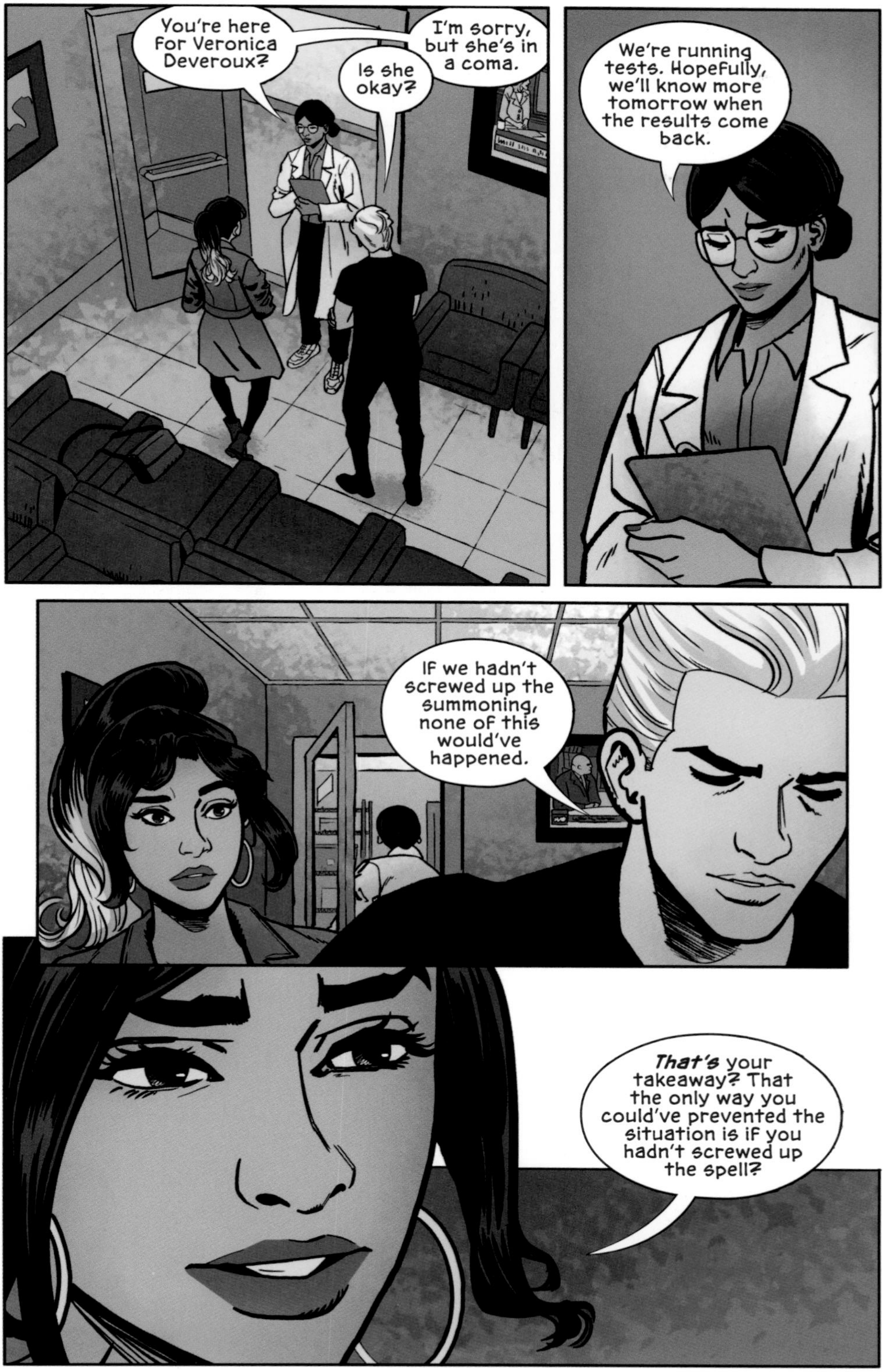
You're here for Veronica Deveroux?
Is she okay?
I'm sorry, but she's in a coma.
We're running tests. Hopefully, we'll know more tomorrow when the results come back.
If we hadn't screwed up the summoning, none of this would've happened.
That's your takeaway? That the only way you could've prevented the situation is if you hadn't screwed up the spell?

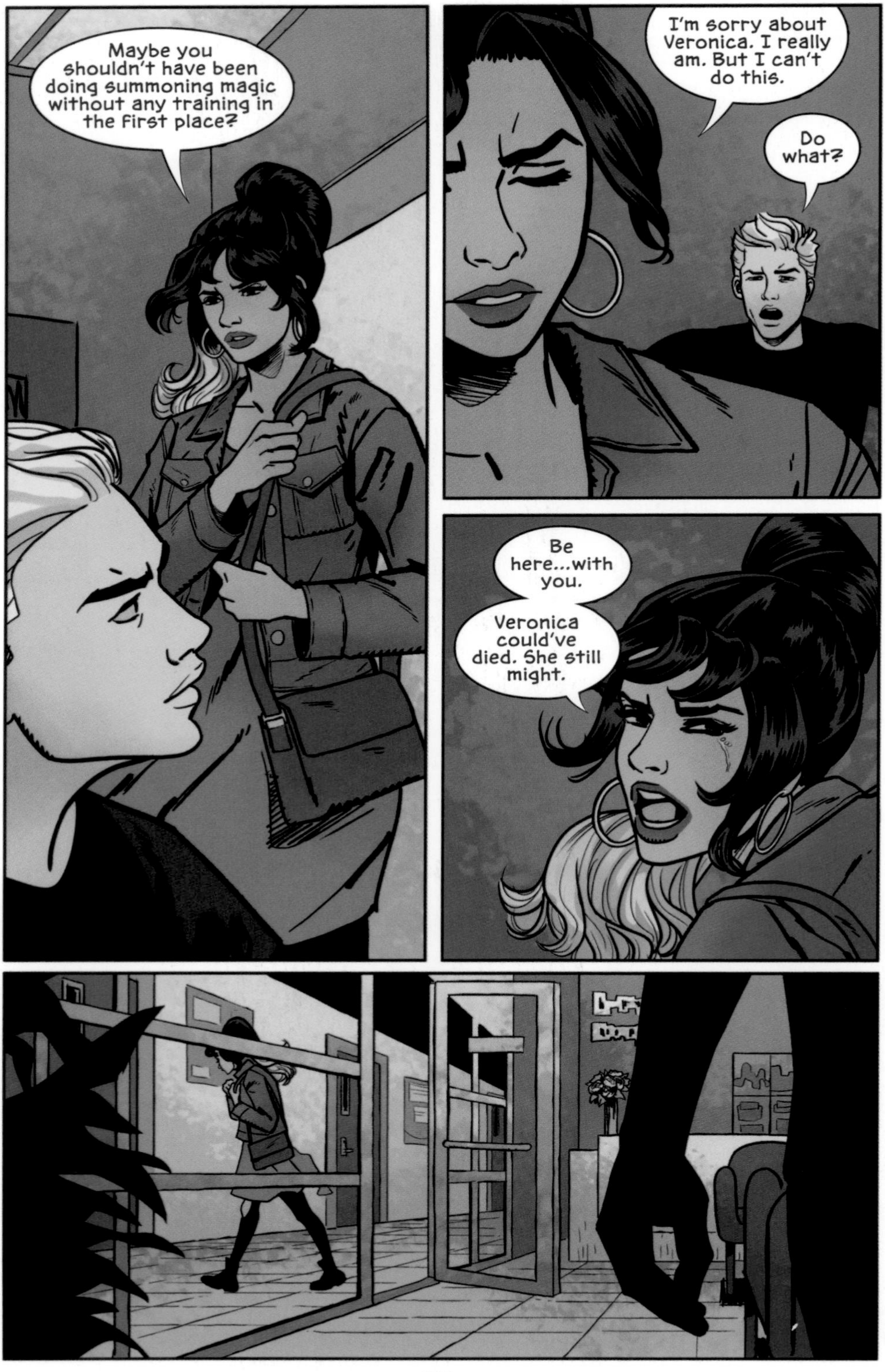
Maybe you shouldn't have been doing summoning magic without any training in the first place?
I'm sorry about Veronica. I really am. But I can't do this.
Do what?
Be here...with you.
Veronica could've died. She still might.

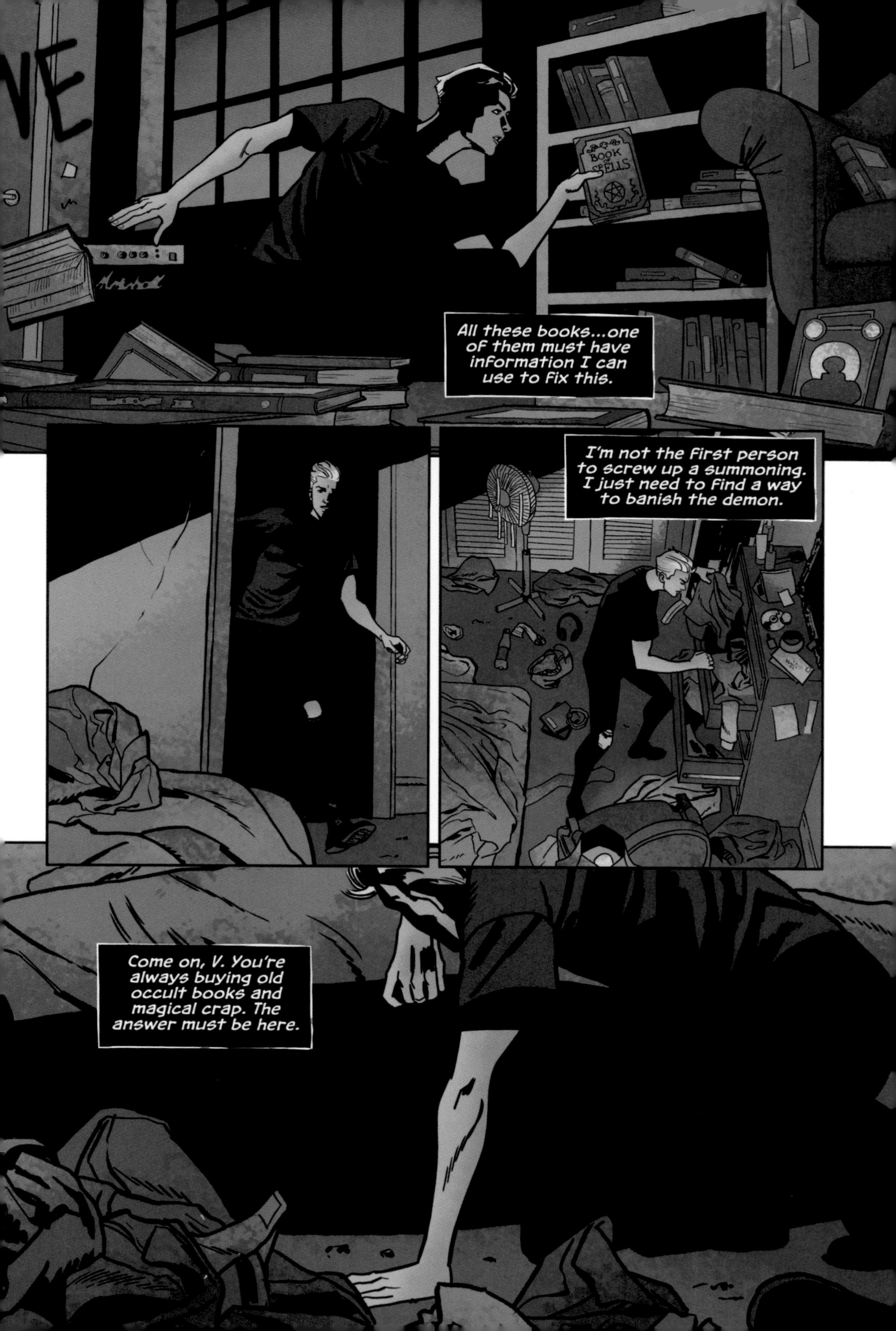
BOOK OF SPELLS
All these books...one of them must have information I can use to fix this.
I'm not the first person to screw up a summoning. I just need to find a way to banish the demon.
Come on, V. You're always buying old occult books and magical crap. The answer must be here.

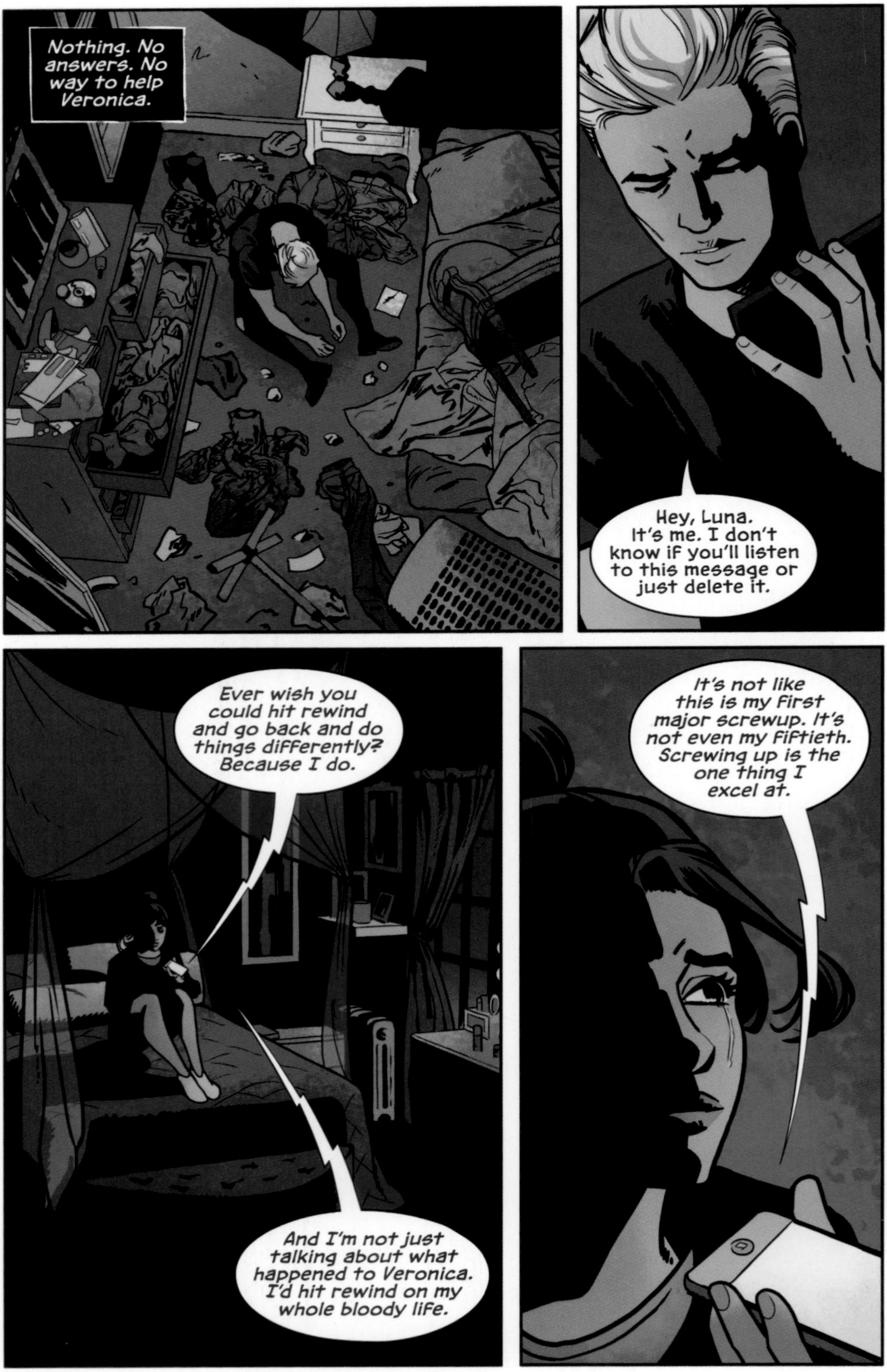
Nothing. No answers. No way to help Veronica.
Hey, Luna. It's me. I don't know if you'll listen to this message or just delete it.
Ever wish you could hit rewind and go back and do things differently? Because I do.
And I'm not just talking about what happened to Veronica. I'd hit rewind on my whole bloody life.
It's not like this is my first major screwup. It's not even my fiftieth. Screwing up is the one thing I excel at.

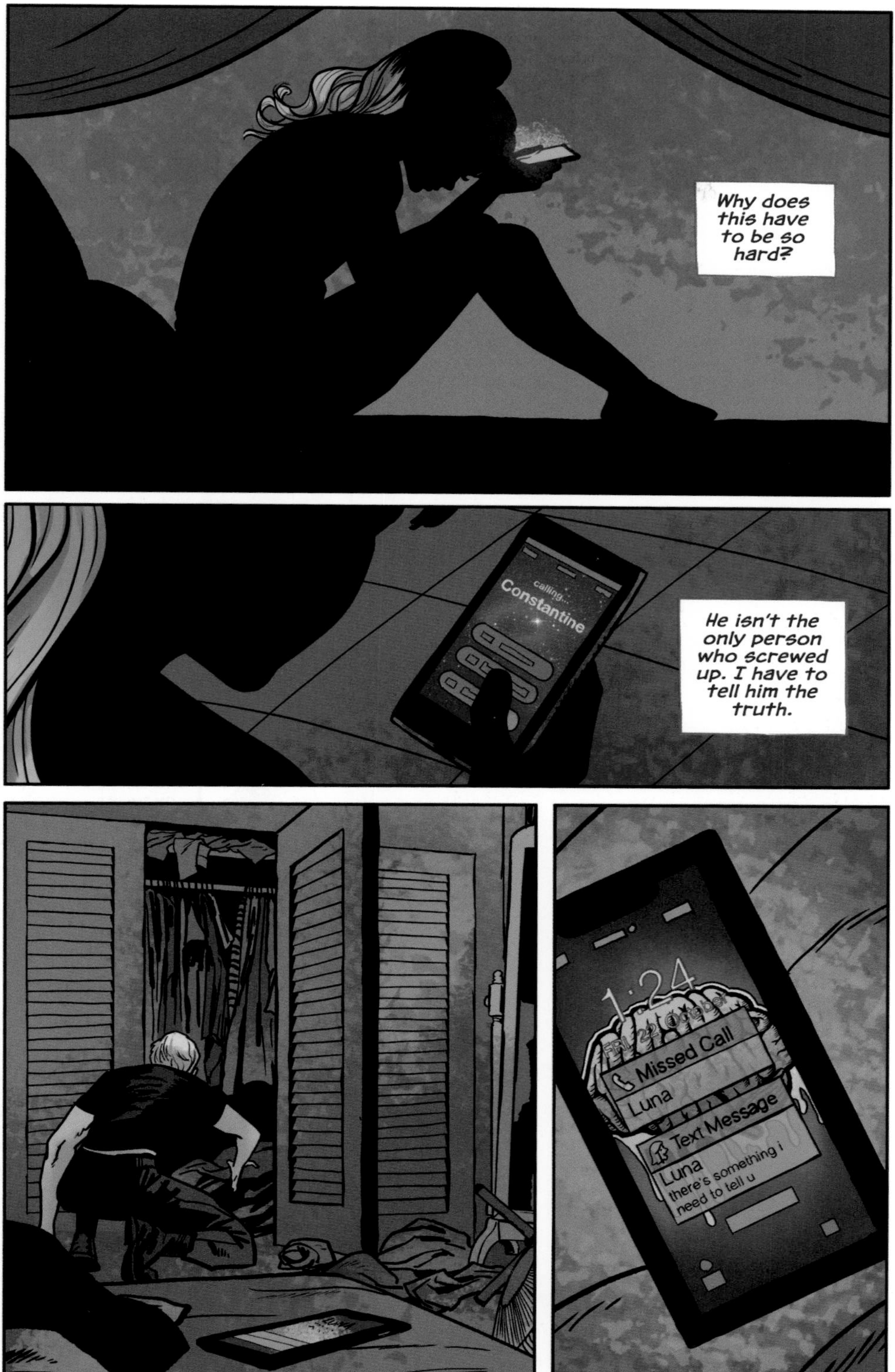
Why does this have to be so hard?
calling...
Constantine
He isn't the only person who screwed up. I have to tell him the truth.
1:24
FRI 22 October
Missed Call
Luna
Text Message
Luna
there's something i need to tell u

CHAPTER 13: Truth and Consequences

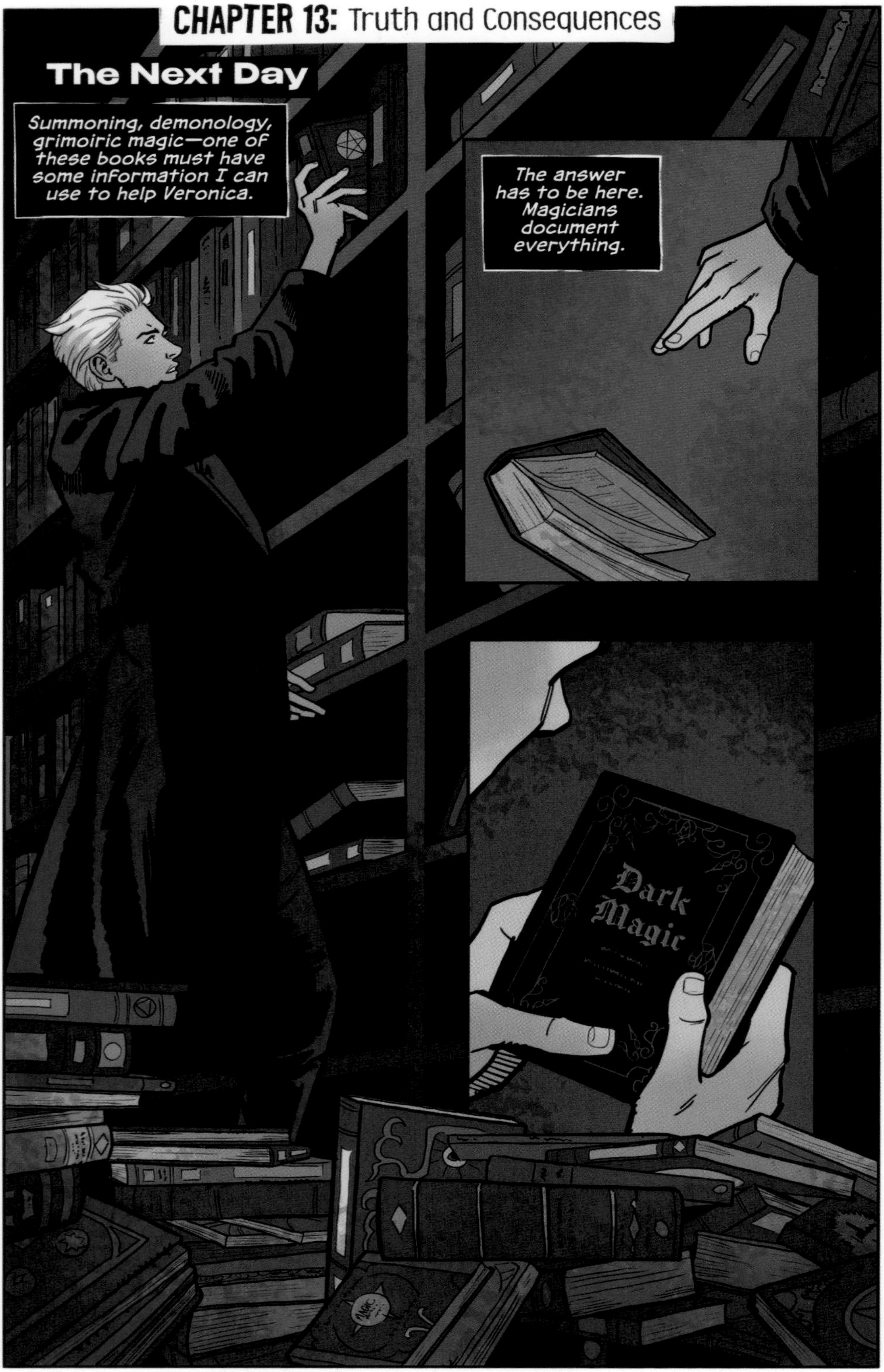
The Next Day
Summoning, demonology, grimoiric magic—one of these books must have some information I can use to help Veronica.
The answer has to be here. Magicians document everything.
Dark Magic

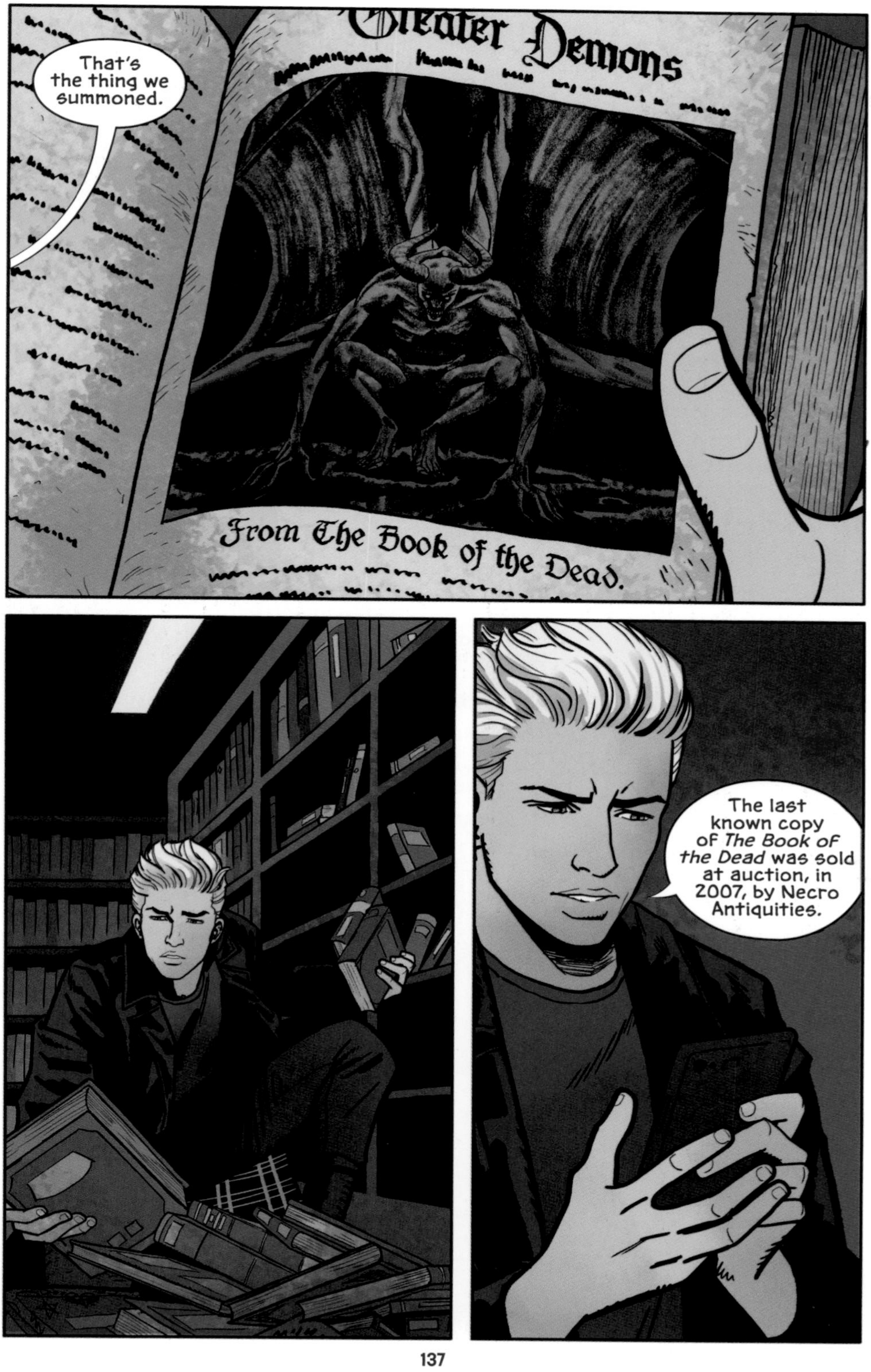
Greater Demons
That's the thing we summoned.
From The Book of the Dead.
The last known copy of *The Book of the Dead* was sold at auction, in 2007, by Necro Antiquities.

May I help you, young man?

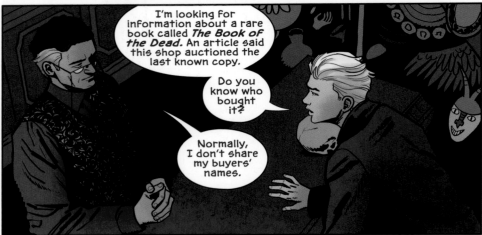

I'm looking for information about a rare book called *The Book of the Dead*. An article said this shop auctioned the last known copy.

Do you know who bought it?

Normally, I don't share my buyers' names.

But that particular auction was public and you won't be able to contact the buyer, so I don't see the harm.

The book was purchased by the famous illusionist Giovanni Zatara.

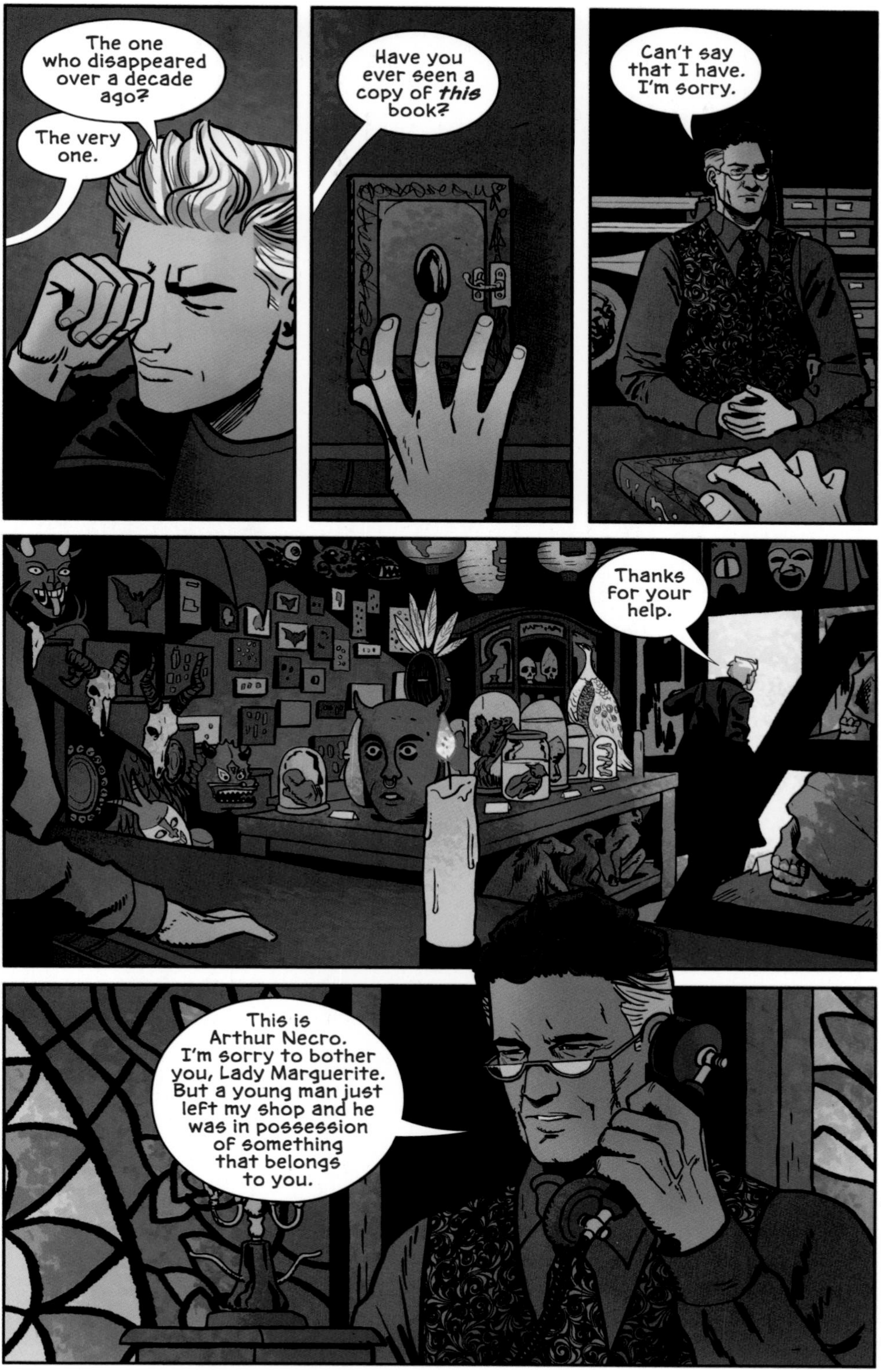
The one who disappeared over a decade ago?
The very one.
Have you ever seen a copy of *this* book?
Can't say that I have. I'm sorry.
Thanks for your help.
This is Arthur Necro. I'm sorry to bother you, Lady Marguerite. But a young man just left my shop and he was in possession of something that belongs to you.

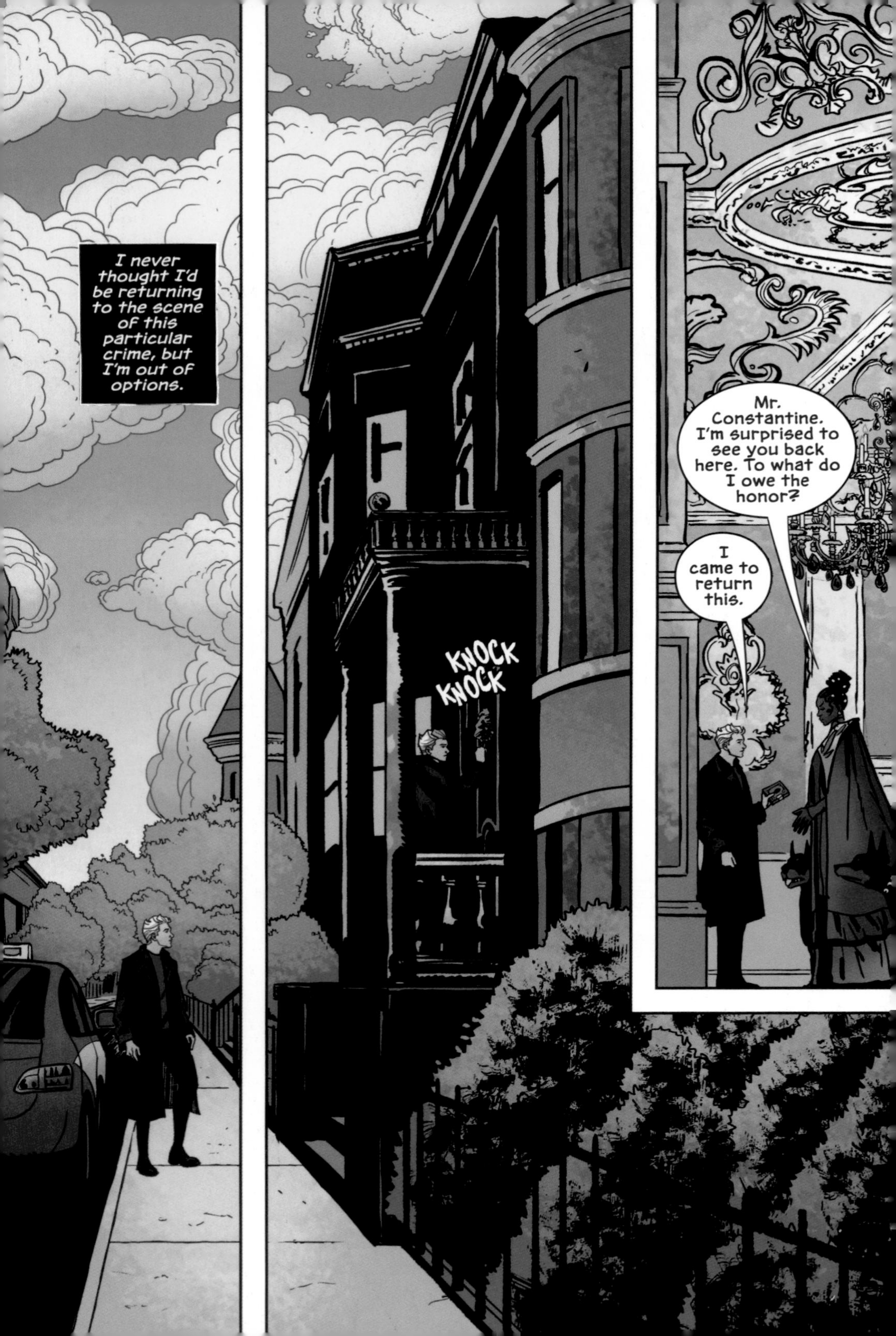
I never thought I'd be returning to the scene of this particular crime, but I'm out of options.
KNOCK KNOCK
Mr. Constantine. I'm surprised to see you back here. To what do I owe the honor?
I came to return this.

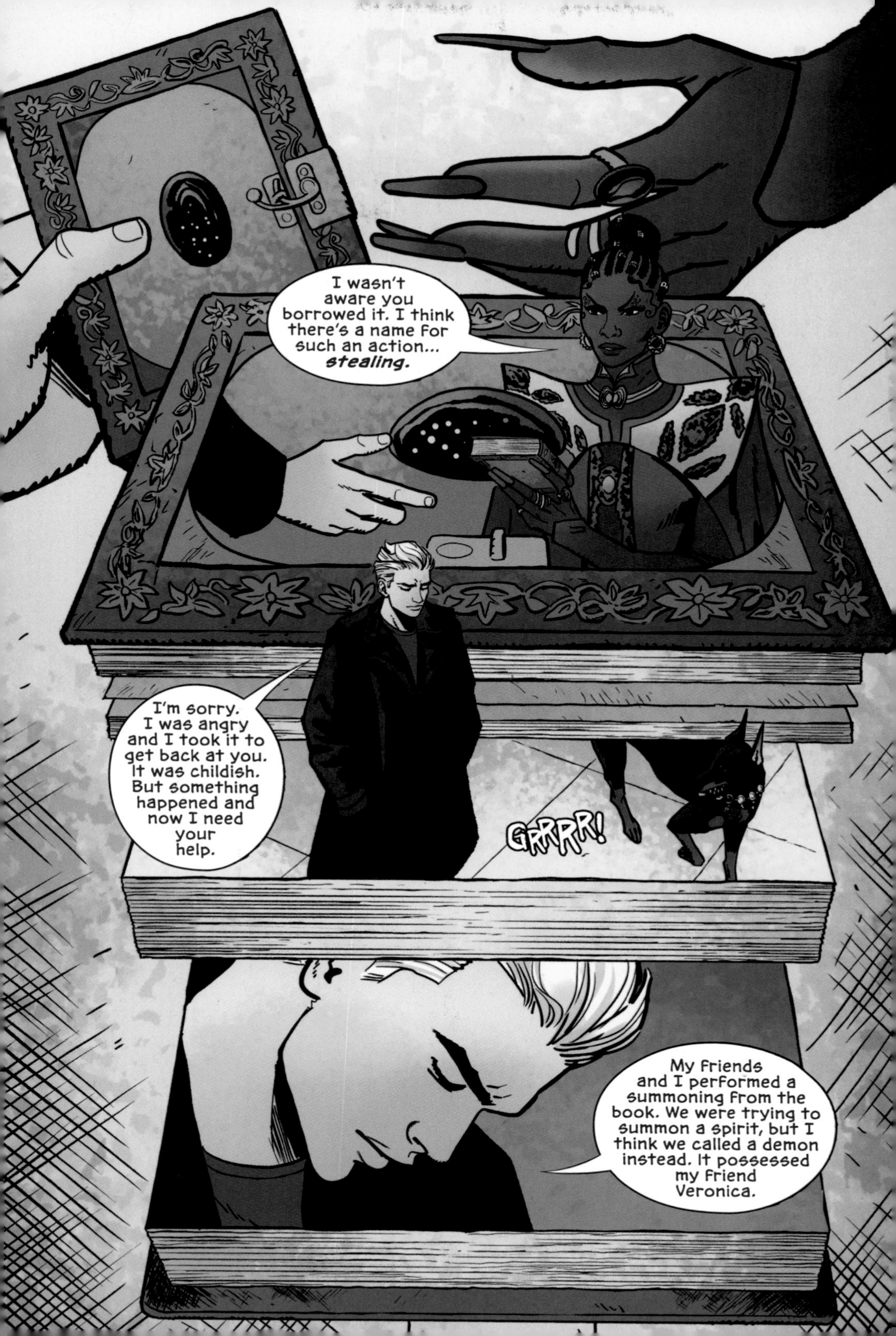
I wasn't aware you borrowed it. I think there's a name for such an action... *stealing.*
I'm sorry. I was angry and I took it to get back at you. It was childish. But something happened and now I need your help.
GRRRR!
My friends and I performed a summoning from the book. We were trying to summon a spirit, but I think we called a demon instead. It possessed my friend Veronica.

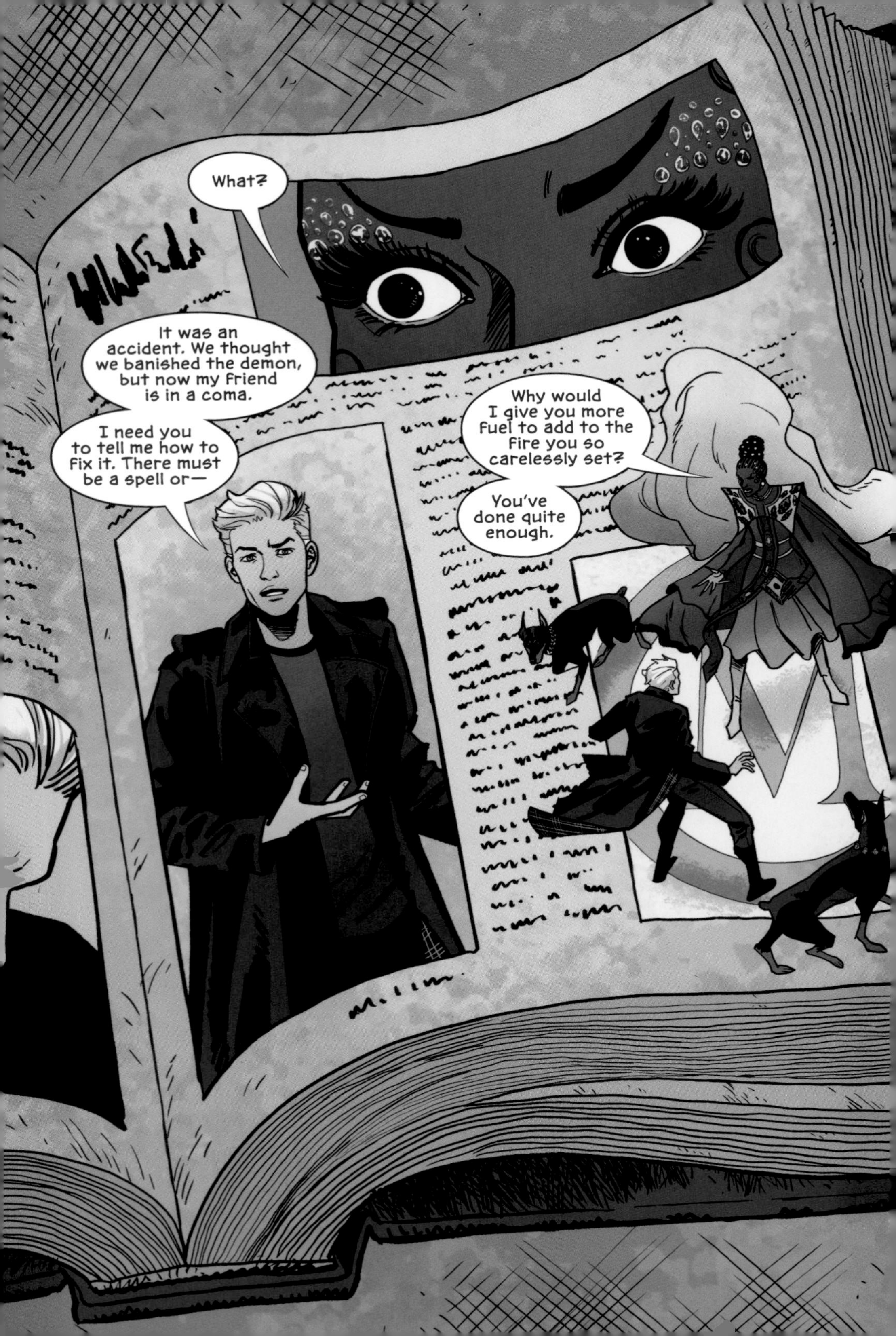
What?
It was an accident. We thought we banished the demon, but now my friend is in a coma.
I need you to tell me how to fix it. There must be a spell or—
Why would I give you more fuel to add to the fire you so carelessly set?
You've done quite enough.

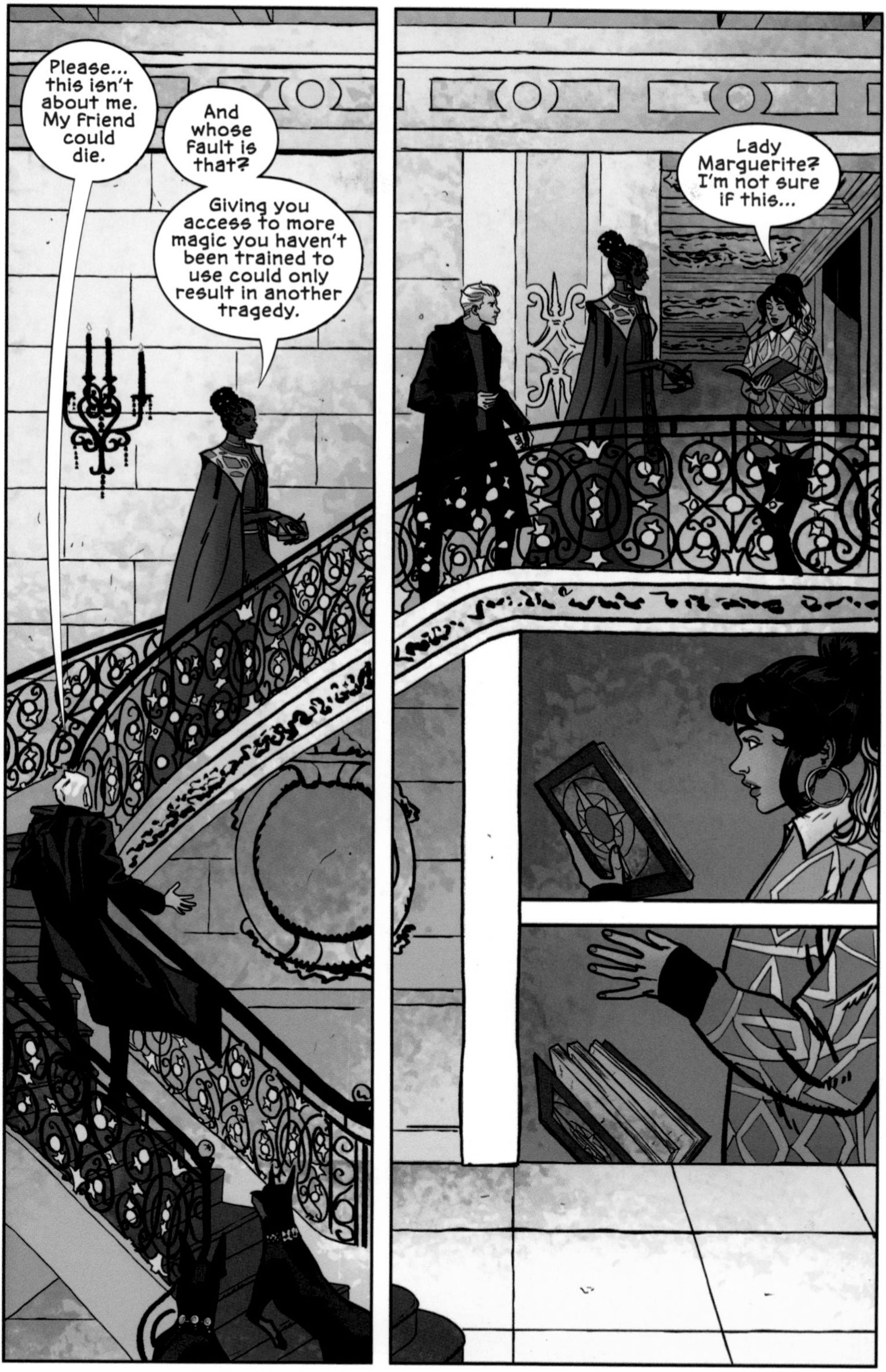
Please... this isn't about me. My friend could die.
And whose fault is that?
Giving you access to more magic you haven't been trained to use could only result in another tragedy.
Lady Marguerite? I'm not sure if this...

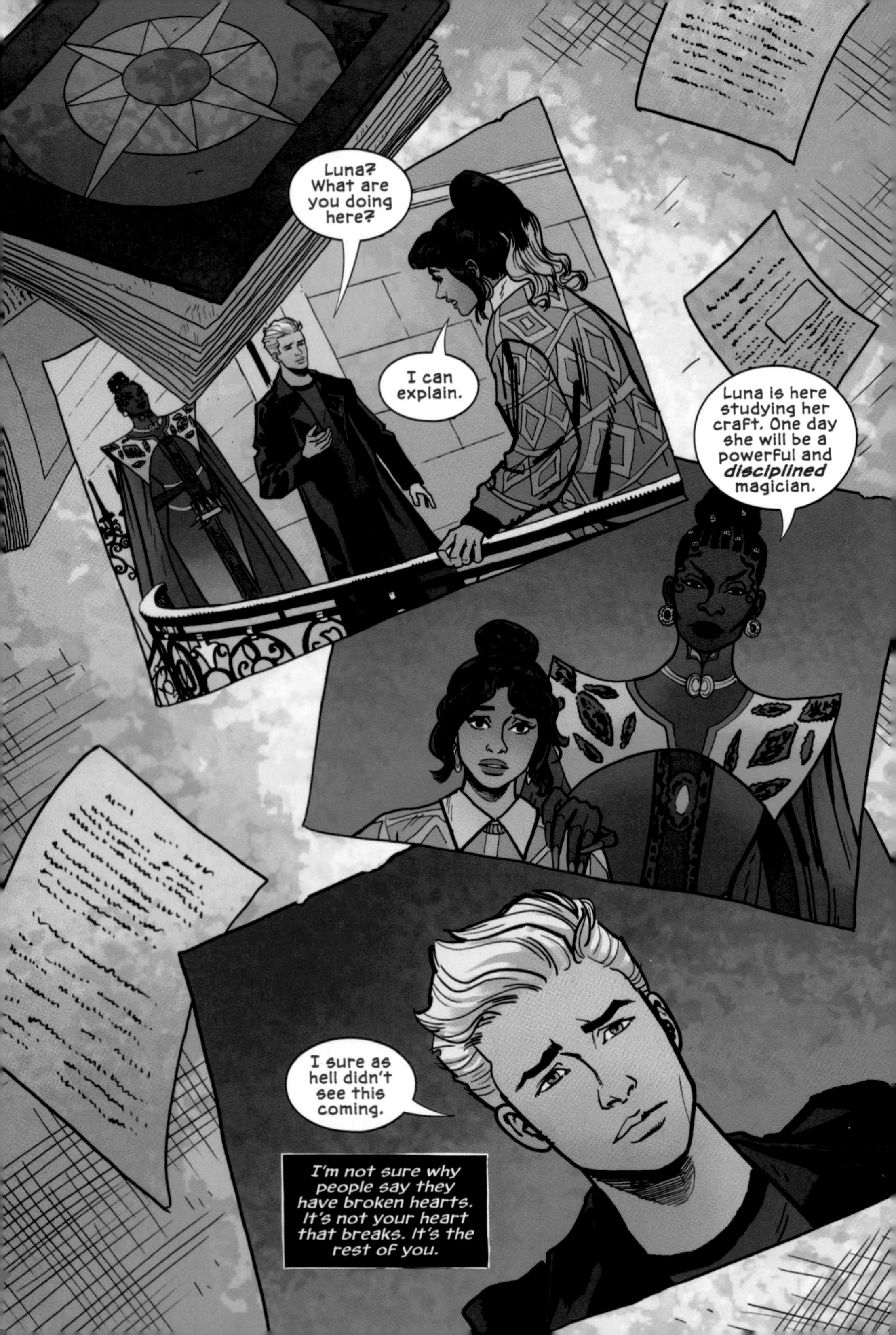
Luna? What are you doing here?
I can explain.
Luna is here studying her craft. One day she will be a powerful and *disciplined* magician.
I sure as hell didn't see this coming.
I'm not sure why people say they have broken hearts. It's not your heart that breaks. It's the rest of you.

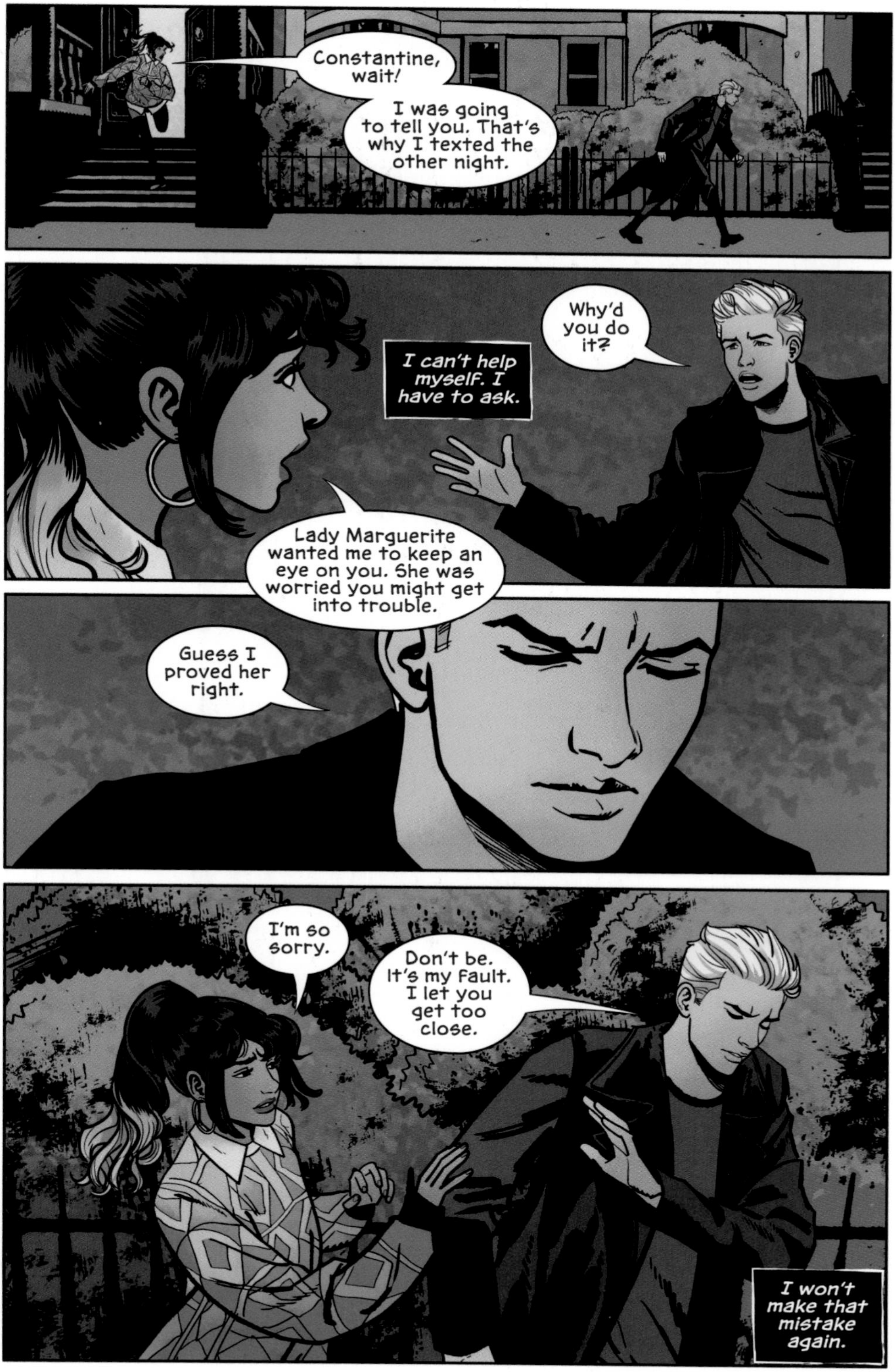

Constantine, wait!
I was going to tell you. That's why I texted the other night.
I can't help myself. I have to ask.
Why'd you do it?
Lady Marguerite wanted me to keep an eye on you. She was worried you might get into trouble.
Guess I proved her right.
I'm so sorry.
Don't be. It's my fault. I let you get too close.
I won't make that mistake again.

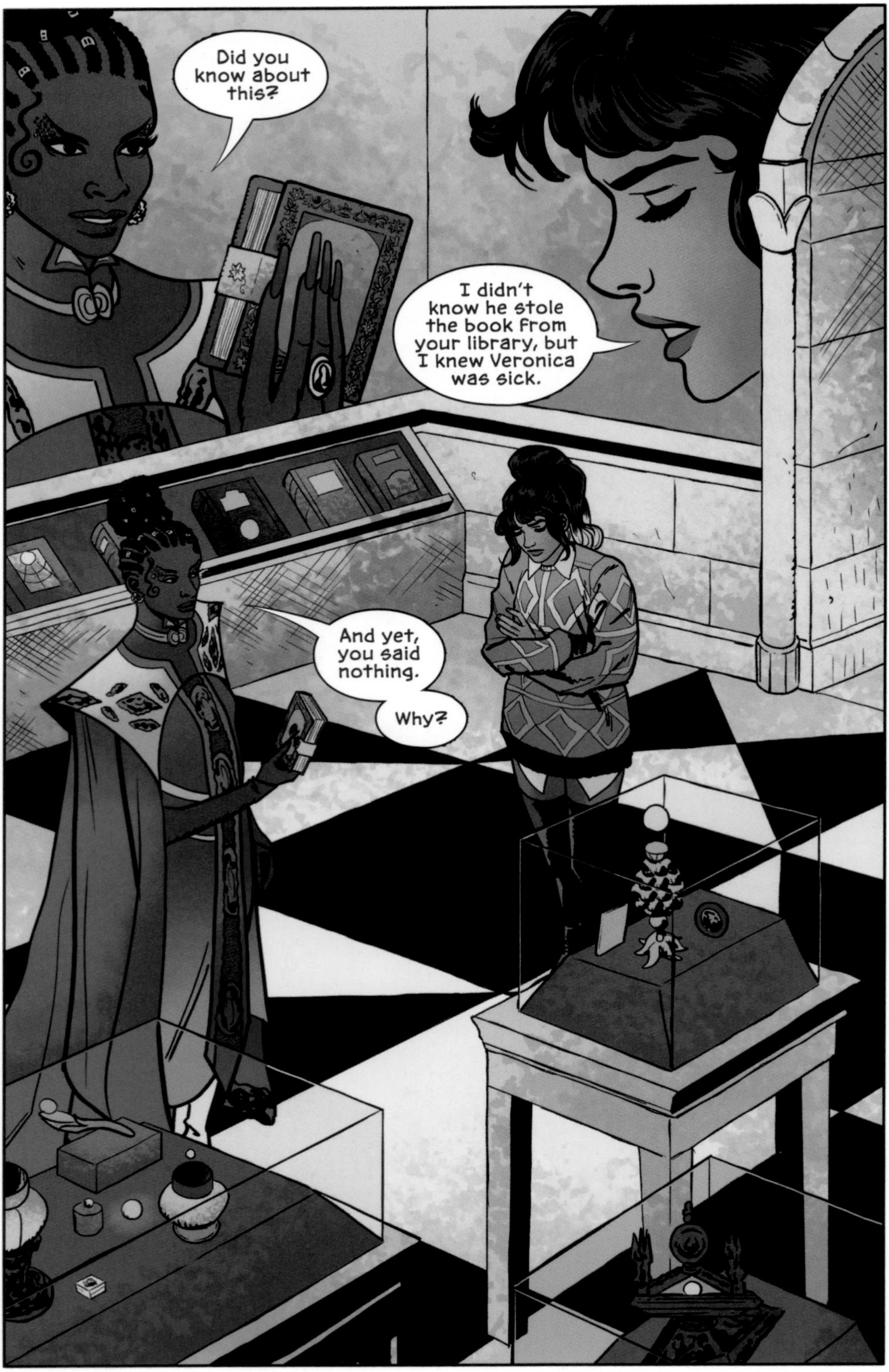
Did you know about this?
I didn't know he stole the book from your library, but I knew Veronica was sick.
And yet, you said nothing.
Why?

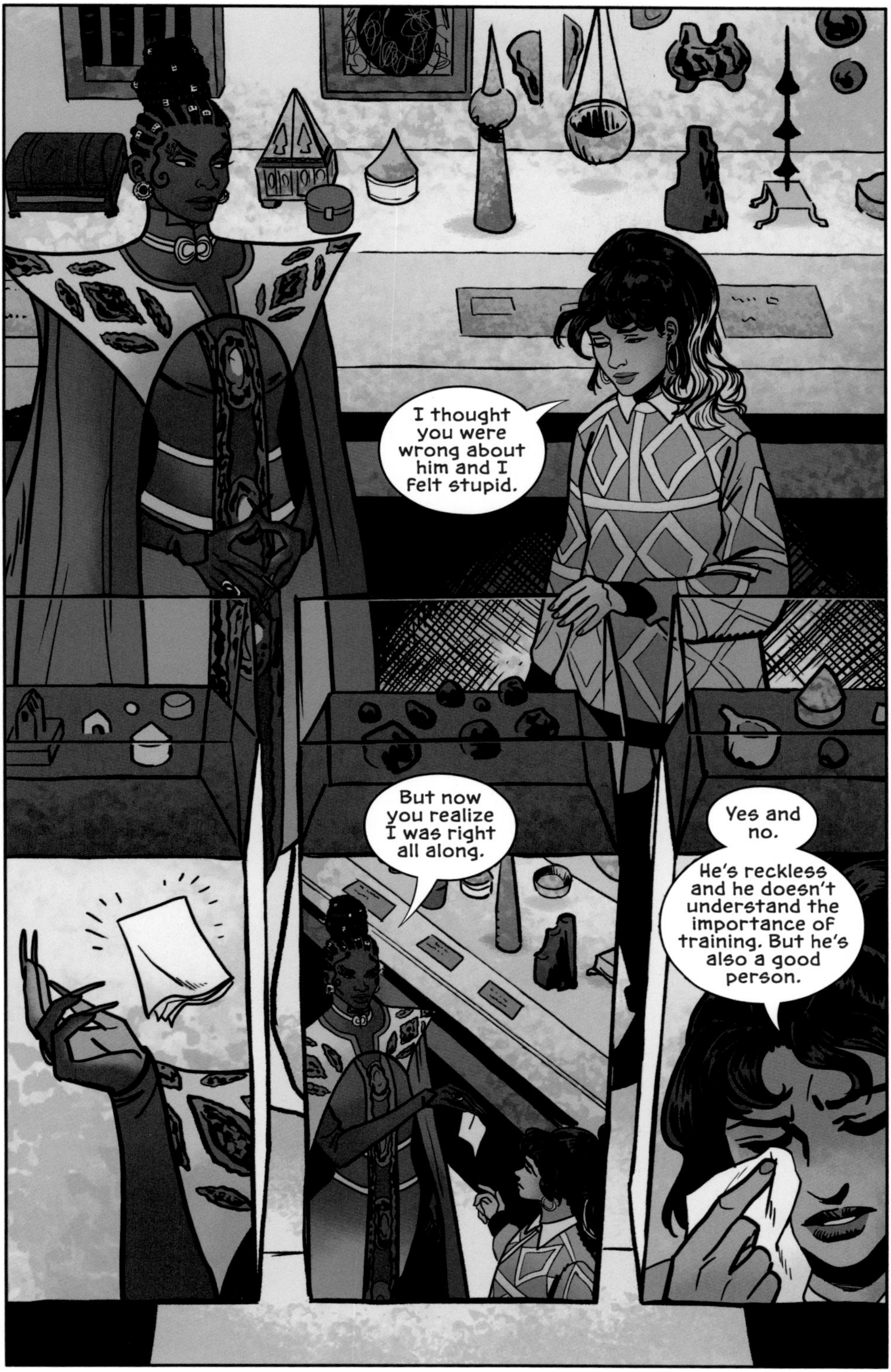
I thought you were wrong about him and I felt stupid.
But now you realize I was right all along.
Yes and no.
He's reckless and he doesn't understand the importance of training. But he's also a good person.

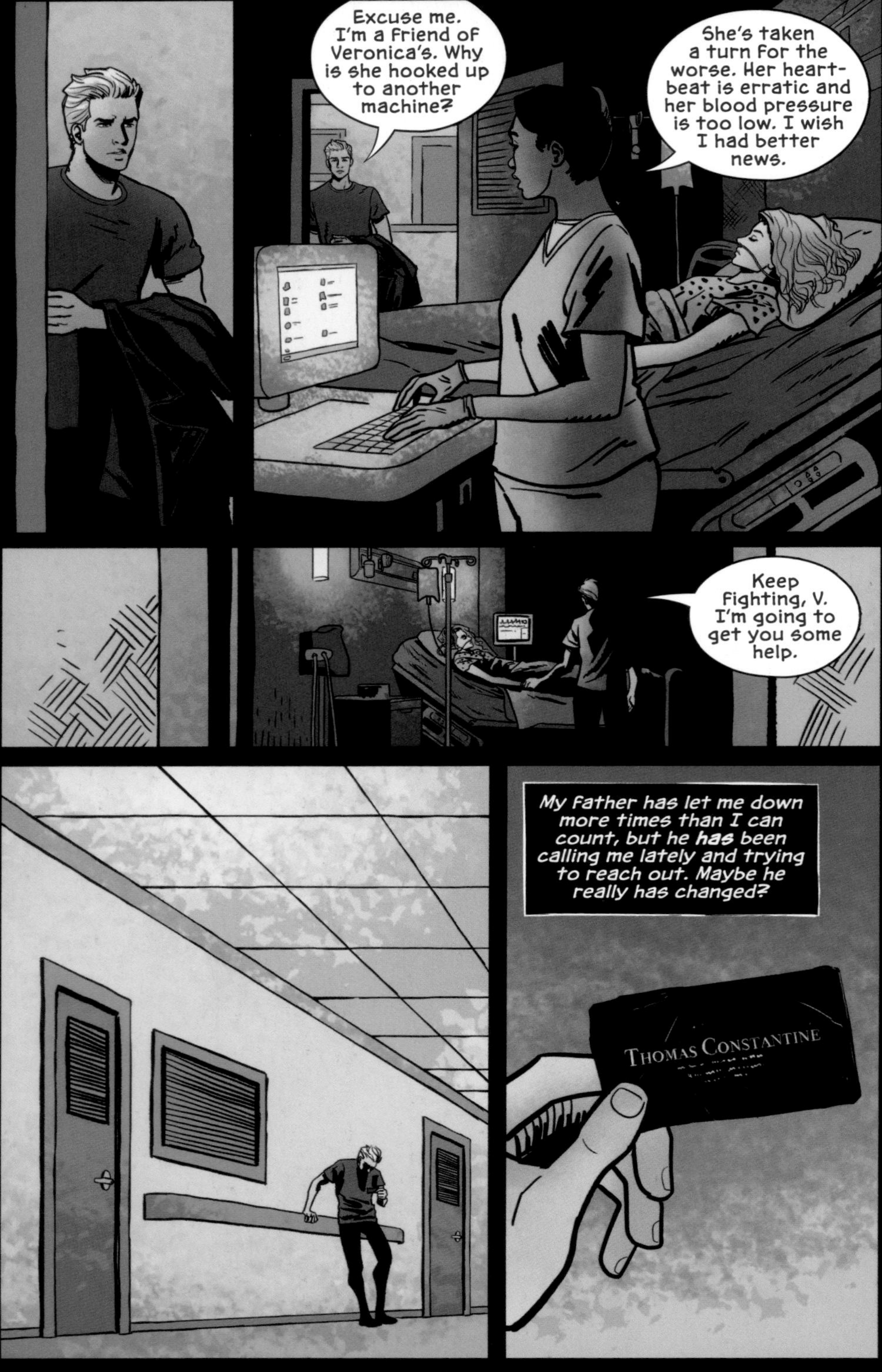
Excuse me. I'm a friend of Veronica's. Why is she hooked up to another machine?
She's taken a turn for the worse. Her heart-beat is erratic and her blood pressure is too low. I wish I had better news.
Keep fighting, V. I'm going to get you some help.
*My father has let me down more times than I can count, but he **has** been calling me lately and trying to reach out. Maybe he really has changed?*
THOMAS CONSTANTINE

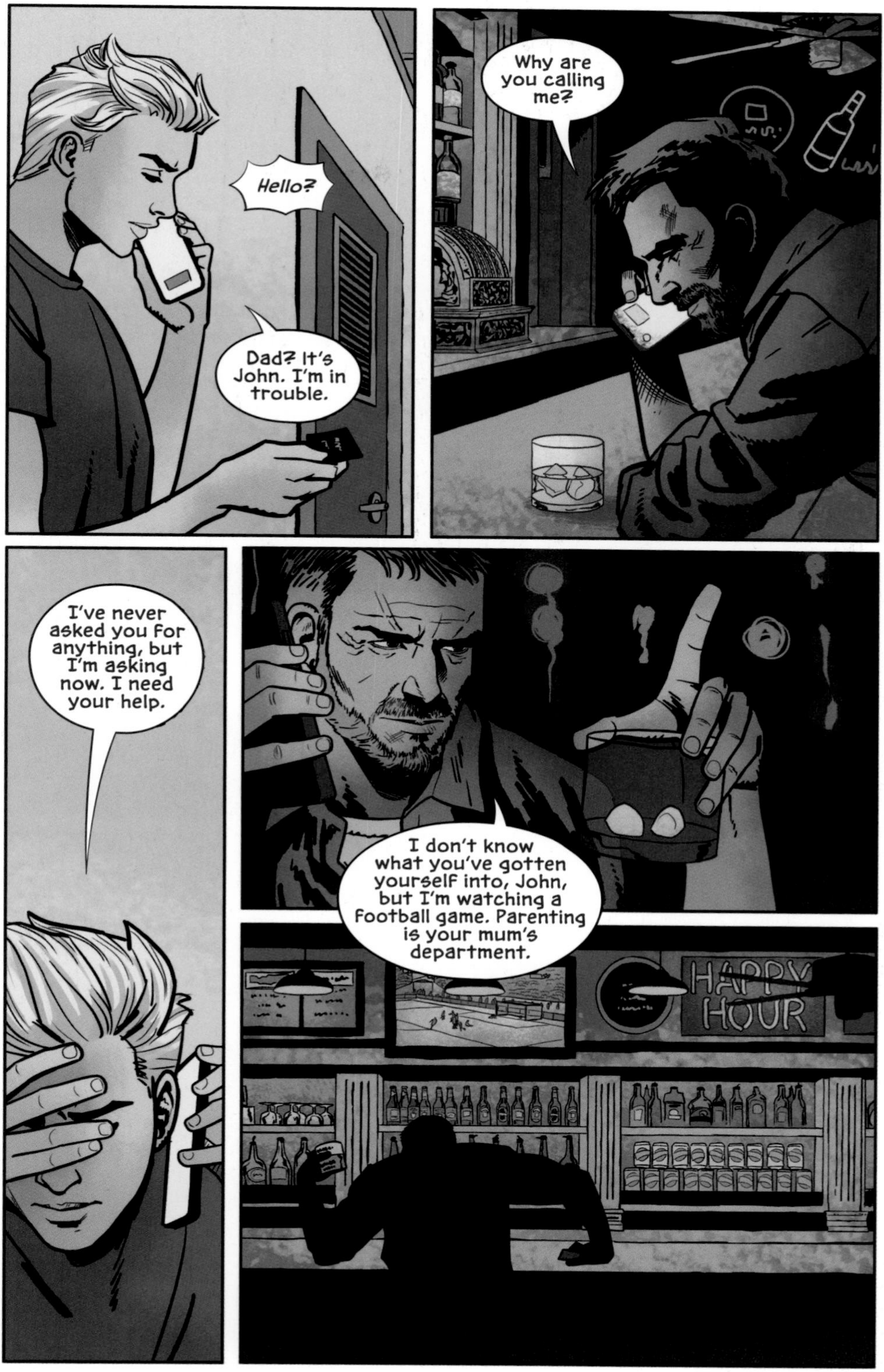
Hello?
Dad? It's John. I'm in trouble.
Why are you calling me?
I've never asked you for anything, but I'm asking now. I need your help.
I don't know what you've gotten yourself into, John, but I'm watching a football game. Parenting is your mum's department.
HAPPY HOUR

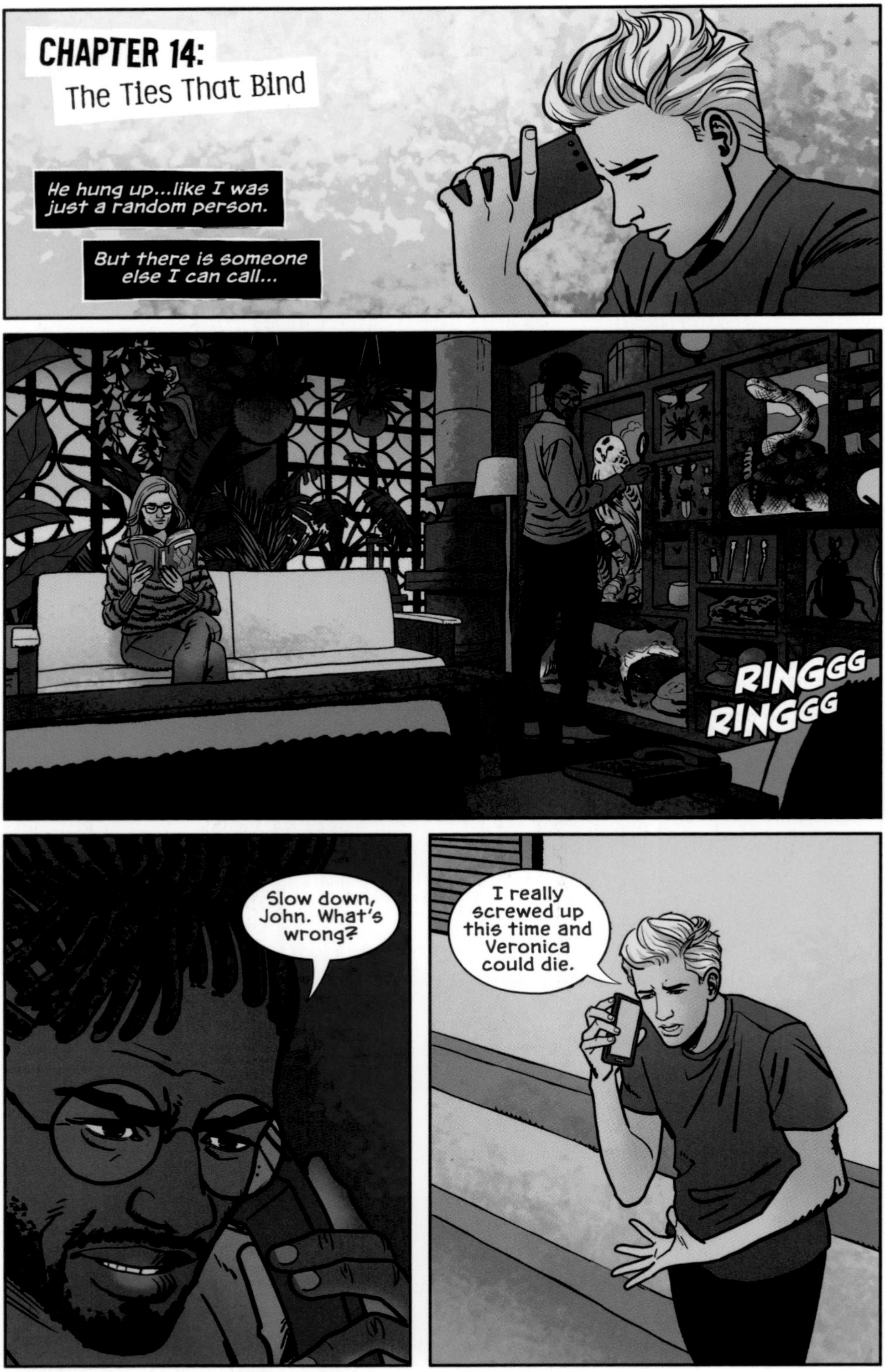
CHAPTER 14:
The Ties That Bind
He hung up...like I was just a random person.
But there is someone else I can call...
RINGGG
RINGGG
Slow down, John. What's wrong?
I really screwed up this time and Veronica could die.

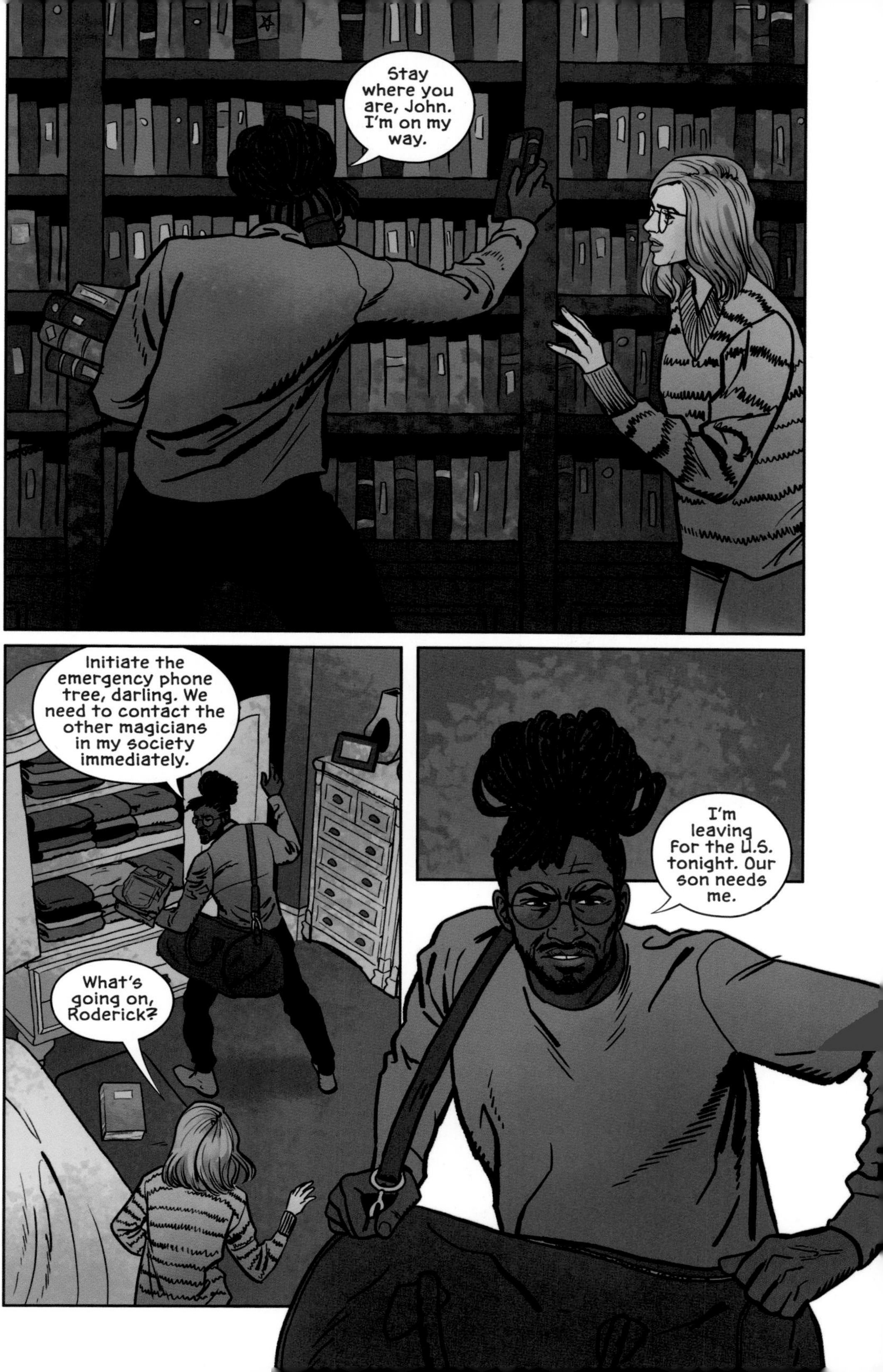
Stay where you are, John. I'm on my way.
Initiate the emergency phone tree, darling. We need to contact the other magicians in my society immediately.
What's going on, Roderick?
I'm leaving for the U.S. tonight. Our son needs me.

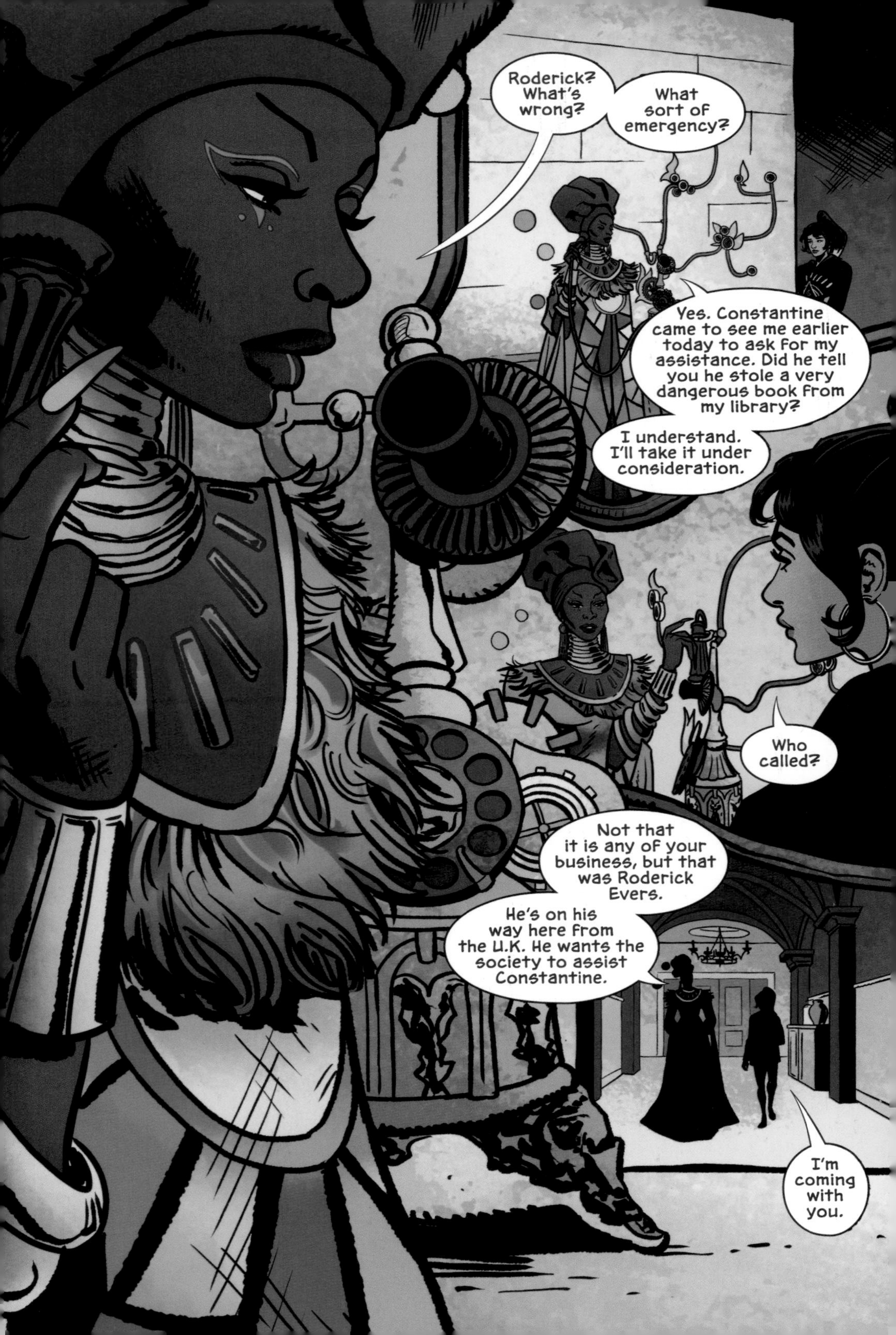
Roderick? What's wrong?
What sort of emergency?
Yes. Constantine came to see me earlier today to ask for my assistance. Did he tell you he stole a very dangerous book from my library?
I understand. I'll take it under consideration.
Who called?
Not that it is any of your business, but that was Roderick Evers.
He's on his way here from the U.K. He wants the society to assist Constantine.
I'm coming with you.

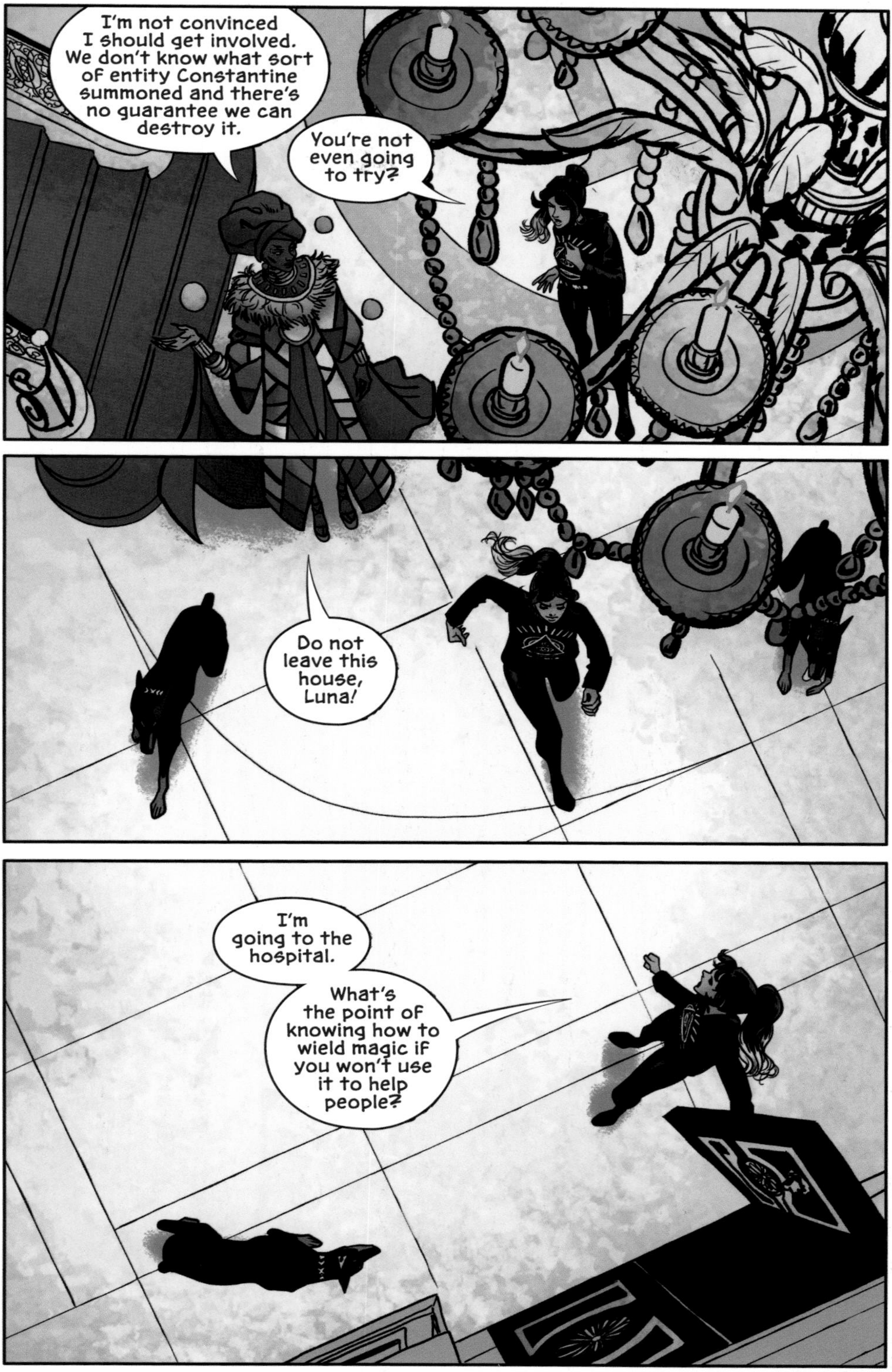

I'm not convinced I should get involved. We don't know what sort of entity Constantine summoned and there's no guarantee we can destroy it.
You're not even going to try?
Do not leave this house, Luna!
I'm going to the hospital.
What's the point of knowing how to wield magic if you won't use it to help people?

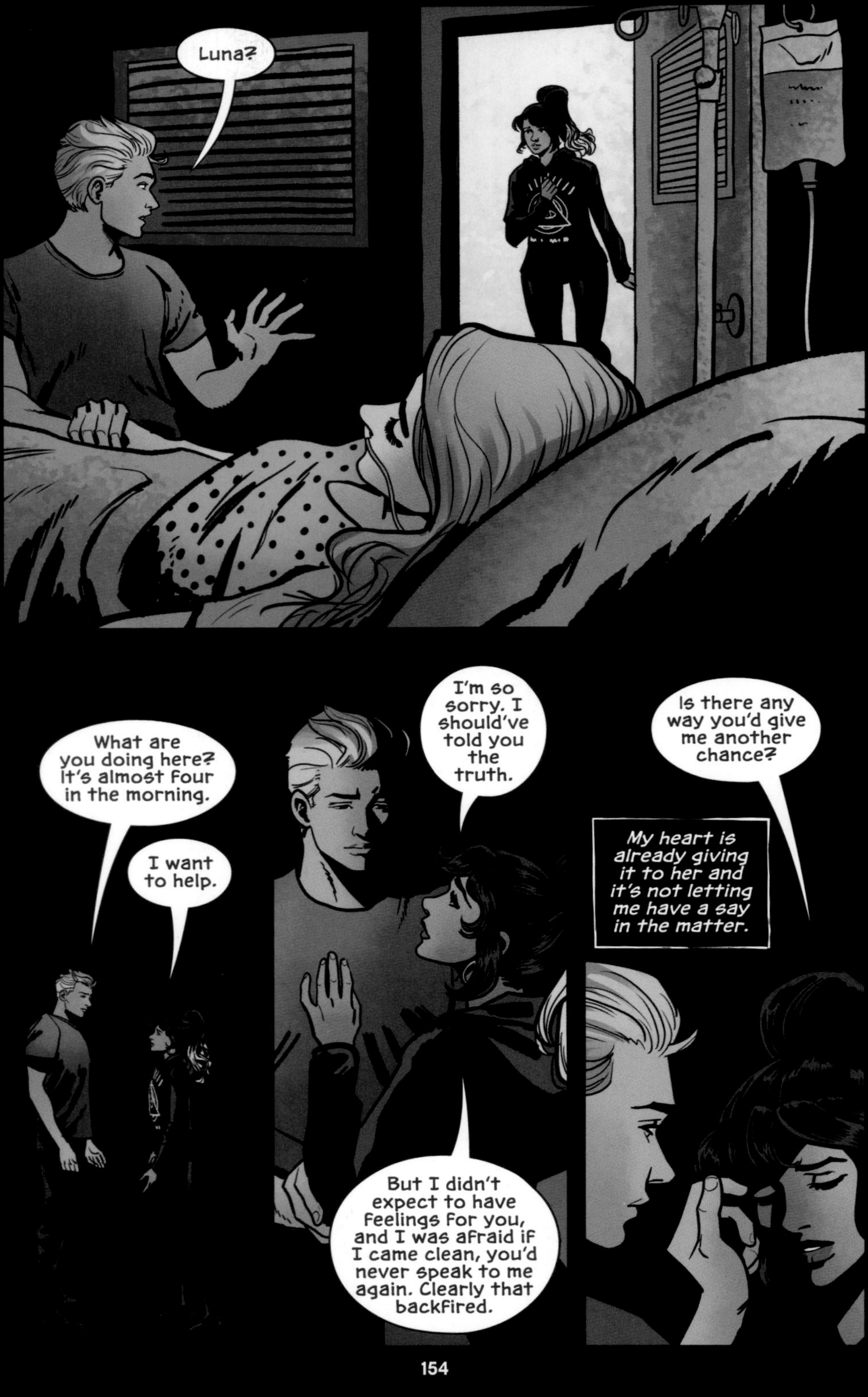
Luna?
What are you doing here? It's almost four in the morning.
I want to help.
I'm so sorry. I should've told you the truth.
But I didn't expect to have feelings for you, and I was afraid if I came clean, you'd never speak to me again. Clearly that backfired.
Is there any way you'd give me another chance?
My heart is already giving it to her and it's not letting me have a say in the matter.

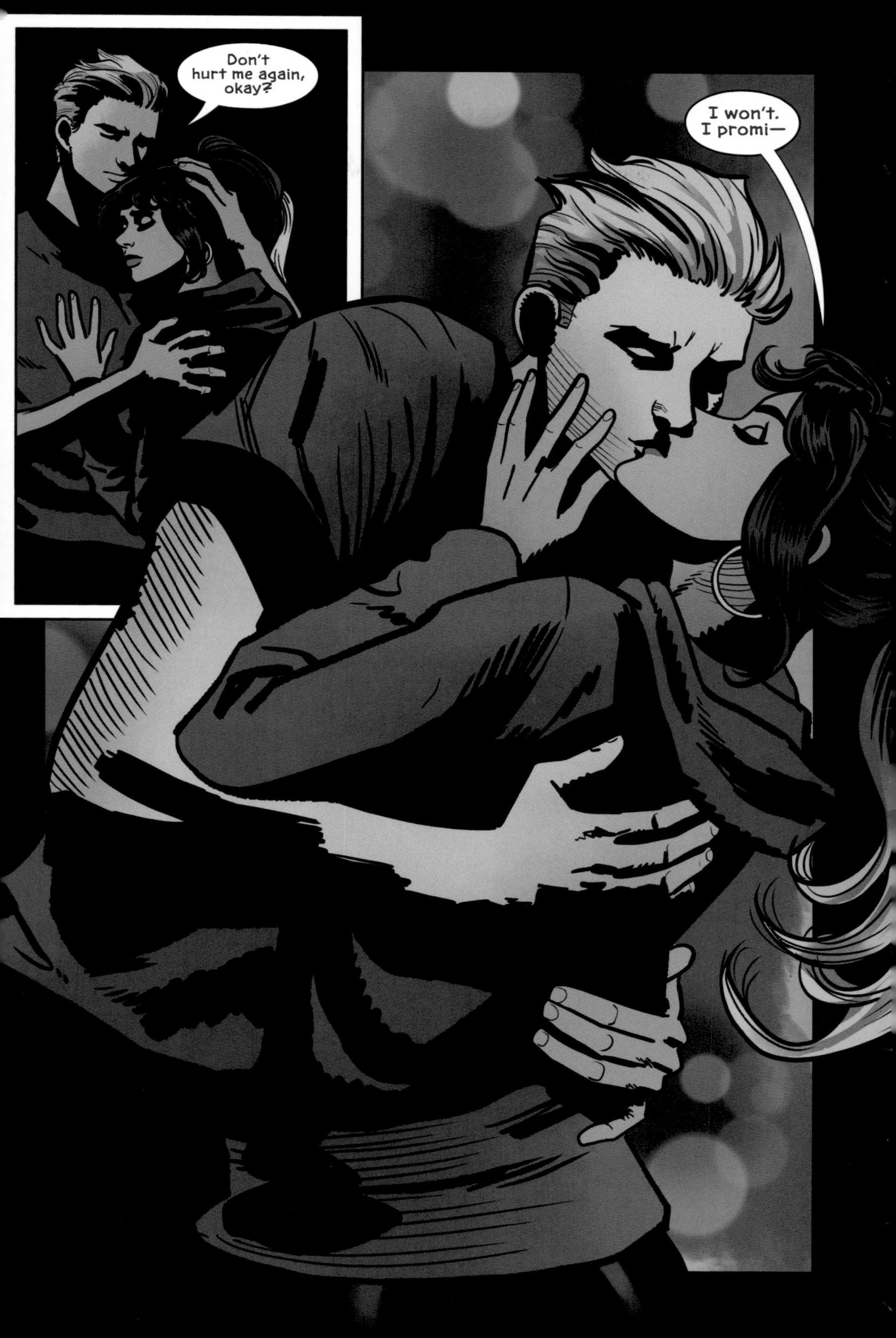
Don't hurt me again, okay?
I won't. I promi—

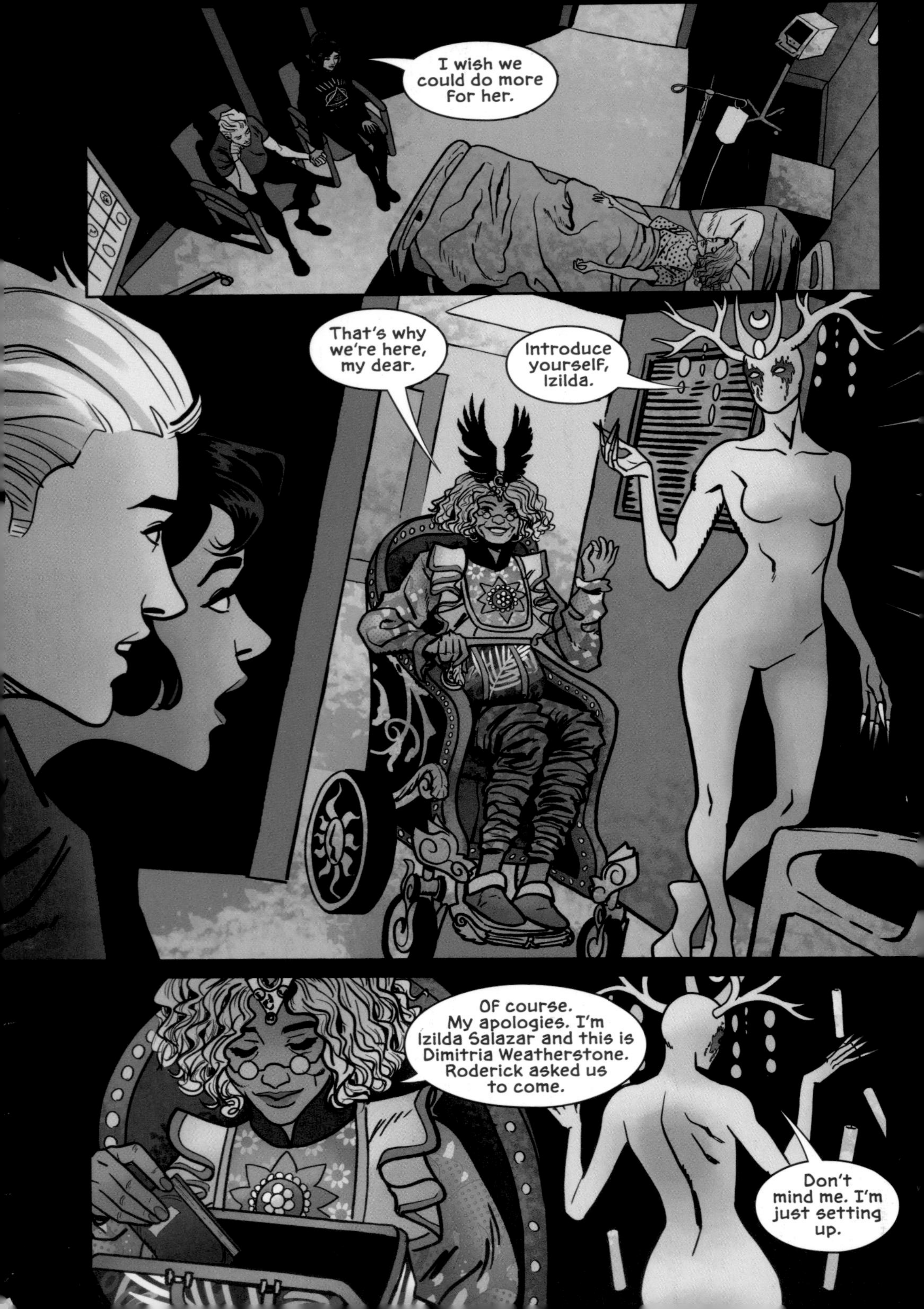
I wish we could do more for her.
That's why we're here, my dear.
Introduce yourself, Izilda.
Of course. My apologies. I'm Izilda Salazar and this is Dimitria Weatherstone. Roderick asked us to come.
Don't mind me. I'm just setting up.

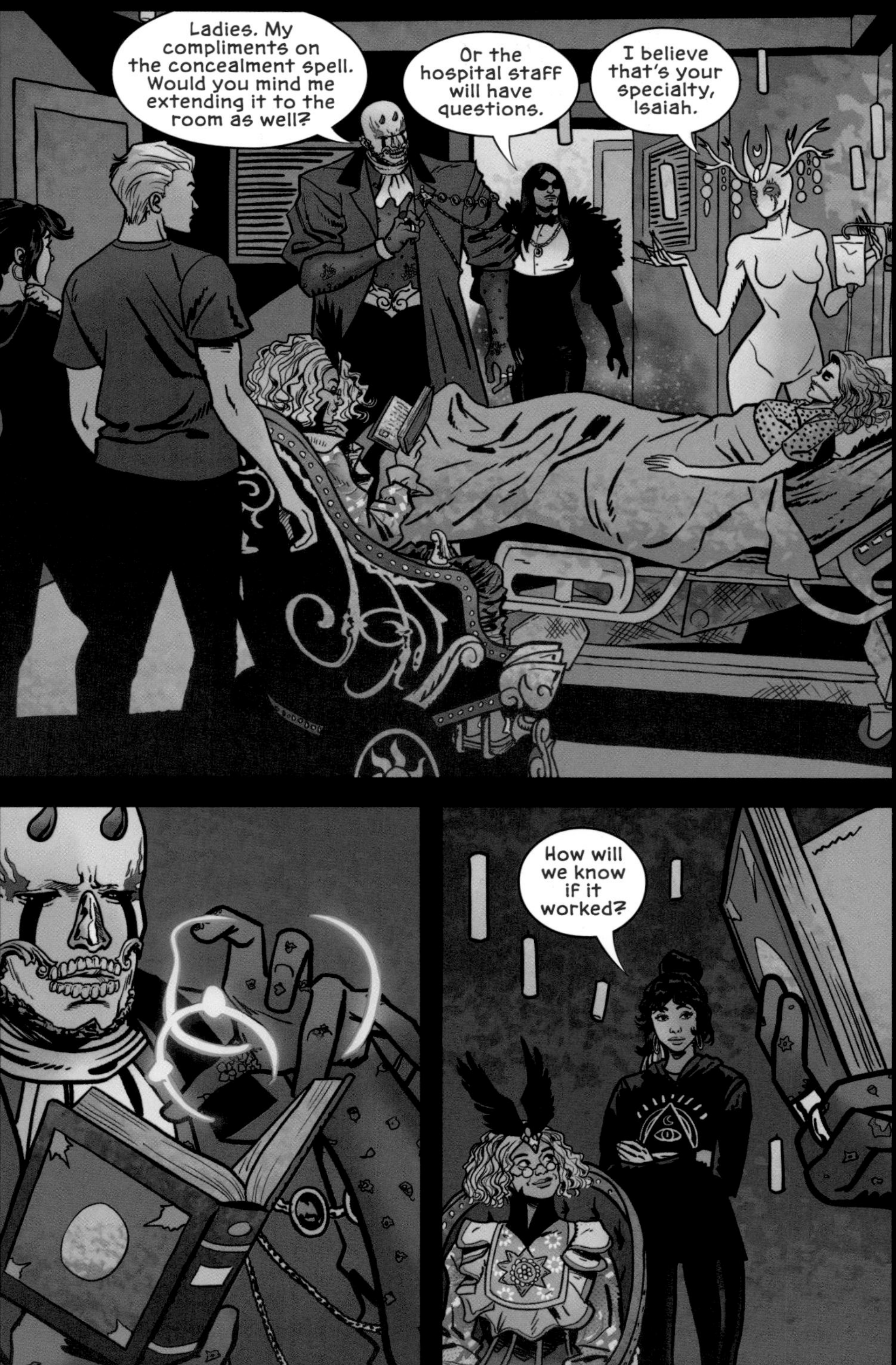
Ladies. My compliments on the concealment spell. Would you mind me extending it to the room as well?
Or the hospital staff will have questions.
I believe that's your specialty, Isaiah.
How will we know if it worked?

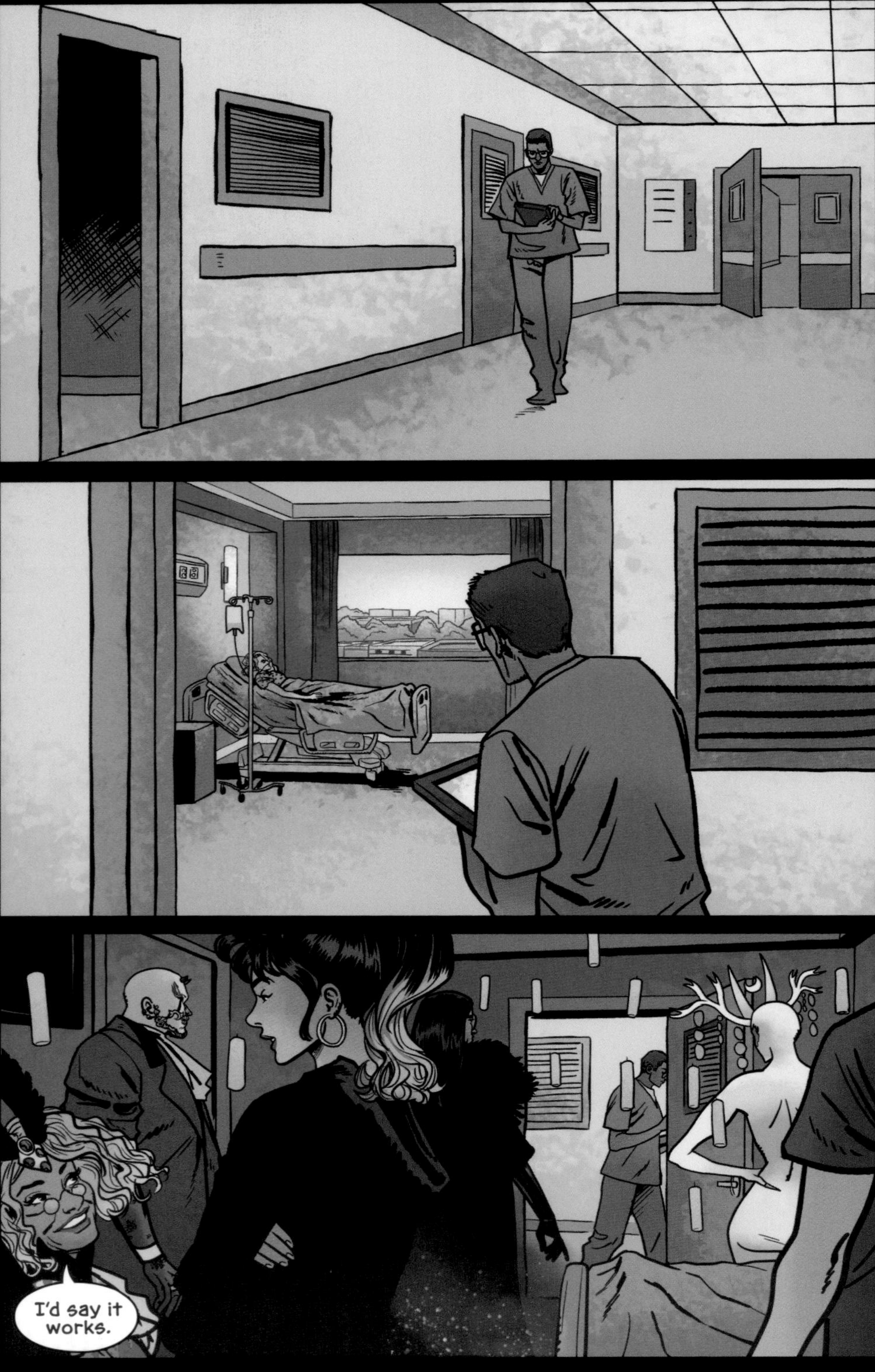
I'd say it works.

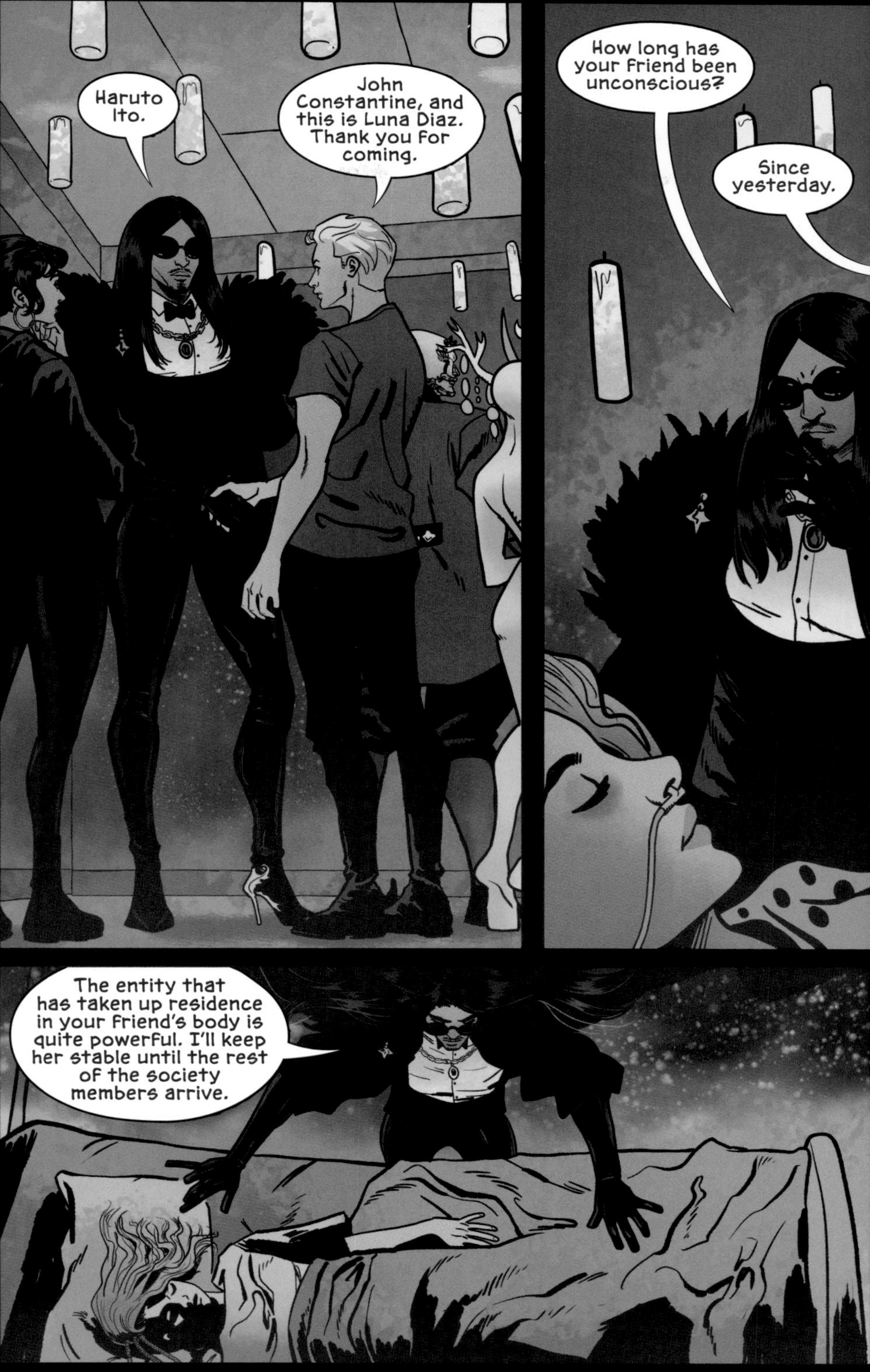
Haruto Ito.
John Constantine, and this is Luna Diaz. Thank you for coming.
How long has your friend been unconscious?
Since yesterday.
The entity that has taken up residence in your friend's body is quite powerful. I'll keep her stable until the rest of the society members arrive.

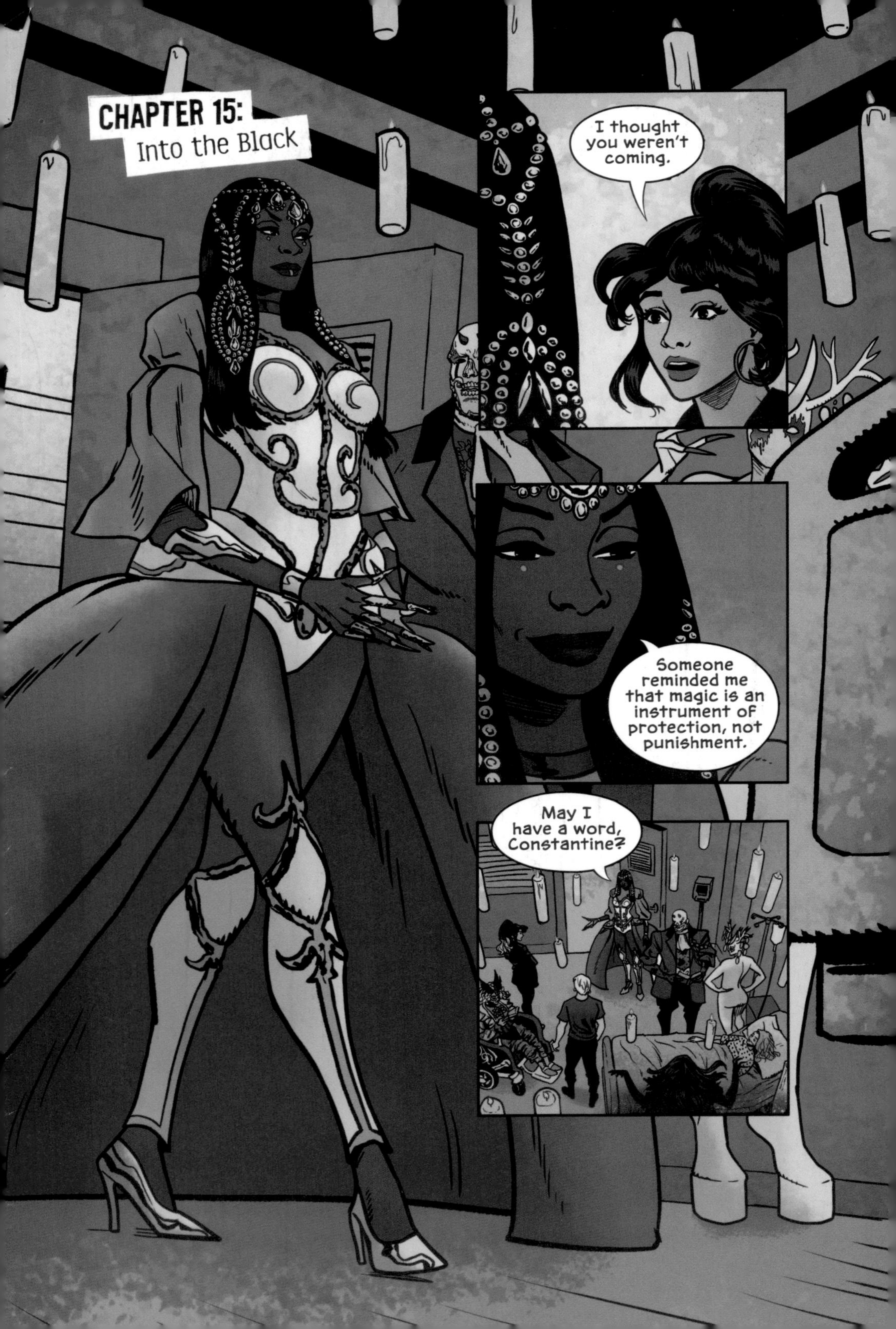
CHAPTER 15:
Into the Black
I thought you weren't coming.
Someone reminded me that magic is an instrument of protection, not punishment.
May I have a word, Constantine?

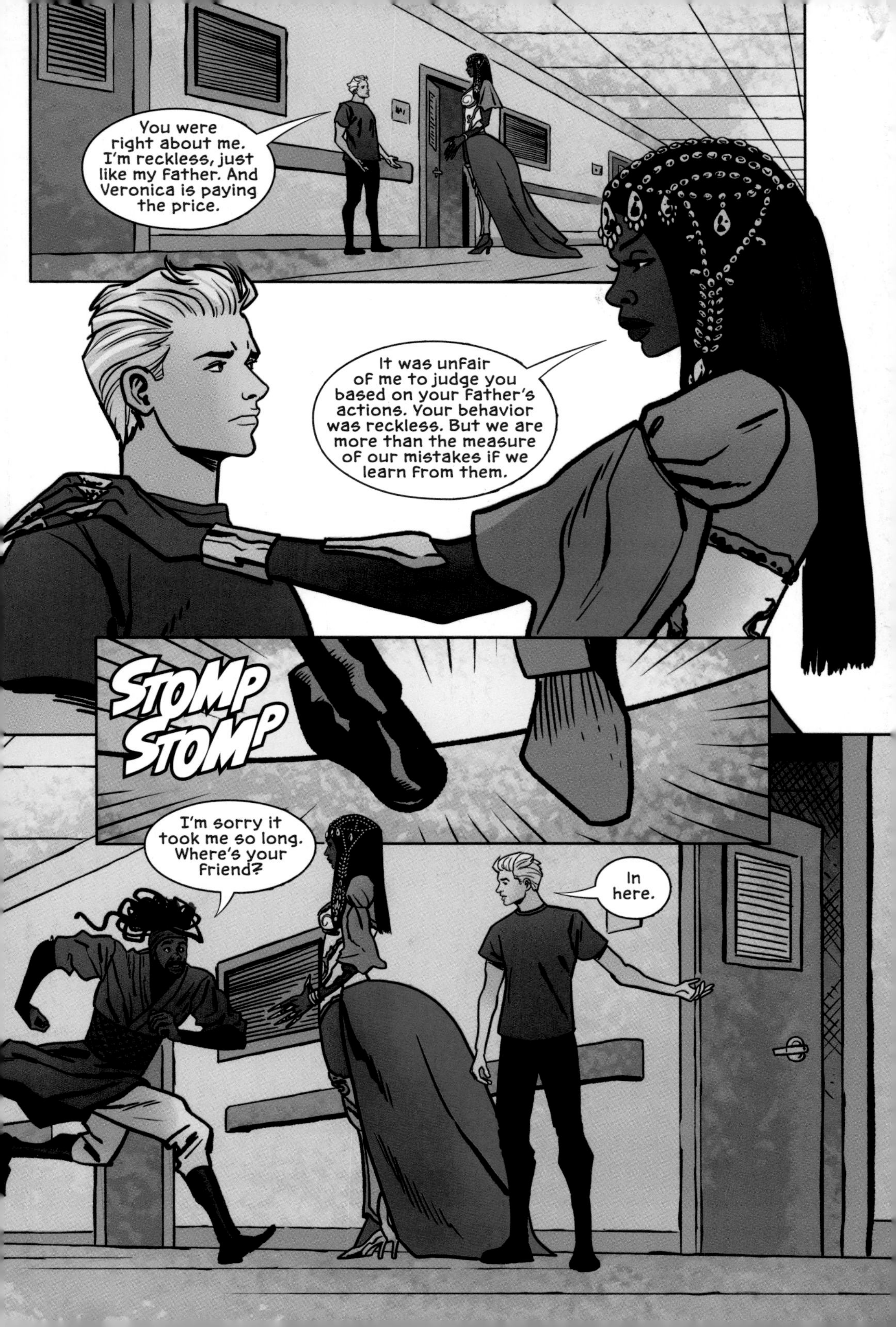
You were right about me. I'm reckless, just like my father. And Veronica is paying the price.
It was unfair of me to judge you based on your father's actions. Your behavior was reckless. But we are more than the measure of our mistakes if we learn from them.
STOMP STOMP
I'm sorry it took me so long. Where's your friend?
In here.

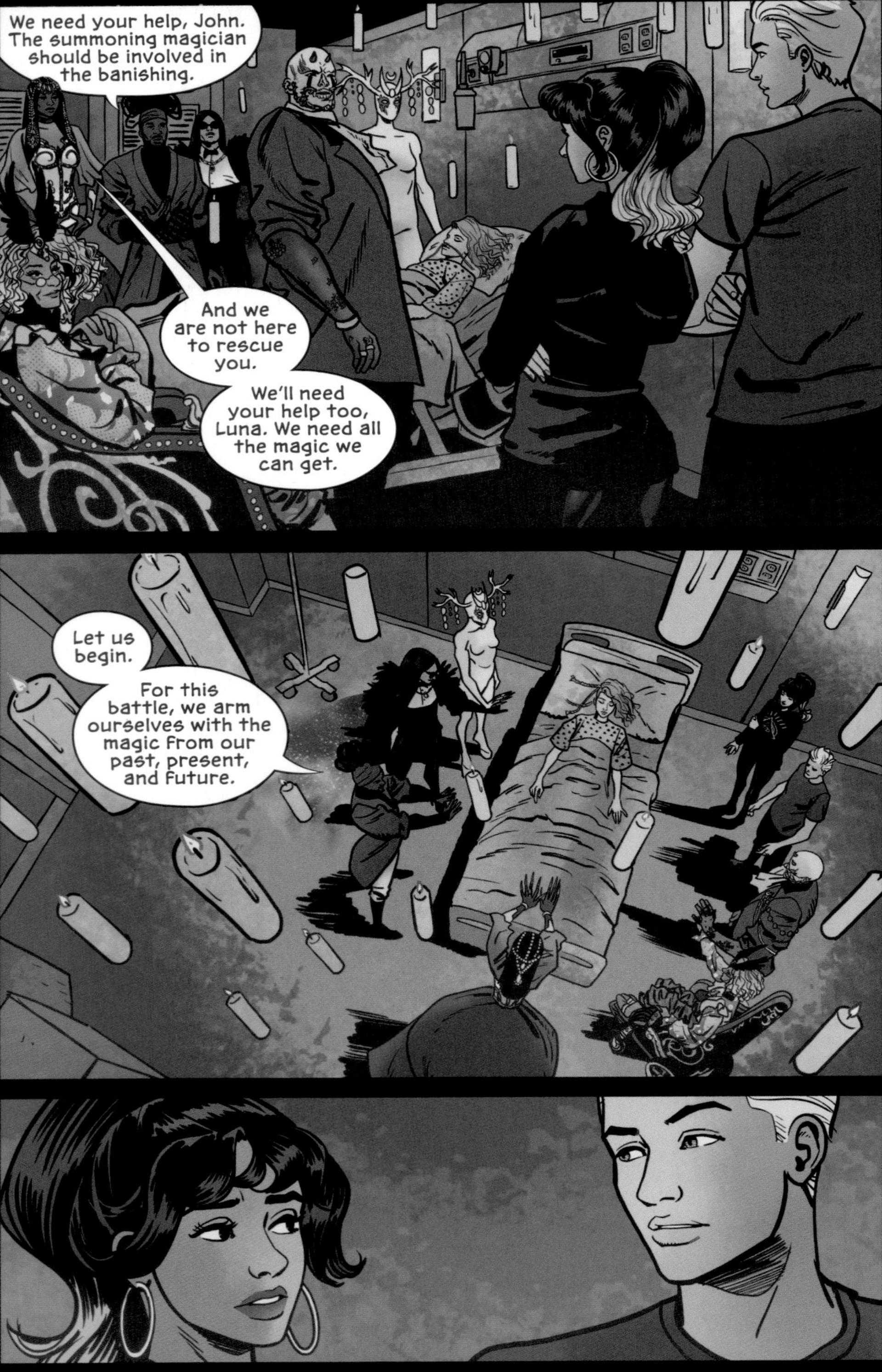
We need your help, John. The summoning magician should be involved in the banishing.
And we are not here to rescue you.
We'll need your help too, Luna. We need all the magic we can get.
Let us begin.
For this battle, we arm ourselves with the magic from our past, present, and future.

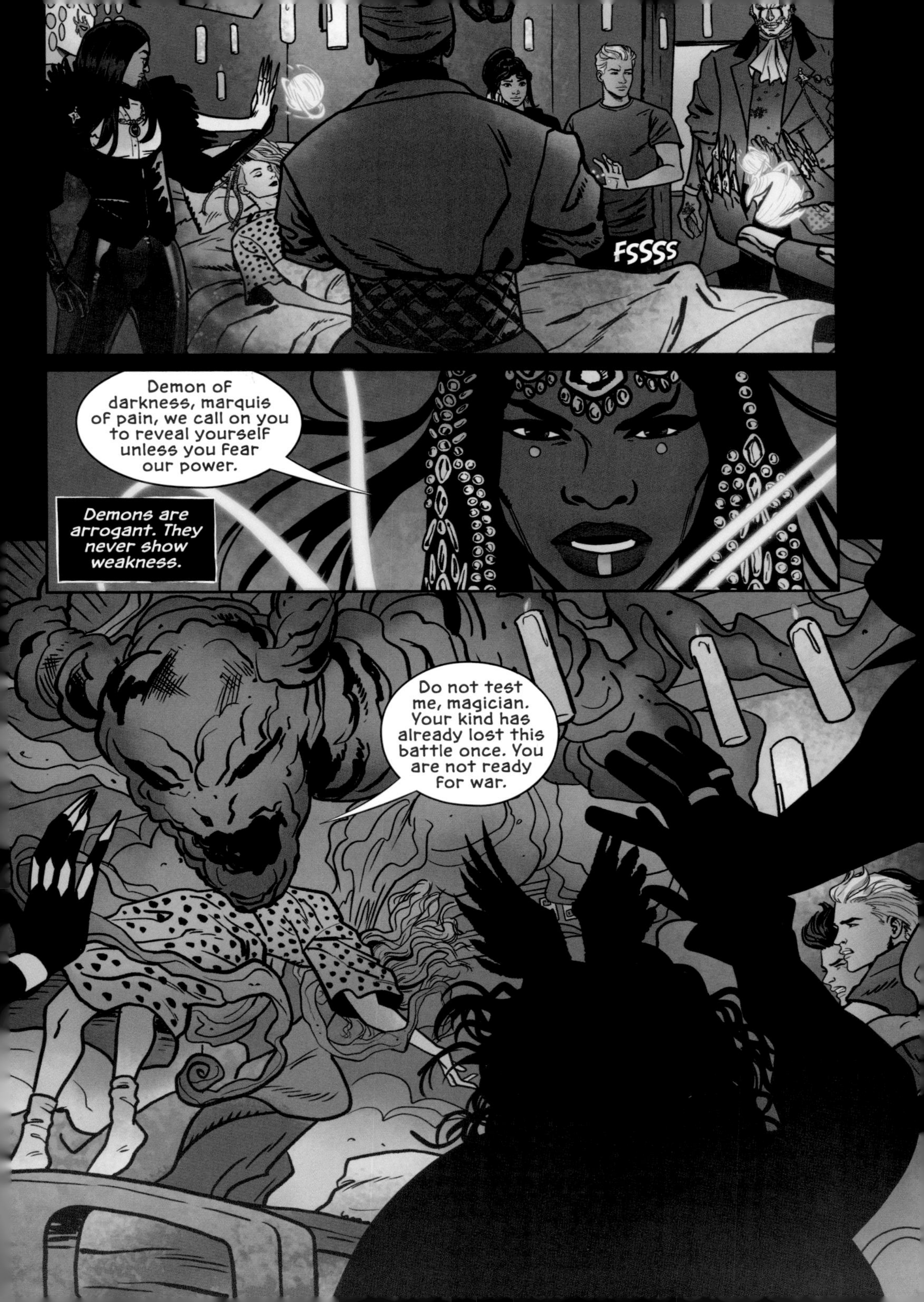
FSSSS
Demon of darkness, marquis of pain, we call on you to reveal yourself unless you fear our power.
Demons are arrogant. They never show weakness.
Do not test me, magician. Your kind has already lost this battle once. You are not ready for war.

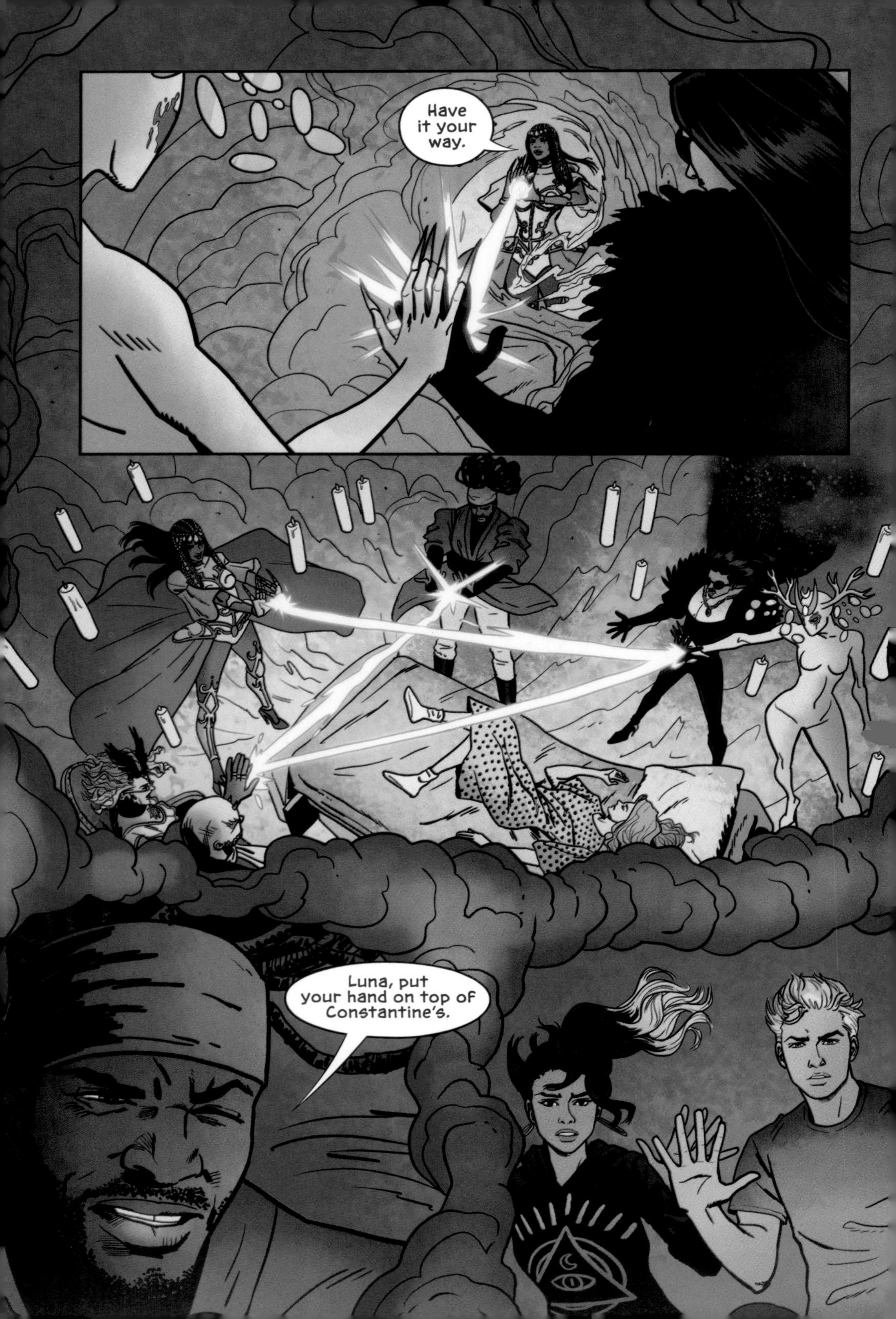
Have it your way.
Luna, put your hand on top of Constantine's.

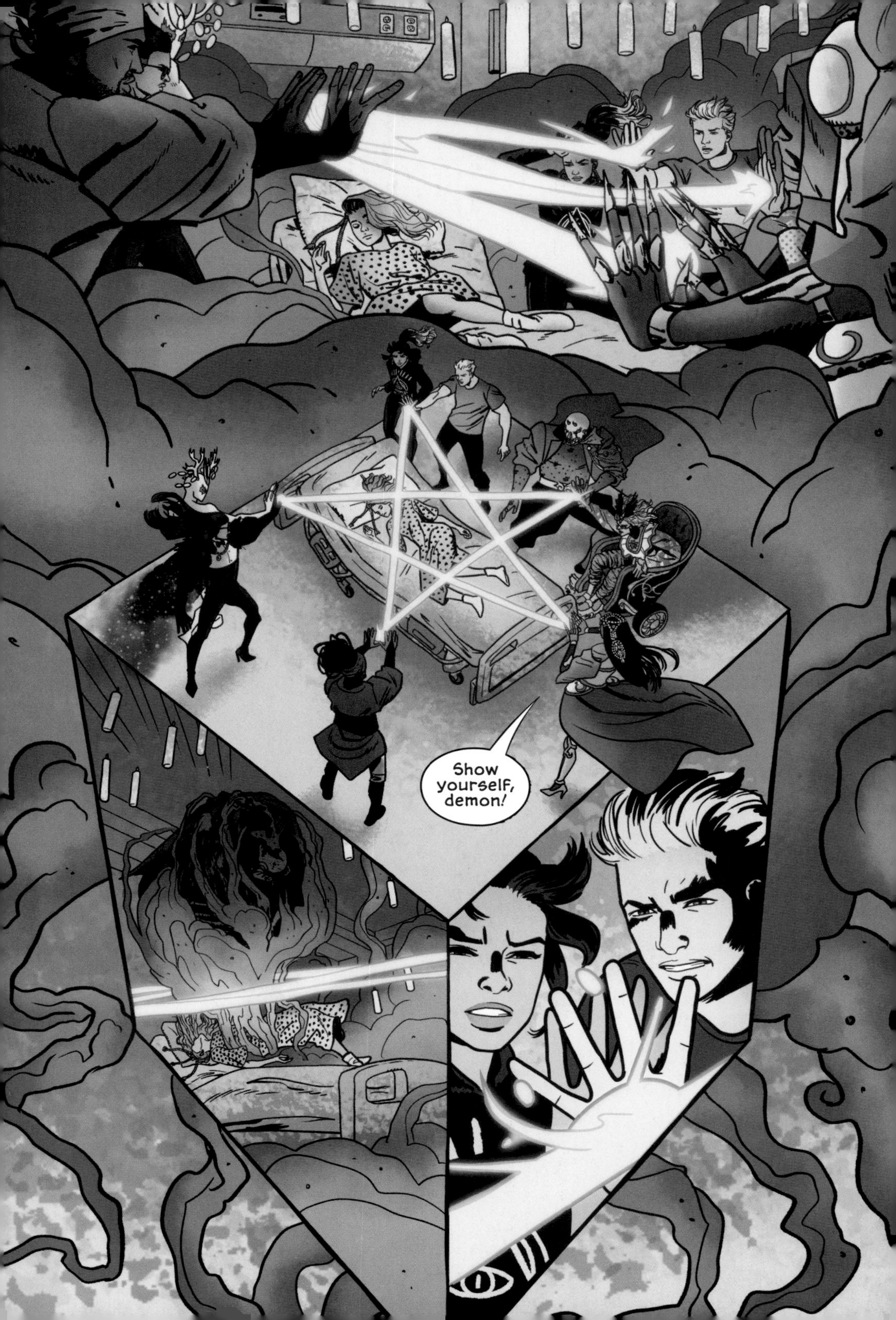
Show yourself, demon!

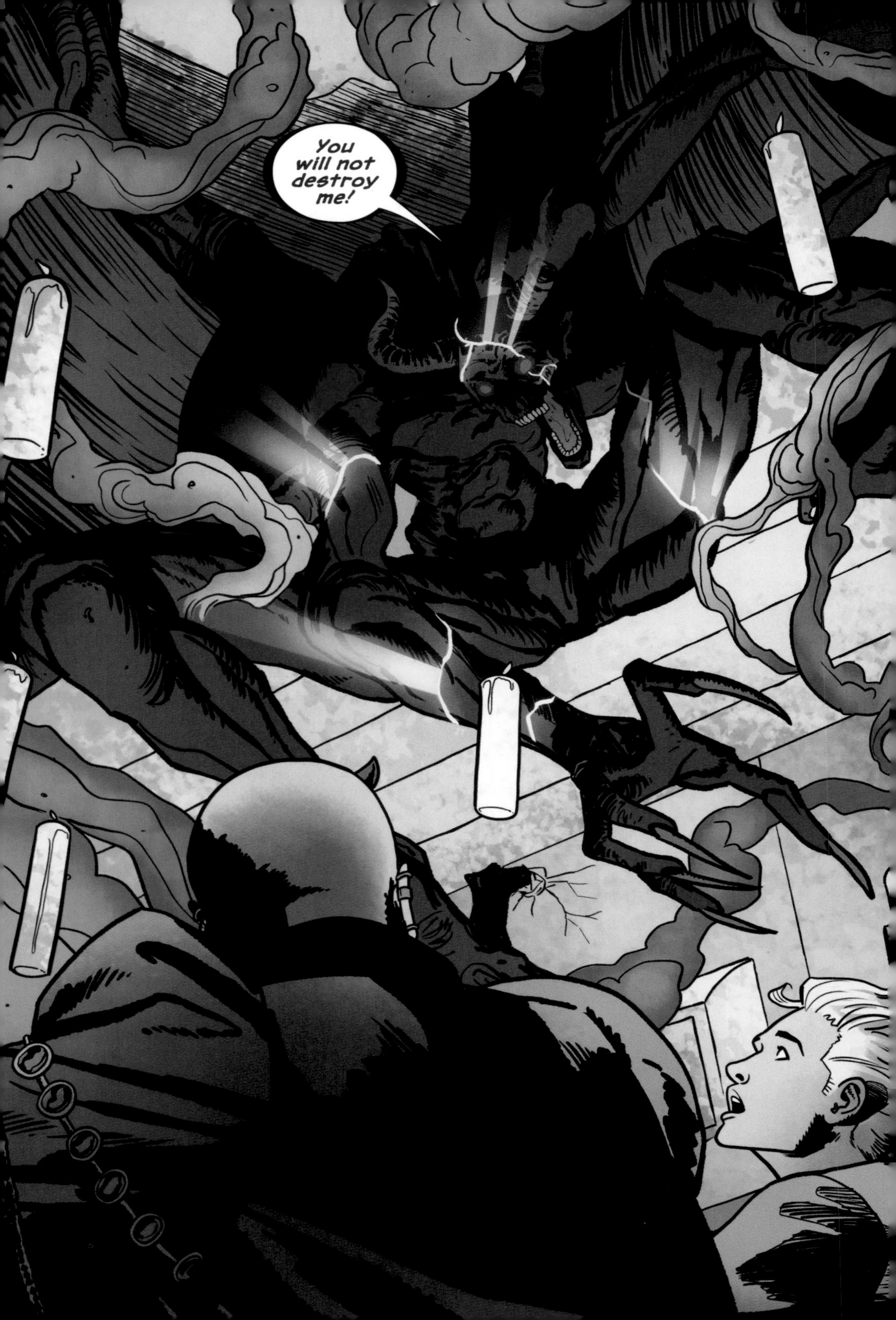
You will not destroy me!

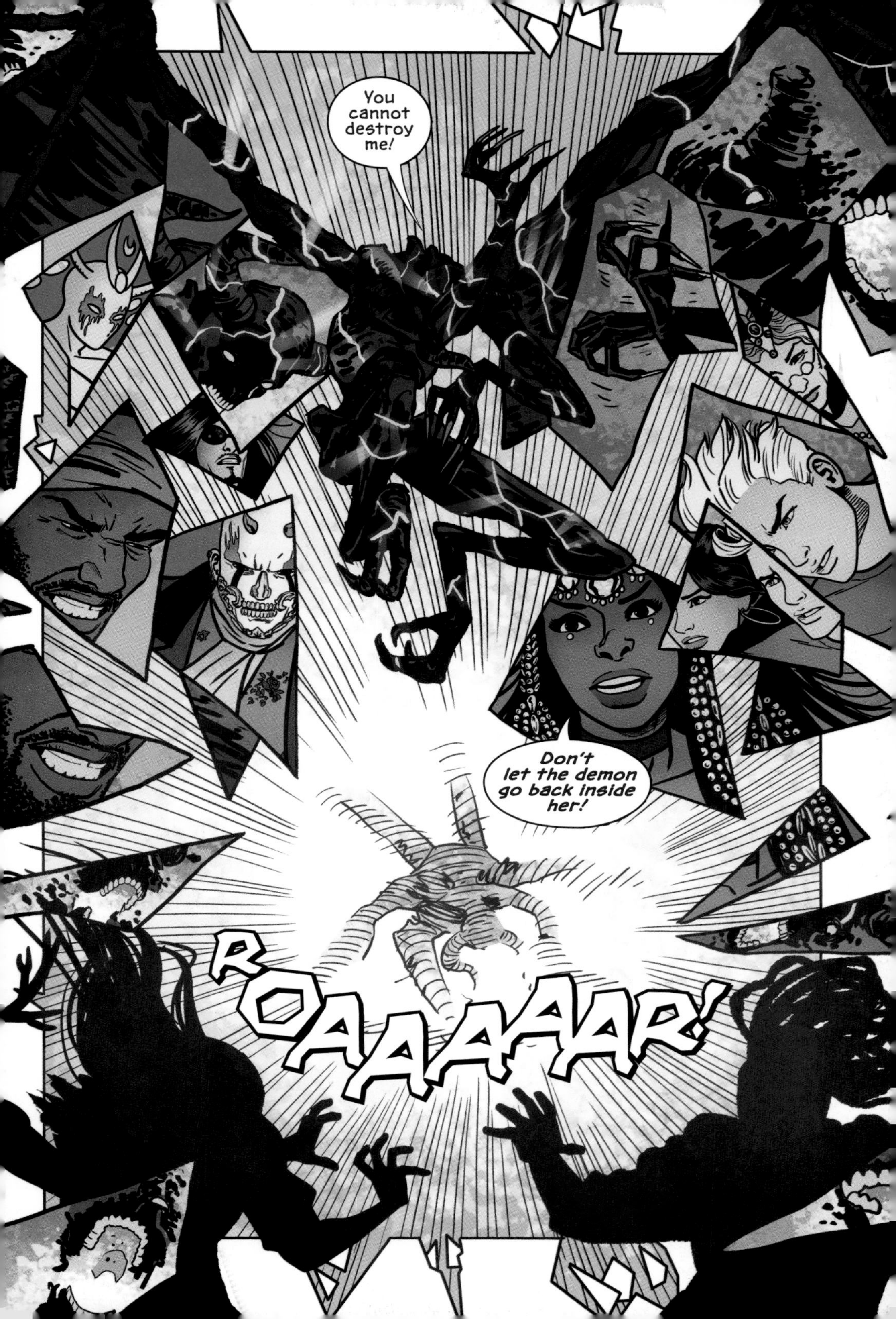
You cannot destroy me!
Don't let the demon go back inside her!
ROAAAAAAR!

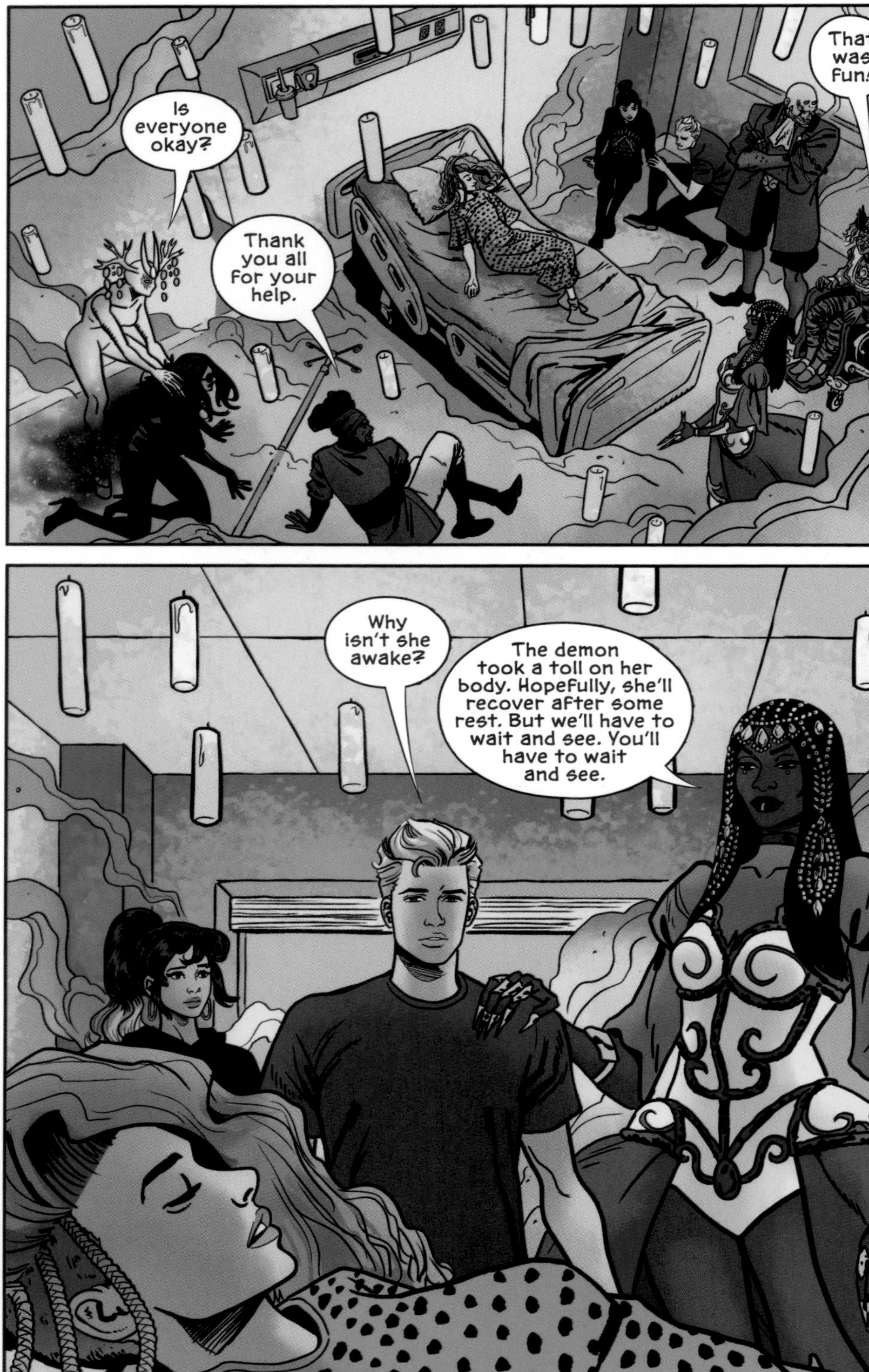
Is everyone okay?
Thank you all for your help.
That was fun!
Why isn't she awake?
The demon took a toll on her body. Hopefully, she'll recover after some rest. But we'll have to wait and see. You'll have to wait and see.

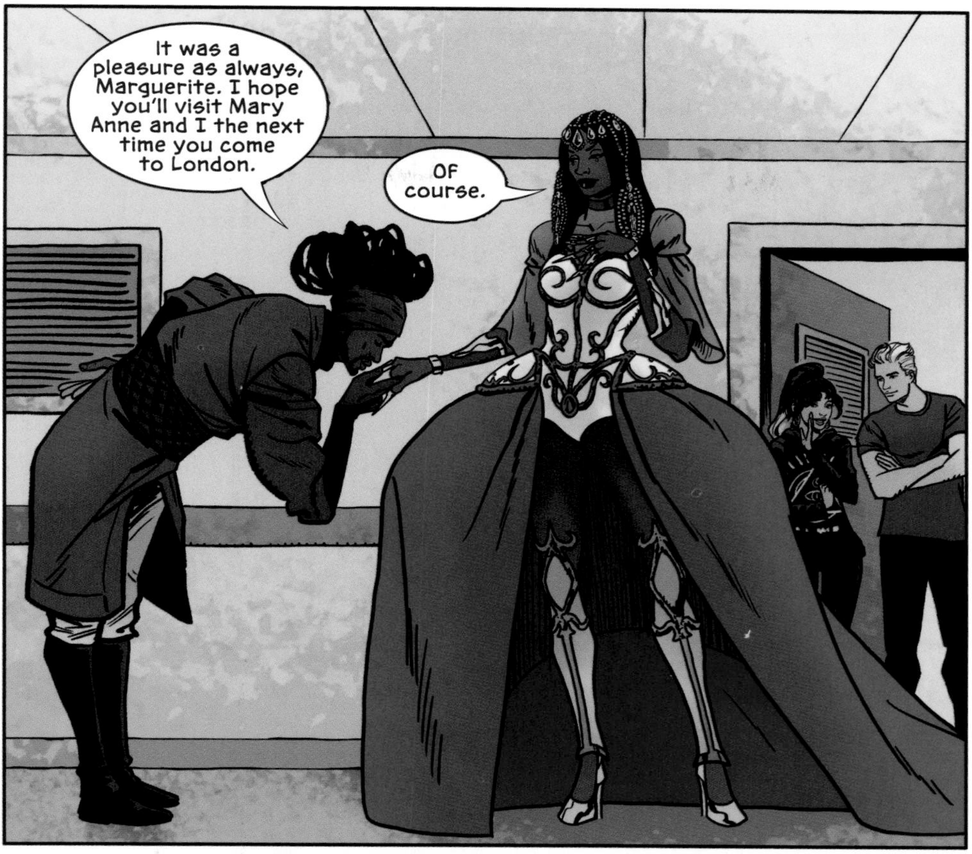
It was a pleasure as always, Marguerite. I hope you'll visit Mary Anne and I the next time you come to London.
Of course.

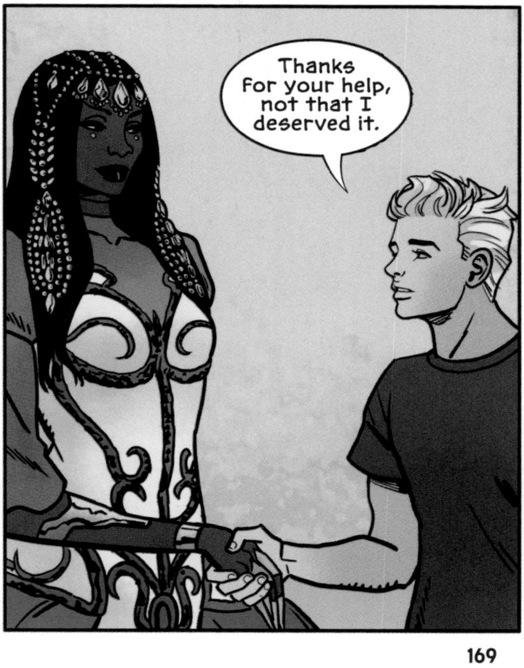
Thanks for your help, not that I deserved it.

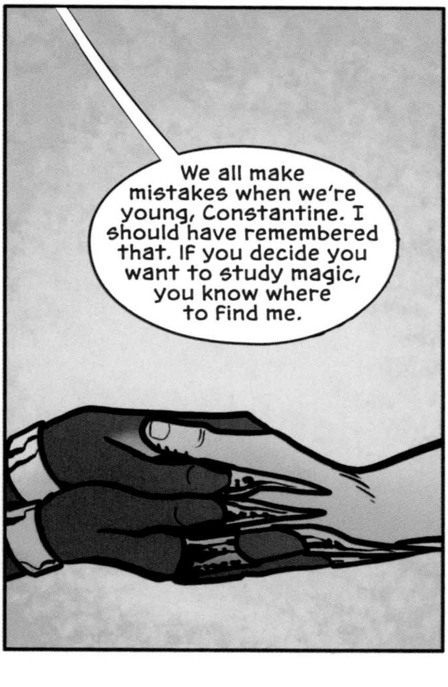
We all make mistakes when we're young, Constantine. I should have remembered that. If you decide you want to study magic, you know where to find me.

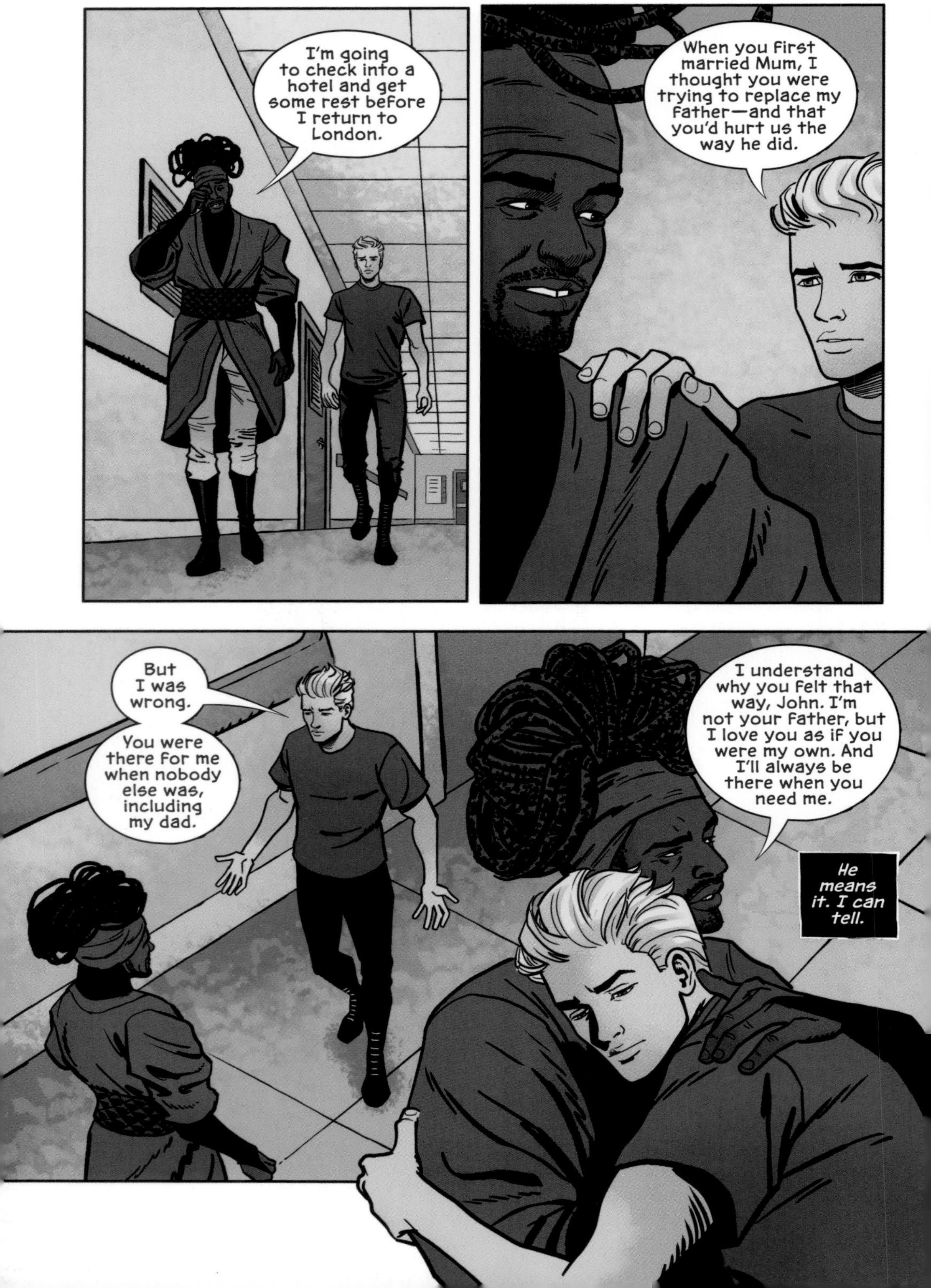
I'm going to check into a hotel and get some rest before I return to London.
When you first married Mum, I thought you were trying to replace my father—and that you'd hurt us the way he did.
But I was wrong.
You were there for me when nobody else was, including my dad.
I understand why you felt that way, John. I'm not your father, but I love you as if you were my own. And I'll always be there when you need me.
He means it. I can tell.

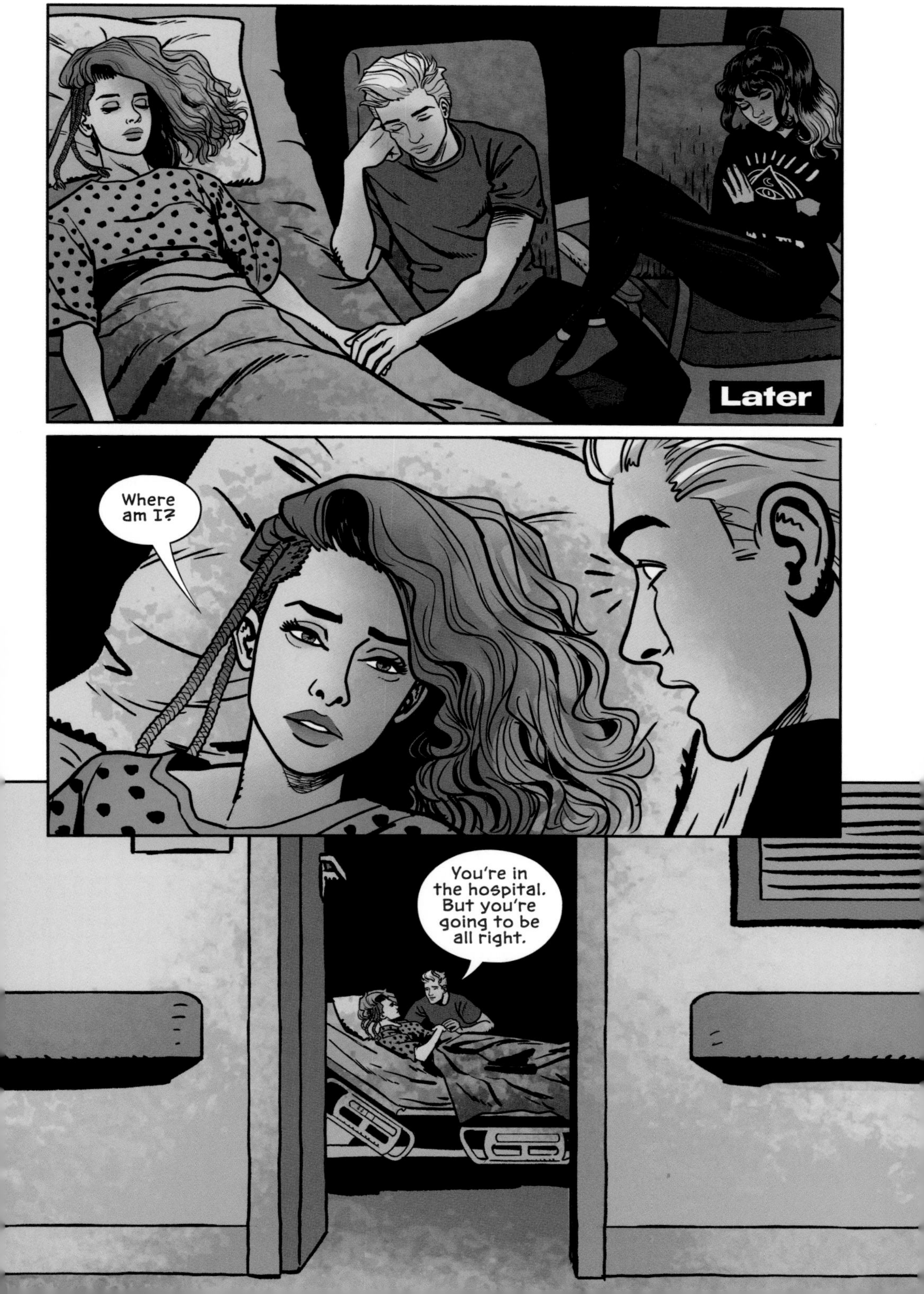
Later
Where am I?
You're in the hospital. But you're going to be all right.

CHAPTER 16:
A Little Less Reckless

How do you feel?

Physically? Like nothing happened. Emotionally? Still a little freaked out.

Three Weeks Later

I'm just glad you're okay.

Have you talked to your parents?

I texted to let them know I was heading to California to stay with my aunt for a while. Not like they care.

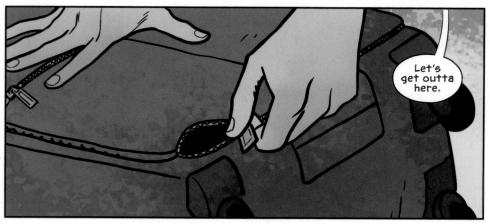

Let's get outta here.

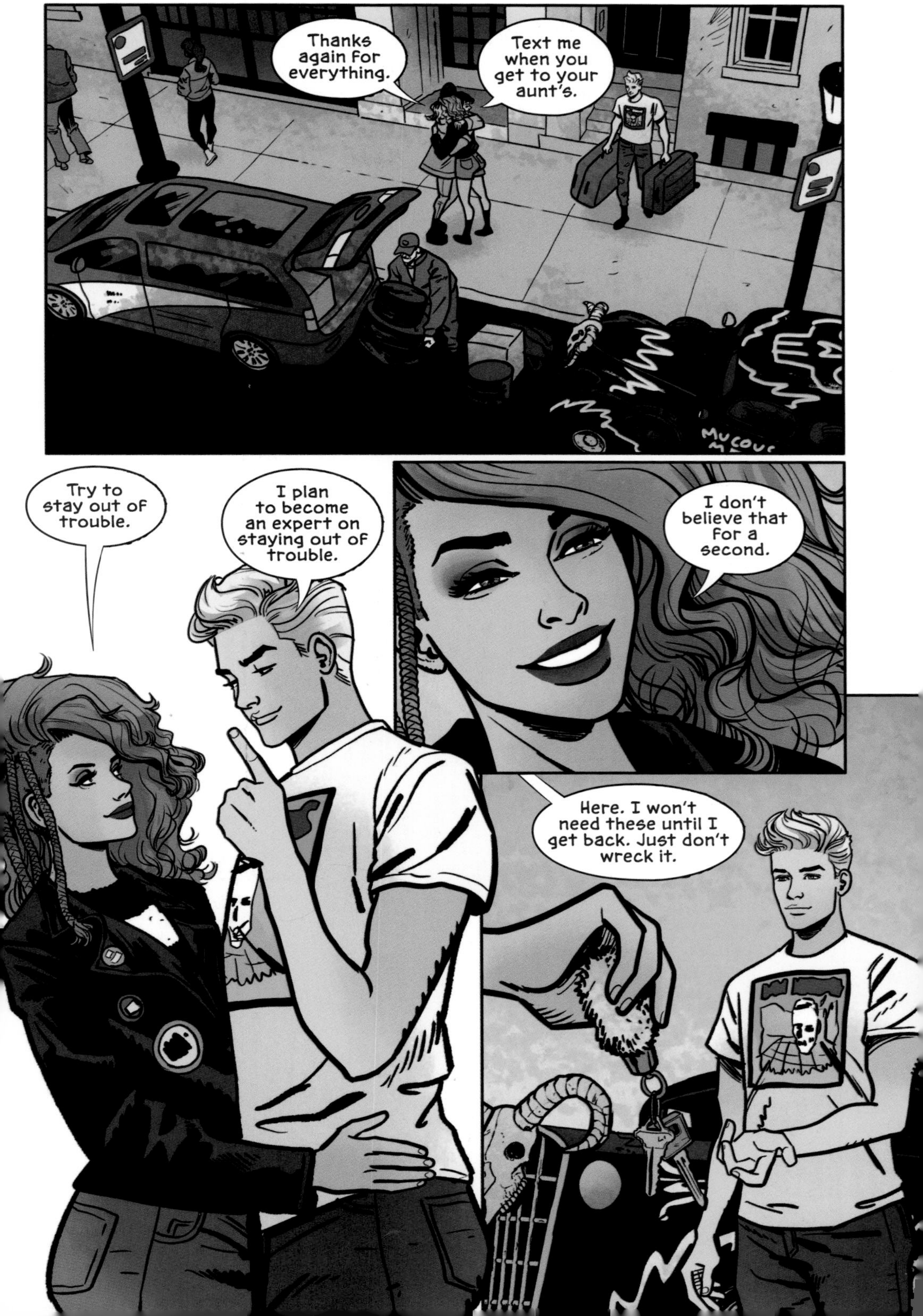
Thanks again for everything.
Text me when you get to your aunt's.
Try to stay out of trouble.
I plan to become an expert on staying out of trouble.
I don't believe that for a second.
Here. I won't need these until I get back. Just don't wreck it.

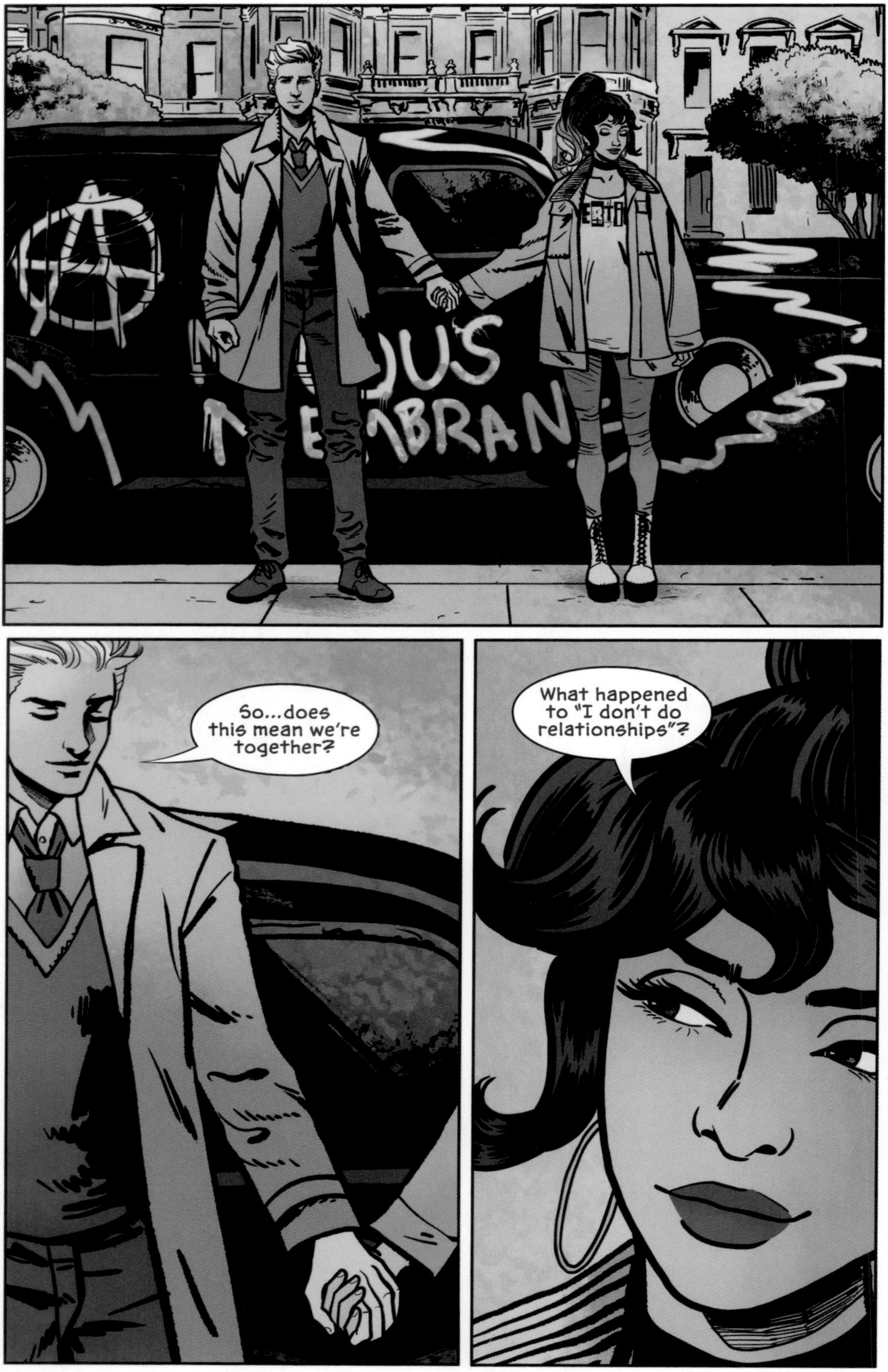
So...does this mean we're together?
What happened to "I don't do relationships"?

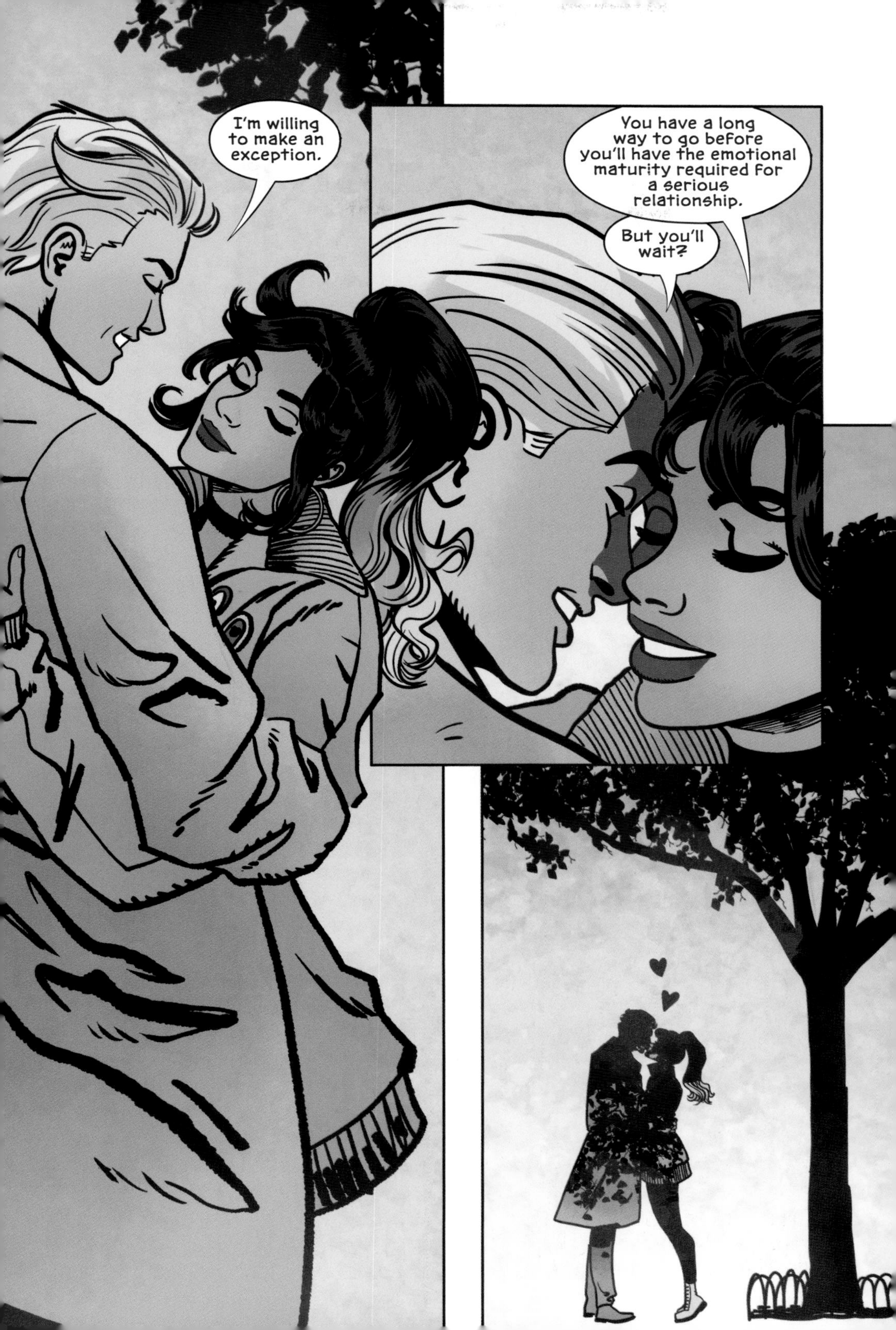
I'm willing to make an exception.
You have a long way to go before you'll have the emotional maturity required for a serious relationship.
But you'll wait?

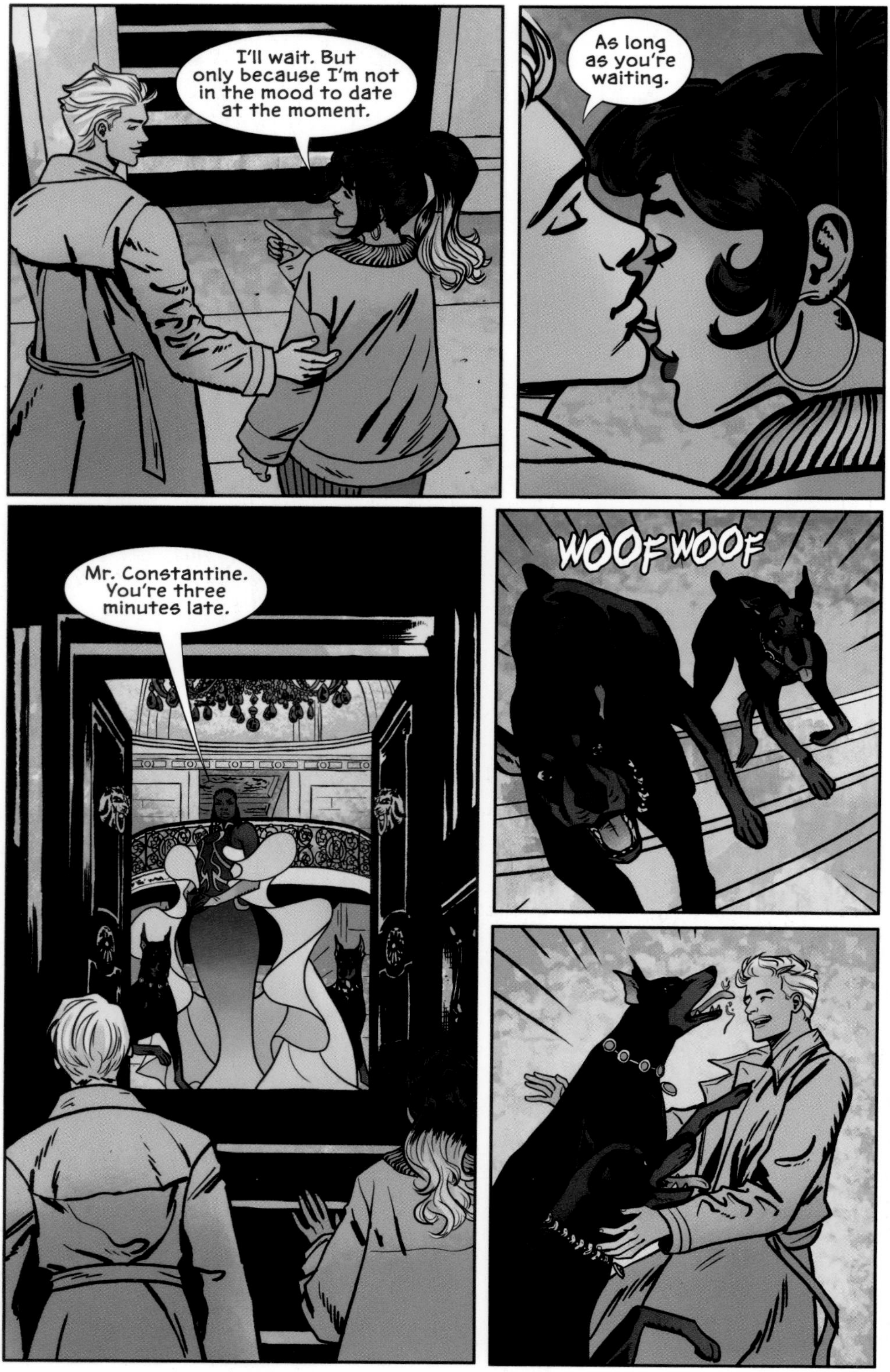
I'll wait. But only because I'm not in the mood to date at the moment.
As long as you're waiting.
Mr. Constantine. You're three minutes late.
WOOF WOOF

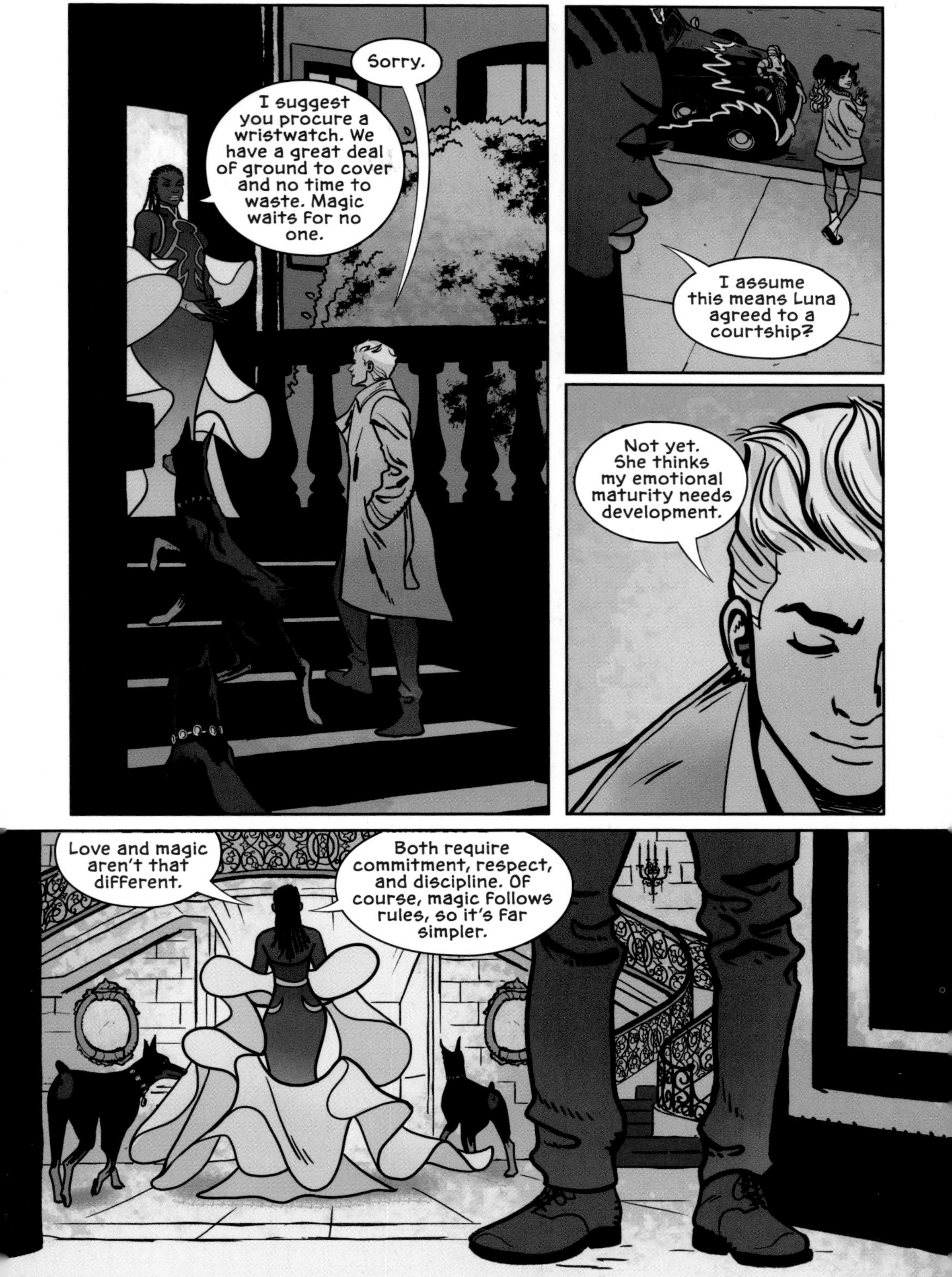
I suggest you procure a wristwatch. We have a great deal of ground to cover and no time to waste. Magic waits for no one.
Sorry.
I assume this means Luna agreed to a courtship?
Not yet. She thinks my emotional maturity needs development.
Love and magic aren't that different.
Both require commitment, respect, and discipline. Of course, magic follows rules, so it's far simpler.

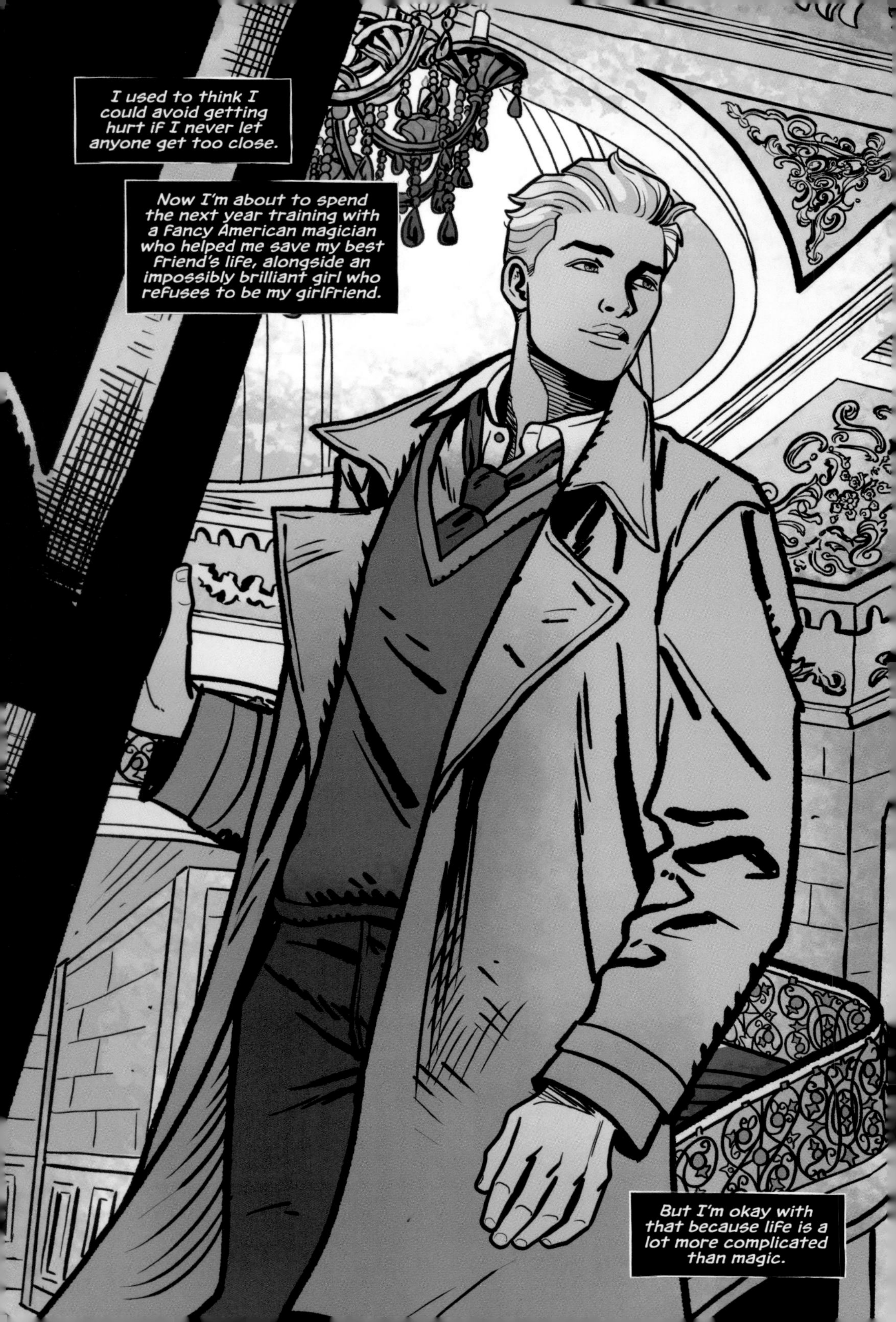
I used to think I could avoid getting hurt if I never let anyone get too close.
Now I'm about to spend the next year training with a fancy American magician who helped me save my best friend's life, alongside an impossibly brilliant girl who refuses to be my girlfriend.
But I'm okay with that because life is a lot more complicated than magic.

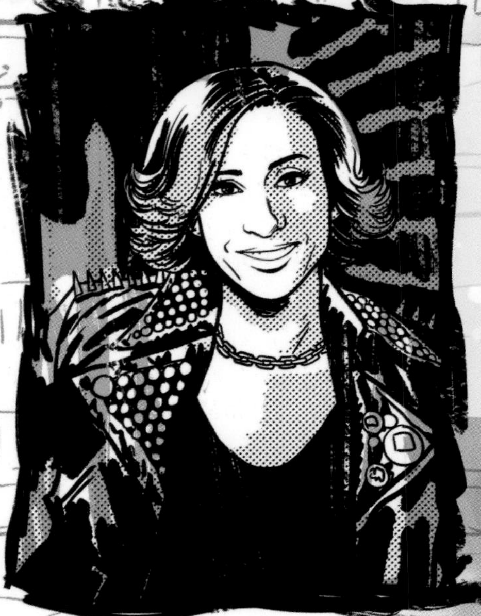

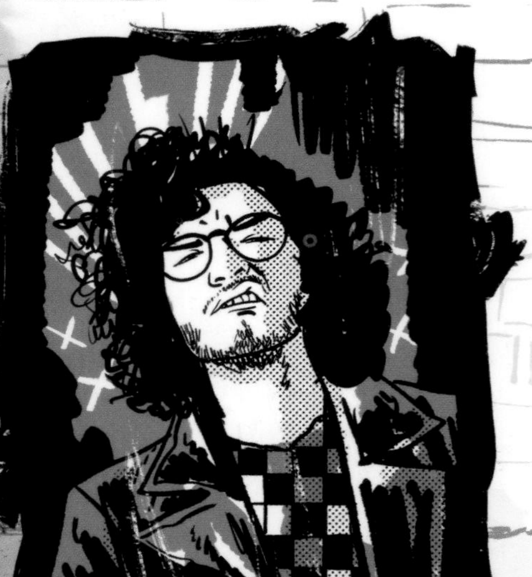

Isaac Goodhart got his start in comics in 2014 as one of the winners of the Top Cow Talent Hunt. After drawing *Artifacts* #38, he moved on to illustrating Matt Hawkins's *Postal* for 26 consecutive issues. He recently illustrated *Under the Moon: A Catwoman Tale* and *Victor and Nora: A Gotham Love Story*, both written by Lauren Myracle and published by DC Comics.

Kami Garcia is the #1 *New York Times*, *USA Today*, and international bestselling co-author of the Beautiful Creatures and Dangerous Creatures novels. *Beautiful Creatures* has been published in 50 countries and translated into 39 languages. Kami's solo series, The Legion, includes *Unbreakable*, an instant *New York Times* bestseller, and its sequel, *Unmarked*, both of which were nominated for Bram Stoker Awards. Her other works include *X-Files Origins: Agent of Chaos* and the YA contemporary novels *The Lovely Reckless* and *Broken Beautiful Hearts*. Kami was a teacher for 17 years before co-authoring her first novel on a dare from seven of her students. She is a cofounder of YALLFest, the biggest teen book festival in the country. She lives in Maryland with her family.

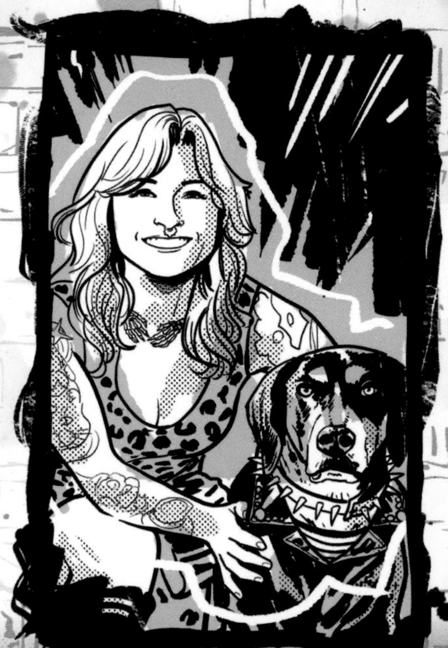

Ruth Redmond began her career as a comic book colorist while studying animation at IADT Dún Laoghaire. Swapping cartoons for comics has given her the opportunity to work on titles such as *Deadpool*, *Worst X-Men Ever*, *Imagine Agents*, *X-O Manowar*, and now *Constantine: Distorted Illusions*. After college, Ruth moved from Ireland to Canada where she now lives with her husband and dog.

Raven Roth, Garfield Logan, Maxine Navarro, and Damian Wayne are on the run...from Slade Wilson, from H.I.V.E., and from the horrible experiments H.I.V.E. conducted at their expense.

Dick Grayson just wants to know what happened to his brother, Damian. Is Damian okay? Does he need help? Why hasn't he been in contact? And why did his tracking device go silent?

One thing is for sure—they all need answers and there is only one person that might be able to help them defeat H.I.V.E. for good.

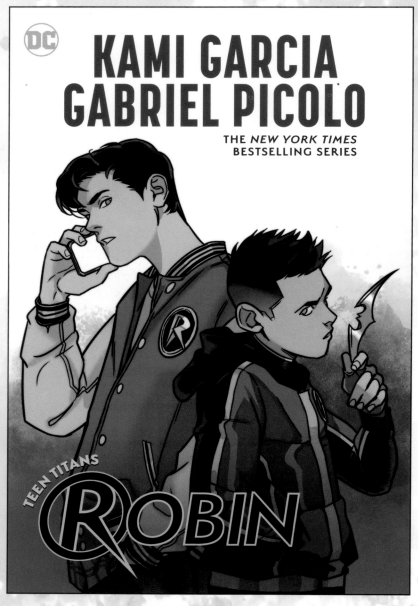

Tag along with #1 *New York Times* bestselling author **KAMI GARCIA** (*Beautiful Creatures*) and artist **GABRIEL PICOLO**, the creative duo behind the *New York Times* bestselling Teen Titans graphic novel series, as they continue with the action-adventure of a lifetime.

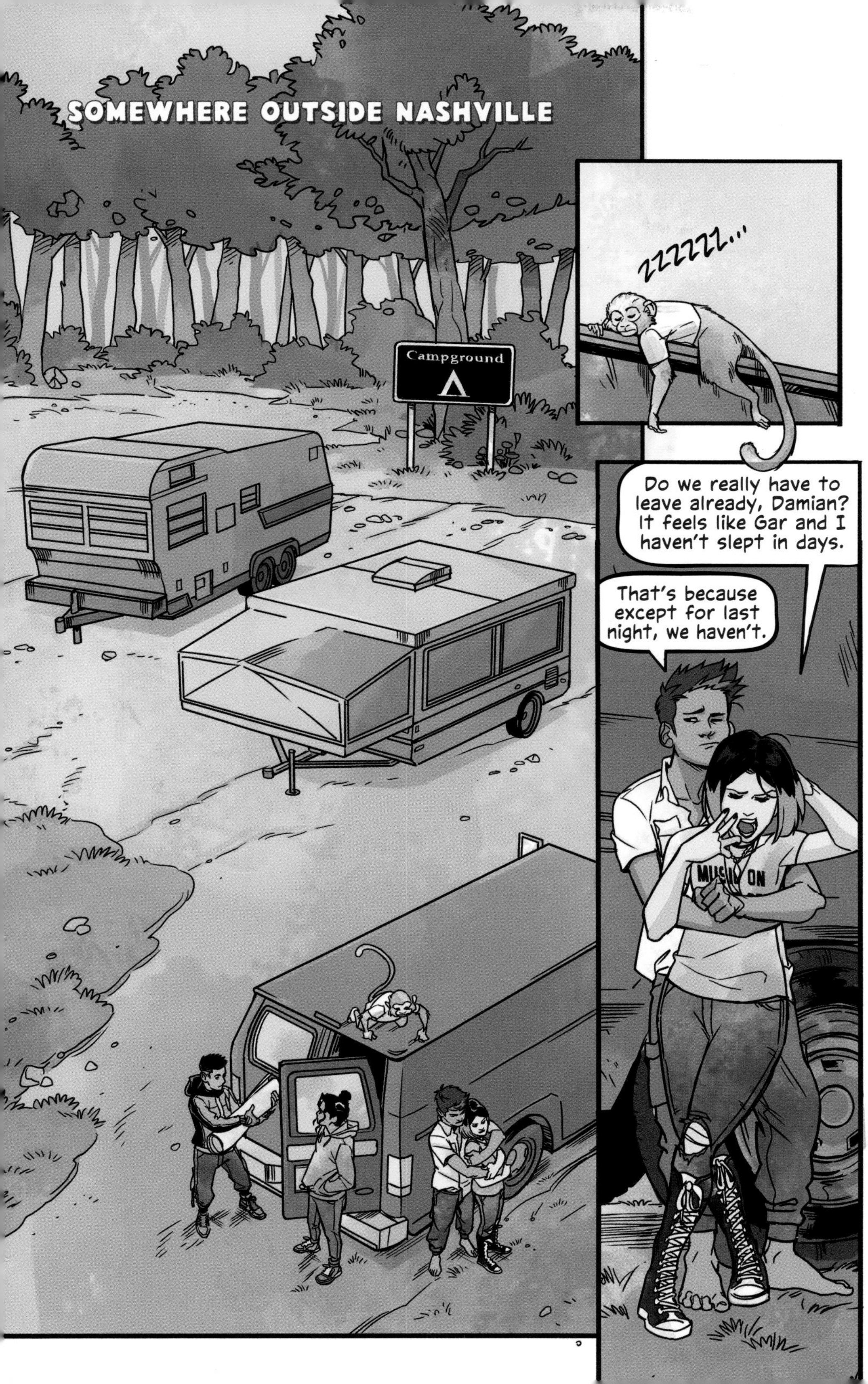
SOMEWHERE OUTSIDE NASHVILLE
Campground
ZZZZZZ...
Do we really have to leave already, Damian? It feels like Gar and I haven't slept in days.
That's because except for last night, we haven't.

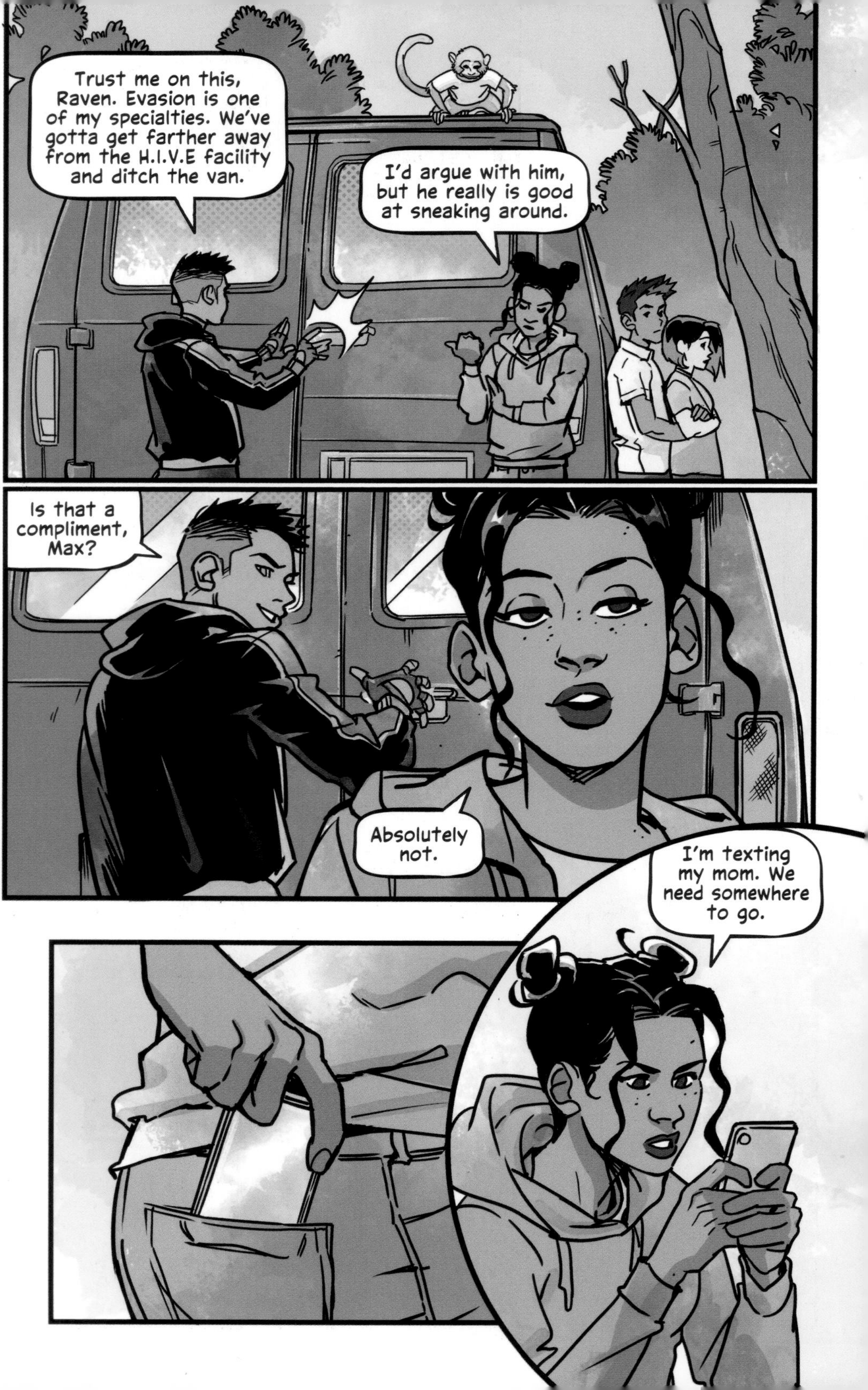
Trust me on this, Raven. Evasion is one of my specialties. We've gotta get farther away from the H.I.V.E facility and ditch the van.
I'd argue with him, but he really is good at sneaking around.
Is that a compliment, Max?
Absolutely not.
I'm texting my mom. We need somewhere to go.

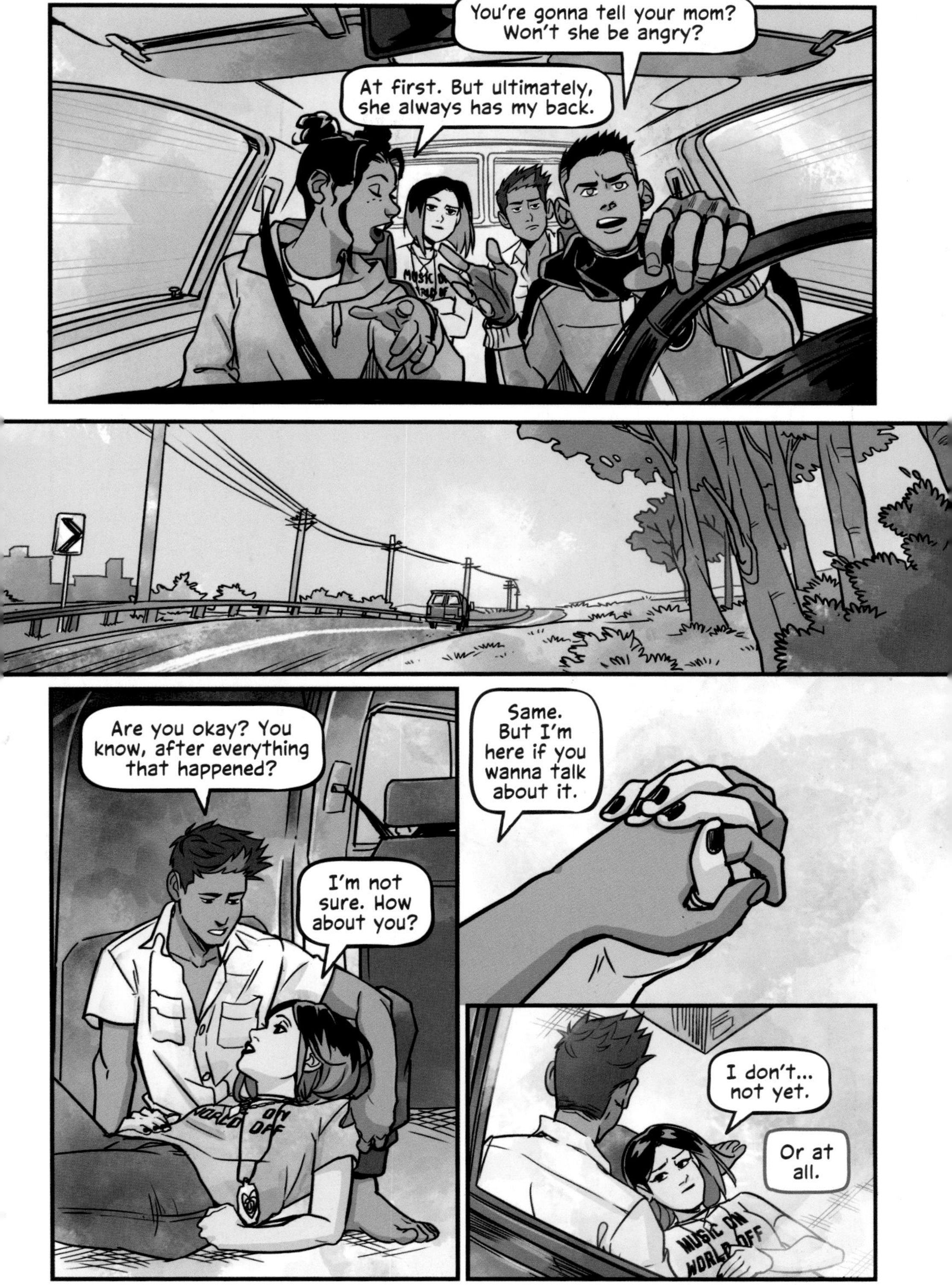
You're gonna tell your mom? Won't she be angry?
At first. But ultimately, she always has my back.
Are you okay? You know, after everything that happened?
I'm not sure. How about you?
Same. But I'm here if you wanna talk about it.
I don't... not yet.
Or at all.

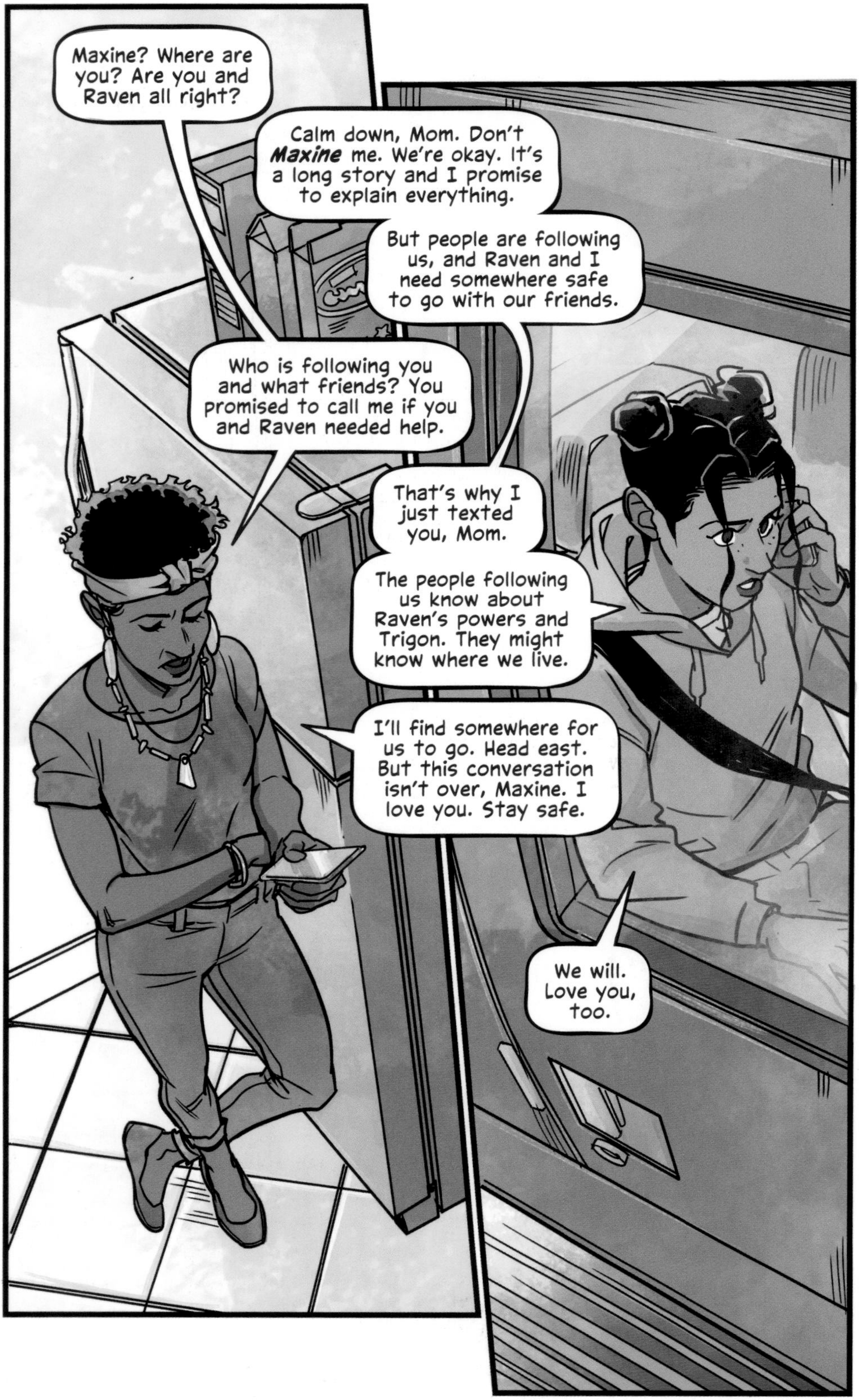
Maxine? Where are you? Are you and Raven all right?
Calm down, Mom. Don't *Maxine* me. We're okay. It's a long story and I promise to explain everything.
But people are following us, and Raven and I need somewhere safe to go with our friends.
Who is following you and what friends? You promised to call me if you and Raven needed help.
That's why I just texted you, Mom.
The people following us know about Raven's powers and Trigon. They might know where we live.
I'll find somewhere for us to go. Head east. But this conversation isn't over, Maxine. I love you. Stay safe.
We will. Love you, too.

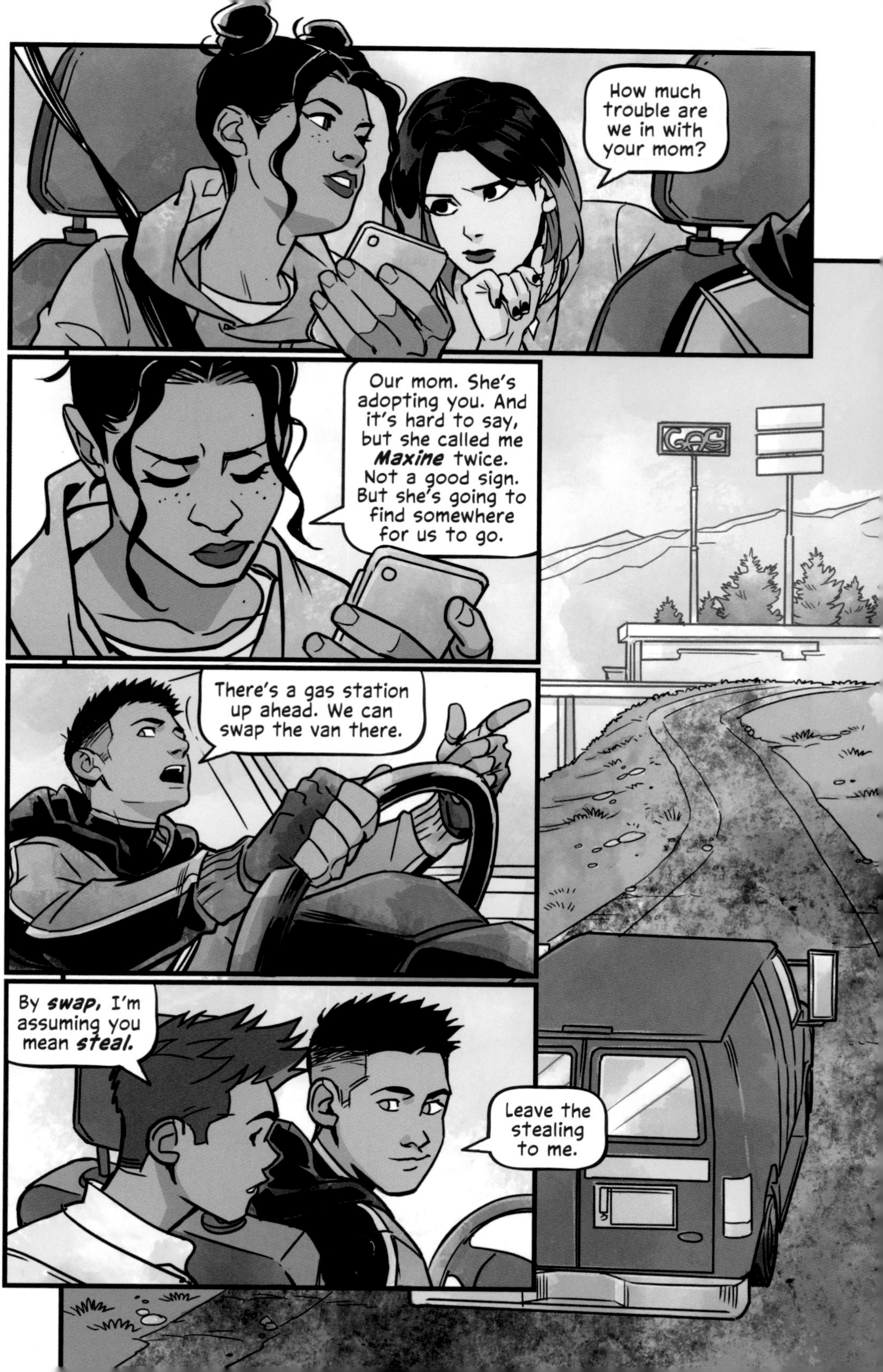
How much trouble are we in with your mom?
Our mom. She's adopting you. And it's hard to say, but she called me ***Maxine*** twice. Not a good sign. But she's going to find somewhere for us to go.
GAS
There's a gas station up ahead. We can swap the van there.
By ***swap,*** I'm assuming you mean ***steal.***
Leave the stealing to me.

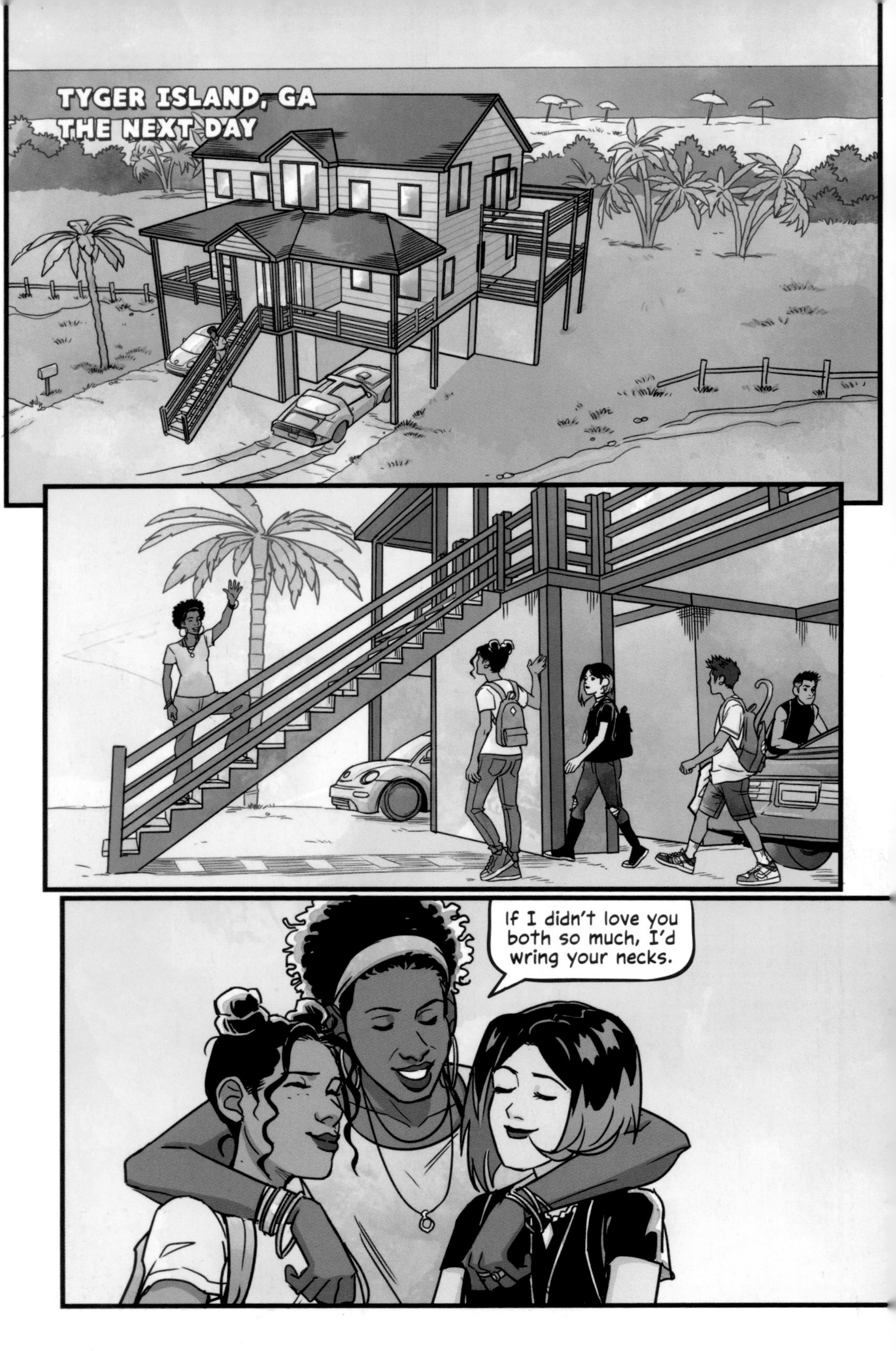
TYGER ISLAND, GA
THE NEXT DAY
If I didn't love you both so much, I'd wring your necks.

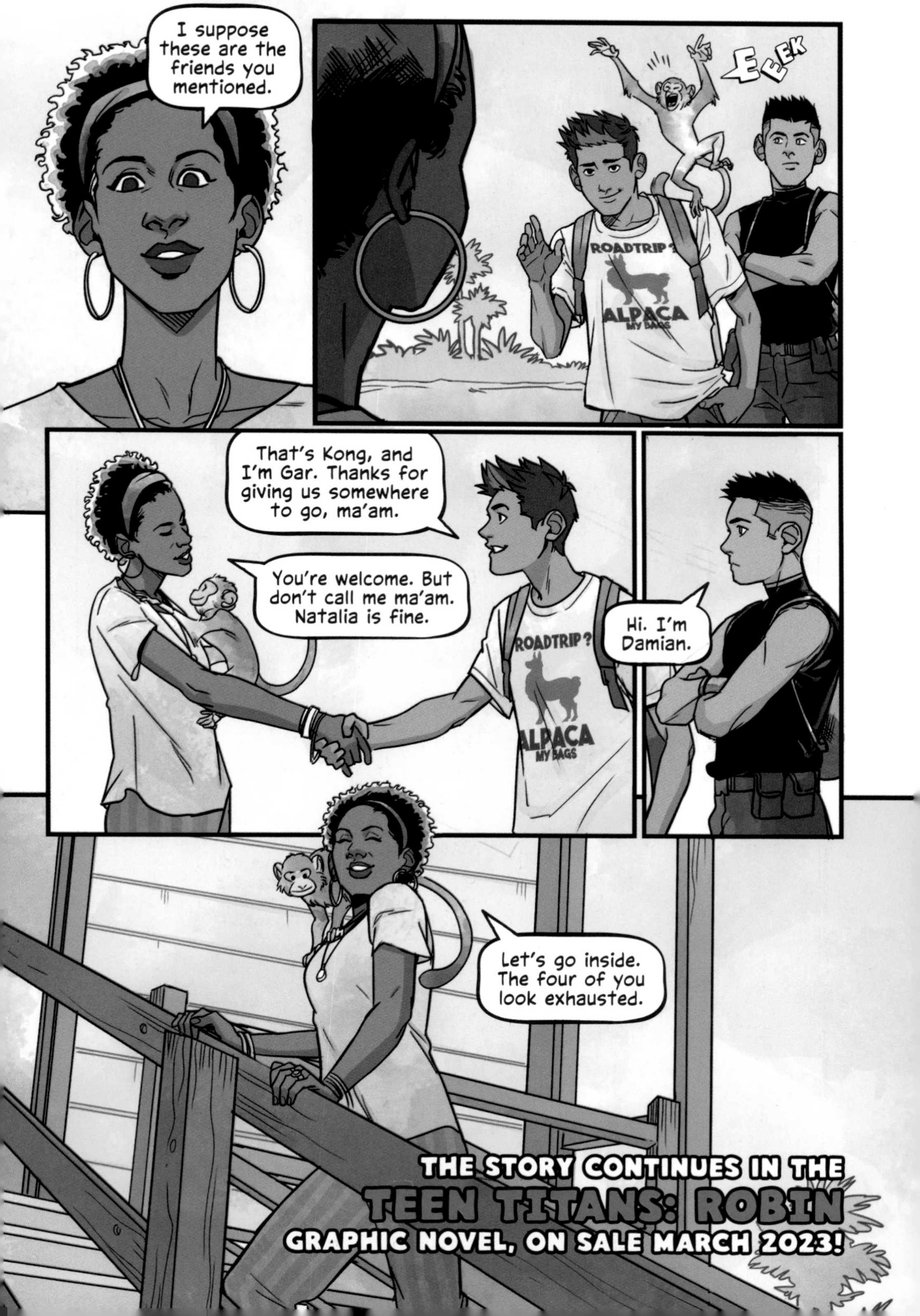
I suppose these are the friends you mentioned.
EEEK
ROADTRIP? ALPACA MY BAGS
That's Kong, and I'm Gar. Thanks for giving us somewhere to go, ma'am.
You're welcome. But don't call me ma'am. Natalia is fine.
ROADTRIP? ALPACA MY BAGS
Hi. I'm Damian.
Let's go inside. The four of you look exhausted.
THE STORY CONTINUES IN THE
TEEN TITANS: ROBIN
GRAPHIC NOVEL, ON SALE MARCH 2023!

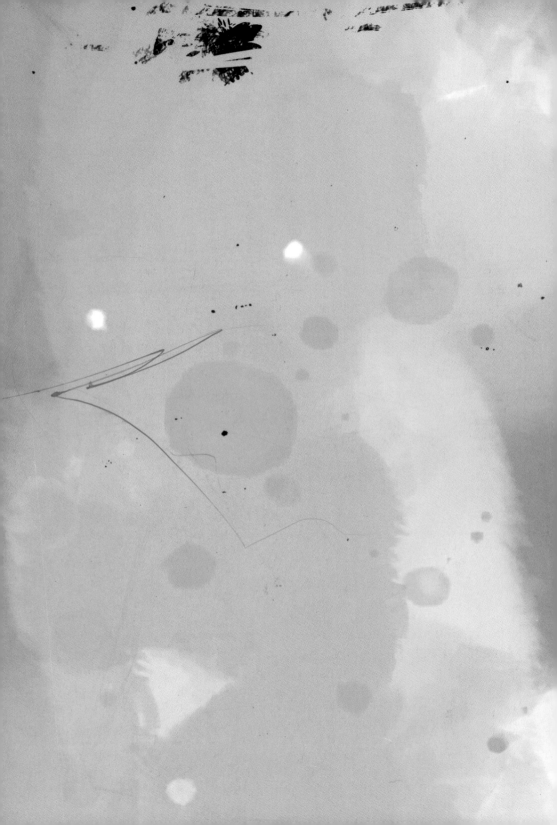